Praise for Sara Ella

"*Unblemished* may have set the stage, but *Unraveling* will forever bind you to this story like a Kiss of Accord. Sara Ella's exquisite writing left me gasping at new revelations and re-reading whole chapters just because. *Unraveling* is a sequel that outshines its already brilliant predecessor. Read it. Now. Then come fangirl with me."

—Nadine Brandes, award-winning author of the Out of Time trilogy

"With plenty of YA crossover appeal, this engaging and suspenseful debut urban fantasy features superb world building and a tightly paced story line. Reading groups will find plenty to discuss concerning self-image, the nature of good vs. evil, and the power of the marginalized to change the world."

—Library Journal, starred review for *Unblemished*

"Sara Ella's debut novel is a stunning journey into a fascinating new world of reflections. Intricately plotted, the story is complex, but not difficult to follow. Eliyana is a strong heroine, yet also has a vulnerable side that readers will definitely identify with. The other characters are also well-developed and have many hidden secrets revealed throughout the course of the tale . . . It will be fascinating to see where the author takes the characters next."

—RT Book Reviews, 4½ stars, TOP PICK! for *Unblemished*

"Ella has created a captivating, relatable protagonist and never hesitates as she keeps things moving briskly through the many twists and turns."

—Publishers Weekly for *Unblemished*

"A breathtaking fantasy set in an extraordinary fairy-tale world, with deceptive twists and an addictively adorable cast who are illusory to the end. Just when I thought I'd figured each out, Sara Ella sent me for another ride. A wholly original story, *Unblemished* begins as a sweet melody and quickly becomes an anthem of the heart. And I'm singing my soul out. Fans of *Once upon a Time* and Julie Kagawa, brace yourselves."

—MARY WEBER, AWARD-WINNING AUTHOR
OF THE STORM SIREN TRILOGY

"Lyrically written and achingly romantic—*Unblemished* will tug your heartstrings!"

—MELISSA LANDERS, AUTHOR OF *ALIENATED*,
INVADED, AND *STARFLIGHT*

"Self-worth and destiny collide in this twisty-turny fantasy full of surprise and heart. Propelled into a world she knows nothing about, Eliyana learns that the birthmark she despises is not quite the superficial curse she thought it was—it's worse, and the mark comes with a heavy responsibility. Can she face her reflection long enough to be the hero her new friends need? With charm and wit, author Sara Ella delivers *Unblemished*, a magical story with a compelling message and a unique take on the perils of Central Park."

—SHANNON DITTEMORE, AUTHOR OF THE ANGEL EYES TRILOGY

"*Unblemished* is an enchanting, beautifully written adventure with a pitch-perfect blend of fantasy, realism, and romance. Move this one to the top of your TBR pile and clear your schedule—you won't want to put it down!"

—LORIE LANGDON, AUTHOR OF THE AMAZON
BESTSELLING DOON SERIES

"*Unblemished* had me from the first chapter—mystery, romance, and mind-blowing twists and turns that I *so* did not see coming! The worlds Sara Ella builds are complex and seamless; the characters she creates are beautifully flawed. Readers are sure to love this book and finish it, as I did, begging for more!"

—KRISTA MCGEE, AUTHOR OF THE ANOMALY TRILOGY

unraveling

The Unblemished Trilogy, Book II

sara Ella

THOMAS NELSON

Since 1798

Unraveling

© 2017 by Sara E. Larson

Published in Nashville, Tennessee, by Thomas Nelson. Thomas Nelson is a registered trademark of HarperCollins Christian Publishing, Inc.

Special thanks to Jim Hart of Hartline Literary.

Maps by Matthew Covington.

Thomas Nelson titles may be purchased in bulk for educational, business, fund-raising, or sales promotional use. For information, please e-mail SpecialMarkets@ThomasNelson.com.

Library of Congress Cataloging-in-Publication Data

Names: Ella, Sara, author.
Title: Unraveling / by Sara Ella.
Description: Nashville, Tennessee : Thomas Nelson, [2017] | Series:
Unblemished ; book 2 | Summary: Eliyana continues her journey towards the throne while she tries to figure out her relationship with Ky and how it might be connected to the powerful magical gifts known as the Callings.
Identifiers: LCCN 2017002678 | ISBN 9780718081034 (hardback)
Subjects: | CYAC: Fantasy. | Love--Fiction. | Kings, queens, rulers, etc.--Fiction.
Classification: LCC PZ7.1.E435 Ur 2017 | DDC [Fic]--dc23 LC record available at https://lccn.loc.gov/2017002678

Printed in the United States of America

17 18 19 20 21 LSC 5 4 3 2 1

For my editor, Becky Monds—
Because when this story was unraveling,
you helped me make it whole.

N

W   E

S

NW NE
SW SE

Starbucks
El's Brownstone

Yankee
Stadium

Upper West Side

Central Park

Belvedere
Castle

The Pond

Subway
Entrance(s)

Empire State
Building

Hudson River

East River

Greenwich
Village

Washington
Square
Fountain

General Giuseppe
Garibaldi Statue

Manhattan

New York

Brooklyn Bridge

Ellis Island

Long Island

B r o o k l y n

Upper Bay
Staten Island

Prospect
Park

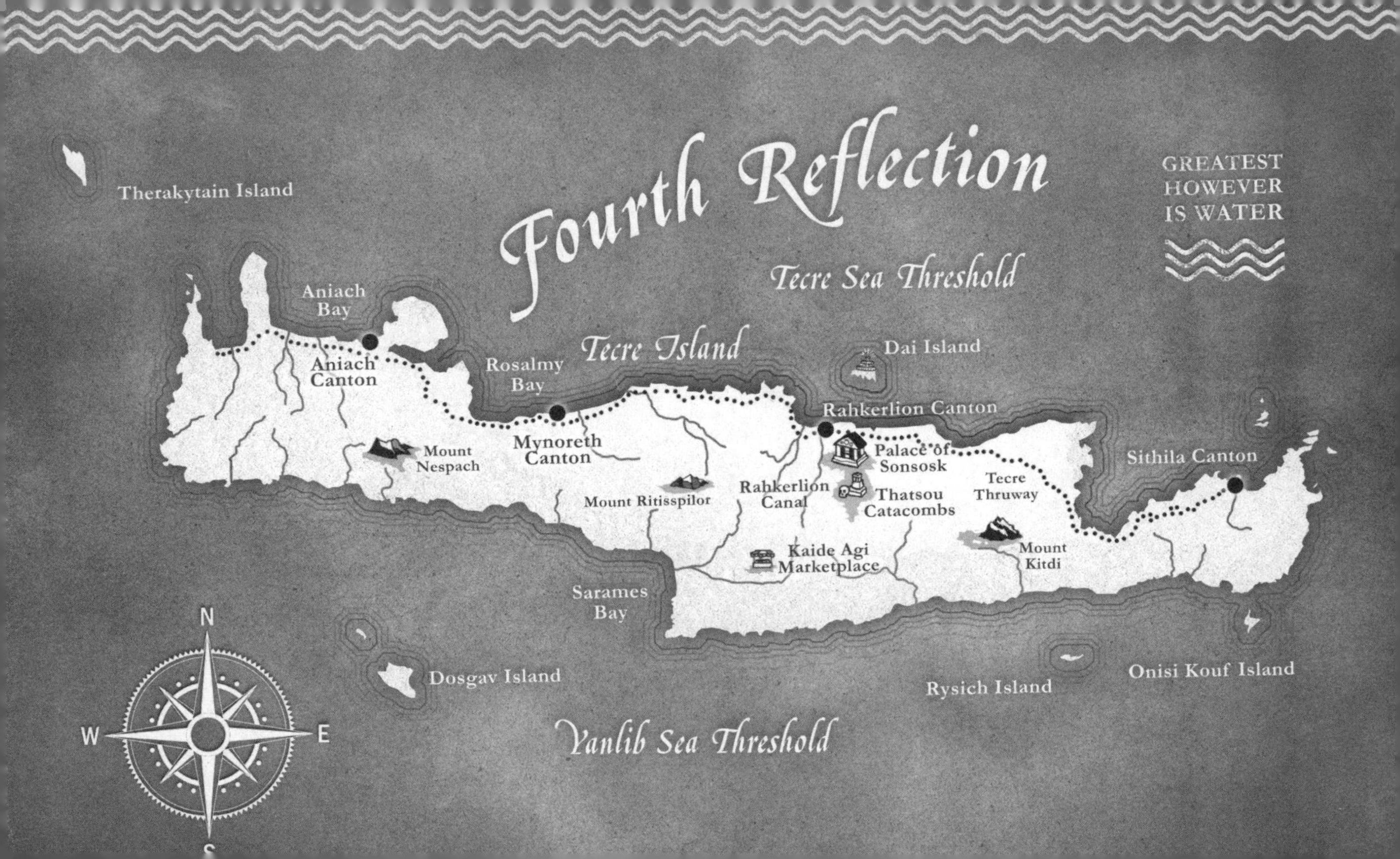

Fourth Reflection

Tecre Sea Threshold

GREATEST HOWEVER IS WATER

Therakytain Island

Aniach Bay

Aniach Canton

Mount Nespach

Tecre Island

Rosalmy Bay

Mynoreth Canton

Mount Ritisspilor

Sarames Bay

Dosgav Island

Vanlib Sea Threshold

Dai Island

Rahkerlion Canton

Palace of Sonsosk

Rahkerlion Canal

Kaide Agi Marketplace

Thatsou Catacombs

Tecre Thruway

Mount Kiidi

Sithila Canton

Onisi Kouf Island

Rysich Island

N E S W

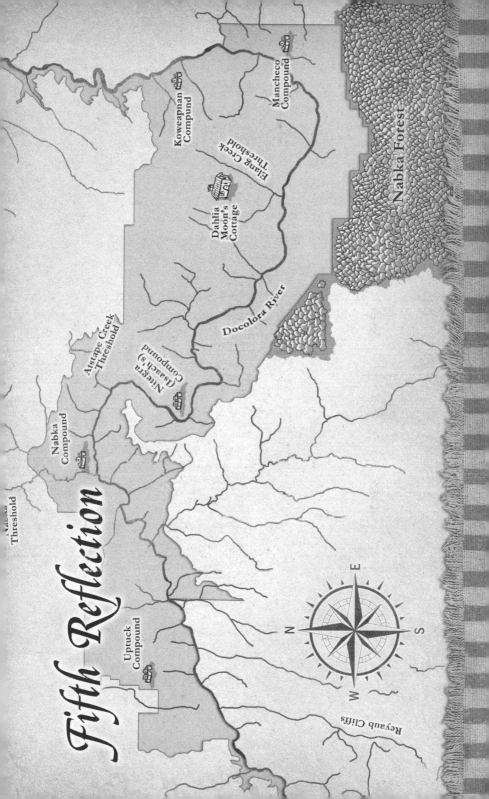

Fifth Reflection

Nabka Forest

Mancheco Compound

Koweapnan Compund

Elang Creek Threshold

Dahlia Moon's Cottage

Docolora River

Acstape Creek Threshold

Ninera (Isaach's) Compound

Nabka Compound

Threshold

Uptruck Compound

Reyaub Cliffs

N E S W

Whence I fell, he left me there.
Lost, nay abandoned; what did he care?
I needed him; away he flew.
I loved him so; he ne'er knew.
When I revealed my soul, my heart,
He turned away; I watched him part.
Without him now, darkness descends.
Where it begins, my light does end.

—"THE SCRIB'S FATE," ONCE UPON A REFLECTION, VOLUME I

prelude

I'm not ready for this.

My shoulder is going to rip from its socket. My bicep is a torch, igniting my forearm. His fingers are sliding from mine, and I can't hold on any longer. All I see is the gorge below, the beads of sweat dewing his temples.

He shouts, "Hold on!"

But the cliff crumbles with each passing blink. If we remain this way, we'll both be swallowed by the chasm below.

I loosen my grip, my clammy palm slipping.

His eyes plead. Beg. Implore. "Don't!" His cry echoes.

The river crashes and curls. Waiting to swallow. Devour. Obliterate anything entering its territory. But it isn't the river I'm afraid of. It's the black hole beyond it. The beginning of the end.

I know if we disconnect he might be lost forever. "I love you" is what I want to say. Instead I ask him, "Find me?"

His expression corkscrews, a mask of raw emotion. "Always." His voice is weak, his energy drained. He's not strong enough. Because of me.

So my fingers splay.

I let go.

ACT I

what once was mine

gleam and glow

Gasp. Ugh. Crud. Drat. Blerg. "Crowe!"

The Second Reflection curse spews from my mouth as I spring from the cushy armchair in the most deserted corner of the castle library. Books and journals fall from my lap and crash to the hardwood floor. My insides cringe. Mom would have a fit if she knew I abandoned a pile of precious tomes lying open-faced and underfoot. But the clock on the wall behind me warns I'm beyond late.

Of all the days to fall asleep studying. What a way to begin the first day of the rest of my life.

I hop on one foot and then the other in my classic dance to get my Converse on. I almost—but don't quite—trip over the book mound. Then I'm lifting the skirt of my now-wrinkled taffeta gown and sprinting from the library. No time to run to my suite and exchange my footwear for something more appropriate. At least I'm in my dress already. Thank the Verity it's too late to change into the shoes Mom selected. High heels, I'm convinced, are a creation of the Void and intended only to torture my poor unfortunate soles.

The white-walled halls are abandoned and my muted steps amp my anxiety. Is this what getting cold feet feels like? My face burns and then freezes. My ears ring and my chest just might explode. I need to get out more. All these late nights perusing tomes older than Beethoven's Fifth may be getting me closer to my goal, but the downside is I'm totally out of shape. The farther I run, the louder my heart pounds because—oh crud—everyone is already in the throne room.

Everyone except the guest of honor.

Everyone except me.

Why did the library have to be in a completely opposite wing?

One corner, then another, a long hall and two short ones. I pass frosted window after frosted window. When I veer closer to the panes, the faintest image of me stares back, the crimson mirrormark climbing up the right side of my face in vines of song and melody. My fingertips trace the notes, admiring the seal of my Calling I once found so repulsive. Then I peer past it, see through the glass to the Reflection beyond.

Something inside longs to escape these walls and bask in the freedom of snowball fights and sleigh rides. But not here, in this all-too-quiet place. No, the place I yearn for bustles with cab horns and— Wait. Did I make a wrong turn?

Ugh, some queen I'll turn out to be. I can't even focus long enough to navigate my way through my own castle. I miss the simplicity of my brownstone. Of New York's structured grid. Impossible to get lost. Familiar. Home.

And then I hear it. The low murmur that accompanies a crowd. A crowd waiting for me.

Stop. Deep breath. Straighten shoulders. Blink. Gulp. *Act like the eighteen-year-old queen they expect and not the terrified little girl trembling within.*

When I round the next corner at the hall's end, I'm there. The scent of roasted chestnuts draws me in. A few feet ahead, one of five tiers of balconies awaits. I'm on the lowest tier so I don't have far to go. I walk with as much regality as I can muster, all at once feeling like a fraud with my non-updoed hair and secret sneakers.

Once atop the grand staircase I pause. This is the part where everyone is supposed to gasp in awe at the beautiful Cinder girl about to descend the steps. And indeed, the guests do cease their chatter. Everyone stares. A chill that has nothing to do with the season wraps me. I twist the white gold engagement ring Joshua gave me around my finger as a jumble of doubts flurries through my brain.

Disappointment.

Phony.

Imposter.

But then a stirring takes residence inside me, like a warm blanket encompassing my entire being. In an instant I recognize it as the Verity. An unfathomable confidence that is beyond out of character. I lift my fingertips, grazing the purple ends of my mocha hair—a tassel to show I stand with the Verity. I lower my hand, smile, and descend the staircase with all the poise of a prom queen.

Toe, heel, toe, heel.

Chin up.

Shoulders back.

Green has overtaken every arch and pillar, the space transformed into an enchanted wood. Fresh pine garlands deck the railings, and hundreds of tea lights gleam and glow on sills and ledges. All eyes attend me, but mine lock on two.

Even from across the throne room the sight of him sends my stomach butterflies into a frenzy. His strong jaw works, lifting his stubble-surrounded lips into a crooked smile. Barely twenty-one, but he holds so much wisdom behind his cerulean gaze. He combs his fingers through his dark hair, then folds his hands in front of him. Waiting for the only one in the entire room I know he sees.

The acoustic quartet to my left plays a Celtic waltz, and I find myself striding in time to the tempo. The familiar sound is oxygen to my soul. Tables crafted from tree stumps sprout beneath the high arched windows on either side of the throne room. Wreaths and moss encircle tea light–filled jars at the table centers. Pine boughs twist around the marble columns supporting the five tiers of balconies above. White globe lights blink at me from the balcony railings, perfectly in sync with the music's elegant tempo. Paper lanterns dangle in a zigzag fashion between tiers, their hearts beating with the light of the Maple Mine Fairies.

The Second Reflection residents watch as I glide toward the dais. Toward him. I tilt my head back and a gasp escapes. Even the artwork on the painted dome ceiling has been freshened, the broad strokes and swirling colors more vibrant than ever. The four-tiered chandelier sends beads of colored light in every direction. I think of my favorite line from *Annie* as I glide across the cherrywood floor, all polished and Chrysler Building shiny. Miss Hannigan would be so proud.

The scents of cinnamon and pinewood welcome me in, and I suddenly find myself aching for a cup of hot cider. I'll have to keep an eye out for Regina Reeves. She *is* in charge of the kitchen staff, after all. She's known Mom since she was a girl, and she acted as midwife when Mom was in labor, so Reggie (and I'm the *only* one who calls her that) has a soft spot for me. Though she bears no Calling, she refers to herself as my "fairy godmother" and insists my desire is her command. Even if cider isn't being served, she'll bring some if I ask.

When I reach the bottom dais step, Joshua David extends a hand. This is it. The moment I've waited for since I took on the Verity two months ago. I'm ready, but I'm also not. *What if I can't do this? What if I can't—?*

But then Joshua's broad hand covers my smallish one. And like the soothing of the Verity, his touch assures me everything is going to be just fine. His gaze holds mine as he lifts my hand and caresses my knuckles with his lips, brushing more than my skin with his not-so-innocent touch. The dark stubble on his upper lip scratches, but I don't mind. For an instant I forget everything but this. Each heart-string pluck, pluck, plucks. "More," they seem to sing.

More.

This is right. This is real. I can do this.

Joshua winks and I release a breath I didn't know I was holding.

The quartet ceases as he guides me in a wide arc just as we rehearsed yesterday. The toe of my sneaker catches my dress hem. My eyes close and I prepare for the *rrrriiiipppp* that's sure to follow. But, as always, Joshua is one step ahead. Steadying me. Saving me from a royal faux pas.

When we're both facing forward, he releases my hand and I let it fall to my side. It takes everything in me to keep from clenching my sweaty palms into anxious fists. I think of what Mom always told me when I'd get nervous in a school play.

"Find me. Even if everyone in the audience is frowning, I'll give you the smile to keep you going."

It takes me all of two seconds to spot her, off to one side, Makai Archer's arms wrapped loosely around her growing belly. His gray-streaked charcoal hair is now long enough to gather into a ponytail. I shake my head, and a smile creeps to my cheeks. As a pair their contrast is undeniable. He's Bogart to her Bergman. An unlikely match, yet it's impossible to picture one without the other anymore.

Mom's brown eyes twinkle and the creases around her smile deepen. She offers an encouraging nod and I return the gesture. Inhale. Face the people once more.

"People of the Second," Joshua's voice booms. "On this, the twenty-fifth day of the First Month, I, Joshua David Henry, being of sound mind and valiant heart, do relinquish this here crown and bestow it upon the rightful ruler of the Second." Joshua removes the mirrorglass circlet at his temples. The same crown his father, King Aidan, wore before Jasyn Crowe took over. A diadem, I'm told, that would've weakened Jasyn had he tried to wear it. The reverse effect of mirrorglass would've counteracted the darkness within him. Put a cap on the Void's power like the Confine on an under-eighteen soul.

Add that to my list of things to research. *Check.*

When Joshua lifts the crown high in the air, the light filtering in through the windows reflects off of it, creating a prism effect and showering tiny rainbows throughout the throne room. Rainbows that remind me of the Verity's true form. Of the beauty and power residing inside.

This is it. It wasn't supposed to happen until spring. I was supposed to have two more months to prepare. But Joshua moved the date up, didn't see the need to wait. As the vessel of the Verity, I might as well be queen already. This is merely a formality.

I swallow. Clench my teeth.

"It is my honor to present to you the vessel of the Verity, the purest soul in this Reflection, Her Majesty, Queen Eliyana Olivia Ember. Long may she reign."

With exceptional care Joshua lowers the crown and places it upon my brow. The mirrorglass is cool on my forehead and I breathe in the finality of it. Something like a spark of electricity jolts my insides. The calm I felt just moments before dwindles, replaced by something dark and new. A hollow ache settling in my gut.

What in the Reflections is that?

I shake my head. It's just nerves. The Verity will soothe me again and I'll be fine. No second-guessing. Joshua has been interim king for two months, waiting patiently as I prepared for this day. But now it's my turn. I feel like Elsa of Arendelle, destined to be queen but terrified of the weight now resting on my narrow shoulders.

Am I good enough?

My gaze falls upon the people and I see them with new eyes. These aren't just *the* people, they're *my* people. Only eighteen and I'm responsible for an entire Reflection? How can I do this? The sole thing that qualifies me is the Verity. I'm no queen. I'm nothing more than an average, blemished—

"May I have this dance, Your Majesty?"

Kuna Lauti's voice draws me from my internal storm. I blink twice and nod. As my insecurities reigned, the world around me shifted. The quartet now plays an up-tempo waltz, and couples glide around the throne room in time with the melody.

Kuna's broad grin spreads from ear to ear, his full lips stretching over whiter-than-usual teeth. He must've stopped chewing tobacco. Stormy never did cease pestering him about it. I can't help but smile in return. Like a big brother, my best friend's husband always has a way of bringing light to the darkest of moments.

For an instant I forget the Verity's sudden absence. Forget tomorrow and duty and what being queen means. I place my pasty hand in his coffee-colored one. "Why, it would be my honor, good sir."

He chuckles and his entire body quakes. "If I didn't know any better, I'd say you were nervous to dance with a good-looking gentleman such as myself."

The knots in my gut unfurl. I look past him and spy Stormy leaning against a nearby column. She rolls her eyes and shakes her head. We exchange a smirk in the way that's become so natural, I can't even remember a time when we weren't joined at the hip.

As we twirl, Kuna lifts me off my feet now and then, making me break into full-on laughter. The Samoan's moves are big and dramatic, forcing me into giggle fits. What was I so worried about? Jasyn Crowe is dead, as is his lackey Haman. My traitorous half sister Ebony is locked away in the dungeons. The lovely but vicious Troll Isabeau and her stooge Gage are nowhere to be found, good riddance. Mom is alive and well, pregnant as can be with her husband, Makai, at her side. The Soulless are no more. All is right with the Second. Even the Void is contained—

I stifle a gasp and squeeze my eyes. *Drat.* I promised myself I wouldn't think about that. Not until I have the answer I seek.

I crane my neck to peer out one of the arched windows. The sun is setting. I'll stay another hour, then slip away. There are more important things than coronation parties. I'm queen now. And as queen my first mission will be to do the one thing no Verity's vessel has ever done before.

Destroy the Void once and for all.

TWO

your power

So much for only staying an hour. The sun has long since sunk into the horizon, and the guests have exchanged dancing for light conversation and sips of champagne. The quartet continues to play low in the background as I take a much-needed moment of solace. I slip off my shoes and shove them beneath the throne where I sit. Wiggle and flex my toes. Seriously, I am so glad I didn't wear heels. If my feet ache this much in flat Converse, what agony would I be in had I donned stilettos? I must've danced with every Guardian in the Second. If I have to do one more box step, I'll end up with blisters the size of Staten Island. #nojoke

Resisting the urge to swing my legs over the arm of the throne and fall asleep right here, I sit a little taller and scan the scene before me. The Second's residents are straight out of a Fairy tale, garbed in silk and taffeta, cravats and cummerbunds. Has it only been two months since these people were beggars and vagabonds? Rebels?

Joshua has done so much in such a short time to restore this Reflection to its previous state. How can I fill his shoes? Never thought I'd see Saul Preacher with a trimmed beard, minus a knit cap, plus a tux. It's quite a sight, especially considering he keeps tugging at his bow tie like it's an electric dog collar. He shoots me one of his classic glares. Guess being queen doesn't matter—some things never change.

My muscles tense and a seedling of fear sprouts. It's been hours since I felt the Verity stir. This has never happened. Could something be wrong?

I shift in my seat and move my focus to Robyn and Wren Song. They stand near the back of the room with their father, Wade, and mother, Lark. I owe a lot to this family. Wren rescued me from Haman. Robyn and Wade tended to my wounds. And Lark? She aided me when Gage tried to kidnap me. The woman offers a soft smile, the kindness behind her black and yellow eyes filling me with warmth.

Wren notices me and my insides freeze over. She glares, then flips her midnight blue–streaked hair over one shoulder.

Robyn follows her gaze. I smile and wave. Robyn does the same despite the elbow in the ribs Wren gives her.

My anxiety eases a smidge despite the Verity's silence. I make a mental note to invite Robyn for tea next week. Mom will be so proud.

When my attention rests on Joshua, he's already watching me He winks from his perch at the bottom of the grand staircase.

I smile and my cheeks flame. He's been doing this a lot lately. Flirting. Wearing his heart on his sleeve. I'm still not quite used to it. After three years as "just friends," it feels a little odd to be so open about our feelings. And there's this other thing, too, this ping of doubt I get whenever he looks at me this way.

What if it isn't real?

What if his feelings are merely a result of our childhood connection—the bond created by the Verity? If we'd met under normal circumstances and he hadn't known his soul was linked to mine, would he have seen me as anything more than a naive teenage girl with a crush?

As if reading my mind, he makes his way toward me. It's like his goal these past months has been to prove his love. To prove his most recent Kiss of Infinity wasn't a product of something artificial. The weight riding on his coattails is undeniable. Whenever we're alone I sense it. In the way his brows pinch when I'm not as affectionate as he is. In the silence festering between us when I can't think of anything to say. I don't mean to be so insecure about us, but how can I not be? How will I ever truly know if his love for me is genuine, or if it's just a result of our intertwined past? Did he give me a Kiss of Infinity because he loves me, or does he love me because he gave me a Kiss of Infinity?

He was a child when he bestowed it. Would he still have chosen me those years later had that been the first time we met? I'm still unsure about the logistics. What truly lies behind such a kiss? Beneath that deepest part of a person, that place in his heart of hearts he may not know exists?

All the more reason to hurry back to the library. There must be something in one of those books to help me solve this puzzle. Question upon question began to surface after Jasyn's demise. If the Void enters the one the Verity's vessel cares for most, why didn't it enter Joshua, or even Mom, for that matter? Who gave the first Kiss of Infinity? Where did the Void originate? It must have had a beginning, right? And where there is a beginning, there must also be an end.

When Joshua reaches me I open my mouth to tell him I'm calling it a night, but he presses a warm finger to my parted lips. Heat spreads through my core. But it's not from the Verity. No, this is what I have officially dubbed "the Joshua Effect," a.k.a. going weak in the knees anytime I think he's going to kiss me.

Because as much as it kills me, I still don't know if I returned his Kiss of Infinity. I do like kissing him though. A lot.

But of course his lips don't brush mine as I wish they would. As open as he's been with me recently, Joshua is still a very private person. PDA isn't his thing. No big deal. It's not like laying one on me in front of the entire Reflection would help me be sure of his love.

Then again, it wouldn't hurt either.

He lowers his finger and smiles.

"Thank you for this. It was perfect." I don't bother to hide my less-than-graceful yawn.

"The night has not yet ended." He turns and claps his hands.

The chatter hushes almost instantly. The ease with which he commands a room will never cease to leave my jaw slack. Is this the easygoing boy I fell for in my backyard what seems like so long ago? He's a common Edmond Dantès turned noble Count of Monte Cristo. Will I ever gain such confidence, such presence?

"Thank you all once again for attending this extraordinary occasion. You honor your queen."

Unexpected irritation pinches. I squint at his back. Shouldn't *I* be the one thanking everyone? Why does he feel the need to speak for me? I'm queen now. And I'm standing right here.

My expression softens. *Whoa. Where did that come from?* I haven't felt such anger—no, I haven't felt *any* anger since taking on the Verity. Any negative emotion—darkness—that has attempted to surface has been quashed by the light. I gulp. *Ignore it. It's a fluke. A glitch.* I'm just exhausted, overwhelmed by it all. Everything will be fine in the morning.

". . . It is a tradition that has been passed down for generations . . ."

Blink, blink. Breathe. What's Joshua saying?

". . . The previous Verity's vessel always bestows a gift upon the new . . ."

My vision blurs. Stomach churns. The crown upon my brow feels a million pounds heavier.

". . . sought a unique gift. A priceless token . . ."

This is it. I'm going to pass out. My first day as queen and everyone is going to see me as weak. Fragile. Opposite of royal.

"El, did you hear me?" Joshua's low tenor comes at me as if from far away.

My mouth is so dry, but I manage, "Huh?" Huh? Could I be any less regal? I am so botching this.

His jaw flexes and I catch a hint of the stern, cold Joshua I saw in the Forest of Night last November—er, I mean, Eleventh Month. He glances between me and the guests. The guests and me. "Will you play with me?" He lists his head toward the baby grand piano situated beside the quartet.

The fog clears. Joshua and I haven't played music together in too long. We've been so busy saving the Second and then getting things back to normal, leisure has been put on the back burner.

Tears well and I blink them away as he leads me to the piano. He pulls out the bench and I scoop my gown beneath me. Sit. My bare feet are visible now, but I couldn't care less. The ivories are slick against my fingertips. For the first time in a long time, I feel at home.

Joshua grabs his guitar from a stand behind the piano, then slips the strap over his head and strums in the same beat. When he begins a tune I'm oh so familiar with, my heart soars. It's a duet I've always wanted to play together but never dared request.

I know the chords by heart and soul, have played them solo dozens of times. My fingers dance along the keys with a grace my two left feet could never muster. Accompanied by guitar the song is fuller, richer than I've ever experienced live. We play the instrumental tune once through before our voices join in at the chorus. The lyrics to "I See the Light" from *Tangled* hold new meaning now. Singing of truth and light and seeing with new eyes. The perfect Verity song. This moment should be flawless. An untainted reflection of our love.

Then why does the churning in my gut return? Why does something feel off?

I trip over my next lyric, then forget the following line altogether. I play the wrong key, then go off-key. I clear my throat. Try again. Fail.

What in the Reflections is wrong with me?

That's when I hear it. A new melody. Haunting. Floating across the waves of my brain like "The Music of the Night" from *The Phantom of the Opera*. It could be that song, but it isn't. It's like every song and no song. Familiar and foreign. Strange and new and thrilling and I have to play it, have to get it out of my head and hear it for real.

A throat clears.

My head whips up.

Oh no.

Joshua stares at me, hurt residing in his clouded blue eyes. His mouth is turned down and I have the urge to kiss him there. To turn that frown upright again. To apologize for ruining his precious gift.

I feel the gapes boring into me from every angle. I don't have to see their faces to know what they're thinking.

Disappointment.

Phony.

Imposter.

But I don't have a chance to face them. To apologize for screwing up as usual.

Pop, pop, pop. Glass shatters.

Gasp. A woman screams.

Rip. A baby cries.

This. Cannot. Be. Happening. Not today. I'm on the ground. Beneath the piano bench. Hands clasped over the back of my head. Joshua is here, covering me. It takes all of one, two, three seconds to push him off. To find my footing. To rise.

I am queen. The vessel of the Verity. I will not allow my past mistakes to define my future decisions. I will not cower like the helpless girl I once was.

A cluster of Guardians has formed a barrier around us. Backs toward us. Weapons at the ready.

I whirl. Jump. Crouch to see something. Anything. The source. Where is it? If this is an attack, it serves to reason there are attack*ers*—

Pain slices my bicep. Am I bleeding? So much spinning.

"Your Highness, are you all right?" some Guardian asks. A woman? Can't tell for all the nausea.

Blink. Focus. *Do not pass out.* The arched windows surrounding the throne room explode in a domino effect, raining glass one after the other. The panes land in shards on the floor, mix with melting snow and ice. The guests scatter. Some bolt for the grand staircase while others seek shelter beneath tables. Guardians beyond our cluster discard jackets and ties, withdrawing weapons hidden at their ankles or strapped to their backs.

It's like some horrible scene from an action film. Except there's no director to yell, "Cut!" No cameraman to stop the chaos or adjust the boom mic. This scene is in real time. No second takes. No do-overs.

Just when I thought everything was good again.

And then the most awful sound I've ever heard pierces the din. Rises above every other shout. Someone is crying . . . no, *wailing*. But the worst part? I know that cry. I've heard it before—in Wichgreen Village right after Ky threw a knife at Gage's heart when he betrayed us all. There's no mistaking Stormy's soul-racking sobs.

The Guardians take action. They move Joshua and me toward the dais, a current too mighty to swim against. Up on the dais they form a line, and Joshua drags me to the throne. The hidden door behind the tapestry depicting a map of this Reflection grates open.

Joshua shouts something, shoves me just beyond the door. He releases me. He's speaking, but I can't focus on his words. I only hear her. I can't make myself ignore the wretched sound.

I lean past Joshua, rising on my toes and swinging my head back and forth. Where is she? Where—?

There! A neon-purple pixie cut. Stormy. She's kneeling over a very still, oversized body. A body resting in a growing pool of blood.

Joshua's grip is firm around my waist. He pulls me back, deeper into the secret space behind the wall.

I twist. Wrench. Slip beneath his arm and stumble past him, tripping on my dress. The Guardian chain stops me, holding me back like some twisted game of Red Rover.

No, no, no. This *will* be just like the other times. Death will not win. It can't.

"*Release me,*" I sing.

Their linked arms fall. And I run.

When I reach them, Stormy's sobs bleed from her lips. "Help him." She's shaking, putting pressure on Kuna's wound. "*Pleeaase.*"

I kneel and force myself to take in Kuna's state. His breathing is so shallow. He looks unnatural this way. Big and strong and helpless, cocoa skin paled as if soaked in cream. His eyelids flutter, the whites beneath them bloodshot. Stormy strokes his bald head with her right hand, her mouth contorted.

Something warm and wet soaks through the fabric at my knees. I can't look, don't need a visual of Kuna's blood staining my dress.

"Hush now," Kuna whispers, the words barely audible. His thick fingers twiddle, and Stormy clutches them so tightly her knuckles whiten.

"Wait," she chokes. *"Wait."*

I lay my hands on Kuna, summoning the Physic within to reverse this unwarranted tragedy. I haven't had much practice with this branch of my Calling, aside from the few scrapes I've healed under the castle Physic's instruction this past month. No time for doubts though. I have to act.

Kuna needs me.

I muster all the love I have for my dying friend and sing new lyrics to my own Mirror melody. They change a bit every time, catering a new song to each situation.

> *"Hear my voice, my friend.*
> *This will not be the end.*
> *Let these words be the remedy.*
> *Stay where you are meant to be.*
> *Stay with us. Stay with me . . ."*

I choke on the last lyric. This must be why my Mirror Calling didn't vanish when I took on the Verity. Because my song is still needed, and maybe the Verity knew. But why isn't it working? Why isn't Kuna's state changing? Healing?

"What's happening?" Stormy's face is trailed with tears. "Why isn't your power saving him?"

I don't have an answer for her. Because when Kuna's eyes stare off into space, it seems surreal. Because when he stills I feel as if I'm watching the shocker ending to my favorite TV series. I can't believe it, but there it is.

And there's nothing I can do to change it.

Joshua crouches beside me then. He drags a dagger over his palm, and pure Ever blood *drip, drip, drips* onto Kuna's open wound.

I'm longing for Kuna to gasp, to blink, to flinch—anything to indicate the Ever blood is taking effect. Ten seconds. Thirty. A minute. Then five. Nothing. We're too late. Kuna is gone.

THREE

what has been lost

When I was ten, my hamster died. I don't even recall the stupid thing's name. I just remember standing there, watching through the plastic pane of its cage, waiting for its furry belly to rise and fall. Rise and fall.

Rise. And. Fall.

As I stare at Kuna's motionless middle, all I can think about is my childhood pet and how, if I had done something more ― different— maybe it *he* would've survived. Despite the screaming and the clambering and the shattered glass reflecting the ruins of my heart, I experience a moment of unequivocal clarity. Time is nonexistent. It's as if I'm standing behind a window, just like with my dead hamster, removed but here. I see but don't feel. I know but can't believe.

Kuna is really dead. And he's not coming back.

Stormy lies crumpled beside him. She pulls her knees to her chest, and she hugs Kuna's arm as if it's a life preserver.

I stroke her short hair, smoothing the fringed locks between my fingers. My chest constricts, and I have to bite my lip to keep my own emotions from surfacing. We all loved Kuna, but no one will be as affected as the Guardian lying beside me, resembling a helpless toddler more than the fearless warrior she is.

Joshua places his palm on Kuna's forehead, then sweeps his hand over Kuna's eyelids. The big lug could be sleeping. I half expect him to sit up, slap his knee the way he does, and laugh, "Gotcha!" Stormy would be furious, and they wouldn't speak for days. But they'd make up eventually. This horrific event would be forgotten.

This can't be the end for him—*them.*

It is.

I glance at Joshua. Any second he'll snap out of his trance, tell me what to do. I'm the Verity's vessel for crying out loud, yet even I couldn't bring Kuna back. It doesn't make sense. First me, and now Joshua's Ever blood? Why here? Why now?

Why Kuna?

"If someone is already meant to die, if it's their time, nothing can change that. Not a touch from a Physic or a drop of Ever blood. Death is a Calling all its own."

Ky's words come screaming back to me. The explanation is so close, so fresh, it's almost as if I hear him speaking aloud. This happens sometimes. When I miss him or feel particularly worried about the burden he carries. That's when his voice calls to me—like a voice in a dream.

"Leave. Now."

It's what Ky said to Gage the night he tried to kidnap me at Wichgreen Village. It's what he'd say now if he were here.

Panic wells as the memory melts away the numbness, giving way to pain and fear. We have to get out. Whoever did this didn't go to such lengths to kill Kuna alone. We need to move. I need to find Mom and Robyn and everyone else I love.

"Joshua, help me get Stormy." I try to unwind her arm from Kuna's, but the attempt only causes her to wail louder.

Joshua doesn't respond.

I touch his knee. "Joshua—"

He pounds the floor with his fist. Tears at Kuna's extra-large shirt, ripping it open. Buttons fly. Joshua cuts his hand again, deeper.

Bile rises into my throat, burns, but I can't look away. I've never seen him so—*gulp*—afraid.

Blood smears Kuna's chest. The rusty scent forces me to cup my hand over my mouth and nose. When Joshua presses his bloody palm onto the wound, his arm shakes and his bicep flexes. He knows as well as I do Kuna is gone. But, just like Stormy, he can't let go.

"Come on," Joshua whispers through clenched teeth. "Come *on*."

"Joshua." I reach out and brush his hand with my fingertips.

He rejects my touch, flicking it away like a pest.

Now I *know* something's off. It's as if we've switched places. The calm that surfaces isn't the same cloaking warmth of the Verity I've grown so fond of, but it's enough to make me act. We're running out of time and I seem to be the only one here coherent enough to see it.

I don't have to worry about Mom. Makai would've made her his first priority.

The Guardians have things under control. The people are well cared for. No question.

The best thing I can do now is protect myself—protect the Verity.

Joshua hangs his head, grabs a fistful of Kuna's newly dyed shirt. Everything in me pleads to comfort him. I can see he's holding back the emotion threatening to break and curl over him like a tumultuous tidal wave. But Joshua doesn't drown. He's a survivor and he won't give in.

Eyes rimmed in red, he faces me. "El, you have to take Stormy." His voice is choked but firm, reiterating what I said only moments ago, as if it were his idea.

I nod, thankful he's returned to the present. The noise surrounding us, warbled before as if we were underwater, pulses against my skull. Guardians bark orders. So much pandemonium. It's hard to tell who's friend and who's foe at the core of it all.

But *where* are the attackers? People bleed. Cry out. Take cover. Popping and shooting sounds resound. Yet there's no one aside from the guests and the Guardians and staff. The Maple Mine Fairies have abandoned their lantern havens, probably returned to the safety of the mines. I know Makai can become invisible, but a whole group of villains? Or maybe there's just one. No way to tell.

Joshua rises and helps me pry Stormy from her husband. Together we bring her to a hunched stand. Pain skewers my arm.

When I notice the blood seeping from the space beneath my torn sleeve, I draw in a sharp breath through my nose. I'd almost forgotten I was injured.

Joshua reaches his bloody palm toward my cut.

I shake my head. "I'm fine." As a Mirror I contain all the Callings, so I heal quickly. But even if I'd lost my Calling, the way I should've when the Verity chose me, it wouldn't matter. My connection to Joshua acts as an automatic repair. Because he gave me a Kiss of Infinity, his life replaces mine. And his Ever Calling takes it one step beyond. It's almost as if his blood runs through my veins, healing me from the inside out.

Joshua knows all of this, yet he presses his skin to mine anyway. But the ache does not subside. We exchange a frown. Kuna was one thing, but now Joshua's blood can't even heal a small cut? My temples pulse against my crown. This is bad.

Stormy slumps into my side as our trio hobbles toward the dais. We climb the steps, skirt the upended table, trip over chairs with legs akimbo, and stand before the wall concealing the passageway where Mom has no doubt already escaped with my uncle-slash-new dad. The tapestry decorating the wall is torn, folding down on itself like a droopy eyelid.

Joshua taps a ten-digit code into the keypad to the tapestry's left. He faces me as the wall grates open. "Once you're inside punch in the code to close the wall. You know it?"

I nod. The code is changed weekly, and only a handful of castle residents are trusted with the information.

"Good." He removes Stormy's arms from around his shoulder, transferring her full weight to me.

I'm stronger now than I used to be, but with Stormy hanging on to me alone, I realize I'm still weak. When this day ends I'll have to work harder. The people now count on me to protect them. My Calling and the fact I'm the Verity's vessel aren't enough. I need to stop relying on these things as a fail-safe and find my own strength.

With one last kiss to my temple, Joshua hurries us through the opening and stands back. I set Stormy down with as much care as I'm able and rush to the interior keypad. It consists of letters, numbers, and symbols.

Five. B. Handprint. Eight. Moon. Four. A. T . . .

When the final piece of the code is in, I train my eyes on Joshua. He stands just past the opening, watching until we're secure. The wall revolves inward, scraping closer, closer, closer. It takes everything in me not to pull him back here with us. Just as I'm about to lose sight of him, my gaze falls to his bloody palm, the one he sliced deep in an effort to save Kuna. I turn my own hand over and trace my fingers across the unharmed space.

The stone wall closes with a finalizing thunder. I clench my fists and swallow back the tears over what has been lost. This confirms the fear I've had for two months.

Because Joshua cut himself.

And I didn't feel a thing.

fOUR

joshua

The expression on El's face before the wall closed was all the proof I required. And now I know the truth about what transpired between us.

Something dies inside me, but I grieve the loss and move on. Even if she didn't bestow a Kiss of Infinity, even if she can't feel my pain the way I feel hers, it doesn't mean she never will. This knowledge only gives me greater determination to fight for her and rid her heart of the pest known as Kyaphus. He and I may share the Void, and he may have the upper hand with a Kiss of Infinity from her to his name, but the better man will win.

And I have something he lacks, as he is gone and won't be returning.

I peel off my tux jacket and toss it aside, then check both shirt-sleeves to confirm they're still intact. Concealing the Void on my right arm has been a breeze these winter months, but come summer I'll have to figure out a reason for staying covered.

I command the dais and take in the scene, scanning each detail and committing it to memory. This is Guardian Training 101—think first, act second. Who would do this? Who would have motive? Who might own the gift of invisibility? An unknown relative of Makai's?

I run the list of possible suspects through my head. My biggest suspicion would be Jonathan Gage, traitor to the Guardians and the Verity. But he is nowhere to be seen, and even if he is involved, he couldn't have done this alone. This unseen attack is some sort of sorcery. I have never witnessed anything like it. People dropping left and right. Bleeding. Dying. Where are the weapons, the arrows, the bullets? Whoever planned this planned well. As chaotic as this seems, my gut tells me that is precisely how it is meant to appear. A sleight of hand. A trick on the eyes. This is merely a framework waiting for concrete to be poured.

As if in response to my questioning, the room shakes and shudders. Several gasps and whimpers resound, and the oak doors beyond the top of the grand staircase bang open. I reach to draw my sword and clench my fists. I'm not wearing it. Excellent, or as my adoptive father Nathaniel Archer would say in his Third Reflection accent, "Brilliant."

Of all the days to let down my guard.

Outside, the wind howls. The people cower on either side of the room, but I stand my ground as we watch the doorway in anticipation. I narrow my eyes and crouch, picking up an oversized glass shard before rising once more. It may not be my sword, but it'll do.

Several Guardians are absent, having evacuated who they could through the tunnels. Those who remain act as medics or consolers. When they notice me they come forward, forming a barricade at the bottom of the dais stairs before me.

A rich cackle echoes just as a figure taller than the grand doors ducks beneath their frame. When the figure straightens to full height—eight feet tall at least—I no longer question the motive of the attack.

The Troll glides forward and down the grand stairs, her Mask form commanding the room. Her scaly dress reveals too much of her leathery golden skin, and I have to force myself not to look away and gag. She's wearing a cape made of hawk feathers that trails behind her, and I feel for whatever poor animal induced the woman's wrath. The staff she carries is topped with shards of steel, making it double as a spear.

Not that she needs a weapon. The curling ram's horns protruding from her head are the sole defense she needs. When I interrogated Ebony Archer two months ago, I discovered her mother, Isabeau, only appears as a Troll when she's on the warpath. This can't be good.

Isabeau halts ten paces from the Guardian barricade and twiddles her dragon-like fingernails against her steel-shard staff. "My, my, what an odd way to greet a coronation guest. I was only an hour late, after all." She sneers, black eyes shifting east and west. Then she palms her chest and throws her head back, giving off another sickly sweet cackle. "Oh, that's right." She levels her gaze at me. "I wasn't invited."

I grip the glass shard tighter, and blood trickles from my hand onto the floor. I do not hiss or clench my teeth despite the relief my Ever blood fails to provide. I'm accustomed to pain. Still, I'll need to be more careful until my Calling is functional again. It's not about what I can endure, but about the strength I'll need to face whatever comes next.

With a hefty breath I ask, "What is your business here, Troll?"

"My business?" Isabeau paces in a circle. Several guests recoil deeper beneath the tree-stump tables. "Why, to offer the mother of our new ruler my congratulations, of course. Where is dear Elizabeth?" She makes a show of glancing around. "The woman has acquired everything she has ever wanted, has she not? First my husband, and now his brother? I hear they are expecting a child." She faces me again. "What. Delightful. News."

I am not oblivious to the Troll's story, as I heard Ebony go on about it while I was restrained behind the dais wall eleven months previous. Tiernan Archer wanted a son and left Isabeau when she could only give him a daughter. Her grudge against El's mother runs deep. Because Elizabeth has everything Isabeau doesn't.

I open my mouth to command the Guardians to seize her, but someone speaks before I have the opportunity.

"You are not welcome here, Troll." Preacher steps forward, always the first to break formation. "But you've done us a favor." His weapon of choice is a bow and arrows, but today he carries a battle-ax. He raises it high as if about to strike. "We've spent months searching for you. Now you've come to us"—he snorts—"you've made our job a crowe of a lot easier."

I'm forced to stifle a snort at the Second Reflection slang. I suppose even with Jasyn Crowe dead, his name will live on in the form of a curse.

Isabeau approaches Preacher. He's the shortest of the Guardians, but his gruff demeanor makes up for his deficient stature. I'm thankful for the distraction, which I know is exactly what Preacher intends it to be. It gives me ample time to form a strategy for capture. With at least a dozen Guardians missing and so many injured subjects present, the feat will be difficult but not impossible. I only need to decipher how to take Isabeau down without harming anyone else.

"What is your name?" Isabeau glares down at Preacher.

"What's it to you?"

I spot Wade Song beneath one of the tables on the room's west end. His wife, Lark, has transformed into her owl state, perched on his shoulder like a sentinel. Her brown and white feathers ruffle, a sign she's prepared to take flight. Their daughter Robyn shields them both, her Bengal tiger coming out to play. She may not be eighteen yet, her Confine still in place, but even with flat teeth and no claws her bite is as ferocious as her growl.

I shift my gaze down and to the left. Wade's other daughter, Wren, stands as one of a handful of female Guardians in my barricade. Tougher than any other woman I've met, Wren is not someone to be trifled with. Her griffin form towers above the Guardians on either side of her.

El's Mirror song along with my Ever blood failed Kuna, but the Mask Calling, at least, seems to be intact.

I catch Wade's eye, listing my head and blinking twice. Wade is a Physic, not a Guardian, but being a father of one I am certain he knows the Silent Code. His brow furrows and for an instant I wonder if perhaps he did not understand. I make the signal again and this time he nods.

As Wade begins to tap people on the shoulder, soundlessly directing them to move as far back in the room as they are able, I return my attention to Isabeau and Preacher.

"You're nothing more than a bully dressed in Troll's clothing." Preacher spits on Isabeau's bare toes. "No wonder Tiernan left you. No man in his right mind would live in a house with that stench." He pinches his nose and leans away. "Oh, excuse me, you don't live in a house, do you? I meant no man would live beneath a bridge with that stench."

Sweat beads at my temples and I'm positive Preacher has gone too far. But the man does not back down, not even when Isabeau raises her hand and claws him square across his bearded chin.

Ah, so her weakness is confirmed. Talk of Tiernan gets to her. I must remember to give my regards to Preacher for his strategy when all is said and done.

"How dare you, a mere peasant, speak to me in this manner." She brandishes her staff and aims it straight at the Guardian's chest. "I ought to rip out your heart for such disrespect." She takes a breath, then steps away, a sunshine smile spreading across her face. Collected once again, she addresses me. "But that is not the reason I have come."

"Then why have you come?" My words are for her but my peripheral vision attends the people. Most have made their way to the far corners. I exhale.

"To collect payment. Haman—"

"—is no longer of this Reflection," I finish for her. "I am well aware of his vow to you." El filled me in, terrified Isabeau would expect her reward despite Haman's death. "But as you and I both know, a Kiss of Accord is no longer binding if one of the parties passes on."

"Ah, ah, ah, better check again. For it is here you are in error."

And here is the line she planned to deliver since her grand entrance.

"What game are you playing, Isabeau?"

"No game. I never fool around when it comes to debts owed.

Haman may be deceased, but I live on. And if the promise was made to the one who survived, the vow remains binding."

"The only debt owed here is yours. I assume a hundred years in the dungeons will suffice."

Isabeau yawns. "Don't be foolish, boy. Her Majesty the Fairy Queen is more powerful than you realize. If you think imprisoning me will hinder her, you are sincerely mistaken."

The Fairy Queen? She's surely bluffing. I have witnessed Fairies with my own two eyes—they lit up this very throne room minutes ago—but talk of a queen is the stuff of legend. A fable Nathaniel Archer relayed to me as a lad. The Fairy Queen is said to be immortal, older than the Verity itself.

"But enough chitchat," Isabeau continues. "I merely dropped by to check on Elizabeth's progress. To ensure she knows I have not forgotten what I am owed."

That is all I require. Isabeau believes she has won this day, but I'm not so easily deterred from my final goal. "Now!" My bellow is sudden but the Guardians don't hesitate. They've been awaiting the command, standing by while I extracted the information I sought.

They surround the Troll, one-story condos to her skyscraper.

Wren snatches a corner of Isabeau's cape in her eagle's beak and soars around the Troll in a spiral, wrapping it around her like a flag about a pole.

Preacher slices at her shins with his ax while a Guardian called Droid scales Isabeau as if she were a wall, holding his knife between his teeth, headed straight for the woman's neck.

I reel my right arm back, ready to fling the broken glass at her eye. But the Troll merely cackles.

And, in the blink of an eye, Isabeau vanishes.

FIVE

shine

I've been through this passage once before, my first week here. The grand tour was a little overwhelming. Secret doorways and hiding places snake between the castle walls. Thank the Verity for my Scrib memory, otherwise I might not be able to keep track of which passage leads where. This one, for instance, heads straight down the hill and then out to some stables in the Forest of Night—er, White. I keep forgetting the name changed when Shadow Territory ceased to exist.

The Flight Stables are stocked with horses and supplies and whatever else evacuees might require. Not that I need a secret passageway. I'm able to pass through any reflective surface using my Calling. I can even take Stormy with me. We could go far away from here, hide out until we think it's safe.

Except we can't. Because we're not the only ones in danger. Better to head to the stables and see who else might need help. It's what a queen would do.

And . . . even if we could go . . . can we? I couldn't save Kuna. What if I can't mirror walk either? Shudder. *Focus. One thing at a time.*

I feel around the wall near the descending spiral stairs for a switch. My right shoulder throbs. I roll it. Stormy gets the hint and straightens a little. It helps. Barely.

Please, please . . . Aha! *Flip*. The stairs illuminate along the sides like the aisles at a theater. Our path now visible, we descend.

The stairs go on forever, taunting us. When we finally reach the hall at the bottom, lit by inverted dome lamps on the low ceiling, Stormy begins mumbling. Several minutes pass before I decipher her words. Either they grow clearer, or I'm an expert at interpreting blubber-speak.

"He saved me. He saved me. He saved me." Sobs release at intervals between each repeated phrase.

I take a deep breath. Earthy air expands my lungs. Question after question batters the forefront of my mind.

Who? *Bam.*

Why? *Slam.*

How? *Wham.*

At last we exit the hall. A hay-strewn path leads to a stack of hay bales, a pitchfork leaning against one end. Stormy breaks away, not even wincing at the strong manure scent. She slumps onto the nearest bale, clutches her head in her clawed hands, tugs at the purple ends of her hair.

I massage my sore shoulder and look around for someone who might sit with her. No one. Maybe the others are outside. "I'm going to see if I can find us some food and water. Okay?"

She doesn't nod. The only indication she's alive at all is the minute undulation of her curved back. I walk away with a backward glance. I won't leave her too long. We just need some sustenance, maybe something to clean the blood—Kuna's blood—off Stormy's arms.

My thoughts disconnect and string together. Will I be able to get her to eat? What kind of sick monster crashes a coronation and starts shooting people? Why couldn't we save Kuna? Where in the Reflections is the stupid supply closet?

Soft soil mutes my footsteps. I peek into a few of the stalls. Where are the horses? Did the others already leave? Uneasiness churns within. It's so quiet. *Too* quiet. Mom, at least, should be here. This was the passage nearest her. She and Makai wouldn't have taken off without me.

Unless . . . she has someone aside from me to care for now.

My new baby brother or sister would've been her first priority. And Makai would've insisted she get as far away from the castle as possible, especially on the chance Isabeau was involved. The Guardians never found her after we defeated Jasyn. The Troll is still out there somewhere, hating Mom, seeking revenge.

Of course Mom isn't here. No one's waiting for us. Everyone would've assumed I was the Guardians' first priority. There'd be no question in anyone's mind Joshua had me covered. He still treats me as if I'm fragile. Breakable. As if I haven't changed.

I thought I'd proven myself by this point. What's it going to take to show him I'm not the girl who runs and hides at the slightest noise anymore?

I huff and pick up my pace. No use worrying about that now. The supply closet has to be here somewhere. I'll grab some necessities, a pack if I can find one, and get Stormy out of here. If I'm still able to mirror walk, we could go to Lisel Island or Lynbrook Province. Maybe even the Third Reflection. My heart skips at the idea.

New York.

Home.

Ky.

It's rare I allow myself to think of him outside my goal to destroy the Void. Because if I don't keep it strictly business, strange things happen to my heart. Unwelcome things. Fluttery, achy, anti-Joshua things.

Get it together. Now.

I've no idea where Ky went, but I do know he left to find his younger sister, Khloe—also my half sister, so weird. Jasyn said she was being well cared for. But by whom? And where? The Third's as good a place to start as any. If we're going away, we might as well make use of our time. I could find Ky, tell him of my secret search. The Void may have already become too much for him to bear. What if he hasn't been able to find Khloe because of it? What if he needs the light of the Verity to quell the darkness within? What if he needs *me*?

Determination motivates my steps. The faster I find supplies,

the sooner we can leave. Calm washes my nerves. Mom's fine, she
has Makai. The people have Joshua, a better king these past two
months than the queen I've been today. But who does Ky have?

I'm sprinting through the stables now. These aren't like the
ones on the castle grounds. Instead of a U-shape, these form a grid.
Maybe around the next corner—

"Em," a voice—Ky's voice—whispers. But not in my head. Not
a memory. I actually *hear* it.

My eyelids snap open. Can't breathe. One. Two. Three. I pivot
on my heel. No one there. I shake it off Taylor Swift–style, turn, and
round the corner. Sigh. The supply closet. I dash to it, clutch the
handle like a lifeline, yank the door open. Jars upon jars of bottled
goods line the shelves. Tan sacks of seeds and nuts slump on the
floor alongside two cases of water in corked glass bottles. It's so cold
some of the contents are frozen. I crouch and lean forward, grab for
two bottles toward the back—

"Ember."

I jerk and hit my head on the shelf. "Bleep." Ebony's wannabe
curse slips out and the bottles drop, crash, splash to the ground. I
fall onto my rear and glance over one shoulder.

Yep, diagnosis confirmed. I'm going insane. Or maybe it's post-
traumatic stress. That's a thing, and I'm totally experiencing it.
Why else would I be hearing voices? No, not *voices*. Just one. Could
this be some morphing of the Scrib within? Instead of remember-
ing spoken words, I'm actually hearing them now?

Three beats later I gather a couple of unbroken, only partially
frozen water bottles, scramble to my feet, and grab a jar filled with
something brownish. Next I snatch a sack off a hook on the door,
open it. Perfect. A flashlight and a few medical supplies rest inside.
I add the water bottles and food, thread my arm through the sack's
single strap, and shuffle back toward where I left Stormy. I pass
saddles. And rope. A giant copper basin. I look left. Right. My
brows cinch. Is this the way I came?

"Em. Please."

I halt, clench my arms so I don't drop anything again.

Something flashes in my peripheral vision. I whip my head left. There. In the basin's reflection. It's— Squint. Couldn't be. I creep closer.

Huff. Nothing but my own disheveled reflection. I tuck loose strands of hair behind my ears and kick the basin over for good measure. I really am off my rocker. The stress of current events has me hallucinating. Unless—

What if I'm seeing through to another Reflection?

No. I wasn't even focusing, let alone using my song. Impossible.

When I find Stormy, she's in the exact state I left her. I offer her one of the water bottles, slipping it through the space between her bent arms. She sips and sets the bottle on the ground.

What do I say to my dearest friend? Loss isn't foreign to me, yet I still have no idea how to react when it happens to someone else. There are no words. No non-cliché ones anyway.

I don't want to be insensitive and rush her. We can spare a few minutes. I take a swig of my own water, lean it against the hay bale, and unscrew the jar's lid. Sniff. Something with cinnamon. Apples? A distant memory. Joshua and peach chunks and—

"He knew. He knew, and he gave his life for mine anyway." Stormy's words are faint, but they're present, hanging in the air like the after scent of burnt toast.

My appetite has vanished. I screw the lid back on the apple gunk. "What do you mean?"

"Kuna." She wipes her nose with her sleeve. "He knew what I did. He knew . . ." One shuddered sob. ". . . about me and Gage."

My nails dig into my palms. Jonathan Gage. Commander of the Guardians in Makai's absence. Supposed friend and protector. Cowardly traitor. All around jerk-wad. "How did he find out?"

She traces little circles over the silky iridescent fabric draping her lap. It's the first time I've seen her in a dress. "I told him. I couldn't live with the guilt of it any longer." Her hands form fists.

Oh. Wow. "When?" I reach over and cover one of her fists with both hands.

"After you defeated Crowe." Her voice sounds far away. She sniffs. "It's weird. Kuna wasn't angry." Two hiccups. "It was as if he knew. He knew from the beginning and he'd forgiven me before I even asked."

"Oh . . . Stormy." I wrap an arm around her shoulders. Dam the emotions threatening to burst free and flood my heart. Kuna was a better man than most. Of course he knew. And of course he'd forgiven. It's who he was.

Stormy sobs into my shoulder for a long time. And I let her. How did we get here? I've noticed there's this moment—an event you can pinpoint—in each relationship. A moment that defines what it will be from then on. With Joshua it was our night singing a duet on Broadway's empty stage, which still makes me ache every time I think about it. With Ky it was when he saved me from Gage, or rather, the embrace that followed. For Stormy and me it was a late night in December—or Twelfth Month as the Second Reflectioners call it. I allow my mind to rest on the memory, reliving it as if it were here and now.

Someone shakes me.

Being awakened in the middle of the night triggers a bad memory. I lurch away, back against my headboard.

"It's just me, El."

I take in the playful joy in Stormy's tone. Relax a smidge. "Just you? The last time you got me out of bed after dark, I almost ended up Isabeau's slave."

"How many times do I have to apologize for that?"

"A hundred more at least." I blink sleep-infested eyes. Night shrouds my west-wing suite aside from the sliver of moonlight peeking through my not-quite-drawn curtains.

Stormy giggles and drags my covers off the bed.

I draw my knees to my chest and shiver. Close my eyes and whine.

She tries to pry my eyelids open with her fingers and I bat her away. "Stor-meeee." I search blindly for my covers. It's too late, too cold for this.

"Come *on*, El. You're going to miss it." Both her hands grasp my wrist as she tugs on my arm.

Yawn. Blink. Eye rub. "Fine." I sit cross-legged on my bed. "This had better be worth it."

She throws her head back, fists on her hips like Peter Pan doing the crow. "Oh, it is. Now come *on*."

Flashlight shoved into my hand, I'm towed through the halls, down the stairs, and outside into the frozen night. As my brain wakes I notice what Stormy is wearing—pajamas. But not just any pajamas, *footie* pajamas. The one-piece kind with the button-drop bottom and the zipper running from toe to neck. Which of course looks ridiculous already. Add combat boots and a camo hat to the ensemble and you've got the funniest outfit ever.

Suddenly I don't feel so bad I'm caught out in the open with my matching flannels. I laugh out loud and Stormy shushes me, dragging me past the hill's wall and down into the forest. I'm freezing my behind off, but I can't stop smiling. If nothing else tonight is worth it, seeing Stormy in footie pajamas totally is.

A deep voice caws into the night.

Stormy yanks me behind a berry bush. We crouch to the ground. We're hysterical, though I've no idea what's going on.

That's when I see the crate shoved beneath the bushes in front of us. It's full of— Oh my chronicles, are those water balloons?

Stormy grabs a couple and nods for me to do the same. My heart is beating so fast and I'm so cold but I don't care. This is awesome.

"Stormy! Come out, come out wherever you are!" Kuna can't be more than ten feet away.

Holy Verity, I am totally gonna pee my pants because I am terrified Kuna will spot us, but I can't stop laughing.

I watch Stormy for the go-ahead.

Her lips move silently. "Three, two, one . . . fire!"

We're on our feet, chucking water balloons into the night. I hear Kuna's bellowing laugh and Joshua's easy chuckle. A water balloon hits me in the shoulder and I squeal. Crowe, that's cold!

Aha. Just as I suspected. Kuna was the culprit. He gives me a grin that says, "What are you going to do about it?"

So I'm snatching more water balloons and cradling them in my shirt and I'm running after him, dodging trees and laughing all the way.

At the end of the Battle de Balloons, Stormy and I are drenched. She slings an arm around my shoulders as we trudge back to the castle. Snow and mud slosh around our shoes. Our teeth chatter. But I don't notice much.

"I knew you were sidekick material." She punches me lightly in the shoulder.

I smile. "You're not too bad yourself." And even though I'm soaked, freezing, and will probably come away from this hacking and sneezing by morning, I mean every word.

❧

I don't know how long we sit there in the stables. I don't know if Stormy fell asleep or if she's merely gone quiet. But eventually she rises, rage trumping her sorrow. "I saw *him* "

"Who? Kuna?"

"*Gage.*"

Impossible. "But Gage is—"

"He was in the shadows beyond one of the burst windows. He had murder in his eyes. He aimed the gun right at me. Kuna saw. He knew it should've been me, and he took my place anyway." She's pacing now. I can almost see the fumes *putt, putt, putting* in her wake. "I still owed Gage two favors. Kuna knew. He knew if he sacrificed himself, the Kiss of Accord would be null. Gage promised not to touch Kuna. Now that my husband has died at the traitor's hands, I'm free."

If this is true, Kuna's death holds more weight than I realized. Except one thing doesn't make sense. "Gage was blinded the last time we saw him. His eyes were clawed out by Lark's owl talons, remember? Are you sure you saw his eyes?"

"Positive." She kicks her water bottle, and its contents create a mud puddle at her feet. "He must've found a Physic or something. I don't know." She hangs her head again. "What am I going to do? I can't imagine a Reflection without Kuna." She makes eye contact for the first time. Her gaze matches her name—stormy. "Can you give me a minute?"

I purse my lips. We really shouldn't stay here, but how can I deny her when she just lost her husband? I nod, then venture outside. Naked forest encompasses me, its clothing stored beneath snow for the winter. Dead vines wind around formerly charred tree trunks, which are now a muted shade of brown. Each day the landscape alters a bit. Darkness washes away with each new snowfall. Come spring, the Forest of Night and Shadow Territory will be all but forgotten.

I massage my arms through the thin material covering them. I feel bare. Exposed. I'd give anything for my parka right now. I scan the trees, cross to a fallen log, and sit. Wait. I'll give her a few more minutes, but then we have to move on.

Snap!

I whip my head up in echo to the sudden sound. I dart my gaze back and forth. Just a rabbit or a squirrel or some other woodland creature. Not every animal hibernates, right? I'm being paranoid.

Another noise. Closer. My nerves electrocute every tiny hair on my arms and neck. One drawn-out blink. When I open my eyes I see him through my fogged breath.

Gage steps forward. His scars shine, a brand courtesy of Lark Song. But his eyes are visible, seeing, glaring. Who or what healed him? "Hello, Your Highness." He bows, mocking me. "It's a pleasure to see you again." He straightens. Moves closer. "Such a shame our reunion can't be a cheery one."

Then he withdraws a gun from his coat and shoots me in the knee.

ASIDE

KY

Son of a Soulless, that smarts. I limp across the ship's cabin, seize a pack of ice from the chest. This means one thing and one thing alone.

She's in danger.

My T-shirt sticks to my chest, damp with sweat. My fingers flex and fist. I hobble to my cot and sit, hissing through my teeth. Since I left it's been this way. I feel everything she feels. Every scrape. Every bruise. But it's more than that. There's a sixth sense, a knowing beyond myself. I can feel her, yes, but I hear her too. Her thoughts carry to mine. It's as if she's with me and somehow I know . . .

I know she senses—*hears*—me too.

Our souls are connected. Could we actually communicate this way, Reflections apart?

Time to find out.

SIX

make the clock reverse

reathe. Stay awake. Do not, I repeat, do not fall asleep." Ky's voice
is so clear. I can almost feel his breath warm my neck, smell
his distinct fresh-cut grass and earth aroma.

I'm on my rear, hands clutching my right knee. My eyes are
squeezed shut and I'm blowing fast breaths through my teeth. I'm
connected to Joshua. This will heal. I'll be fine.

Except Kuna wasn't fine. The cut on my arm is still fresh.

Holy Verity, I've been shot. And I have zero clue if I will ever
walk again.

"Deep breaths. Listen to the sound of my voice."

I shake my head. *You're not really here.* My Ever and Physic
Callings may not be working, but my Scrib memory is clearly
intact. *This is just a reminiscence of your voice manifesting—*

"You know this is something else. Something more."

Gulp. *I know no such thing.*

Gage gives no indication he hears Ky's instructions. I don't
have time to freak or attempt to comprehend what lies behind my
lunacy. This goes beyond the recollection of Ky's voice in my head.
I'm hearing him as if he's standing a breath away.

"My apologies for the inhumane tactic." Gage's tone is too-
much-sugar-in-my-coffee sweet. "But we had to know for certain."

We? And know what, moron? That people bleed when you
shoot them? Surprise, surprise—they do.

Gage pockets his gun and crouches before me. The look in his
healed eyes is—what? Curious? Crazed? Excited?

I feel five familiar fingers wrap around my left arm, and my stomach does the Macarena. I sneak a sideways glance. Ky's not there. My teeth chatter, and I force myself to level my gaze with Gage's. This traitor will not see my weakness. I'm not the girl he tried to abduct in November.

At least, that's what I'm going for.

"Gage, what have you done?" Stormy's sudden presence adds to my composure. She's kneeling beside me in a blink, placing her dainty Barbie-like hands over my blood-spattered ones. She's both best friend and Guardian, all traces of distress and despair having thawed from her demeanor. No one would ever know she just lost her other half.

"Move aside, love." Gage jerks his buzz-cut head. I notice his dark-blue braid behind his ear is missing. Of course it is. He doesn't serve the Verity and he probably never did. "This isn't about you," he says to Stormy.

"You made it about me when you killed Kuna." She speaks of her man as if he were no more than an acquaintance. Coping mechanism?

Gage rises, withdraws his gun once more, and twirls it around one finger.

Show-off.

"Yes, well, that was unfortunate. It was you I aimed for." He jiggles the gun at Stormy as if it's a finger and not a deadly weapon. "I thought a little maiming was due, a little convincing in the way of returning the favors you owed. Of course, thanks to your dim-witted husband, none of that matters now."

"How dare you." Stormy stands, mirroring Gage. How can she be so . . . with it? When I thought I lost Mom, the fog lasted much longer.

"What's wrong, sweetheart? Offended I speak ill of the dead?"

"You'll be the dead one soon enough. The cost of your crime is termination by sword." Her voice wavers, hinting at the turmoil beneath her collected surface.

Gage shakes his head. "We'll see about that. I have more than you know on my side. Kuna was an unfortunate loss, as now you owe me nothing. If I could, I'd bring the imbecile back myself."

"Hold your tongue!" she screams, letting loose the storm.

And then she charges.

I reach out to grab her ankle, her leg, *something* to hold her back. Pain sucker-punches my wound and I clutch my knee once again. Ky's touch vanishes and my heart falters.

Gage laughs, the sound resonant of an out-of-tune clarinet. He deflects Stormy, tossing her aside like a rag doll when she reaches him. It's not like her to act so rashly. To use physical force instead of relying on the strength of her water Magnet Calling.

Grief's a witch. It changes you. Makes you do things you'd never do.

I know all too well.

Gage cracks his neck. Returns his focus to me. "Looks like it's just you and me, kid. And I'm betting you're not so tough without your protector to rescue you this time. Tell me, where is Kyaphus?"

Chills. Everywhere. My pulse thrums in my ears. Something about his question makes me think he knows the answer. He knows where Ky is. He has the upper hand there. But I have an advantage. Because Gage has no idea what I'm capable of.

Insert maniacal laugh here.

He advances again, his steps sure. Not at all afraid.

Suspicion confirmed. My heart beats out of sync with my breaths. My body's off beat but my mind is perfectly in tune.

Bring it on, dude. Cuz this chick's ready to rumble.

I brace my injured self. I may not be a physical match for him, but the mind—the soul—is better than brawn. My heart swells, my Mirror song begging to release, to order Gage to his knees. If it didn't work on Kuna to power my Physic ability, will it let me down on another aspect of my unique gift?

Only one way to find out.

Click. Gage cocks his gun.

"Stop!" My voice quavers.

"Oh, how the Thresholds have turned. Doesn't feel so good being helpless, does it?"

I force calm into my voice. Then new lyrics to my Mirror melody rush out.

> *"Don't you dare move, don't you dare breathe.*
> *You are finished, you will not succeed.*
> *Fall to your knees, it's time to go—"*

My insides convulse without warning. A sharp pain takes up residence in my throat, inhibiting my voice. I hug my middle and retch onto the snow. *Gross. What in the Reflections is wrong with me?*

Gage takes one step. Another. Heel, toe, heel, toe. His combat boots crunch the snow like teeth crushing ice. When he's standing over me he asks, "What's the matter, girl? Is the Verity within not enough to overtake even me, a Calling-less traitor?"

He knows? But how? "I'm not sure what you mean." *Why can't I be a good liar?*

"I'm not daft. Mistress Isabeau has eyes and ears within the castle walls. We're well aware of who you are and what you are capable of, as well as who you've kissed."

I have the urge to puke again but I contain it. *So Isabeau is involved. Which means Mom's in danger.*

"Don't worry. I have no intention of killing you. Ending you would allow the Verity to latch onto a much-less-tainted soul. And we can't have that."

Tainted? No. The Verity chooses the purest—

"I only desired to see you bleed. To see if your link to David's Ever blood would still heal you now that you are queen."

Dizziness clouds my vision. I close my eyes. Open them. Blink. *What's happening? How does he know?*

"As Isabeau suspected, the Ever Calling was the first to go. Now we need only bide our time until every last Called is weak. Vulnerable. Defenseless."

I glance at the spot where Stormy landed. It's empty. Vacant.

My pulse ramps. "Isabeau is a Mask." If I could stand, I'd spit in his face. "How can she want the Callings harmed?"

"Isabeau Archer is more than she seems."

"A jagged surface doesn't always allude to what truly lies beneath."

Another Ky-quote memory. They seem to pop up more and more these days.

Stormy appears then, launches her toothpick self onto Gage's meatloaf back, locks the crook of her elbow around his neck.

Gage's eyes bulge. His gun falls to the snow and I lurch to snatch it. It's wet and cold and slips between my numb fingers. My knee throb, throb, throbs. *Do not pass out, do not pass out.*

Gage claws at Stormy's arm, gasps for air.

I dry my fingers on my dress, try for the gun again. This time I capture it.

Stormy is stronger than she looks, wrapping her legs around Gage's waist, refusing to give as he tears at her skin with his fingernails.

I thrust my nausea to my toes, force myself to ignore the pain splitting my leg open. My arm shakes but I steady it.

Gage pries Stormy's arm off and flings her against a nearby tree for the second time. "That was stupid," he growls, advancing on her.

Stormy whimpers. She shields her face with her arms. Thunder roars in the distance, but it's faint. Rain sprinkles but doesn't pour as it should. "Something's wrong." Her arms lower and her eyes find the sky. "It shouldn't take this much effort to summon a storm."

She doesn't need to explain. The ache in my throat says it all. Something is definitely affecting the Callings. Which means we're left with fewer options of defense.

I widen my gaze and level the barrel at Gage's center. He's too focused on Stormy to notice. One. Calming. Breath. And then . . .

Bang!

Unprepared for the gun's force, I drop the weapon. Did I hit him? Is he down? Gah, my ears are ringing. My leg—I can't feel it anymore.

A moan breaks through the din inside. Stormy? Gage?

"El."

My heart reaches for Stormy but my body can't move. "It's okay. We'll figure this out." I wish my words weren't so halfhearted.

Gage sputters behind me. "It has begun."

Panting, I turn. He lies feet away, ripped arm encompassing his middle. He moves to his knees and blood *drip, drip, drips* like red tears onto the snow.

He coughs and crimson spurts from his mouth. "This is the beginning of the end. It began the moment you kissed—"

Fwit! An arrow soars inches past my left shoulder and sinks into Gage's chest before he can continue. He releases his hold on his stomach, and blood oozes with the loss of pressure. Arm shaking, he grabs the arrow and yanks it out. Then he collapses.

In an instant I'm surrounded. Guardians rush past. Preacher scoops Stormy into his arms, cradles her against his chest. No doubt Preacher was the one who fired the arrow. Gone during the coronation, his quiver has returned to his back, right where it belongs. Two burly Guardians I recognize but don't know by name hoist Gage by his arms and legs, carrying him away. And of course it's Joshua, limping as if his knee were shot, who kneels by my side.

Anger chisels his jaw, pleats the space between his dark brows. But something else is shadowing his demeanor. Fear. His right hand trembles as he lifts it to my cheek and brushes a loose lock away. "Sorry it took so long. I'm here now."

I shake my head, press my frozen face into his palm. I want to say we were fine. To explain I was handling the situation on my own, without him. But Joshua has this need for me to need him. As if this somehow proves the connection between us is real, stronger, deeper than our childhood bond.

He draws his hand away and I spy the cut that has not healed. The cut I didn't feel him receive. His Ever blood should've healed him, but somehow that's the least of my worries. Because this cut is the ultimate proof I didn't give him a Kiss of Infinity. I didn't connect my soul to his in the way he linked his to mine.

Joshua catches me staring and curls his fingers into a fist, as if we can somehow ignore the truth. He draws me into his arms, lifts me, and says, "Everything's going to be fine now. We're together. The threat has subsided. We're all going to be fine."

I nod despite the war inside. I want to scream at him. Because we're not all going to be fine. Kuna is dead. Something weird is going on with the Callings. Even the Verity within couldn't empower me. According to Gage, Isabeau is involved, which means Mom isn't safe. No, we are all far from *fine*.

"*The beginning of the end.*" Gage's words. As Joshua hobbles toward the passage with me in his arms, I can't ignore the dread circling my navel. Because Gage was about to divulge something important, and I can't help but feel it's no coincidence he was muted just in time.

We can't turn back time to this morning when all was well, can't make the clock reverse to a moment when life was good. This isn't a movie, some carefully constructed act in a play. This is real life. There are no coincidences. Gage was silenced, which makes me wonder . . .

What was he about to say about a kiss that Joshua doesn't want me to know?

joshua

Would you care to explain why my father—a man of mere traditional medicine—was the only Physic able to help the injured at the coronation? Why the other Physics could not heal with a single touch? Why Kuna is, in a word, dead? Even if the Physics could do nothing, your blood should have worked. Does it have something to do with our new queen?" Wren Song stares at me from across my study desk. She may be grown now, but this woman is no different from the fiery girl I came to know in my youth, before I traveled to the Third Reflection and the course of my life was altered forever.

A creak sounds from beyond my study door, so I lean to the side of my chair and focus my attention there. The cut on my hand is healing but still causes discomfort. The pain in my knee from El's gunshot wound continues to throb. I ignore both and will myself to focus on any sound outside this room. My pulse is a hammer to nails. I cannot divulge my theory to Wren here and risk another soul hearing about it. I must rectify this predicament before anyone else attempts to take the matter upon themselves.

"I am looking into the issue." I exhale, shove away from my desk, and rise. My wingback chair slides with ease against the cherrywood floor. My sport coat is draped over the chair's back, but I let it be. Turning away from Wren, I gaze out the bay window behind my desk where a faint reflection stares at me. My top two shirt buttons are undone and my face needs a shave. I scratch my cheek, noticing the filmy taste in my mouth. When did I last eat?

Five days have passed since Kuna's death, but I have not gained a moment's solace. Complaint after complaint has arrived at my doorstep. The people want answers. Those with Callings in particular have lashed out, and rightly so. The loss of their Callings, after all, could ensue. Nothing such as this has ever occurred, and they expect me to act. I may no longer be king, but they continue to seek my guidance and counsel. I was groomed for this role. How can I turn my back on them simply because I do not bear the crown?

"It's that girl." Wren drums her fingers on the desk. "The Verity sources the Callings and she contains the Verity. There are rumors she gave a Kiss of Infinity to Rhyen. Something is . . . wrong with her."

Irritation flares, but I clear my throat and force calm into my voice. "Need I remind you how you helped rescue that girl? How she saved our entire Reflection? She defeated Crowe and extinguished the species known as Soulless." I face her. My words border on harshness, but this must sink in.

Wren bristles as she steps away from my desk, spewing no retort, as one does not exist.

"Even so." Zipping her green Guardian jacket, she moves toward the door. "I find it highly suspicious the Callings were just fine before the Verity transferred to her. Now Physic and Ever are useless. What next? The people expect answers, and they expect them soon."

I offer a nod before she slips out the door and into the hall. She does not bid me good-bye or offer so much as a bow. No, I am not king, but I would think I have earned a measure of respect, at the very least from an old friend like Wren. I should call her back and demand some semblance of veneration, but I cannot bring myself to do it. How can I order respect from her while I am losing respect for myself?

I should be able to fix this. Indeed, I will.

I circumvent my desk and pace before the floor-to-ceiling bookshelves lining the east wall. I have scoured the volumes of *The Reflection Chronicles* cluttering these shelves. Pages upon pages of histories, but not a jot regarding the subject of faulty Callings. There are holes in the collection, of course, not every volume accounted for. El has a volume of her mother's, but I doubt it contains the information I seek. No, what I need is something much older.

I need to speak with Nathaniel Archer.

EIGHT

Bring Back

I stared out the bay window in Stormy's suite for five days. I should be lamenting my shot knee. Wade fixed me up better than any Third Reflection surgeon could, but that means I have to heal the old-fashioned way. Thankfully the bullet only grazed me—though it felt much worse at the time—and I came away with my knee fully functional. Illusoden helps, and I've gotten the uneven walk down to a science. Still, my bum knee is the least of my concerns. My head swims and my throat aches. The eyelids in my reflection droop and the tip of my nose shines bright red. I sniff and swallow, wince against the pain it causes.

It's just a cold. My voice will be fine. What happened with Gage was a fluke. And Ky. I heard him. Felt him. Could it have been real?

I pick at a loose thread on the hem of my crochet-lace blouse. Why does my world feel as if it's unraveling? Thread by thread, seam by seam, worry tears at my heart. I unfold the note Reggie gave me upon my return to the castle the night of the attack. Rub my thumb over Mom's rushed and out-of-character scrawl. I've read this dozens of times, but the words hit me fresh with each pass. Contradicting emotions consume me. Relief because Mom and the baby are safe. Anxiety because she's not here—with me.

Dear brave girl,

Makai has taken me far from this Reflection. I will not divulge

where and risk this letter falling into the wrong hands. All I can say
is I am out of harm's way. I will send word again when I am certain it
is safe. Do not forget you are now queen and all the position denotes.
You are the woman I always anticipated you would become. I believe
in you continuously and support you no matter the choices you make,
but be chary in whom you place your confidence. I am leaving this
with Regina, as I would trust her with my life. Keep that in mind
going forward.

All my love,
Mom

I refold the note along its premade creases and slip it between
the pages of Mom's sketchbook-slash-journal—the one I've held on
to like a security blanket since Ky returned it to me in the Forest
of Night. Mom, at least, has begun to see me in a new light since I
took on the Verity. She treats me not as the girl I've always been but
as the woman I'm *trying* to be.

Most everyone else, however . . .

Sigh.

Why are people tiptoeing around me, avoiding me even?
Guardians look the other way in the halls, and maids turn their
backs and whisper as I walk by. I could almost mistake their re-
actions as reverence for their new queen. But naïveté is no longer
my middle name.

Because there's no denying the emotion etched on everyone's
face.

Fear is tangible. I sense it seeping through the walls, hanging
heavy like the notes in Chopin's "Funeral March in C Minor." This
week has been a reboot of *Freaky Friday* in which my high school
and the Second Reflection have switched places. Except this time
it's not my mirrormark that's causing the chatter.

I just wish I knew what was.

As the questions scroll by like summer clouds, the Second's
highest point seems to sharpen in the distance. Stormy's suite faces
south, overlooking the Forest of White and what's beyond. I think

of the tapestry map in the throne room. Of all the places in this Reflection, or even the next, Pireem Mountain is one I've yet to visit.

"I still want to take you there, you know. To Pireem Mountain."

My ears perk and I sit up straight. Such a casual comment and the first I've heard his voice since coronation night. What would happen if I . . . ?

Why not? Doesn't hurt to try.

"You'd actually have to be here to do that." The out-loud retort sends a tiny thrill through my center.

"You know why I left. I had to bring back Khloe."

My breath looses, relief canceling my reservations. "I know," I say. If I can talk to him, really talk to him, maybe it is real.

And if it's real, maybe I can find out where he is.

I rest my elbow on my knee, smush my cheek into my knuckles. "But you could've said good-bye, or even taken me with you. I could've helped you with the Void." Pause. "Ky . . ." Swallow. "I'm looking for answers."

"I know, Em. Me too."

"Ky . . . where are you?"

"Who are you talking to?"

I flinch and fall off the window bench at Stormy's sudden appearance. Oh, for Verity's sake. Scrambling to my feet—man, my knee stings—I push my overgrown bangs from my eyes. "I didn't know you were awake," I say—croak.

Her glazed eyes don't focus on me, or anything for that matter. The crimson tank of her Guardian uniform is rumpled, and her bra strap hangs off her right shoulder. "I don't get much sleep these days." She scratches the back of her matted bedhead.

Right. When I thought Mom died, insomnia was my middle name.

"So, who were you talking to?" She snatches a now-stale biscuit off the coffee table, turns it over in her dainty hand.

Say something. "Uh . . . myself?" *Nice one, genius.*

"Hmm." She doesn't comment on my unconvincing response.

Instead she zombie-walks across the suite's common area, enters
the bathroom, and shuts the door. The sound of rushing water filling the tub follows moments later.

I cross haphazardly to the cushy love seat in the common area
and sink onto it. The antique coffee table sits before me. I open
Mom's book, laying it across my thighs. I've taken to studying it each
day, learning what I can from her experiences with this Reflection.
There's the loose sheet of parchment with Queen Ember's "Mirror
Theory" as well. It's been unfolded and refolded so often it's beginning to yellow and wear along the creases. I should copy it onto a
fresh page before it falls apart.

After a few minutes the rush of water ceases, and steam begins
to seep beneath the door. I moved into Stormy's suite the day after
Kuna died. Was that only last week? She insisted she was fine, and
at first she seemed so. But I wasn't buying it. I know all too well the
façade one tries to put on after such a loss. No way was I leaving
her alone.

"It wasn't your fault, Em."

I give a physical shrug against Ky's internal comment. "I don't
know what you mean."

"Kuna's death. It wasn't your fault."

Except maybe it was.

I close my eyes and curl my fingers around the edges of Mom's
book, feel the worn leather slide against my fingertips. This was
everything to me a couple months ago, held every answer I needed
to become who I was meant to be. Now I long for more. With
Stormy up and about, perhaps it's safe to venture back to the library
and continue my search. Or perhaps I'll grab another volume of
The Reflection Chronicles from Joshua's study.

Huff. This presents another problem. Because then I have to
come out of hiding too. Which means risking an encounter with
Joshua.

Since the run-in with Gage I've been avoiding him. We can't
talk about the Kiss of Infinity I obviously didn't give him, but how
can we evade it? And what's worse is I think he *wants* to discuss it,

as if somehow talking will fix everything. He's ever the optimist, always believing he can find a solution to every problem.

But that's not reality. Sometimes there *is* no solution. Sometimes there's simply an end.

A single sob sounds from the bathroom and I rise. Wince at the pressure in my knee. Hold my breath. Stormy has hardly spoken since Kuna's death. She's like a ghost haunting this Reflection. Her guest appearance a few moments ago is the most I've seen her all week.

Another sob. Then another. I move to the bathroom door and place my palm there. Wait a second.

And then she's bawling.

Dread pinpricks my sternum. Kuna's Reminiscence is tonight—a Second Reflection tradition much like the memorial services held in the Third. This is why Stormy's mobile. Tonight she says good-bye. We all do.

My most recent meal tumbles in my gut, banging around like a sneaker in the dryer. Good-bye. Such a simplistic, trivial detail, but oh so necessary. Closure finalizes things, allows those left behind to move on.

I move away from the door and stand before the bay window. My face contorts. I cross my arms. "Couldn't you have given me that?" I ask no one. "After all we went through, couldn't you have at least said good-bye?" I shake my head, unable to finish my sentence past the emotion looming just below my throat.

Good-bye.

The beginning of the end.

Gage's words are a broken record. I've been itching to head to the dungeons to question him, to see if he does in fact know where Ky might be. There's more to what happened than Gage's, or even Isabeau's, revenge. He mentioned her, so she must be involved. If only I could get down there without anyone seeing me.

The last thing I need is another suspicious glance.

It has to happen soon. In fact, Gage may already be dead. With the Physic and Ever Callings out of commission, the castle Physic was forced to resort to natural remedies. Wade Song remained after the coronation to assist. Still, no telling how long Gage will last without a miracle. My knee was one thing, but the bullet and arrow that hit Gage sank deep. Wade said as much when he stopped by to check on me before heading home to Wichgreen Province.

My palm meets the foggy pane, and slick moisture cools my skin. When I draw back, a sweating handprint forms a window of its own. Fresh snow hasn't fallen in weeks, but the weather is frigid enough that nothing has melted either. Down the hill, a frozen Threshold, nestled in the Forest of White, stares at me like a glass eye.

"I wish . . ." A hoarse rendition of the opening notes from "Into the Woods" dances from my tongue. I swallow and clear my throat. "I wish . . ."

My translucent reflection shimmers. Short, blond waves replace my longer, darker ones. The soft curves of my face harden, and one brown eye shades to green.

I gasp and draw back. I've been without my voice—my song—all week. Is it returning?

Once more I lean forward, so close to the glass my nose almost touches. Short breaths mist what is now merely my reflection. But just like with the copper basin in the stables, I know I saw something.

Someone.

A hasty glance over my shoulder informs me the bathroom is still occupied. It's quiet. Stormy's cries have ceased. Still, no way to tell how much longer she'll be in there.

This is a bad idea, but the desire to see Ky again outweighs reason. I gaze at my reflection once more, place my hand on the glass. Was it my imagination? A glimpse into another Reflection? If I can see him, maybe I can figure out where he is.

But before I can utter a note, movement at the hill's crest distracts my focus. It's a man, familiar, with shoulder-length charcoal hair and—

My hand slips from the pane as my heart slides to the floor.

Even from here I can make out the ditch between Makai's brows.

What's he doing back?

He wouldn't leave Mom wherever she is unless something is wrong.

I gather the skirt of my dress and half limp, half bolt for the door. Down the spiral staircase, through the hall to the balconies framing the throne room. *Ouch, ouch, double ouch,* but whatever. I'm one tier above, leg shaking, when Makai enters the massive double doors just beyond the grand staircase.

"Makai!" My call might as well be a whisper. He doesn't look up, but even from a distance I notice his face is hard. This is another Makai, the man I met back in New York when my world turned on its end.

This is Makai, Commander of the Guardians.

Makai on a mission.

Makai without Mom.

what has been hurt

"Eliyana, please." Makai combs his fingers through his shaggier-than-usual hair. "There is no need to panic." His tone is hushed and it's obvious he's trying not to make a scene. He's at least a foot taller than me so his head is bowed close to mine, and he speaks through the corner of his mouth.

I take a deep breath and puff it out, then exhale a burst of fog. This is Kuna's Reminiscence. It should be about him. And Stormy. But I can't help it. When it comes to Mom, to anyone I love really, that all-too-familiar terror kicks in.

"No need to panic, Makai?" *Dad?* I haven't quite figured out what to call him. "You just told me the stress of the attack caused Mom to go into premature labor. She's out there somewhere with my brand-new baby brother—my brother who is two months early—and you're telling me there's no need to panic? Isabeau is dead set on finding her. On taking the baby."

He shakes his head. "Elizabeth is resilient, just like you. She and Evan—"

"Evan?" I'm so unnerved I forgot to ask his name. Weird. I went from only child to sister of three in less time than it takes to rehearse for a theater production.

A twitch of a smile perks Makai's lips. "Yes. His name means 'fighter.' He's a tough one. Came out wailing. A full set of lungs, that one."

It feels wrong to do so here, while waiting to honor Kuna. But how can I not grin at Makai's words?

I have a brother.

His name is Evan.

In all the chaos and tragedy, this small bit of something is . . . something. A lit window in a dark alley. A high C in the midst of a solemn composition.

We exchange a new sort of glance. One different from the distant Guardian-charge, or even the less distant uncle-niece looks we've given. This time we share a knowing. Bonding, I think they call it. Strange. Foreign.

I like it.

Makai wraps an arm around my shoulders and squeezes. "I assure you, I would not leave your mother or Evan unless I knew for certain they were protected. Isabeau will never find them. I returned to give you the news myself, and Elizabeth insisted I see what I can do to aid the Guardians. I intend to get to the bottom of last week's attack, Your Majesty." He winks at that, the natural dad in him coming to life.

"Now more than ever I am needed here. I will not rest until the Troll is either behind bars or extinguished altogether." He squeezes my shoulder once more, then releases me and heads through the crowd toward a cluster of his men.

My gut roils at the thought of Mom and Evan alone. But if Makai says they're safe, I have to trust they are.

I turn and meander through the courtyard's throng. Preacher, my Guardian for the evening, lingers just a few feet away, eyeing my every blink. A quiver attached to his belt slaps his hip whenever he moves. He clutches his bow in his right hand, as if begging for an opportunity to present itself for a little target practice.

I've been trying to tell Joshua I don't actually *need* a Guardian anymore. But the debate is pointless. I could be Wonder Woman and he'd still insist I have a chaperone wherever I go. Especially now, with the Verity stagnant and the Callings malfunctioning.

Ignoring Preacher, I rise on my toes, stretching beyond my kinder-ballet ability. An ocean of cool hues eddies around me. Azures and indigos. Violets and periwinkles. Not a black pinafore or charcoal tunic in sight. Just as a blue- or purple-dyed lock of hair—a tassel—represents loyalty to the Verity, so these colors revere the deceased at a Reminiscence. Even the Guardians, circling the crowd like NYPD officers in Times Square on New Year's, have shed their standard uniforms and replaced them with navy jackets and slacks.

I skirt a family of three and sit on a marble bench. The same bench Jasyn Crowe occupied upon our first encounter. I lift the hood of my plum-colored parka. Shrug my shoulders to my ears and squint. The family seems to be in a bubble. The mother and father wear drawn expressions as they swing their toddler girl by her arms. She giggles and cries, "Higher! Again!" oblivious to the purpose of this evening's outing, not understanding what has been hurt and lost and broken.

When a human shadow blocks what little sun remains, a shudder jolts my body from the curve of my neck to the spaces between my toes.

"Sorry I'm late." Joshua's words lack oxygen, as if he sprinted a mile to get here. "I lost track of the time."

"It's fine." When I look up I'm careful not to meet his gaze.

Joshua exhales, his breath vaporous. From his coat pocket he withdraws wool gloves, tugs them onto his hands. He touches the hilt of the sword at his hip, as if checking to make sure it's there. "Can we talk about this?" His hushed question is a hot coal on my blaze of irritation.

I abandon the bench. "You think now's the best time?"

He sighs. Runs a hand over his face. "Stop avoiding me. We can't ignore this forever." His hands find my waist. He draws me in.

I stiffen and my stomach bungies to my feet. My gaze finds his face, but I still can't look him in the eyes. "I don't know what you want me to say." I bite the inside of my cheek. Why do I feel guilty? A Kiss of Infinity isn't something I can choose to give. I shouldn't feel bad.

But I do.

Joshua's expressions pass through a wheel of emotions. First his brow furrows. Confused? Then he shakes his head. At last his jaw tightens, each individual muscle beneath his skin hardening into a countenance I'm all too familiar with.

"Very well." He releases his hold on my waist, then turns on his heel and traipses to the courtyard's other end, toward Stormy. He climbs onto the half wall at the edge of the hill. When he speaks I don't register the words but stare without seeing in his general direction. After his speech fades, he hops down, wraps an arm around Stormy, and leads her through an archway overrun with dead ivy.

The crowd moves as a unit, a massive game of follow the leader, and I trail behind. Preacher marches toward me, Scrooge-like as ever, and forms the caboose of our train. I'm the slowest of the bunch with my gimpy knee, but I don't mind the separation for now. Gives me time to think. To breathe. To absorb.

We stroll down the stone steps embedded in the hillside, through the forest, and toward the nearest Threshold. It was dubbed Midnight Lake when the Void shrouded this area. But like the Forest of White, it received a new name—Dawn Lake. The stark-silent atmosphere is a welcome escape. I can almost hear the snowcapped trees gasp for breath, feel the gravel path soak what little warmth I have through my soles.

Kuna's sun-ray grin enters my mind, a distraction from the chill. Why him, the sweetest, most jovial person I've ever met?

I'm reminded of Mom's words from the past. *"Some things are beyond our understanding,"* she'd say when something bad would happen. There were times as I got older when I thought it was an adult cop-out to say such a thing. I used to think grown-ups knew everything. Now I see how far that is from reality.

Kuna's body was buried the day following the coronation. It was an informal affair. Just a few Guardians with shovels in a small graveyard located west of the stables.

"It's how things are done here, darlin'," Reggie said this morning over hot cocoa the same color as her skin. We sat beside the kitchen hearth as she soothed my nerves about Mom's absence. "The people here don't find it necessary to watch their departed rejoin the earth. Kuna's soul sleeps until it awakens in the First. His body is no longer connected. The First is the only place where a soul can survive apart from a physical vessel."

No longer connected? Physical vessel? Still seems more complicated than the toughest Sudoku puzzle never solved. Life after death isn't something I've given much thought. Perhaps because it always sounded impossible. But now . . . I'm not so sure.

"Good girl. You're learning."

I slow, glimpse Preacher over my shoulder.

The Guardian appears to stare straight through me as per usual.

Facing forward, I answer Ky under an exhale. "Not a good time, Ky."

"You see it, don't you? You see nothing is ever as impossible as it first seems."

"Yes, okay? I see it. Now stop making me talk before someone notices."

His voice doesn't return and I sigh. For the briefest instant I allow myself to miss him. His confident smirk. The way he got under my skin. The honesty we so freely shared. He was always straight with me, and I never hesitated to let him know exactly what I thought.

Most of the time.

Once we reach Dawn Lake—which looks more like an ice rink than a Threshold leading to the Third—those paying their respects split north and south, line up along the shore. So many familiar faces yet foreign at the same time. I hardly know them. A meeting here, a conversation there. If I'm being honest, most are simply acquaintances and nothing more.

Sunset has passed, and a small clearing in the clouds reveals a gibbous moon. I draw a candle from my coat pocket and trudge to stand between Stormy and Joshua, her on my left and him on my right. It's a tight squeeze and I can't avoid it when our arms brush.

Joshua bristles but doesn't move away. He clears his throat, strikes a match, lights his candle, and then ignites mine. My flame kisses Stormy's wick, and she leans over and lights the next person's. The ritual goes on and on until every attendee's candle is ablaze save one. The lake is a circle of light. Fire's life encompassing the deadly ice.

Then the singing begins.

The tune isn't one I recognize, but as the lyrics press in, the melody pulsing, I feel as if I know this song. Perhaps it's my Calling that allows me to pick up on anything musical. Whatever the case, I'm able to join in after the first verse, singing the words as if I've practiced them over and over again. My voice remains hoarse, but no one seems to notice.

> *"He lies down. He will not rise.*
> *Until all is gone, he cannot be roused.*
> *Sleep infests his heavy-laden eyes,*
> *And though sorrow arrives with night's dawn,*
> *Joy lives in morning's song."*

Sniff. Blur. Tears dawdle on my lashes.

"It's beautiful, isn't it?"

My jaw sags. Stormy?

"He would've loved this. Kuna wouldn't have wanted us to grieve."

I turn my head, and shock steals my breath. Though her cheeks exhibit damp trails, splitting and joining like a network of rivers, the corners of Stormy's lips stretch toward her glistening eyes. She reaches over and clasps my free hand, shakes it a little. Her grip is almost painful, but I squeeze back, speaking my love for her through the silent gesture.

And somehow, this tiny hint of the "before" Stormy fills me with a sense of hope. I turn my head, peek up at Joshua. His eyes are closed, head bowed as his lips release song. His familiar tenor melts the ice inside. The memory of how I felt the first time we met tugs at my lips, forcing them to curl up. Just like then, the promise of a better tomorrow adds an inch to my height.

I close my eyes and sing for Kuna, adding harmony to the tune on this round despite my sore throat. Each note carries hurt and hope. Pain and healing. If Stormy can find joy amidst ashes, surely Joshua and I can find a way past this Kiss of Infinity thing. I didn't give him one. Okay. But does that mean I never will?

"You gave me one. Isn't that enough?"

Everything in me wants to respond to Ky's voice. But I can't. Not now. Maybe I've been going about this the wrong way. Maybe the best thing for me is to let Ky go.

"Em, no."

After giving Stormy's hand an extended squeeze, I release her, guard my flame with a cupped palm, and free my right hand. I lace my fingers with Joshua's, hold fast to the tangible. The real.

Joshua pulls away.

My spirit droops.

But then his arm slips around my waist, fingers sliding through the space between my arm and midsection. He draws me into his side.

Sigh. We're going to be fine. I inhale his Thanksgiving dessert scent, press my cheek to his life-filled chest. Our voices become one as we continue the ballad in Kuna's honor—Joshua singing the lyrics, and me "ah-ing" the repetitive melody. My throat burns and my song is off-key, but I press on.

"The Void holds no power,
A soul it cannot own.
Though it may seem night has won the hour,
It is the day we live to storm,
Until the battered no longer—"

A sound like thunder. A deafening shriek. A collective gasp. All seem to happen at once.

Voices cease midlyric, stalked by an unnatural quiet.

My head jerks around. My gut bottoms out. The earth shakes. Someone has fallen through the ice.

joshua

Iron brushes leather as swords emerge from sheaths. Firearm after firearm is cocked. Bows are brandished and arrows are drawn. All attendees, save the Guardians, retreat from the ice's rim and creep toward the trees. I draw Eliyana into my side, tightening my grip around the one I can't bear to lose. She may be queen, the vessel of the Verity even, yet to me, she remains fragile as ever. Someone breakable and delicate and all too good to be true. El is mine, and with my Ever blood failing I refuse to risk her enduring so much as a scrape. Her pain will always belong to me, regardless of whether our connection heals her or not.

I hone my focus and glance south. Wren Song stands two long-sword lengths away. Her arms are folded over her chest and her gaze penetrates mine. I grunt beneath my breath. She doesn't need to speak. I know she believes this is related to El.

And perhaps she's right. I drop my candle and the flame snuffs out. I comb my fingers through my hair and run my palm over my face. Have I been ignoring what's right in front of me? I haven't had an opportunity to go to Nathaniel as of yet, but I can't put it off any longer. I will see him tonight. But first I must get everyone to safety, El to safety.

I scan the frozen Threshold. Aha! There. About three yards east—an opening in the ice. I squint. An opening, yes, but nothing more. No flailing arms, gurgles, or screams.

"El." I grip her arm, though I keep my eyes trained on the Threshold. "Take Stormy, follow Preacher, and lead the guests back to the castle. Everyone will be safest there. Reggie and the kitchen staff already have food prepared. Preacher will inform the Guardians on perimeter duty of the situation."

She looks around, eyes wide. But it isn't fear I detect there, it's awareness. She is so different from the timid girl I met over three years ago. Something has changed within her. The Verity lives there, yes, but it's more than that. As if a fire has been ignited. Even so, this alters nothing. Verity or not, fire or none, she still needs me. And I will protect her no matter the cost.

The Guardians tread the bank's edge and anxiety taints the air like sour milk. The only noise is the distinct hush preluding fresh snowfall. Wait for the opportune moment. That's the first thing they teach you in Guardian training. Patience is key in a crisis situation. Acting too soon could cause disaster, while waiting too long could trigger an equally treacherous outcome.

Preacher appears at my right. "All bodies accounted for, sir."

I nod. As I suspected.

I face El. Her oaken gaze pierces like a wooden dagger. We know each other so well, yet somehow this doesn't help. She's aware I will send her away, and I expect her to fight it. "Do not question me on this," I say.

"This isn't like before." She pulls away and rounds on Preacher. "I am your queen. You answer to me now. I'm staying."

He avoids her gaze. Half of me is enraged by his indifference toward his queen. But the other half? The other half is still me, and if Preacher's indignation aids in my efforts to protect her, so be it.

"I'm not weak. I can fight." Her eyes plead with mine.

Must she resist every time? Doesn't she realize I'm trying to keep her alive? "Not this you can't." I have my suspicions, but I won't know for sure until I speak to Nathaniel.

"If you would just tell me what's going on, I know—"

"Enough!" My raised voice catches the crowd's attention, and all eyes attend us. I swallow and inhale, regaining composure. Where the crowe did that come from?

"This is why." She wrenches away.

My pulse speeds but I remain collected. "Why what?"

Her lower lip quivers and her gaze darkens. "Nothing. Never mind." She wraps an arm around Stormy. "Lead the way, Preacher," she says straight through me.

My best Guardian looks to me for confirmation, and once I give the nod, he's off with the girls and the remainder of the guests in tow.

I watch their departure, keeping my eyes fixed on El until the last possible second. When she's out of sight I find Makai. He's already giving orders, placing Guardians around the lake's perimeter, sending groups of twos and threes to search the forest.

"At least ten Guardians will be stationed here at the Threshold around the clock," he says to Wren. "No one goes in or out."

"Yes, Commander." She wears her war face, usually not a good sign, but in this case a relief to witness. She can be trusted to guard and protect. No fear, this one.

When I approach she glances in my direction, and her expression alters. Guilt settles in my gut. I bring my fist to my lips and clear my throat. "Wren."

"David."

I wince. I have yet to tell El of my history with Wren. One more secret I have kept.

Wren marches away, leaving me alone with my commander. Though I was king, I still feel as if I answer to Makai, my honorary older brother.

I already know but still feel a need for confirmation, so I ask, "The Threshold at Dawn Lake? It is draining?"

"So it would seem, but the situation is under control." He pulls his unkempt hair off his face and secures it at his neck with a leather tie. "Do what you must."

Makai always knows before I utter a word.

"Give Father my regards. I have not had a chance to visit him recently."

I clap him on the shoulder. "I'll tell him."

As I head toward Wren I think of the last thing El said. *"This is why.*" I acted as if I didn't understand, but I knew precisely what she meant. Because I know her better than anyone. She wanted to say more but refrained, always concerned about others' feelings. But I know. Oh, I know.

This is why.

This *is* why.

This. Is. *Why.*

The reason she didn't give me a Kiss of Infinity. She takes my actions as mean and cold, stubborn, when really it's my love for her fueling me. How could she give me such a kiss when she doesn't truly believe I love her?

I shake my head. She doesn't see my love. Time to rectify that.

I tap Wren on the shoulder.

She turns slowly, her expression blank.

Fist to my mouth, I clear my throat. "I require your services."

It's difficult to perceive, but I think I see a hint of a grin surface. She doesn't respond but her pupils dilate.

We stare at each other, and for the first time in years I wonder if we have a chance at being friends again. I smile. "How do you feel about going on a little journey?"

She folds her arms over her chest and raises one eyebrow. "I thought you'd never ask."

ASIDE

KY

And so it begins.

  She doesn't know it yet, but this will lead her here. The Threshold in the Second isn't the first to be affected, and it won't be the last. I could tell her, call to her, but it must be her choice.

  And so I wait.

ELEVEN

change

I f I wasn't in my right mind I'd chuck this blasted mirrorglass
crown off the hill. What good does it do me? No one looks to
me. Listens. They still think of Joshua as their leader. And can I
blame them? One look at him and people think, *Noble. Worthy.
King.*

What do they think when they look at me? Imposter? Intruder? Wannabe?

*"Don't be ridiculous, Em. This insecurity is the old you. You know
better. The Verity chose—"*

"Just leave me alone." The smallest burst of Verity burns in my
gut. As if it's staging a silent protest to my words. I tug at the ends
of my hair. Regret my harsh tone. None of this is Ky's fault. "I'm
sorry."

"I know. It's fine." Though his words reassure, his voice in my
head reveals a pinch of hurt.

Ugh. This sucks. Joshua and I are at odds—again—and now
I've hurt Ky? Maybe. I don't know. He's probably not even real. Of
course he's not.

Or is he?

I'd like to scream my head off now if you don't mind. Okay,
thanks.

Anxiety revs my nerves as I enter the door leading into the
kitchens. Old memories lift from storage. I take them out, dust
them off, and see them anew. The frame around a not-so-long-ago

scene shrouds my vision, gives me the smallest intermission between act one's cliffhanger and the impending twist awaiting me in act two.

It's last November and our final night in the Maple Mines. Only one day left until we reach the Haven. The other half of our group sleeps soundly a few feet away. Stormy lying on her side near the tunnel's wall. Joshua slouched against a tree root thick as a log. Kuna and Preacher sitting back-to-back, chins digging into their chests. What happened with Gage in Wichgreen Village seems like a lifetime ago rather than days. I'm exhausted to the bone. But for some reason, whenever Ky takes the lookout shift, I can't sleep. I don't think he minds though.

After four days spent navigating root-infested tunnels with nothing but the undersides of maple trees on the horizon, I should be more than thrilled about the prospect of a warm bed.

Except the thought of leaving moments like these behind pinches my pulse. Sometime between Ky saving my life and now, a change occurred. We became . . . friends? He still doesn't know Tiernan Archer, the despicable man who raised him, is my father. How can I tell him? It would ruin what we have, and I'm not willing to give that up. Not yet.

"Give me your hand," Ky whispers. The kerosene lantern on the ground between us washes his face in amber light, causing the flecks of gold in his green eye to glimmer. His brown eye lights up, too, like a warm cup of cocoa inviting a first sip.

I eye him. "Why?" Suspicion laces my tone.

He dons a knowing look, chin tucked in and one brow quirked. "What's the matter, Em?" He offers his hand, palm up. "Afraid I'll bite?"

I roll my eyes. "Whatever, *Edward*." I jut my fist forward, not at all sorry it pokes him in the ribs.

A huff escapes his lips. "Comparing me to sparkly vampires now? You're losing your touch if that's the best you can come up with."

Ky's pop culture fluency isn't so surprising anymore. He did live in the Third with his adoptive mother and younger sister, Khloe—my *actual* younger sister—for several years. They hid from Tiernan, who had given himself over to the Void. The more I learn about Ky, the more I find we have in common. A connection both foreign and familiar. Ky takes my upturned arm, pushes my sleeve north, and runs his fingers over my skin from elbow to wrist.

All *Twilight* puns elude me. "What are you doing?" I draw back. Take in a breath. Finger the rose-button necklace at my collarbone. It's only been a few days since Ky gave it to me—*made* it for me—but it feels as if it's always been right here.

"I'm helping you relax." He grasps my arm again, initiating tingles as he runs his fingers back and forth. Back and forth.

My muscles grow heavier as my fist curls open. My lips part, and I close my eyes without preamble. "Now what?" The words release on an exhale.

"Shhh. Wait. Trust me."

Trust me. Joshua made the same request the night at the Pond in Central Park. It should be easier to trust the boy I've known for years rather than one I just met. But there's something about Ky. Something causing my heart to put faith in him even when my brain warns me against it.

One deep inhale. Two. Then something small and round drops into my palm. My eyelashes lift. Gasp. "Where did you get candy?" The sugary scent alone, like maple syrup, forces my mouth to water.

"Keep your voice down. Otherwise it won't work."

I huff but don't allow another question to escape. Curiosity wins. For now.

We remain motionless, our breaths plateauing. I watch the candy in my palm. Inhale. Exhale. After a while I make the mistake of meeting Ky's gaze.

He's staring at me, his regard so intense I can't tear my eyes away. He inches closer, bumps the lantern with one knee. Using his knuckles he strokes my arm again, only adding to the heat building between us. This time his touch doesn't relax me. It kindles something. His fingers are matches.

And my skin is on fire.

Gulp.

Flit. Flicker. My head whips right. "What was that?"

Ky touches a finger to his lips.

Another flash, this time to my left. An insect? Firefly, perhaps? A tap against my palm. More candy?

I look down. Oh my chronicles—definitely not candy.

A stubbly cheeked boy Fairy no taller than my thumb stands next to the treat, chiseling at it with the smallest pickax I've ever beheld. Grimy overalls hug his miniature frame. He removes a handkerchief from one pocket and wipes his brow. He could almost be human if not for the gray, mothlike wings, twitching every so often, protruding from his back.

This Reflection continues to astonish me. A beautiful Troll. A hulking merman. A childlike leviathan. I'd always imagined Fairies as tinkling little women with topknots on their heads and pom-poms on their shoes. Wrong again.

When I glance up at Ky, he's beaming. We don't move, barely breathe. Just watch the Fairy excavate chunks off the candy and drop them into a sack at his hip. It's like this is our little secret. The knowledge invites an intimacy I'm not sure I'm ready for. Not with Ky, anyway.

Once the Fairy's bag bulges to the brim, he takes flight. His wing tips light up, glow orange like an airplane on a dark runway.

Just as abruptly as he arrived, he's gone.

⌒∞⌒

"Ain't ya gonna eat, darlin'?" a voice asks from behind.

"Huh?" I stop in my tracks. Blink. Too skittish to retire to my suite, I've been pacing the stone hallway outside the kitchen for at least half an hour. I hold the Verity, yet here I am.

Useless. Unneeded. Invisible.

I haven't told anyone about my trouble with the Verity since the coronation. How its calming presence has nearly vanished, only a blip here or a flicker there to grasp on to. In its place sits a coldness centering around my chest. It does feel similar to an actual cold with my sore throat and itchy eyes. Maybe I am just sick. I'll get better and things will return to normal.

Who am I kidding? I'm not fooling anyone. A measly illness wouldn't harm the Verity, the most powerful entity in the Seven Reflections.

But something must be hurting it. If only I could figure out what.

In an attempt to occupy my overloaded brain, I try to think on things other than the here and now. The mixture of aromas wafting from the kitchen through the archway to my right sent my thoughts to a place I didn't want to venture. Rosemary. Cinnamon. Nutmeg. Maple. Maple Mines. Ky and candy and Fairies.

I touch four fingers to my chest. The treble clef–heart necklace Joshua gave me is there, resting outside my blouse for all to see. But it's not what I'm looking for. I feel around until I find it, the button charm hidden beneath my clothes. Sigh. Ky's gift remains, resting against my heart. I haven't been able to let it go.

I haven't been able to let *him* go.

I shake my head. *No. Focus.* I'm queen whether the people think of me as such or not. And Ky? He's my past. My future lies here, with the Second and Joshua. One kiss doesn't dictate who I spend my life with. I choose Joshua.

"*Wrong. You already chose me. I'm your past and your future. I'm both.*"

I whirl at Ky's voice, trip over a sack of potatoes, and nearly collide with Reggie.

She steadies me with her flour-dusted hands. "Everyone else has already gone to bed, but I'll make whatever you fancy. Maybe one of those cheese sandwiches you're so fond of, hmm?" Her southern accent, all fried chicken and country gravy, warms my bones.

I finger-comb my bangs to one side and roll my shoulders. "Sure, Reg. Thanks."

"Comin' right up." She smiles and tucks a wisp of graying black hair into the bandanna covering her head. Since she was raised in the Third like me, being near Reggie is sort of like going home. She may be from Georgia, but her carefree manner and Third Reflection knowledge make her the closest thing to a neighbor I have. Plus, she's my greatest connection to Mom while she's gone. Regina "Reggie" Reeves practically raised Mom. Her stories about Mom's childhood—before Jasyn took on the Void, of course— always make me feel better when I'm down.

As she meanders through the kitchen archway her hips sway, and I swear it's a Dolly Parton tune she's humming.

Pacing once more, I will my mind not to wander into forbidden territory. Sacks of flour and grain lie piled against the walls on either side of me like sandbags damming a flood. They make the hallway seem narrower than it is, and a bout of claustrophobia revs my apprehension. This is the same hallway Ky and I passed through when he rescued me from the dungeons. I didn't admit it then, but that was the night I first began to trust him.

I sigh and wander into the kitchen. The guests were fed hours ago and the aftermath of dishes and trays, goblets and mugs, lies piled in the farmhouse-style sink straight ahead. Makai decided it would be dangerous for the guests to travel back to their various provinces in the dark, especially considering recent events. He, at least, was straight with me. Whether it's because he actually respects me as his queen or just feels obligated to me as his new daughter, I don't know. And I don't care. All information is good information, no matter the reason given.

"The Threshold at Dawn Lake is draining." He reloaded his quiver as he spoke. "We have not yet determined the cause or the source. But rest assured, we will."

I watched from my perch on the courtyard fountain as he made his way back down the hill and toward the Threshold. While everyone was inside eating their fill and chattering about what happened, I remained outside. Away from the gossip and stares. Away from the questioning glances and awkward half smiles.

Is this to be my life? Never living up to their expectations? Failing before I've even begun?

Stormy came and sat with me in silence for a while, neither of us knowing what to say to the other. She gave my hand a squeeze before heading to bed. On any other day she'd be among the Guardians on duty. She even attempted to join them after we led the guests back to the castle. But Joshua sent her away, insisting she take the night off.

Joshua. Where *is* Joshua?

He hasn't come to find me and no one has seen him. When I asked Makai where he'd gone, he avoided an answer. Uneasiness pinpricks my brain. He wouldn't just leave. Joshua does nothing without purpose.

"Sandwich is ready, sugar," Reggie calls from the island to my left. "You can eat by the hearth. Nothing like a little warmth to soothe what's ailin' ya. I'll let Saul know you're staying down here for a spell." She turns and strolls down the hall toward the stairwell leading into the west wing. Reggie's one of the few people who calls Preacher by his first name. He pokes his head around the bend, and they speak in hushed, non-eavesdroppable tones. If I didn't know any better I'd say Reg is . . . flirting with him?

I head toward the hearth at the far end of the kitchen and grab my food off the island as I pass by. I don't bother taking a seat at the table where the staff eat their meals. Instead I plop onto the soot-infested rug, cradle my plate between my crossed legs, and stretch my hands forward. Clench, flex, clench, flex. Mm. Cinderella got it right. Coziest spot in the castle.

I pick up the sandwich and bite. The sharp, yeasty taste sends another sigh through my lips. *This* is food. Not fancy or special. Just good. Comforting.

"The first meal I made for you was a cheese sandwich."

I swallow. "Don't you think I know that, Ky?"

"Irritated?"

I return the half-eaten sandwich to my plate. Rub my throbbing knee. The Illusoden I took earlier is wearing off too fast as usual. "Not at you."

"Tell me."

I open my mouth, but Reggie returns and I snap it closed. She bustles around the kitchen, carrying about her work as if I'm not here. She whistles a happy tune Snow White would be proud of, and I'm half tempted to cover my ears. She means well, but I can't focus this way.

And then I hear it, the song from my dreams, the one I played on accident at the coronation. It's slow and graceful. Deep. Almost sad. Reggie's chirpiness fades into the background, and all I hear is this. This haunting melody that seems as if it were written just for me.

The fire's heat dries my eyes and I allow my lashes to descend. My scattered thoughts organize. The ambush at the coronation. How secretive everyone's been. My lack of song. Today's incident. They line up, but one image stands out among the rest—the expression on Joshua's face. Fear. But not of the mysteriously broken ice.

Joshua was afraid of *me*.

It's all connected. To me. But how? I need answers, but no one seems willing to give them. If Mom were here, she would. But she's not. She said to trust Reggie, but how would she know anything about any of this? I love her, but she's just a cook, spent her whole life in this castle. I need someone who's been places, who's seen what others haven't.

I seethe in silence, allow loneliness to weigh but never surface. I'm ice shards on the floor, each piece of me melting into the rug until all that's left is damp ash.

Is there no one I can rely on?

The invisible piano crescendos and I find myself rocking back and forth, back and forth. Like Ky's fingers on my arm, the motion is soothing. Relaxing. My shoulders sag and a shaky sob releases. I'm burnt out. Exhausted to my core. Who do I turn to for help? It'd have to be someone who doesn't care about protecting me.

Someone who'd be willing to make a trade. Someone with nothing to lose.

My head snaps up in sync with a crackle of the fire. The song dies. Mom has always said sometimes the answer is right in front of you.

Close, Mom. This time it's right beneath me.

fate's design

"She'd never admit to it." Reggie shakes from laughter, her more-than-adequate bosom bouncing in her too-tight blouse. "But Elizabeth was quite the mischievous child. Always sneakin' 'round the castle, searchin' for secret passageways and trapdoors or somewhat. Found a key once. Never did learn which door it opened." She shakes her head and closes her eyes, an endless smile stretching her worn face.

Any other night I'd be content to sit here for hours, listening to stories about Mom, letting Reg refill my mug with spiced cider and my plate with chocolate chip cookies.

But tonight is different.

I fake a yawn, hoping she'll notice. She doesn't, of course, continuing one story into the next.

"Did I ever tell you about the time—?"

I stand, grimacing at my own rudeness more than the pinch in my knee. "I'm so sorry, Reg, but I'm exhausted. To be continued another time?"

Her smile doesn't falter as she dusts off her apron and rises beside me. "Course, darlin'. Don't you mind me. Old Regina's gotta know when to zip her trap." She shoos me through the kitchen archway. "Scoot along now. I'll be up in the mornin' with your breakfast tray as usual."

I give her a tight hug and kiss her cheek.

She blushes and sways away, humming some old country

song or another. Shania Twain? Oh brother, it is. Can't stop my own smirk. Reg is a character if there ever was one.

The easy part is over. But what comes next? Will my plan work? Preacher isn't an idiot, and he's not exactly the sentimental type.

"He's not so bad once you get to know him."

Ky can't be serious. He and Preacher have never been on good terms. No way the real Ky would speak on the old grump's behalf.

Still, I'm out of options. And time. It's now or not at all. Who knows when I'll get another opportunity like this.

Preacher trails me as we circle the stairwell ascending into the west wing. The sound echoes, acting as the overture to what I hope will be my best performance yet. If my Calling weren't faulty, I could simply use my voice, sing him to sleep, and head straight for the dungeons. But with each passing day, my Mirror song fades. It worked at the coronation on the Guardians but just as quickly failed me when I confronted Gage. I want to brush it off as a winter cold, but I know it's more than that.

Which is exactly why I'm doing this. I gasp and halt on the step above him. "My treble clef–heart necklace, it's gone." I fling my hand to my neck and widen my eyes.

"You can look for it tomorrow." He adjusts his jacket, nudges me onward.

"No." *Stand your ground. Don't take no for an answer. You are the queen, after all.* "Joshua gave it to me. If he finds out I misplaced it again, he'll be so hurt." This part, at least, bears truth. The memory of his face the last time I lost it stabs at my chest.

Preacher huffs, crosses his arms, and starts back toward the kitchen. "Let's make this quick. I don't want to be down here all night."

Turning sideways, I push past him, stopping a step below him this time. "It's fine." I can't bring myself to look him in the eye. My poker face wouldn't win me many chips. "You go ahead. I can make it to my suite on my own." I slide one foot back, lower it onto the next stair.

One furry eyebrow shrugs, meets the bottom of his knit cap. "Nice try, *Highness*. You know the rules. You are to be escorted by a Guardian at all times."

Ugh. *Highness* is almost worse than being called *girl*. The way he says it, as if mocking, makes me want to put *him* in the dungeon for a night. How can he be so insolent? Did I not save this entire Reflection from the wrath of the Void, for Verity's sake?

I clear my throat, forcing calm into my frog-plagued voice. "I am the Verity's vessel. A Mirror and your queen." I hold my head high, stare him down. "I think I can make it to my room without reenacting a scene from an eighties slasher flick."

Ky snorts inside my head.

It's all I can do not to copy the sentiment.

"I have my orders, and they do not come from you."

"That's where you are mistaken." Darn voice. Stop trembling. Sheesh.

Preacher shakes his head. Is that compassion softening his scowl? "You don't get it."

"What don't I get? Enlighten me."

His lips purse. He looks away.

"What aren't you saying?" My heart pounds. He knows. He knows why most everyone has been acting so strange around me since the coronation.

"It's not my place." He pauses, shuffles from foot to foot. I've never seen him at a loss for words. "But the people are . . . concerned."

I furrow my brows. "Of course they are. With the attack and—"

"No." He rubs his nose. "What happened last week is the least of their concerns . . ." He meets my gaze then, eyes narrowing but not in the mean sort of way, as is his custom. No, this time his expression is more studious. As if trying to read what my reaction to his next words might be.

I touch his arm, connecting with him in a way I never believed possible.

He exhales, sending the whiskers above his upper lip flapping.

"They're . . ." He clears his throat. *"We're* all concerned perhaps the Verity isn't the best . . . match for you. David was the one—"

"Hold on." I palm my forehead. "Are you implying . . . What *are* you implying? The Verity chooses the purest heart." It's black and white, night and day. The Verity selected me, which means I have the purest heart, which means I am fit to be queen.

The bag beneath Preacher's right eye twitches. "Indeed. But in light of recent events, there are those who wonder if, perhaps, the Verity got it wrong this time."

And now I've forgotten my line. Someone send in the understudy because I can't even improvise this one. I don't know which question to ask first. Who all thinks the Verity got it wrong? Obviously Preacher does, but who else? Joshua? Mom? Haven't I proven myself? Is it not enough I killed my own grandfather? Not enough I was willing to take on the Void and sacrifice everything for those I love?

Am I ever going to be enough?

"You are enough for me."

Tears well. Ky's whisper is so clear, his statement so sure. My heart patters and doubt creeps in. If the Verity is capable of making a mistake, aren't I? What if I'm not meant to be here? With Joshua? I bite my lower lip and allow the question to form, to become real and tangible for the very first time.

What if I'm meant to be with—?

"Go find your necklace." Preacher's concession yanks me from my epiphany. He pushes up his jacket sleeve, checking the time on his out-of-date Rolex. "I'll wait here. You have ten minutes." He relaxes against the curved stone wall and tugs his cap over his eyes. "A minute longer and you won't take so much as a leak without a Guardian nearby, you hear me?"

Mouth agape, I stare at him. Why the sudden change of heart? Pity? Guilt? I guess it doesn't make a difference. I'll take what I can get.

"Now you only have nine minutes."

I pick up my skirt, descend the stairs two at a time.

"I won't be far," he calls after me. "No Dragon games."

I roll my eyes. I may have given Preacher the slip, but I doubt my cunning is any match for a Dragon. Or so I hear. "Okay."

The lie ricochets up the stairwell as I withdraw my treble clef–heart necklace from my pocket, reattach it, and slip soundlessly through the archway leading into the dungeons.

❧

During my half-star stay last November, compliments of Jasyn Crowe, I only had the opportunity to visit the highest level of dungeon cells. My mind wanders to the prisoner who helped me. The one who called to me through the wall. Did he die? Is he still there? I make a note to ask about him later.

But now is not the time.

Thanks to my snooping skills I know the prisoner I seek hasn't been afforded such luxury. No, she'll be enjoying much more . . . moderate accommodations. And if I happen to come across Gage, too, well then, bonus round. Maybe he can tell me where Ky is, or what he meant by "the beginning of the end."

Maybe. If he's conscious. Or still alive.

I creep down sconce-lit steps. The stingy light has me wary of my own shadow. Every move and shift plays tricks on my tired eyes in shades of gray on the walls. And then there's the memory of a boy with blond locks and a cocky grin. Of how he rescued me in more ways than one.

About every thirty steps or so a new archway waits, signaling I've reached the next level down. I pass each one without pause, the theme from BBC's *Sherlock* playing in my head. When I reach the final arch at the bottom, I exit the stairwell. How deep am I anyway? I must be at least five stories below the hill's surface. Where are the Guardians? They can't all have gone to the Reminiscence. At least a few must have remained behind to attend the prisoners. Right?

But the absence of a "Halt, who goes there?" assures me it's safe to continue. I'm inspired by my favorite Broadway lead. If *Wicked*'s Elphaba can learn to trust her instincts, so can I, even when no one else does.

"*I do.*"

Ky's constant reassurances are becoming commonplace. I almost hate to admit I wait for them. Expect them. Any moment his voice could vanish. And then he'd really be gone.

Iron doors mark my path to the right and left every ten paces. Sconces are positioned between, though only a few produce light. The doors bear no windows, just slender slots at eye level, and iPad-sized cat doors at the bottom. A familiar scent puckers my nose, and I opt to breathe through my mouth. It's not too far removed from the pungent aroma of a subway tunnel. Urine blended with a hint of spray paint fumes and BO.

I check every peep slot, sliding them across—*shick*—and back again—*clank*. Empty, empty, empty. Faster. Five doors. Ten. Three left turns . . . now four. How vast is this level? And how much longer before Preacher realizes I'm not in the kitchen?

Around a fifth corner I careen, stop dead at the brink of yet another identical hallway accommodating more doors, which I have no doubt also host vacant cells. Is it designed as a labyrinth on purpose? Maybe that's why I haven't come across a single Guardian. Who needs them when I can't even locate one measly prisoner?

Hmm, better retrace my steps, see if I missed something. Retreat, run right, sprint right, jog right, walk, *ouch-my-knee*, limp, slow down—

Wait . . . Is this the way I came? Whirl. Squint. Crud. Nice plan. Maybe everyone's right. If I can't navigate a dungeon, perhaps I do need a babysitter.

Shallow breaths and dizziness take precedence. My knee is really starting to throb now. I half expect my heart to beat right out of the pulse residing there. If I just sit for a minute, regain my bearings, I'll be fine. Using the wall for support I slide onto my rear, good leg sprawled in front of me, bad one bent to my chest. The earthy floor cools my thigh through the fabric of my skirt.

I press my palms to my cheeks, swipe sweaty cowlicks from my temples. *Drip, drip, drip.* A leak plinks into a pot somewhere, washing a memory to my mind's shore.

To think I believed Jasyn would put me up in a penthouse suite. It had all seemed so real. The comfy bed, the crackling fire, the French pastries. What a joke. I'd been in a dungeon cell the entire time. Thankfully, it didn't take long to see through his tricks—

My body rigidifies, and my head smacks the wall. *Ouch and duh.* I rub the sore spot through my thick tangles. Why didn't I see it? I rise and search the surrounding space. An Amulet has put a façade over this level. Has to be. But I'm usually quick to catch an Amulet's work. I see through façades before most. It's one of my strengths as a Mirror.

Fear spreads deeper, winding its roots around my gut. Something is definitely wrong with my Calling. Stormy had trouble with her Magnet when we were with Gage. Joshua couldn't heal Kuna. Who else has been affected? And how is this possible? If the Callings are sourced by the Verity—

My breath ceases. How did I miss it?

If something is wrong with the *Callings* . . .

Then something is troubling the Verity, causing it to remain stagnant . . .

Which means the problem lies within *me.*

This is the reason for the whispers and stares in the halls. Why Joshua won't let me help. Why Preacher believes the Verity may have been in error.

A wave of nausea sends my hand to my mouth. Something is . . . *wrong* with me. The thought makes me feel unclean. Could Preacher be right? Did the Verity make a mistake? What if I'm like cancer and something about me is eating away at the Verity, hindering it from empowering the Callings?

Gasp. And the Thresholds. They're sourced by the Verity as well. Whatever happened at Dawn Lake wasn't an accident or a mere case of someone walking on too-thin ice.

Fury spreads like wildfire through the fabric of my soul.

Just when I was getting used to my mirrormark—accepting it as strength and beauty and so uniquely me. This is almost worse than a blemished reflection. Because true beauty comes from within, from the person you are. And if my soul is weakening the Verity, what does that say about me?

My eyelids migrate south, and I inhale a controlled breath to quell my shaking limbs. The truth is so clear it slaps me in the face. Is this fate's design? To keep me the forever screwup? My greatest fear comes to life. Concrete. Final. It's one thing to hate my reflection, to think I'm ugly, or to worry about how others perceive me. It's entirely another to realize, deep down, I was right all along.

I am damaged. And not just on the surface. Not just where others can see.

My very soul, my essence, my heart is not good enough to house the Verity. I'm no better than the person I came down here to find.

"Em, no. You've got it wrong."

I ignore the sadness in Ky's voice, rise with leg shaking, and move forward. But instead of turning around the next corner, I walk straight through the wall before me. Within moments I'm in a new hallway. Terra-cotta tiles replace the grimy floor, and track lighting above sheds a homey glow. Two doors await ahead, plain white with a tiny window in each like at a hospital. Situated between the doors, a C-shaped nook sinks into the wall, privacy curtain pushed to one side. A cot topped with a ratty comforter and a single flat pillow sits at the back. And there, sitting with legs crossed and red lips sneering, is none other than Quinn Kelley in the flesh.

I release an exaggerated sigh. At least someone's Calling is working fine. "Knock the Shield off, Ebony."

She stands but doesn't approach. Plants pristinely manicured hands on her hips. She may look like my ex-bestie with her platinum hair and ice-blue eyes, but it doesn't matter what persona she takes on. Deep down she's just my traitorous half sister.

Her eyes narrow. "What the bleep took you so long?"

THIRTEEN

mine

You know those moments when you can't think of anything to say?

Now is not one of them.

Every jab and nasty comment. Every unkind word. Every lie Quinn has ever uttered buoys to the surface, breathes and expands. I've spent so much time suppressing my hurt, trying to get over it, but now it boils over. A white-hot ball of pent-up woundedness. I have so many things to say to her. So many questions.

Why?

How could you?

What kind of person does what you did?

Instead I spit out, "Is that all you have to say to me?"

She blinks. "What am I supposed to say?"

I emit an irritated gurgle in my throat. "An apology would be nice, for starters."

"Life isn't scripted, El. Get used to it." She flicks her hand flippantly and hops off the bed.

"I don't have time for this."

"Makes two of us."

I scan the length of her, absorbing her appearance. Torn fishnet stockings run up her legs, disappear beneath a wrinkled black dress. She's barefoot too. I never realized how short she is without high heels. A closer glance at her "bedroom" reveals a chamber pot tucked in one corner.

Quinn shifts. Her shoulders lift as if trying to shrug off my scrutiny. "My Shield has been faulty. I can alter my person, but my clothing remains the same."

I recall the first time I saw her shift, when she revealed herself as Mom's conniving art dealer Lincoln Cooper and I discovered just how deep Quinn's—*Ebony's*—deceit ran. The way she'd played me to exact revenge. Now, as her face contorts, the transformation doesn't seem out of place. Instead I find it suits her superficial personality. Her sharp features soften, and everything from her hair to her skin fades from bright to shaded.

Shaded. Like her soul.

Ugh. And mine apparently.

Ebony Archer stares back at me, a knowing glare in her espresso eyes. "But that's why you're down here, isn't it? You already know something's up with the Callings."

"What do you know? Why are the Callings"—*what's a good word?*—"malfunctioning? Do you know which cell belongs to Gage? Maybe I can question him—"

"Relax, little sis. Don't be so rushy-rushy. Lucky for you I eavesdropped on Gage's interrogation. I'll fill you in. But first you're going to do something for me."

This part, of course, is unavoidable. "What do you want?"

She yawns, makes a show of ghosting her hand over her mouth. "Nothing much. Just a small token, some collateral to ensure you don't screw me over."

As always her word choice proves tactless. A hurried glance over my shoulder allows me to breathe easier. No Preacher. Yet. "Get to the point, Ebony. Name your price."

She meets me at the nook's edge where the tile on my side meets the carpeted floor on hers. Next she reaches forward, palms facing me, and pushes as if an invisible wall separates us.

I step back and examine the air before me. No, not air, glass. Glass so clean and clear it's hardly detectable. Ebony's in a cage.

"Only David knows the way in and out," she explains. "But that is irrelevant. Because you, my dear sister, are a Mirror."

My face numbs. "How did you—?"

"I'm not clueless. Your display last Eleventh Month pretty much alerted everyone and their horse to your Calling."

My display. I touch my right cheek. Ky and I discovered Queen Ember's "Mirror Theory" together. I guess most people know my ability based on what they've seen me do. Sometimes I forget only a select few know how my birthmark—*mirrormark*—is related. Every Calling has a symbol associated with it, a tattoo that appears when the Calling manifests. But unlike the seven main Callings, which are revealed by the intake of Threshold water, the Mirror Calling can only be given to one person at a time. And nothing but a Kiss of Infinity bestowed by the Verity's vessel can create a Mirror.

Could this be the problem? I'm a Mirror *and* the Verity's vessel. Perhaps my Calling needs to be passed on to someone else. Could the Mirror in me be hindering the Verity from functioning properly?

I shake my head. None of this adds up. If the Callings are sourced by the Verity, why would mine hinder it? Joshua was an Ever *and* the vessel. It didn't cause him any complications.

But Mirrors are different. Special. Rare. Ugh. My brain hurts. Once again I sense this is all connected. But how?

"En-ee-waaay." Ebony curls her upper lip and examines her nails. "What I seek is a trifle. You release me, and I'll tell you what I know."

"That's it?" No way. Not buying it.

She smiles. I almost believe it's genuine. "That's it."

I lift one eyebrow the way Ky does when he doesn't believe someone. "Yeah, right. Tell me what I need to know first, *then* I'll release you." Maybe.

In the past moving through a reflective barrier would've been easier than playing "Chopsticks" on the piano. But I haven't attempted mirror walking in a while. If my song is dying and my hands are unable to heal, what other abilities am I losing?

"Let's make a deal." She leans her head to one side and begins braiding her mocha tresses. "I'll give you what you want, and vice versa." When the braid is finished she secures it with a black tie from around her wrist. "We can be sure the other will follow through because we'll seal the promise with a Kiss of Accord. Fair enough?"

A Kiss of Accord? Hmm. "How do I know this isn't a trick? How do I know you can help me?"

"I guess you don't. But let me add this, sweeten the deal a bit. I'm aware you didn't just come down here to chat about Callings, or even Gage's interrogation." She doesn't miss a beat when she says, "You want to know where Rhyen is."

I blink, keeping my expression as neutral as possible despite the thudding in my chest. This confirms my intuition was correct. Ebony won't tiptoe around me. She's exactly who I need. "Where is he?"

Ebony clicks her tongue. "Do we have a deal?"

Before I can weigh the pros and cons of her offer—and there are most definitely more cons than pros when it comes to Ebony—the ground shakes. The cell doors rattle on their hinges and rubble tumbles from the ceiling. My half sister's face turns ghostly, contrasting against her pink lips and darker-than-mine hair.

Our eyes meet. She pounds the unaffected glass. "Get me out."

I glance over my shoulder. Then back at the transparent wall separating us. I could book it or even attempt to mirror walk to a safer place. Alone. Without her.

Would serve her right.

"El, come on!" Her shrill plea only grates my nerves. Where was she when I needed her? When I was the one in trouble and could've used a real and true friend?

"El, pleeeassse." The ceiling in her cell begins to crumble. She covers her head with her arms.

I consider her for another second. Then I groan and press a palm to the glass, clear my throat. My song is scratchy, off-key, and breathy and barely a melody at all. But it's enough. A sensation like having the air knocked out of me takes over. It's as if my lungs are being squeezed through a pipe. Normally the transition from here to there is smoother, and not at all painful. This is so not a good sign.

Once I'm inside the cage, Ebony flings her arm toward me.

I can't believe I'm doing this. I should leave her here, make her pay.

"But that's not who you are," Ky says, and I swear that's a smile in his voice.

"Get us out of here," Ebony screeches.

With her hand in mine, I return to the glass wall. I begin my song but my voice is so raw, I might as well be lip-syncing for the amount of sound coming through my lips. I swallow, shake my head, begin again. Pain shoots up and down my throat and I cry out, making a noise like a beaten donkey. It's not working.

"Because you're relying on the wrong thing."

Ky? Sigh. Help me.

"Think, Em. What did you learn at Nathaniel's the first time you passed through a mirror?"

I close my eyes and picture it. The musty attic. My cynical grandfather in his ratty old bathrobe. Ky encouraging me, believing in me.

How could I forget?

My eyes open and my soul jolts. Preacher stands on the other side of the glass, his face wrinkled with a mixture of anger and disappointment. He's pointing a finger at me, commanding me to come out. An all-too-familiar guilt returns and prick, prick, pricks my chest. Preacher's mad because I lied to him. Because he's trying to protect me. Maybe Ky was right and Preacher isn't so bad.

"Finally she gets it." Ky laughs in my head. "When are you going to learn I am pretty much always right?"

I roll my eyes.

"Reflections to El." Ebony snaps her fingers in front of my nose. "Now is not the ideal time to pursue a career as a space cadet."

Where was I? The attic . . . my song . . . the way I felt . . .

Love. Not song alone, but love. I wonder . . . could it work?

Only one way to find out.

This time when I close my eyes and press my palm to the glass

I don't open my mouth. Instead I experience the music, the lyrics, within. I allow the notes to glide across my soul. I feel their re-verberations around my heart. They fill me up and undo me at once. I think of Mom and my new sibling. Of Makai, and of course Joshua. And then . . . then I think of Ky. I see his face. Feel his hand in mine.

That's when the song comes alive, as if it's awakening my soul. The glass turns liquid beneath my touch.

Ebony and I step through.

ACT II

poor
unfortunate
souls

joshua

The air on Lisel Island is thin and briny. I breathe deep, my chest expanding as I take it all in. This is where I grew up. Here I am at home.

"Do you think he's expecting visitors?" Wren asks.

"Nathaniel Archer raised me. I've no need for an invitation here."

"If you say so." She shrugs, leaving a substantial amount of space between us as we contemplate the remodeled brownstone.

One of my first tasks as interim king was to have a team fix it up, and a fine job they did. I have not had a chance to witness it since the remodel. The caved steps have been demolished and replaced, the door repainted a deep shade of green. The windows are quartz clear, their sills sanded and coated with fresh varnish. Even the planters have been cleared out, at the ready to host flowers come spring.

If only I could have worked on it myself. Perhaps when this is over I can build one for El. She would love that. A place for us alone, away from duty and responsibility. My father had this one built for my mother. A grand gesture would be just the thing—

Wren coughs and I consider her with a sideways glance. She rubs and rolls her neck, breathing deep and stretching. She had a more difficult time than usual transforming into her Mask state tonight, and even then her griffin didn't appear quite right, her feathers thinned, her beak not fully grown. It was a relief she was able to shift at all. So far it seems Physic and Ever are the only two Callings that have vanished completely, but some of the others have also begun to show signs of wear. Stormy's shaky Magnet and now Wren's off-kilter griffin. What will fail next?

Grinding my teeth, I bury my anxiety. My new mortality has made me more cautious as of late, holding me back like a cage. This is why we have come. Nathaniel will have answers.

Wren proceeds up the steps and I follow. Blueprints for El's country home occupy my brain, filling me with hope for our future once more. She will require a room for her music, a space magnificent enough to house a grand piano. Would she want a sound studio as well, a place where she can record her own music? Where we can record together?

I shake my head, forcing myself to focus on the task at hand. First things first. If I desire a private haven where El and I can be us again, I must stop what's happening to the Callings and Thresholds before it ventures too far.

Wren knocks on the front door. I chuckle and move past her, twisting the knob and walking straight in. The foyer is not at all how I remember. The wood floor is clean and buffed, the ratty rug removed. "Nathaniel?" I cough and wait. When no answer returns I try again. "Nathaniel. It's Joshua. Are you home?"

Wren arrives beside me. "Maybe he's out of town." The slight lilt in her voice tells me she's joking, but this does nothing to ease my apprehension.

"Natha—"

A creak sounds from the floor above, and Wren and I look up in unison. Two more creaks follow, continued by a scuffle, a cough, and another creak.

Nathaniel appears at the top of the stairs. His squinted expression portrays annoyance, but then he rubs his spectacles on his robe and blinks. Now his face softens, the hard lines smoothing. He does not smile, but I know this man well. For him this *is* a smile.

"Joshua, my boy. To what do I owe this pleasure?" His accent is the same as ever. I always found it odd as a child. It was not until I spent time in the Third that I discovered the way he speaks is common for those from overseas. A British accent, they call it.

He hobbles down the stairs, clutching the refinished railing as if his life depends on it. When he meets me at the bottom, we embrace. He was not able to attend the coronation, the return to the castle so soon after Crowe's expiration too much for his aged bones.

After a few good hacks he says, "Come in. Come in." He meanders into the room to my left and Wren and I follow. "Forgive me for the mess. I was not expecting visitors." A cloud of dust rises when he plops into an armchair. "Nice to see you as well, Miss Song. How is your father, my old apprentice?"

"As good as can be expected." Wren folds her arms and leans against the frame separating this room from the foyer. "He keeps busy as a trome-visiting Physic these days."

"Very good," Nathaniel says. "Taught Wade everything he knows. A fine Physic, that man."

"Yes, sir."

I place my hand on Nathaniel's shoulder. "I wish you would reconsider my offer and come live in the castle. There is no reason for you to remain here. We have plenty of room and you would be well cared for. You could be near me and Makai and Elizabeth and El. No traveling back and forth—"

"Bah." He waves a hand. "I have no need for servants or pampering. It was time for me to be done with all the brouhaha. I have lived here many years and manage just fine on my own. Besides, I like it on the island. It's quiet."

I shake my head and kneel before the fireplace across from him, stacking logs in a crisscross fashion the way Makai taught me when I was eight.

"So, what brings you to my humble abode?"

"I came to seek your knowledge." I grab some parchment from a nearby stack, crumple it, and stuff it here and there among the logs. "I suppose you may have noticed your Physic abilities have ceased?" I glance back at him.

He rubs his chin. "Indeed. Just the other day I cut my finger on a paring knife. What should have been a simple repair required salve and a bandage. Very odd. Then again, I am old and weak and tired. Tell me, what is the latest on the mainland?"

I find the matches on top of the mantel and light the fire. The draft from the chimney challenges the flames, but after a few tries the parchment begins to crackle. I relay the events of El's coronation, sharing the details of our run-in with Gage and Isabeau. I explain Kuna's death and my failure to save him. "Even El's Mirror song had no effect."

"I see." He sneezes and rubs his nose. "And Makai and his bride?"

I fill him in.

Nathaniel steeples his fingers and presses them to his lips. He closes his eyes and now I know to wait. This is what he does when he's thinking. He runs everything through his brilliant mind and pieces details together, making connections before coming up with possible answers or solutions.

At last he releases a long, phlegmy exhale. "Continue, please."

I glance at Wren. She offers the slightest nod and for some reason this relieves my fear. It's as if she's saying, "I'm here. I support you." So I continue. "The Threshold at Dawn Lake. It appears to be . . . draining."

Nathaniel's eyebrows arch, but his eyes remain closed. "Is it, now? How very interesting. Yes, how interesting indeed."

I rock back on my heels and rise, wiping soot from my palms onto my thighs. "You know something. I knew you would."

"I can but speculate. Such a situation has never occurred in the history of the Reflections. That we are aware of, anyway."

Wren straightens and moves farther into the room.

I gaze down at my adoptive father.

The fire is ablaze now and the orange light reflects off his spectacles. "The Void. How are you handling it?"

My heartbeat halts. He knows, but how? I haven't told anyone, not even Makai. My gaze shifts to Wren as sweat beads on my temples. I expect to find a disgusted glare. Instead I recognize the look she gives as sympathy. I roll up my sleeve, flex and clench my right hand. "It was stagnant for a while, but recently it has begun to spread."

"I see. The day of the coronation?"

I nod.

"Interesting." Now he opens his eyes and slowly turns his attention to me. "When Eliyana took on the Verity, am I correct in assuming the burden of the Void did not fall solely to you?"

Neck pulsing, I swallow and relent. "Yes."

"Kyaphus took on half?"

My pulse is in my ears now. "Yes." I hesitate before relaying the next bit, but finally add, "He and El shared a Kiss of Infinity shortly before." Might as well get it all out in the open.

"And I suppose you believe because the Void enters the one the Verity's vessel cares for most, Eliyana cares for you both equally?"

My stomach clenches. "Yes." Except, not quite. Otherwise she'd have given us both a Kiss of Infinity. But I can't bring myself to admit this part out loud.

"Interesting theory," he muses. "Any idea where it came from?"

His question makes me cock my head. Is he being rhetorical on purpose? "The Reflection Chronicles. Where else?"

"And in exactly which volume did you find this information?"

I scan my thoughts, racking my memories for an answer. When I can find none I admit, "I never actually read it. It is common knowledge." Correct?

"And therein lies the problem." Excitement tremors his voice. "Relying on word of mouth rather than going to the source yourself."

My brain illuminates. How could I have been so careless? Why didn't I research more? Why didn't I search beyond the volumes in my study?

"The truth is," Nathaniel says, "it is precisely the opposite. The Void does not enter the one the Verity's vessel loves most. No, no. The Void inhabits the one—or ones in this case—who cares most for the one who retains the Verity."

Of course. El may not have given us both a Kiss of Infinity, but we each gave her one.

Wren snorts and when I look at her she rolls her eyes. "Of course she'd have two guys in love with her."

My lips flatten and I scratch the back of my head. She is not El's biggest fan, and the blame for that falls to me. Will Wren ever forgive me for what happened between us four years ago? She can hold a grudge better than anyone. At some point I hope she can let it go.

"It is more complicated, Miss Song," Nathaniel says. "I knew someday it would come to this. I knew eventually I would be forced to explain." With a groan he rises from the chair and looks me square in the face.

Whatever comes next, the seriousness in his stare tells me I'm ill prepared for it.

"Joshua," he says. "Kyaphus Rhyen is your twin brother."

FIFTEEN

Turn

"You saved me?!"

Ebony's shrill whisper—if such a thing exists—plunges a dose of oxygen into my chest. Is it a question? A statement? An accusation? With her, I never can tell.

My eyelids snap open. I'm lying on my back. My lungs expand and I breathe deep. Gasp. Cough. Choke. Gulp. Moonlight spills through the bay window at the other end of my suite. The chandelier above rattles and the drapes between my bedposts tremble. The earthquake seems to be ongoing, but the force of it is much less abrupt so high aboveground.

"Why would you do that?" She's standing above me now, hands on her hips and toe tapping. Doesn't she know any other way to stand?

I sit up, rub the back of my head. "Good question," I rasp.

She reaches down and helps me rise. "We didn't even exchange a Kiss of Accord. You basically just gave me a get-out-of-jail-free card."

I scowl. "So leave then. Pass go. Collect two hundred dollars. Take the whole flippin' bank, for all I care." I turn my back on her, pace to the window, and cross my arms. I'm boiling, bubbling over with no way to lower the heat. I have more important things to worry about than Ebony Archer.

What's happening to me?

Why was mirror walking . . . painful?

Why do I feel drained and weak and ready to sleep for a hundred years after traveling such a short distance?

Verity, where are you? Where's your soothing calm? Why can't I feel you? Did you abandon me?

Shuddering from the hollowness within, I gaze out over the Second. My suite is in the same wing as Stormy's and I can just make out Dawn Lake from here, or the lack thereof. The ice is broken, bobbing about in chunks across the shallow water. Makai was right. The Threshold is draining. But why? My mind is a spinning record. Too many tracks. They tell a story, but they're out of order. What's the pattern, the rhythm to this album?

Ebony appears beside me. She mirrors my body language and I make a point to let my arms rest at my sides. We are not alike. No. Not at all. Nuh-uh.

"I should leave." She just stands there.

I hurl a sideways glare. "So leave."

"I will." She doesn't budge.

"Fine."

"Bye."

"Bye."

Five minutes pass. Neither of us moves.

"You stay then." I push past her, making a point to bump her shoulder as I do. When I flop onto my bed, I bury my face in my pillow and scream. It's all of three seconds before I hear the creak of the wood floor, the *click* of the door to the hall, and the rattle as it slams closed.

I turn on my side and hug my middle.

Should've known better than to turn to a traitor for help.

In my sleep I toss and turn. Throw the covers off. Drag them back on. My pillow is on the floor and the sheets are twisted around my legs. My dry mouth and throat beg for water, but my body is lead and I can't bring myself to get up.

Wretched nightmares.

"El, come on, you've been in here all day." Joshua's shadow blocks the lamplight, casting a gray film over my work space in the back of the library.

My brows pinch and I subdue the annoyance begging to grunt from my throat. I don't look up from the book laid out on the table in front of me. I skim my notes, trying to make sense of what I've found. My eyes are dry and itchy. My nose runny from the dust in the air. But my obsession—er, interest?—takes precedence. Where was I? Oh yes. Here. According to this author, the earliest record of the Void dates back to—

A hand reaches out. Snatches the book away. Tosses it onto an empty chair. "Enough is enough," Joshua says. "It's the first day of First Month. We should pause and celebrate."

I want to ask him what we have to celebrate when the Void is still alive and well. When it isn't destroyed—not really—it's always hurting someone even if it's not hurting everyone. Is it so easy to forget another's pain as long as it's not your own? How can Joshua ignore it? The Verity within keeps me calm, quelling whatever darkness I might feel from Ky. Does it keep Joshua at peace too? I'm still not quite clear on how this triangle-soul-connection thing even works.

I pick up my pen and scribble in the margin of my notes:

research soul links (also see Kiss of Infinity)

Joshua takes my writing hand, removes the pen, and kisses each finger soft and slow.

Breaths cease. Time? What is that?

He kneels and that crooked grin of his surfaces, making it impossible not to return the gesture. "One hour?" He lifts a brow. "I only ask for sixty minutes of the future queen's time and then I promise, on my honor as interim king, I will return you to your task." Now his eyebrows wag. "It'll be worth it, I guarantee."

This. *This* is the Joshua I remember. The one I've hardly

glimpsed since arriving in the Second. How can I miss an opportunity to spend a moment with the boy I fell in love with? The one I was afraid, for a spell, had disappeared altogether?

I sigh. Blush. Defenses down. "One hour." He helps me stand and our hands remain connected. "This had better be good."

"Oh, it will be." He winks then. Of course he does.

Outside it's freezing, like ice-cubes-sliding-down-my-bones-and-turning-my-blood-reptilian cold. New York wasn't this frigid, not even close. No, this is a whole new level of frostbite. My entire body quakes as we crunch through the snow toward the castle stables—the same stables Ky and I escaped through in November. The memory wraps me with an unwarranted chill and I shiver it away. Should've brought my coat. How is Joshua not an icicle in his meager long-sleeved button-down?

"Don't worry," he says as if reading my arctic brain. "You'll be warm soon."

Teeth chattering, I pick up my pace to match his longer stride. One of his steps is three of my hobbit ones. At the stables, which are U-shaped with their own sort of courtyard at the heart, I stop. Lively, Celtic-feeling music with an urban flair wafts through the entry arch. I glance up at Joshua. It's city meets country, a Manhattan-slash-Second Reflection mash-up. Most days I wonder if he's forgotten me—us. But then a pinprick of sunlight beams and I see . . .

He knows me all too well.

When we enter the courtyard, winter fades. Large space heaters are stationed throughout, and a bonfire blazes at the center where Reggie roasts marshmallows bigger than my fist. Couples skip and dance. Children race and tag and tumble. Band members play and slap their knees. Horses whinny and nod. A triple-row horse-drawn sleigh waits to one side where passengers board. There's even a mini ice rink in the far southern corner. It's like a Fairy tale come to life.

"This is all for me?" My jaw won't stay closed.

Joshua chuckles. The sound has always teetered between an

old man's laugh and a child's giggle. "It is tradition to ring in the New Year with a small gathering of family and friends. With a little light in the darkest of seasons. You will officially be our queen in less than a month. I thought it only fitting to amp the festivities up a notch and add a few of your favorite things." He releases my hand and offers his arm.

I link mine through his, let him lead me toward the fire. My insides thaw and the Verity washes me with serenity. What was I so worried about? I almost can't remember why I've kept myself holed up in the library. Life is here and now. How have I allowed myself to miss it?

Joshua twirls me around and around, the perfect gentleman. He knows every step and sway, never faltering or missing a beat. Everything about him is methodical and planned. Purposeful. He knows each move before he makes it, each word before it's uttered.

With Joshua I am safe. With Joshua I am home.

Reggie's deep laugh rises over the crackling fire. Mom and Makai join in the dancing, her smile brighter than a full moon. When the music slows, Joshua intertwines his fingers with mine once more and takes me to a stall where his white stallion (because, why not?) Champion waits, saddled and ready.

Joshua lifts me onto the back of the saddle, then mounts. I wrap my arms around his waist, inhaling his warmth and spice and all things Joshua. When we've cleared the stables, Champion transitions from a trot into a gallop. I hold fast to my knight on a white horse as we circle the castle. He's quiet until we halt near the rose garden.

That's when I stop breathing. Because holy Verity, how is this possible?

What was dead under Jasyn's rule has now burst to life. Vibrant roses bloom everywhere, a maze of crimson and scarlet. Joshua dismounts, then helps me do the same, leading me along the rosebush-guarded path until we reach a marble bench at the center. And there, sitting on the bench, atop a pillow embroidered with purple thread, is the white gold, diamond-studded band I returned to him weeks ago. The one that hung from my necklace chain like an anvil. The one I asked him to keep until I was ready to wear it for real.

I guess he thinks a month is ample time to wait to re-propose.

How can I disappoint him? How do I tell him I'm still not ready?

My heart. Oh, my stupid, unsure heart.

I know the answer, but I won't admit it aloud. Instead of *A Tale of Two Cities*, it's a tale of two boys—men. But I have to believe my feelings for Ky stem only from wanting to save him as he saved me. That's why I gave him a Kiss of Infinity. Because I didn't want him to die. That's why I search for a way to end the Void now. Because it's not fair he's taken on such darkness only to live with it, alone, while I act out my light and fluffy happily ever after.

Guilty much?

"El," Joshua says, oblivious to my internal dilemma. "I think you know why I've brought you here."

I swallow hard past the boulder in my throat. No need to panic. Cold feet are uncalled for. I expected this, even if later rather than sooner.

Joshua tilts my chin up and kisses me. The Verity dances, swirling and twirling around my pitter-pattering heart, weaving in and out of my soul. Why was I worried again?

"*Cheer up, sleepy Jean,*" Joshua sings in my ear, rocking me back and forth. He's the bluebird's wings I hide beneath. The six o'clock alarm that never rings.

I stir in my sleep, the memory begging to end there. Where it was good and perfect and right. But of course it doesn't.

Before Joshua can get to his knees to ask for my hand, I'm on the ground. Aching, crying, and I don't know why. It's as if I'm being burned, seared to my core. What feels like a knife slitting my jaw forces a yelp from my lips.

Joshua joins me where I kneel, his face a contorted mess. My pain is his. And what's worse? There's no denying where my pain stems from.

Ky is in danger. And there is not a single thing I can do to stop it.

I bolt upright in bed, the clothes I've worn for the past day damp with sweat. It's still night, the darkness casting an eerie quiet over every rug and drape. My room is static, the earthquake ceased. Moonlight no longer spills into the room. When I slide out of bed and move to the window, I can no longer spy Dawn Lake or its contents. Clouds fill the skies, making it too dark to tell how much water remains in the Threshold below.

I rub my jaw from ear to chin. The pain I felt that day was so real. Too real, making the ache in my knee a mere bruise in comparison. The brain is a funny thing. Dreams are merely devices that allow us to relive memories we don't want to lose. They're a way of idealizing relationships, of putting them in our perfect little boxes where no one can touch them. But this dream—this memory—has a dark side. All memories do, if you know where to look. This dream, this memory, always turns nightmarish. Except, instead of waking to find it was just my imagination, I feel as if a bucket of ice has been dumped over my head, reminding me what I must do. I twist Joshua's ring around my finger and straighten the crown on my head.

I've scoured the library ten times over and have unearthed nothing of consequence. I'm making my way through *The Reflection Chronicles*, too, though the feat is slow and dull. Reading Mom's words is one thing, but so far the other journals I've perused have been nothing less than the textbook definition of boring. There must be an account with more meat in it, but which one?

Even though Jasyn destroyed much, hundreds of volumes were still uncovered. The people worked together to stash and stow the accounts passed down to them. Then those accounts were brought here to be archived.

Problem is, even though each one is dated, they all seem random. I've no way of guessing who would know anything about the history of the Void. No starting point. And without a starting point, I'm lost.

I've read Mom's account of *The Reflection Chronicles* so many times I have it memorized, along with Queen Ember's "Mirror Theory." I could recite the thing word for word and pass with flying colors. Have I missed something? Could there be a clue connecting me to another chronicle? The "Mirror Theory" and information on the Kiss of Infinity are the closest things I have to a beginning. My brain scans the uploaded information. Searching. Skimming. I squeeze my eyes and press my fingers to my temples.

And there it is, a single snippet of information standing out among the rest. How could I have missed it?

No time to waste.

I know where to look.

It's time to pay an unscheduled visit to Joshua's study.

joshua

I'm dry heaving on Nathaniel's front steps. It is, in a word, humiliating. How can this be? Ky Rhyen, my brother? No, not just my brother. My *twin* brother. It's the most impossible, unfathomable thing.

And yet it makes more sense than anything has in months.

The front door creaks behind me. I'm aware it's Wren without so much as a backward glance.

"How are you doing?"

I wave her off. "Fine."

"You are not *fine*, David." She places her hand on my back.

I flinch and her touch vanishes. "Apologies." Another dry heave. "I didn't expect . . ."

"I get it." The bitterness in her tone lets on she still hasn't forgiven me for the past. "I'm not her."

I shake my head and then realize she might not understand the reason behind my reaction. "It isn't that. I'm just unaccustomed to being touched when I'm . . . weak." I despise the taste of the word.

"No." Wren's hand returns. This time I don't jerk away. "You're not used to needing someone." And she leaves it at that. I know she understands. Wren is a lot like me. Independent. Self-sufficient.

A loner.

I take another minute before I straighten and head inside, Wren beside me. Nathaniel waits in his chair and gazes at the dying fire. We linger a good while. When at last he rests his elbow on the arm of his chair, head propped by his thumb and index finger, I know he's about to relay a story. I sit on the floor and motion for Wren to do the same.

"The night of your birth," Nathaniel begins, "your mother was at perfect peace. I had never seen Ember so calm in all the years I'd known her. It was as if she knew it was her final night and she'd accepted it."

This is a tale I've heard a thousand times over. It always opens this way, with my mother. But this time will be different. Because this time the story will be complete.

"It was as if her deepest desire was to truly experience her last moments, bringing her boys into this world."

And there it is, the slightest alteration. Not *boy*, but *boys*. Oh, what a difference the change makes.

"I offered to put her under, to ease her pain. Against Aidan's and my wishes, Ember refused." Agony fortifies his voice. My mother was his student, yes, but in the end became more like a sister to him. "She was in labor for hours. Kyaphus, as it so happens, came first."

I work my jaw. It shouldn't bother me he's older.

But it does.

"Ky was effortless and did not struggle against the inevitable. You, however, were quite the task." Eyes narrowed, Nathaniel goes on. "You held on as long as you could, unwilling to adapt to the change without a battle. When you finally arrived it was mere moments before your mother inhaled her final breath. She never even got a chance to hold you."

My chest tightens and a lump lodges in my throat. I have forever felt at fault for the deaths of my parents. It was their soul bond that killed my father. I used to wonder if the birthing process had been easier for my mother, would she have survived, saving them both?

I suppose I'll never know.

The light in the room dims as the sun sets beyond the window behind us. Nathaniel leans forward, resting his elbows on his knees. "Upon Aidan's dying breath, I speculated which soul the

Verity would choose—which son contained the purest heart. You or Kyaphus?"

He rises and crosses to the grandfather clock in the room's southeast corner. The clock has long since stopped ticking. I don't believe it ever worked, come to think of it. Nathaniel opens the clock's face and reaches inside. Next he withdraws something small and square. A photograph?

"I watched you both for signs." Out of breath, he hobbles back to his chair and sits. "You see, the Verity changes you, and sometimes that change manifests physically. For Kyaphus it was his eyes, turning one green and one brown. For you the alteration was much more understated—nearly unnoticeable—but a difference nonetheless." He passes me the square.

I turn it over in my hand. The photo is old, the quality horrid, but there, sitting side by side, are two boys. They couldn't be more opposite. One with brown hair, one with blond. One with blue eyes, one with green and brown.

And yet I notice similarities too. My thumb smooths over their—our—faces. We share wavy locks, and our smiles are crooked. I mourn inwardly for the brother I never knew, and now don't care to know. Blood or not, he's a traitor. No one takes what belongs to me.

No one.

Nathaniel retrieves the photo, looks at it over his spectacles, and sighs. "As I was saying, the Verity altered your voice. The moment it inhabited you I could discern the variance in your cry. To this day I cannot describe it in words—it was almost like a song." The corner of his mouth twitches.

I scratch the back of my head, casting a side glance at Wren. I am generally a private person and not at all inclined to have my personal history laid out for another to hear. But Wren won't judge me. I needn't even ask. She'll never speak of this to another soul.

I return my regard to Nathaniel. "So the Verity split and inhabited us both." This explains much.

"Indeed." He leans back and the chair's springs whine. "Which brings us to your current situation with the Void."

"The Void." My brows turn down. "Could there be some sort of . . . connection . . . between me and my . . . brother?" The last word tastes wrong. It's like an admission, concrete and final.

Kyaphus is my brother.

"My thoughts precisely," he says.

My brain works, its gears grinding. My connection to El from childhood, my strong feelings toward her. Could this be why Kyaphus holds feelings for her as well? Perhaps he only thinks he loves her. Because as my twin he is connected to me and I am connected to El. But . . .

"It was I who gave El a Kiss of Infinity as a baby, correct? Not Kyaphus?"

Nathaniel nods. "Yes. You won't remember my youngest son, Tiernan, but he kidnapped Kyaphus a mere month prior to Elizabeth's appearance on my doorstep. I never saw Tiernan again after that. He raised your brother as his own. When Ky and Eliyana came to me last autumn, I recognized him straightaway. It was his eyes, you see. I saw the way he looked at her, and"—Nathaniel pinches the bridge of his nose—"the way she looked at him. I was concerned they had become close. Despite the fact you both housed the Verity, it was you, Joshua, who I raised to become king. You who were trained and prepared and honed for the task of defeating Jasyn and imprisoning the Void within a vessel you could control. I worried Tiernan had corrupted Kyaphus, and he in turn would corrupt Eliyana. And now we see I was, to our dire misfortune, correct."

I hang my head, rub my right hand down the side of my face. "We share the Void though, just as we shared the Verity. If he is corrupting her, so am I."

"Ah, but that is where you are mistaken. The problem lies in the one her soul is fully linked to. The one to whom *she* gave a Kiss of Infinity."

This is the hardest part, and I hate to finally admit it aloud. "I kissed her on her eighteenth birthday. It was a Kiss of Infinity. But for her . . ." I palm the back of my neck and rub hard. "For her the kiss was not as deep. The feeling wasn't mutual."

"And with Kyaphus?"

"I believe they shared one, yes. From what I saw the night of Crowe's defeat, their connection . . ." I close my eyes and picture it. Release a sound that's part exhale, part groan. "Yes. They are intertwined, heart and soul." The ache in my chest makes it hard to breathe.

Nathaniel lifts a finger. "And that, my dear boy, is your answer. Never has the Verity been bonded to a soul containing the Void. Because their souls are linked, and the link made complete, the Void within Kyaphus is disturbing her greatly. The contradiction— the light of the Verity within her versus the darkness of the Void within Ky—is too much. Eventually one element or the other will take over. And I'd wager my favorite bathrobe, if her feelings for Ky deepen, the Void will win.

"Love is powerful. Both you and your brother love Eliyana, which is why the Void is shared between you. But furthermore, it is clear our new queen loves Kyaphus, even if she won't readily admit it. And if she loves him, by default she loves the Void. And light cannot remain light if in love with darkness. It is impossible."

His explanation is a punch to the gut. This explains why the Callings are suffering. Why the Threshold drains.

"If the bond between your brother and your love is not broken"—he yawns—"before long the Verity will die. Should such a fate come to pass, it will be as if the Callings and the Thresholds never existed."

I rise and roll my shoulders. "So their bond can be broken then. How?"

"I hesitate to offer this information. You are as a son to me, and the risk is weighty." He adjusts his glasses. "Perhaps we should mull this over. Take some time to research other options besides the sole path of which I am currently aware."

Unexpected agitation ramps my pulse, but I contain it. I've never been angry at Nathaniel and I am not about to begin now. "We don't have that kind of luxury. We must act now."

"You have never been one to act in haste, Joshua. I wonder if you might need to lie down—"

"*No.*" I pivot and pace the room's length, scratching the scruff at my jaw. When I face my adoptive father once more, I exhale and say, "*Please.* Just tell me what you know."

Nathaniel stares at me a long time. "Does the name Rafaj Niddala ring a bell?"

I shake my head.

"He was the Void's vessel before Jasyn Crowe. An Ever same as you and your father."

His suggestive tone ignites a spark. An Ever? "We're related. Aren't we?"

"Indeed. He is your paternal grandfather."

"*Is?* That means he's still alive."

"Quite." Nathaniel doesn't miss a beat. "He holds valuable information pertinent to your dilemma."

My feet itch to get out the door. "Where can I find him?"

"I'm surprised you don't know more about your own castle."

I cock my head, but it's Wren who speaks up. "He's a prisoner?"

"Smart girl," Nathaniel says, twiddling his fingers. "He is, in fact."

Before we take our leave I ask my final question. "Exactly what information does he hold?"

"He discovered something—an unbinding elixir. Potent stuff, its effects are nearly irreversible." With a sniff, he eyes me. "Are you certain you want to do this? Once the bond is broken, it is difficult to repair. If Eliyana and Kyaphus share true feelings for one another, you may destroy any chance they have of a future together. Are you willing to pay that price?"

I don't answer. Instead I ask one last question. "What do you know of the Fairy Queen?"

"No more than the stories let on. She is said to be an immortal soul jaded by heartbreak. A being with the power to grant any wish, except her own. That is a myth, of course. Though I never doubt anything absolutely. Not unless there is certain proof against it."

His answer isn't much to go on, but it's still more than I arrived with. If the Fairy Queen exists, and she is indeed helping Isabeau, then our problems are grander than we first realized.

I nod and bid Nathaniel farewell. When I have one foot out the door, he adds, "Son?" I turn my head enough so I can view him through the corner of my vision. "Sometimes the quickest solution ends in the most treacherous outcome."

I swallow, step outside, and close the door. He may be correct, but what other option lies before me? This isn't about doing what is easy or fast. This is about so much more than me or Nathaniel or anyone. This is about everyone.

Wren has already made her way down the steps and into the snow. Once she's a griffin again, I mount and we take flight. With the wind cold on my face, I consider Nathaniel's question. I didn't voice my response, but that doesn't mean I don't have one.

Whatever it takes to break El's bond with my brother is what I'll do. Because I love her. Even if my actions hurt her. Even if they cause her to hate me.

So be it.

SEVENTEEN

made a switch

Locked. Of course it is. And drat, he still has the master key set. But I've been in Joshua's castle study before. Which means I can get in again.

Phantom pain sharpens my breath. Never have I dreaded mirror walking more. The shot of Illusoden I took before leaving my suite is starting to kick in, but I doubt its effects will extend to this sort of pain. Good for mortal wounds, yet it's done nothing to abate the ache in my throat. Which probably means it doesn't work on ailments related to the Verity and Callings.

A framed mirror hangs ten feet down the hall to my left. This time of night the walkways are deserted. Preacher hasn't thought to look for me in the most obvious place yet. Or at least I haven't seen him. My door was unguarded when I slipped out of my suite, and Ebony was long gone, surprise, surprise. With half the Guardians tending to the Threshold and the other half on the hunt for Gage and Isabeau, the castle is pretty empty. I may not have much time, but I have a little.

Here goes a body full of *oh man this is going to sting.*

The trip through the mirror is even more agonizing than my walk with Ebony. My voice is barely more than a whisper now, and my right arm has begun to go numb. I've heard that's a sign a heart attack is on the horizon. Or is it the left arm? I can never remember. Either way, I've already established this must be more than a physical ailment. Each time I attempt to use my Calling, my symptoms grow worse.

When I land face-first on the rug before Joshua's desk, it takes a full minute of controlled breaths—pants—before I'm able to move. I want to die so much right now. Like literally, I could just lie here and be content to never get up. But I won't. Because Joshua has been hiding something. And I'm betting somewhere in this office is the answer I seek. Or at least something to lead me there.

Once on my feet I switch on Joshua's desk lamp. It sheds just enough light to provide a good view of the floor-to-ceiling bookcases on the east wall. I cross to them, pressing a finger to my lips as I squint and scan the titles. Which one—?

Joshua's desk chair moves, the legs scraping.

Frozen doesn't even begin to define my statuesque demeanor. Breath on hold, I turn my head.

The chair tips, crashes to the floor. I glance between door and desk, desk and door. Slide sideways. Inch, inch, inching toward the door. Reach, reach, reaching for the knob . . .

Ebony pops her head up over the desktop.

I lower my arm. Roll eyes.

She glowers. "For the love of crowe, you scared the living Void out of me."

"What are you doing in here, Ebony? How'd you get in?"

She waves her hand like a homecoming queen on parade, then stands and proceeds to pilfer through Joshua's desk drawers. "Don't tell me you don't know how to pick a lock." When I refuse to answer she stares at me, mouth agape. "Oh my word, you don't. Wow. That's lame, El. Not gonna lie." She opens one drawer, slams the next. Once she's done she starts on the filing cabinet beside the desk, taking out folders one by one and thumbing through them.

"What are you looking for?"

No response.

"And stop being so loud." I snatch a folder from her hand. "Preacher's probably alerted the entire castle we're missing by now. He'll have Guardians searching every nook and cranny faster than we can say Dewesti Province." She's wasting my time. This was supposed to be a quick in-and-out operation. Leave it to Ebony to fudge up everything.

With the fakest yawn I've ever seen, she removes another folder from the cabinet. "(A) What I'm looking for is none of your concern, and (B) if you're so worried about getting caught, you can leave. You forget I can transform—"

The doorknob rattles.

Double crud.

Ebony and I exchange a glance. Despite her confidence in her Shield ability, there's no mistaking the dread whitewashing her face. She doesn't want to get caught any more than I do.

Ha. For once I have the advantage. Sayonara, sister.

Think. The bay window on the room's other end is where I came in and is my obvious exit. My gut tells me my next mirror walk may be my last for a while. Maybe I shouldn't go too far, just to be safe. Then again, what do I care if Preacher finds me? I'm the one in charge. What's he going to do? Tell the queen on me?

Yeah, I'm saving my next trip for something important. I'll deal with Preacher and whatever other Guardians come through that door. Ebony's the one who should be nervous, not me.

I came here for a reason and I won't run before I find what I seek.

Volumes of *The Reflection Chronicles* span the shelves of Joshua's bookcase, along with some of his favorite classics from his trome at the Haven. I run my fingers along the textured spines. Some bound in oily leather, others coarse and tied with twine. His collection is incomplete, only containing what was recovered after Jasyn's defeat. I wish I had time to read and study them all. Maybe I will, but for now I only need one.

I scour for the single volume I've heard of besides Mom's. I've no idea if Dimitri Gérard's account exists among those recovered, but I have to look. He's the one who discovered the Kiss of Infinity—or he was the first to write about it, at least. How could I forget? Why didn't I think to look for it when I started my research?

And there it is. I remove the eighth account of *The Reflection Chronicles* from the shelf and fan the pages. Nothing beats that old-book, been-on-a-shelf-for-years smell. The yellowed pages are covered in elegant calligraphic writing. Each entry is titled and dated. Stuff on the Kisses of Infinity and Accord. A chapter on mirrorglass. A map of the Fourth Reflection, and . . .

Holy Verity, yes! This is what I've spent the past two months searching for. It's been here all the—

The door handle rattles again.

Someone in the hall lets out a muffled shout.

I don't even waste a glance in that direction. Instead I pop a squat on the floor, criss-cross-applesauce my legs, and begin to read.

Inference of Time by Dimitri Gérard

Hmm. He already sounds like a professor. Must be a Scrib.

Eleventh Day, Fifth Month, Eighth Year of Count VonKemp

Count VonKemp? Not king? I make a mental note to inquire which Reflection is ruled by a count or countess rather than a king or queen.

Time is, indeed, a strange and wondrous thing. It has no beginning or end, it seems. Time goes on, forward and backward, this way and that. But perspective is an illusion, for we know all things begin somewhere . . .

Yes, yes, they do. At last I'm getting some substance.

Someone's pounding on the door now. It trembles on its hinges. Whatever. I lower my head and read on.

. . . the humble fact that we are mere mortals does not

conclude time is endless. On the contrary, this trivial detail
but implies we are merely less than time. Because it goes
on without us, and was present before us, we somehow fool
ourselves into believing time is equal to infinity. This is
simply not the case . . .

Ebony is pacing the room now. Except she's not Ebony. She's
made a switch into some generic female Guardian or other with
red hair, a tight bun, and pursed lips. I've seen the woman before,
but her name eludes me. Doesn't matter though. Ebony's clothes
remain the same. She's not fooling anyone.

I snort before turning the page.

. . . which is why I hold the theory: If time has a
beginning and an end, somewhere it meets itself. It is
a loop, as all life is. From dust we came and to dust we
return. Time is a circle. The beginning is the end, and the
end is the beginning . . .

"Okay, you win." The journal slides through my hands as my
thief of a sister confiscates it. "Give it back," I say in the weakest
whisper-voice ever.

"Who's gonna make me? You?" Now it's her turn to roll her
eyes. "Please, you're losing your touch, sis. This mission you're on
to find out what's happening to the Callings and the Thresholds?
You can't go it alone, especially when your own ability is ama-
teur at best. You need help." She tucks the journal under one arm.
"Lucky for you I'm feeling generous."

She doesn't know what else I want—to find the Void's origin
and destroy it for good. If I told her, she'd think I'm insane. But the
problem at hand takes precedence. First I need to stop and reverse
the downward spiral of Calling loss–slash–Threshold drainage.
Then I can work on ending the Void.

But Ebony? Generous? No way. Not buying it. "You need help
too. Don't you?"

She curls her lip and makes an "as if" sort of noise.

Oh yeah. She needs me. But why? I stand and we begin the stare-down. The commotion in the hall is impossible to ignore at this point.

"Let's just go. *Please.*" She flips a glance over her shoulder. Back at me. Her expression is in full panic mode now, eyes wide, hands shaking.

"Why do you need to get out of here so badly?"

Glare time. What else would I expect? "I don't."

I shrug. "Have it your way." I move to sit back down.

Ebony grabs my shoulders. "I can help you."

Nice try.

"I can show you how to hone your Calling."

I blank my face. "My Calling is dying." I don't have to say it. My nearly nonexistent voice gives it away.

"Only because you're letting it. A Calling has to be mastered like any other talent. You can't just expect using it to be a breeze. Yes, something is wrong. No, the Verity isn't doing its job. But I can still transform. I have to work harder now, but I'm able to change. I can help you change too." She eyes me. "I'm betting you haven't discovered the Mask within yet?"

My pride shrinks. Why am I so easy to read? And how does she know so much about Mirrors?

"Do we have a deal? You get me out of the Second and I'll help you strengthen your Calling."

I consider her for all of half a second. Then I nod.

Ebony returns the journal then flings her arm toward me.

I take her hand in my free one, grasp it loosely.

"I promise to help you sharpen your Calling," she says.

I swallow, say the words I know are required. "I bind you to your vow."

She leans down and places a kiss on the heel of my palm. "By a kiss I am bound."

When she straightens I free a breath. My turn. "I promise to take you from the Second."

"I bind you to your vow." Her eyes twinkle.

I press my lips to her palm.

My stomach churns.

No turning back now. "By a kiss I am bound."

EIGHTEEN

Joshua

I lean closer to the griffin's back, clutching her feathers and keeping my head down against the frigid altitude. I'm forced to close
my eyes to shield them from the wind's whipping. Wren's shoulder
blades roll and I readjust, my thighs and knees digging into her
sides. The ride is jerky and takes longer than necessary due to the
weakening Callings. Fear grips me. If she loses her ability midair,
we'll both be dead in the water.

She soars lower and my thoughts venture to another chilly
evening winter last. One El and I spent together before *normal* was
no longer a word in our vocabulary.

"Are you sure this isn't too expensive?" She kept her face
shadowed behind a curtain of dark hair. I never understood her
reasoning. Why would someone so lovely want to hide?

We passed beneath the red awning at Sardi's. I opened the
glass door and we approached the restaurant podium. The gaunt
hostess raised a brow, as if expecting we'd be ill prepared. But I
knew better. "Reservation for two under David, please."

The woman considered us over her pointed, and most certainly false, nose. I stared her down, unblinking, and stood an inch
taller. El and I may not have been her typical guests, but I'd been
planning the dinner for weeks. I knew a winter formal wasn't El's
scene, especially considering she hated high school to begin with.
When Elizabeth requested I escort her, I'd agreed, but I never carried any intention of actually attending the stuffy event.

El and I had been friends for over two years. Though I felt

more for her than she realized, I couldn't tell her. But that didn't mean I wouldn't treat her like the princess she was. She deserved everything and more, and I wanted to give that to her, even if she and I could never be what I desired. She'd been talking about eating at Sardi's since I could remember. I was sure she'd enjoy this much more than a dance.

"Ah yes," the hostess said. "Here you are." She invited us onward with a pointy, traffic-cone orange fingernail.

I offered my arm to El and she hesitated only a moment before linking hers lightly through mine. My pulse raced from her nearness. It took all the willpower I had spent years perfecting not to hold her and kiss her the way I ached to.

We were seated at a table for two in the center of the room. I withdrew her chair and she sat awkwardly, tucking her hair behind one ear and then, as if realizing she didn't intend to emerge from her shell, letting it fall back in her face.

The hostess set menus before us and took her leave.

I rested my elbows on the table, interlinking my fingers and watching El, waiting for the change to occur. It generally took a moment but always transpired, like a butterfly breaking from a chrysalis. I didn't want to miss this. The day was drawing near when nothing would remain the same. She'd be eighteen by year's end. I intended to relish every last ordinary moment we had together.

When she peeked beneath her lashes, I smirked and leaned forward. Her head lifted as if in slow motion, followed by a widening of her eyes. She took in the room corner by corner and wall by wall. Portraits of Third Reflection celebrities hung everywhere, and the light on El's face let on she spotted a star or two sitting at nearby tables.

I smiled and shook my head. She was the sweetest thing I had ever laid eyes on. Even without our soul bond I would have found her attractive. How could I not? That face. Those eyes. Her voice. She was unlike any girl I'd met. Soft and fragile, feisty but insecure. So different from me, mysterious in ways others were not—

I bite back the notion, blinking and bracing as Wren evades

Pireem Mountain. What I did prior to leaving for the Third those years ago was heartless, almost cruel. But it had to be done. I couldn't have any romantic attachments, with Wren or El or otherwise. I was raised to be king, the vessel of the Verity. And with that came loneliness. The Void would enter the one I cared for most. By default, it was El, but if I truly allowed myself to love her, watching her take on such darkness would break my heart. And heartbreak would destroy me.

Of course now I have learned otherwise. According to Nathaniel the Void enters the one who cares most for the Verity's vessel, not the other way around. Would that still have been El? Since Kyaphus entered the picture, things have grown complicated.

I gaze down at Wren, imagining her hard human face and even harder heart. She admitted she loved me before I left, but I had become well versed in the art of pretending not to care.

"I know you feel the same, David." Wren is not a crier. The fuming expression in her blazing eyes more than made up for it though. "Tell me you don't."

My jaw tensed and I swallowed. I hated to hurt her. I cared. But my heart belonged to another, even if I hadn't met her yet. "I don't."

It wasn't like when I told El I didn't love her. That was one of the most difficult lies I've ever been required to utter. With Wren it was painful, but not an untruth. She was beautiful, smart, and strong, but the emotion was not mutual.

When at last we land at the base of the castle hill, I turn my back as Wren transforms and redresses. I wait longer than is necessary, and when I pivot to offer my gratitude, she's standing there, arms crossed, waiting.

"The dungeons?" she asks. The smirk stretching her lips stings.

"That will be all, Guardian Song." I scratch the back of my head. "Thank you for your services." I cross my heart with a fisted hand and add the Guardian mantra, "To the crown until death."

Her head cocks and her lips part. It must be a half minute before she responds in turn. "To the crown until death." Then she spins on her heel and marches away.

The trek up the hill toward the castle provides me much time to think. My Void arm throbs and I massage it up and down, rolling my shoulder and neck. What I'm about to do is necessary. There is no other way.

Yes, no other way.

I whip my head around. "Hello? Wren?" I didn't realize I spoke aloud.

When no one replies and the eerie quiet is too much for my numbed ears, I finish my journey and head inside. The voice must have been my imagination, my own exhaustion playing tricks. Whatever it was, it was an illusion. Everything will be made right once I alter things.

Everything will be fine when El's bond with my brother is severed for good.

NINETEEN

Longing

I whirl and examine Joshua's study. The hall outside is calm, but that's not saying much. Either someone has gone to find Joshua and the keys, or they're planning to break down the door.

No time to waste.

If we're leaving the Second we'll need supplies. I move to the desk, set Dimitri's book down, and rifle through the drawers. Their contents clatter as I open and shut, open and shut.

Ebony walks to the window. "Guardians are running around like mad down there. Preacher must be flipping out."

"If you want to help, you can start by finding things we might be able to use."

She meanders around, picking up a knickknack here, moving a chair an inch there. Some assistant. Was she this incompetent when she worked for my grandfather?

Once I'm finished with the desk, the only loot I've produced is a small pocketknife, a lighter, and a comb. I wish the medical wing were closer. It would've been useful to take first-aid supplies. With my Calling withering I've seen firsthand I won't heal faster than normal, and medicines don't wear off as quickly as they once did.

I pivot. Run fingers through my hair. My chestnut locks are longer than they've ever been, hanging past my shoulder blades now. I keep meaning to recolor my faded purple ends, but why bother? If my heart were truly loyal to the Verity, we wouldn't be in this mess. The outward symbol means nothing if I'm black inside.

"Don't talk like that."

I feel someone touch my arm.

A smile surfaces.

Hi, Ky.

"We'll fix this."

I want to believe him. I wish with all my soul the voice I hear truly belongs to Ky. That it's not some figment of my imagination. But how can I trust anything anymore? I thought life would be perfect after Jasyn's defeat. Maybe it was all just a lie.

"The Verity chose you," Ky says.

"The Verity made a mistake." The words are out before I can stop them.

Ebony titters. "Talking to yourself again?"

I ignore her and continue exploring the office. When I'm beside the window I peer down. Ebony was right. Flashlight beams and lantern rays bounce like scattered fireflies below. Guardians comb the area. Some even head down the hill, sinking from view.

Do they search for me because I'm important? Because they care? Or do they look because I'm a danger? Could it be I've been a prisoner since taking on the Verity? Trapped and babysat until they figure out what to do with me?

I've been so stupid. This is no different from before. Secrets and lies. Agendas. Why am I always the last to know anything?

A draft chills my ears. Shiver. Joshua's green Guardian jacket hangs on a rack to one side of the window. I haven't seen him wear it since taking on his duties as king. I run my fingers over one sleeve from shoulder to wrist. I miss this version of him. Simple. Joshua. Then again, which version is real? I'm still not sure I ever knew him. Perhaps I never will. Is this why I couldn't give him a Kiss of Infinity? How can you love someone you don't know?

Then again, I didn't know Ky . . .

"You know me. You just don't realize it yet."

I lift the jacket off its hook, gather it in my fists, and touch the collar to my nose. The distinct scent of Joshua mingles with the musty smell of unworn clothing. I swing the jacket over my shoulders, slip my arms through the too-long-for-me sleeves.

The jacket's weight mirrors the heaviness in my heart. My fingers slide into the pockets, and each hand wraps around an object. The right around something bulgy, crumpled. The left around what feels like the hilt of a knife. I withdraw the crumpled item, hold it up to the moonlight. An envelope? I flip it over in my hands. A name printed in quick scrawl glares at me, and immediately I know who it's from.

For Ember

My heart plummets to the floor, and I sink beside it. Throat constricts. Jaw goes slack. Why does Joshua have a letter? For me? From Ky?

And why has it been opened?

I lift the flap and remove a folded sheet of paper, cutting my index finger in the process. *Ouch.* I wince, suck on my fingertip, and read.

Twenty-Sixth Day, Eleventh Month, First Day Apart

The day after Jasyn's defeat. The day after the last time I saw Ky.

Em,
If you've found this letter, you are on the right path.
The path toward me.

Tears of anger well. *Found?* He must've given this to Joshua. And he knew Joshua would hide it.

I'm sorry for leaving without a word. Never think it's
because I don't care. I refuse to say good-bye to you.
I won't.

Oh, my heart.

You're smart, so I'm sure you've figured out I've gone after my sister if no one's told you. Khloe is with Countess Ambrose in the Fourth. Once I've acquired her, I'll return to the Third. And it is there I will wait for you. Because I will always wait for you.

I have no words. No thoughts. Only tears and the humming-bird wings beat, beat, beating in my stomach. The lyrics to Mumford & Sons "I Will Wait" strum across my soul.

Seek the truth, Em. Don't rely on others to pave your way. Only you can decide what path you'll take, how much you'll risk—sacrifice—to get there. Sometimes the road less traveled is the one that leads you home.

Yours,

Ky

"Look what I found." Ebony's sudden presence makes me jump. I stuff the letter back into the jacket pocket and stand. "What?" My question lacks oxygen. My voice is fading fast. My right arm is throbbing worse than before. My chest feels tight and constricted.

Ebony either doesn't notice or doesn't care. She holds up a black Coach bag. "It was in one of the cabinets. David confiscated it when I was arrested. Lucky for us he stowed it for safekeeping." She places one hand on her waist and pops her hip. "Ready?"

I nod and dump the things I found in Joshua's desk, along with Dimitri's journal, into her purse.

We stand before the window together. The lights below are sparse now, either because many have ventured into the forest to look for me or because they've come indoors. I slip my hand back inside the left jacket pocket. I don't have to withdraw the knife to know what it is—whose it is.

Ky's mirrorglass blade.

Time to return it to its rightful owner.

I inhale a shuddering breath and stare at my reflection. One palm on the cool pane, I allow myself to think of Ky. I smile when his face appears clear in my mind. My fingers tap out the rhythm to the song playing in my heart. But it's not my Mirror melody playing. This time it's the song I hear in my dreams. The one I played at the coronation. New lyrics form and I feel them lift my soul. Feel them guiding me home.

> *I never thought I'd find myself here,*
> *Looking for someone like you.*
> *I never knew it could ease my fear,*
> *Watching for someone like you.*
> *I never felt so sure, so secure,*
> *Hoping for someone like you.*
> *I never thought, never knew, never felt,*
> *Never. Until I met someone like you.*

When the song within ends, I open my eyes. My reflection shimmers, transforms. The image in the window transforms. A familiar street replaces the Second's night sky. Parked cars line the curb. A dying streetlamp is a blinking ball of warmth beyond the sunroom window.

I peer through my Second Reflection side of the pane at my brownstone in Manhattan overlooking a sleepy Eighty-First Street. I didn't realize how much I missed home. Until now.

A passerby on the sidewalk just below stops before the window—a man with cropped hair and a thick wool peacoat.

Could it be?

The stranger turns, faces the window. His coat collar is turned up, touching his car-door ears. Gaze fixed just above the window, he stares as if longing for something.

Or someone.

He lowers his head, two-tone eyes visible in the lamplight, and I force myself not to waver.

Can he see me?

"We're going to get caught." Ebony's impatience spoils my focus. "You need to create a façade before they burst through the door."

My jaw hits my chest. Is she insane?

She grabs my wrist. "Just because you never have, doesn't mean you can't."

Ugh. She's right. I pull away. Wait for instruction.

"Half your ability comes from confidence. Believing you can do it—believing the *Verity* can do it—and actually doing it go hand in hand."

Okay, Tinker Bell. Sure.

She either doesn't read the doubt in my expression or she just ignores it. "Imagine a wall. Picture it."

I gape. How does she know so much about this?

"Just do it, El."

Huff. *Fine.* I close my eyes.

The door shudders. "Who's got the key?" Preacher bellows from the hall beyond. *Wham, whack, bam! Knock, bang, slam!*

"You are a Mirror," she says, voice panicked. "Stop thinking of yourself as the picked-on girl from the Third and act like the person you are now. Today."

Whoa. I open one eye. Who is this person? When did we enter the Twilight Zone?

"You have the power. You've always had it. You just didn't know how to use it."

I squeeze my eyes. The memory of the first time I mirror walked plays fresh in my mind. The thrill I felt. The love.

"Own it." She shakes my shoulders now. "You have all the Callings. All. Of. Them. Now bring out your inner Amulet and hide us."

My heart swells. I feel my melody rising, swirling about my Verity-infused soul. I've about lost my voice, but not my song.

My song was never about my voice. Because it was always about something more than me. The Verity sources the Callings.

It is not by my own power but by the strength of the Verity I have any ability at all. And though the Verity may be dim, I still believe in its light. I have to.

Taking Ebony's hand, I let my song go once more. It's noiseless, at least to human ears, but oh so real.

A horde of Guardians explodes through the door, Preacher at their helm. He looks left, right, up, down. Scratches his head. Barks an order I can't hear, as if he's behind an invisible wall blocking out all sound—

He's behind an invisible wall.

I did it.

Ebony and I exchange a glance and a nod. Then I turn toward the glass once more, moving through it as my inner orchestra plays on. It's even more painful than last time, the walk like a vise pressing, clamping, squeezing the life out of me. But I don't care. I let my body weight take over, pull Ebony with me, and fall through my reflection.

I'm coming, Ky. I'm coming.

TWENTY

Body Language

O *of!* Hands and knees meet cold concrete. Scrape.

Rats! My foot catches on my long skirt, ripping the hem, tangling the loose fabric around my boot. Twist. *For Verity's sake!*

I try to stand, but the desire is much too optimistic. I'm a jumble of legs and arms in this ridiculous Second Reflection getup. Joshua's jacket is gargantuan, swallowing me, only adding to my incoordination. Too much fabric equals me on my rear, salted sidewalk grating my palms.

Ebony—surprise, surprise—stands on all twos, shoulders squared and head erect. No sign she was recently sucked through a window, then catapulted onto a wintry sidewalk.

Ugh. How am I related to this person? And why did she get the better end of everything?

When at last I disentangle my skirt hem, I glance around. It's as if I never left. Same brick apartment building across the street. Same Manhattan aroma—smoggy, overcrowded city meets basil and roasted nuts. But where'd Ky go? He was just here. Or did I imagine him?

My heart thunders as I make it to my feet. My breaths pant and fog. I whip left, right. If he's not really here, where do I look? I wouldn't even know where to start—

"Helllloooo." Ebony waves her hand in front of my face. "If you're going to have a nervous breakdown, can we at least go inside?" She rubs her arms in a dramatic, Quinn-like fashion.

Doesn't bother to comment on my awesome Amulet show back there. "I'm freezing."

I open my mouth to speak, but no sound emerges. It's official. Voice is toast. Man, does my right arm smart.

I purse my lips and offer a quick nod, then I take the brownstone steps two at a time. Like most people, we have a spare key. But instead of hiding it under the mat—because, duh—we keep it somewhere inconspicuous. Obvious, but not. The door's knocker is loose, and when I lift it the backing pulls away just enough to release a single silver key. It pings to the cement and I snatch it, thrust it in the lock, and turn the bolt.

When I open the door, Ebony shoves past me and makes a beeline for the first-floor restroom to the right of the foyer. But me? I take my time, lingering in the space between outside and in.

This is home.

I'm home.

I inhale, long and deep. The house smells different, forgotten and unattended, resting beneath a layer of dust. But somehow it's the same too. A combination of me and Mom, the scents of oil paint, canvas, sheet music, and veggie stir-fry all present. Or maybe it's my memory making it seem so. Either way it doesn't matter.

Because I'm home.

The flush of the toilet alerts me Ebony's about to emerge, so I book it up the stairs. I'm in total need of an introverted moment, and my extroverted half sis won't allow for many. I turn the crystal doorknob and slip inside my room, then push the door closed with my rear.

Click. Sigh.

The space is just as I left it. Inside-out tees strewn across the hardwood floor. Space heater stretching into the room's center. I almost trip on the cord as I cross to my bed. Once I'm there, the cushy mattress giving beneath my weight, I can't help but lie down. Close my eyes. Breathe.

Why can't I sleep through times like these? No worries. No responsibility. No Void or Verity or Ky or Joshua. No Callings or

Thresholds or death or losing my voice or getting shot in the knee or feeling as if my arm will fall off. Just sleep. Rest. Nothing.

Nothing. At. All.

The stairs creak beyond the door and I cringe, my fingers clutching my rumpled sheets. I expect Ebony to interrupt my momentary relief, but her footsteps fade down the hallway. Probably headed to Mom's room in search of clothing. Knowing Ebony, she'll be all bright and fresh before I find a clean pair of jeans.

And that's my cue.

Whining and rolling my neck, I peel myself off the bed. At my dresser I dig, open, shut, slam, rummage. Where are all my clothes? At least half are missing. I decide on a short-sleeve Mets tee and a pair of black skinny—but not too skinny—jeans. I slip out of Joshua's jacket and the remainder of my layers. Ah. Much better. Who knew I missed modern clothing so much?

A plaid shirt hangs from a hook on the back of the door. I grab it and tie it around my waist. One hand on the knob, I pause. A small mirror rests on top of my dresser. I rarely used the mirror, and even then it was in small spurts. It's upside down and half shoved beneath a stack of way-overdue homework. Did anyone at school even notice I was missing, or did they think I moved away?

I picture the jerk-wads from Upper West Prep. Nope. They definitely didn't notice my absence. Not unless they ran out of people to bully. And then they'd be like, "Hey, what happened to the girl with that ugly thing on her face?"

I bite my lower lip and return to my dresser. If they only knew just how awesome this "ugly thing" on my face turned out to be.

Or rather, how awesome it *was*. Sure I created a façade, but the accomplishment is minuscule compared to all we've lost. All we're still losing.

I pick up the mirror, turn it toward me. Hold it at arm's length. Hmm. My hair is a disaster, all flyaways and cowlicks curling away from my temples. Seems unfitting with the mirrorglass crown resting there. My complexion is oily and pale. Purple half-moons droop beneath my tired eyes.

A knock at the door jolts my system. Fingers open. Mirror drops.

Crash!

Ebony enters. "Nice one." Her tone remains sarcastic as ever.

The mirror is in shards at my feet, the plastic frame now vacant of reflection. It's not as if it was an expensive gift, but it was a gift just the same. A gift from Mom.

I miss her.

"Are you ready?" Ebony asks.

Her purse hangs from one elbow, as is her custom. She's dressed in some of Mom's old clothes—chocolate leggings, a pine-green sweater dress, ankle boots. Not Ebony's style but more so than if she'd borrowed my things. How does she manage to appear as if she walked straight off the runway? Her rich brown hair falls softly past her shoulders, a just-brushed shine gleaming atop her crown like a halo. Clear skin. Sparkling eyes. Perfection.

Except nobody is perfect. No matter how much they seem so on the outside.

Ebony surveys the mess that is my room. In the past this would've bothered me. Her scrutiny. Judgment. Now I don't care. My room is me. Deal with it.

"You upheld your end, now it's my turn," Ebony continues. "We should probably move to the back or the roof. More space to practice. Amulet was only the beginning."

Practice. Right.

Later, I mouth. I try to slide past her, but she blocks my way.

"Where are you running off to?"

I move left and she echoes the move.

"Are you really going to see your man looking like a hobo-girl from the back alleys of Chinatown?"

I stop dead. A blush creeps to my cheeks. Brows furrow.

She slips her hand into her purse, withdraws Ky's letter. "Found it on the sidewalk. Must've fallen from your pocket when we landed."

How does she still manage to embarrass me? I wish I had some semblance of a voice so I could set her straight.

First of all, it's bad form to read someone else's mail.

And second, Ky is *not* my man.

He's not.

Ebony is beside me now, dropping her purse and the letter onto the bed and sweeping my hair on top of my head in one motion. "Now hold still." Before I can argue she's behind me, removing my crown and twisting and pulling, tucking hairs in here and loosening some there. She takes my shoulders, spins me toward her, and begins on my face. Removes things from her bag to pat and dab, curl and brush. Stepping back, she examines her work, sweeping her fingertips over my eyebrows and wiping beneath my eyelids.

"There." She leans away, narrowing her eyes. "Now you look on purpose. You're welcome." One by one her things return to her bag, all except for her silver compact, my crown, and the letter. She hands the compact over, snaps her purse closed, and waltzes out the door.

Privacy. Wow. How very unlike her to let me face my reflection alone. I push up the lip of the compact with my thumb. Stare. My hair sits in a messy bun atop my head, slightly off center, but somehow perfectly in place. Strands frame my face and ears, but my bangs are long enough to be pulled back now. My lashes are darker, fuller, my lips pink but not unnatural looking. My face is clean but not covered, my mirrormark standing out in all its crimson vines and music notes.

I've not worried much about the mark these past months. Since Joshua can't see it, it's almost as if it vanished altogether. But now, a reunion with Ky on the horizon, I almost want to hide. To pull my hair down and slink behind the curtain of my bangs.

And then a memory surfaces, faint and fragile, but there just the same.

Ky sweeping my hair off my face.

Smiling.

"*Cool tattoo,*" he'd said.

At the time I thought he was a nut job, but it turned out he was right. My mark ended up being so much more than I'd ever dreamed possible. A unique composition framing my eyes, playing the strings of my heart.

I smile and close the compact. I'm ready.

Almost.

I swipe Ky's letter off the bed. I gaze down at the crown, which looks small and insignificant atop my mountain of covers and sheets. Instead of donning it once more, I shove it in my sock drawer for safekeeping. No reason to wear it where I'm going.

Next I steal the mirrorglass blade from Joshua's Guardian jacket, which lies crumpled like a discarded candy wrapper on the floor. The letter gets folded again and again, then hidden in the compact, which I stuff in my pocket. But the knife, hmm . . . what to do? Whirl. Search. Think. Aha! Old sock to the rescue, it makes the perfect wrap. I don't have a sheath or anything to make one with so I tuck the socked dagger in the back of my jeans. It'll do for now.

In the kitchen Ebony is searching the cupboards, removing snacks and dropping them into her purse. I wish I'd thought to bring the pack Ky made me, but there wasn't time. Oh well.

"Look what I found." Ebony holds up a wad of cash. "You really ought to rethink your hiding spot. A cereal box, really? You might as well have hidden it in a cookie jar."

I shrug and return to the foyer. Retrieve a couple jackets from the coatrack. Ebony is already opening the front door when I try to pass her a jacket.

Hair flipped over one shoulder, she makes a stopping motion with one hand. "Thanks, but no thanks. I'd rather freeze than not match."

Typical. I have to refrain from shaking my head. I drop one jacket on the floor and slip my arms through the other, my right arm shaking from the constant pain residing there now. It's my jean jacket from middle school and fits a little snug. Wish I had my parka, but this is better than nothing.

When we're out the door, I lock it and pocket the key. With a last glance at my home, my heart sinks. So much chaos ensued last fall, I didn't get a proper good-bye. Now we head down the street, and it feels like the end of something. As we aim for the nearest subway entrance, I recall the lyrics to a Christina Perri song.

"This is not the end of me. This is the beginning."

The words repeat over and over. I've always fought change, but sometimes things have to end. They disappear as if they never existed. Never were.

And only then can a new beginning . . . well . . . begin.

Eleventh Day, Ninth Month, Twenty-Second Year of Count VonKemp

Ky mentioned Countess Ambrose in his letter. Was Dimitri from the Fourth as well?

It is with a heavy heart I pen these words. Yet another dame has broken my heart. Yet another love lost at sea, if you will. Is there nothing strong enough to bind two people, heart and soul? Will no one ever remain?

So this was before he discovered the Kiss of Infinity. Interesting.

Tomorrow I set sail for a new Reflection. Perhaps it is there I will find what I have searched for my entire existence. Perhaps it is there true love waits.

I press the open book to my chest. True love. Do I believe in such a thing?

"Are you even listening to me?" Ebony elbows my rib cage as the train lurches forward.

I snap the book closed. Set it on my lap. Sigh. Nod.

"I said we need to go to Coney Island. If Ky was headed to the Fourth, that's where he would've sailed from." She crosses her legs. Smooths her sweater dress over her knee. "You need to brush up on your Reflection knowledge now that you're queen, FYI. Everyone knows the nearest entrance to the Fourth is in the Atlantic."

Maybe she *can* help me. I smile my thanks, trying to communicate my gratitude with my eyes.

She ignores the gesture. And why wouldn't she? This is business, not friendship. We both want to be as far away from each other as possible when this is all over.

Don't we?

It's at least an hour before we reach the Coney Island stop at the south end of Brooklyn. Since it's the dead of winter, Ebony and I are pretty much the only commuters to exit the train. This area of the city is mostly deserted. Dusty apartment buildings and hotels constructed of brown brick tower over us, casting wide, frigid shadows. The rides, games, and other attractions are closed for the season. Crushed soda cans, discarded cotton candy cones, and empty popcorn buckets litter the ground. I kick one and it hurtles into a vacant hot-dog stand.

I've only been here during the summer, when the wait to get on the Wonder Wheel is at least forty-five minutes long. When the cacophony of voices and music and Cyclone rider screams is so loud, I can't hear myself think. But in the winter it's a ghost town. Lively carousel music is nonexistent. No laughing children or popping balloons. Gone are the stilt-walkers, weight-guessers, and strongmen. We walk in silence, the sound of our shoes *clap, clap, clapping* the pavement.

Eerie.

When we're nearly to the beach, I freeze. A single Coast Guard boat bobs just off the shore. Odd. Out of place. I veer toward it. Why would the Coast Guard be all the way down here this time of year?

I grin and slip beneath the railing separating concrete and sand. We're close.

Ebony groans, staggering and sinking across the dunes in her unpractical ankle boots.

I'm faster in my black Converse sneakers. Moving, running, sprinting for the shore. I'm paces ahead of her now, but I can't wait. He's here. I feel it.

A wisp of another Ky memory returns. Standing on a much grander vessel with him, trying to escape a mob of Soulless. Me asking if he knows how to drive a ship. Him looking at me with one eyebrow raised, almost laughing as he replies, "You don't drive a ship."

There's so much more to him than I'd allowed myself to believe.

Sand flings against my calves with each step. The shirt around my waist loosens and I cinch it tight. Almost there, a few more feet—

Someone grabs my arm, yanks me back, says in a thick Scottish brogue, "Well, what do we have here? A spy, is it?"

I twist and stare into the face of a dude with two missing teeth and an eyebrow piercing. Ratty dreadlocks frame his tan, leathery skin. Blue eyes so light the blacks almost seem to touch the whites glare at me.

Where did he come from? He just . . . appeared.

I lurch away. *Ha-ha, very funny, El. Without your voice you're nothing but an insignificant, five-foot-nothing girl.*

His grip tightens. "Feisty, are we? We'll see what the cap'n has ta say about tha'." He lugs me through the shallows, then up, up . . . up? A ramp? This wasn't here. I crane my neck. My mouth forms an O. Gasp.

Not the Coast Guard. A ship. A *pirate* ship. Holy Verity, it was hidden by a façade. I hang my head. I couldn't even see it.

What is happening to me?

Dreads pitches me onto the deck.

Ouch. I back away crab-walk style. Brainless cretin.

"Who's this, Streak?" a tinny female voice asks above me.

I glance up, squint. The clouds part and sunlight shines into my eyes. I shade them. A girl who can't be much older than I am moves to the side, blocking the rays. Teased, fiery hair is pulled off her face into a half pony. Jet-black liner edges her robin-egg eyes. The corset-like bodice of her dress curves over her torso, feathers out into a colorful skirt made of ripped fabric scraps in shades of turquoise, mauve, and gray. Her body language suggests she has no doubt just how gorgeous—and intimidating—she is.

"Spy by the looks of it," Dreadlocks—Streak?—informs Red. He withdraws a pocketknife, digs beneath his dirt-encrusted fingernails.

Gross.

"What do you reckon we do with her, Charley?"

"Throw her in the brig with the other spy, of course." Charley nudges me with the toe of her boot as if I'm something she fished from the ocean. She whistles and two more men appear over the ramp, Ebony captured between them. "Captain Warren doesn't tolerate spies," Charley says. "He'll deal with them once we're out at sea."

Brig? Sea? Captain? What have we gotten ourselves into?

TWENTY-ONE

Joshua

W hat do you mean she's gone?"

Preacher wrings his cap in his hands. The poor garment should have unraveled by this point.

"I mean, she left and took the Troll's daughter with her."

"Where did they go?"

He shrugs. "Beats me. We've scoured the grounds and the castle. Secret passageways as well. They're gone." He coughs and tugs his cap on over his ears. "They were in here and then they just . . . vanished."

My mouth turns down. Everyone may know El is the vessel of the Verity *and* a Mirror, but not all are aware of the specific capabilities a Mirror possesses. Even I was in the dark until she shared my mother's "Mirror Theory" with me.

"Thank you, Saul." I brace myself against the desk, my knuckles like paste against the dark grain. "That will be all."

He lingers, moving in a ruler's breadth. "Is it true what everyone's been saying?"

I pinch the bridge of my nose. "And what is that?"

"Eliyana and Rhyen shared a Kiss of Infinity, and now her soul is tied to the Void."

I heave a sigh. "Might I suggest you ignore rumors, Saul? Speculation gets us nowhere."

With a nod he takes his leave, and I welcome the *snap* of the closed door. My answer wasn't a lie, not really. The people carry no proof of El and Ky's bond. They merely go off what they hear. If I don't confirm their assumption, it's still a rumor. And I'd like to keep it that way.

The night has dragged on, but the blue-gray haze of dawn has finally begun to break. I swivel in my desk chair and rest my head against my thumb and forefinger. What I would pay to remain in solitude for a day, to recharge before accomplishing what I must. Of course, that isn't an option. It never is these days.

I can give you rest.

My head jerks and cocks, a gun's barrel ready to fire. "Who goes there?" My sword hand hovers above the weapon at my side. "Show yourself. Enough Dragon games."

But there is nothing aside from the furniture-cast shadows.

Have I misplaced my mind? Lack of sleep will do that. I'll stop by the kitchens on my way to the dungeons. Regina's coffee will be just the thing to get me through the day ahead.

But first thing is, as always, first. I open my filing cabinet and thumb through the tabs. Why are these out of order? I had them organized alphabetically—

My hands clench the cabinet drawer. Ebony. If she was with El she would have searched for her prisoner file. No doubt she wanted her name erased from our records. Why would El help her? She knows Ebony can't be trusted. Where would they have gone?

Terminating my hunt, I shove the drawer closed. It clangs and causes the entire cabinet to shudder. Pulling at my hair, I pace to the window. But before I reach it, something on the coatrack catches my eye. Or rather, the lack of something. My Guardian jacket, where is it?

The lines fall into place like a finalized blueprint.

El left to find Ky.

She helped Ebony escape.

So Ebony would help her.

My mission is now more vital than ever. I stomp to the files, locate the one I require, and storm out of my study and into the hall.

Rafaj Niddala, I hope you enjoy visitors.

⤜∞⤏

Rats. I hate rats.

The sooner I'm out of the dungeons, the better.

Motivation drives me onward, Regina's coffee still warm in my gut. I tread beyond the rodents scurrying past my boots and over the water trapped between cracks in the cement. Rafaj's record stated he's on the third level down, in cell 33. The odd detail, however, is his record gives no indication as to the reason he remains imprisoned. His sentence was to be for the length of time he held the Void, stating Rafaj became a danger to himself and others, and thus captivity became essential.

As an Ever Rafaj is the ideal inmate. Food and water would make him more comfortable, but he does not require them. In fact, it would be easy to forget his existence altogether. Now that he's Void free, what would have kept him down here all these years?

I suppose I will discover the answer soon enough. My mind weighs on the side of restraint, causing my footsteps to dither. Seeking help from a prisoner is indeed a last resort at best, and not to be taken carelessly. But what I'm doing is not just for El, it's for everyone. Every Called. Anyone who has a loved one in another Reflection. This is about our existence, our way of life. About ensuring the Callings and passages to other Reflections remain intact. It goes beyond a mere romance. Some things are simply too important—sacrifices must be made.

The Void cannot snuff out the Verity.

I will not allow it.

My steps resume.

At cell 33 I pause. Whatever lies on the other side, whatever information Rafaj relays, there is no turning back.

I shove the key in the lock and after a half turn the bolt bangs, the door opening toward me. I step inside and close it, the *clang* echoing finality. But the cell is . . . vacant? Did I choose the wrong one? I was certain—

But no. There, in the shadowed corner of the space where a

fraction of daylight touches, is where Rafaj waits. The eager expression on his sagging face gives him away. He was, at the very least, expecting someone. His eye sockets are sunken holes, but the eyes they hold are bright with life and color. Despite his aging body, the Ever Calling inside keeps his soul young.

But soon this too will fade, should the Verity's light continue to dwindle.

Perhaps Rafaj has something to gain here after all, if he wishes to live, that is.

"Rafaj?"

"It is I." His voice sounds as if it has not been used in decades.

"Rafaj, my name is Joshua David. I am—"

"Silence, boy. Don't you think I know my own grandson?"

"How did—?"

"You sound like him, my son, Aidan. Your voice is the same. I knew Ember was with child when they departed for Lisel Island those many years ago. You are what, twenty-one, twenty-two? I may be old, but I am far from senile."

Good. We can forgo the niceties then. "You know why I've come?"

He wheezes. I can just make out his contour, nothing but skin and bones. "You are after the Unbinding Elixir."

"Yes."

"You and everyone else. It is the only reason I ever get a visitor at all. In fact, I have had contact with no one aside from the girl in the next cell. I spoke to her through the wall months ago, or I believe it has been months. Quite difficult to gauge time down here." His words are a jumble of wheezes. "Tell me, did she make it out all right?"

Girl? I've no idea who he's talking about, and I can imagine all the years he's spent down here have played tricks on his brain. I almost feel sorry for him. But then I remember my surroundings. He's imprisoned for a reason. I cannot be too careful. I must obtain his knowledge without losing my head. Or being fooled.

"So tell me," he says. "What is your purpose?"

I swallow. "The Callings are in danger."

Head shaking, he croaks, "Not good enough. Try again."

"The Thresholds are draining across the Reflections. Without them everyone will be sentenced to one Reflection forever." Surely the complexity of the problem is enough to convince him to share. This is about our life, our worlds.

"You do not fool me, Joshua David." Suspicion lowers his tone. "The desire to aid the greater good is a cover-up, a façade. Tell me *your* truth. What is it *you* desire?"

My body tenses. "This is not about me, old man. I would not have come if it were."

"Nonsense." He waves his skeletal hand. "It is always about the individual. You may pretend you care for sacrifice, pretend you are indeed selfless. But no one is entirely selfless." His bony finger wags. "No one."

Something triggers deep inside. My entire life has been about selflessness and sacrifice. But have I once asked myself what it is I truly desire? All considerations aside, have I ever thought, *What's in it for me?*

No. Because I always suppressed the notion, held it back, refused to let it surface. Yet here, now, talking to Rafaj Niddala, is when my will takes its initial breath.

Face hardening and chest expanding, I say, "I want to unbind my love's soul from the soul of my brother."

He leans forward. "And?"

"She is the Verity's vessel, and he holds a portion of the Void. Their mutual feelings are corrupting her. I need to break their soul bond to save the Verity."

"Is that the only reason?"

I clench my jaw. "No."

"Speak *your* truth."

My truth. My truth is, "I love her." This is the simplest explanation I can give. "I want her to be with me. Always. I want her whole heart."

"You want her to forget he ever existed." Wobbling, he rises.

His skin is so translucent he could almost be a ghost. "You want her to forget she ever loved him at all."

I nod.

"Well then, come close." He beckons me with one finger. "Let me share my secret."

not to say a word

Charley lugs me to a stand, her fingers curled around my wrist. She's forceful. Careless. Who does she think she is?

I lurch away. How can I explain without my voice? What was the word on *Pirates of the Caribbean*? The word Elizabeth Swann used to ensure temporary protection? Parfait? Par . . . par . . . parley! My mouth opens, but there is nothing. Not a squeak or a rasp. Drat. I'm in for it now.

"Excuse *me*." Ebony pitches against her captors. "You don't have to hold on so tight. I'd rather walk away from this unscathed, thankyouverymuch."

Charley and Streak whip their heads in her direction.

"You'll be quiet, girl, if you know what's good for you," Charley says.

But then Streak squints and a smile spreads across his sun-worn face. "By the Reflections, if it isn't Bones."

Bones?

"I 'aven't seen you since . . ." Streak lists his head. "When was it?"

"November, dimwit." If Streak is bothered by Ebony's insult, he doesn't show it. "When I brought Khloe to you to be transported to the Fourth. Looks like you've upgraded vessels though." She gives the ship a once-over. "This craft is much grander than your dinky little fishing boat."

"Aye." Streak winks. "The *Seven Seas*, she's called. She be a sturdy one, at tha'."

Charley's face quirks from lip to eyebrow. "This is Bones? *The Bones?*" She elbows Streak. "Why didn't you say something?"

What did I miss?

"I thought I jus' did," Streak says.

Charley plants her hands on her hips and shakes her red head. "We've been shore ridden far too long. You're losing your marbles."

Scratching his scruff, Streak whines, "Am not."

"This little back-and-forth is fun and all, but would you mind telling your minions to release me?"

The men on either side of Ebony let her go. She rubs her arms, swaggers her way out from between them.

My neck burns. I trusted her. Again.

Stupid, stupid, stupid.

"I assume your captain is interested in fair trade?" Ebony—Bones—saunters over, glares down her snobbish nose. "This girl here is worth at least five thousand Third Reflection dollars, if not more."

Streak and Charley exchange amused glances.

"You'll get wha's comin' ta ya, Bones, don't ya fret now." Streak claps Ebony on the shoulder.

She wobbles, then brushes his hand away as if it's infected. "Carry on, then."

Teeth bared—the ones he still has, anyway—Streak grabs me, throws me over his shoulder. His stained white shirt is taut over his back muscles and smells of alcohol mixed with used mop water.

Ick. I pound him with my fists. Try to scream but no sound emerges. Why do I bother? I'm nothing without my Calling.

"Not true."

Ky? Where are you? If you're near, why are you letting them do this to me?

My thoughts go unanswered as Streak laughs and marches across the deck, shoulder quaking against my waist. Charley remains behind, chuckles racking her form. So glad I can be the onboard entertainment for these two.

Ebony doesn't give a second glance as she glides in the opposite direction. How can she do this? We shared a Kiss of Accord. Our contract is binding. She has to help me. She has—

Unless, hmm. Is she up to something? Could it be she *is* helping me?

I watch her walk toward a short flight of stairs. Wait for it . . .

There! A peek over her shoulder. A wink.

My heart sashays. Maybe she won't let me down this time. #fingerscrossed

I cease my resistance and relax. A breeze gusts, sends a loose sail flapping. The ship groans and creaks, and my stomach churns along with it. A bout of seasickness—or maybe it's Streak's pungent odor—threatens to upend my last meal. *Do not lose it. Clear your mind. Think.*

Could Ebony and Ky be in on this together? What reason would they have to make it appear as if they're against me?

My mind wanders and I survey my surroundings. Rope and line cover everything, wind around railings and hooks, snake up a mast toward a crow's nest. Streak angles left and we descend a staircase, the railing wrapped in more rope. *Stomp, creak, stomp, creak.* My courier doesn't bother to step lightly. I'm nothing but unsolicited cargo.

At the bottom, a long room stretches. On either side canons are rolled against the walls, their mouths sticking out of pane-less square windows. Between the sixteenth-century weaponry, canvas hammocks hang from the low ceiling. A border of copper-colored trunks and dark-brown barrels divides the space in half. One trunk is open, revealing curved swords and throwing knives. Streak lifts one leg and kicks the lid closed before moving to the far end of the room.

I'm hauled through a door and down a spiraling metal stairwell into the ship's core. Scarce light peeks through the floorboards above in slivered shafts. I blink hard, force my vision to focus. Barrels upon barrels line the walls. Crates are situated into rows, forming a sort of maze. Coils of rope sit atop several, while sacks of flour and other food supplies are stacked on top of others.

Streak maneuvers his way toward a barred cell in one corner—a human-sized cage scarcely taller than me and not much
wider than a bathtub. I'm set on my feet and shoved inside. No
chair. No cot. Just floor and the musty aroma of damp wood.

Clang. Rattle. Streak shuts the cell door and locks me in with a
key chained to his belt. He grips a bar and jiggles it. Then he pivots
and strides away.

My fingers wrap around the cold, rusty bars. I sink to my
knees as the sound of Streak's footsteps fades into the shadows. I
wait five minutes. Ten. Fifteen. Half an hour? With each tick of my
heartbeat my hope dwindles. Perhaps Ky isn't here. Maybe Ebony
sold me to a band of pirates in exchange for passage to the Fourth,
or wherever it is she's headed. Was the Kiss of Accord not binding?
What if the kisses are affected by the weakness of the Verity as
well? No, not the Verity's weakness.

My weakness.

I scooch back into one corner and hug my knees. Déjà vu
wraps me like an itchy blanket. I'm not cut out for this. Another
cell. Another betrayal. Except, who will rescue me this time, and
furthermore, why should they? I should be able to rescue myself. I
am the Verity's vessel.

And I am helpless. Insignificant.

Alone.

⚬⦾⚬

"The dress is perfect." Mom beams at me from below the small
platform where I stand.

I hold still as Reggie, who doubles as a coronation gown seam-
stress apparently, measures my bust, my waist, my height.

"Don't move, darlin'," she says through the pin caught between
her teeth. "Wanna make sure we don't end up with the wrong
numbers."

Mom crosses her eyes at me. My upcoming coronation
has made her giddy. She's shed her serious demeanor for one

much more fitting for a woman in love. Silly. Not a care in the Reflections.

Thank the Verity for Makai. I laugh, then hold my breath when Reggie eyes me. Oops.

"That'll do for now." Reggie stuffs her measuring tape into the front of her apron. "I'll be back tomorrow with some sample fabrics." She sways through Mom's suite, grabbing an empty tray off the table before she waltzes out the door.

Mom glides to the common area and sits on the sofa. She may be pregnant, but her poise and grace are ever present. In the way she carries herself. In how she reaches for her cup of Earl Grey.

I join her, though my coffee is nothing but a few stray grounds at the bottom of my cup.

"Are you getting excited?" She sips her tea, holding her cup by its too-tiny handle.

I am not so proper, grasping my mug in both palms. "For the coronation? Of course." Why do my words lack enthusiasm? Maybe I'm just tired.

She swallows. Lowers her cup to rest on her growing belly. "Baby girl, I know you better than anyone. What's on your mind?"

The Void. My connection to Joshua. I love him, but do I *really* love him? Is it my choice or was it orchestrated? Sigh. I wish I knew. If I could just find a way to destroy the Void once and for all, perhaps this feeling of obligation to Ky would vanish. Then I could decide who it is *I* want to be with. Not who the Verity says I care for most, but who I do.

Mom takes another sip. "Your coronation will be the event of the year. I know you are nervous, but you will be splendid. The belle of the ball."

Hands shaking, I set my mug on a side table. "To be honest, I haven't thought about it much."

"You should." She sips again. "It's the first day of your new life."

New life. Right. I chose this, I suppose, when I ended Jasyn and imprisoned the Void.

Then why does it feel as if I have no choice?

"There's always a choice."

My body trembles and my eyelids snap open, the memory-slash-dream fading with each blink. I squirm. Ugh. My arm's asleep. Hate that.

Charley stands above me, her face upside down and tilted. I sit, massage my tingling arm.

"Captain Warren will see you now." Traces of fear slither into her words. This Warren guy must be as unpleasant as they come.

Lovely.

I trail her up to the deck. My clothes are wrinkled and damp. My bun loose and falling. The sun is buried beyond the horizon now, dusk's marbled-gray tint shrouding the sky. A shiver quakes my tired bones. The deck is deserted aside from us. Charley leads me up another set of stairs, onto an upper deck. Two doors stand to my left and a brass bell hangs to my right, overlooking the main deck. I stop and lean closer to examine the bell. Words etch its bottom rim.

Dive deep if you ever hope to rise.

Why are the words familiar? Have I seen them before?

An exasperated sigh draws me from the bell. Charley waits on a curving set of steps, ascending to another, higher deck. It's small, with barely enough room for two people. A large steering wheel stands proud, and behind it a lone door with an iron knocker waits. Charley raps the knocker three times. Must be the captain's cabin. I may not be able to distinguish stern from bow, but I do know the captain of a ship generally has his own private quarters.

We stand there, Charley with her arms crossed, refusing to make eye contact. Me fidgeting from foot to foot.

Thirty seconds. A minute. "Come in," a muffled male voice says from beyond the door.

Charley turns the knob, opens the door, and stands aside. When I don't move, she jerks her head, signaling me to enter first.

The modestly furnished space is warmer than I expected, not a hook or an eye patch in sight. Several oil lamps send shadows wavering against the walls. A drafting desk sits off to one side, maps unfurled over its surface, their edges curling. A map on the wall behind the desk showcases pins poking every major city across the world from Hong Kong to New York, Athens to Phoenix. Just beneath it, a globe rests on a small, circular table.

And there, at the room's end, a wide, curving window sectioned into at least two dozen miniature ones looking out over the sea. A small kitchenette flanks the window's right, and a full-length mirror leans against the wall to its left. But it isn't these modern accessories or the gorgeous nautical view with its rippling silver waves that catches my eye. It's the boy with his back turned toward me, hands clasped behind him as if he's waiting for something. For someone.

For me.

Ky.

Since when did I forget how to breathe?

I step forward, but Charley's hand on my shoulder stops me. I shrug her off. I'd almost forgotten she was here.

Ky turns. Gives no indication he knows me. No smile of recognition. No jaw set in anger. His expression is passive. Stoic. Indifferent.

It's like looking into the eyes of a stranger.

Something inside jolts my feet into action. I don't think. I move toward him.

Charley grabs my arm. "You will wait for Captain Warren to invite you to approach. Do you know nothing of protocol?"

Swatting her away, I toss a glare over my shoulder. My eyes meet Ky's—Captain Warren's?—and plead with him to tell her he knows me. This is all a huge misunderstanding.

Ky narrows his eyes, then focuses on Charley behind me. "*This is the girl Miss Archer delivered earlier today?*" His voice carries a deepness that wasn't there before. It's been less than two months. How is that enough time for this boy to grow up?

"Yes, Captain."

"She doesn't look like much, does she?"

Charley snorts.

Gee, thanks.

"Thank you, Second Mate Hallen. You may report to the galley for supper. Please inform Chief Cook Toshiro I will take my meal in my quarters again this evening."

What's with the formalities? The fake name? This isn't Ky. Why must everything change? Everyone? I thought I could count on Ky to be himself.

Wrong again.

ASIDE

KY

She's *here*.
  She's here.
  I run my hand down my face.
  At last. Our journey can begin.

TWENTY-THREE

A Lady who's withdrawn

The door clicks closed behind me. A clock on the wall *tick, tick, ticks*, echoing my time-bomb pulse. Charley is gone. I'm alone with someone who knows me so well, but he's a stranger and maybe I never knew him at all.

Then, as if twenty thousand leagues of ocean have been lifted from his shoulders, Ky exhales. Drags a hand over his face. Pinches the bridge of his nose.

In the silence I take a moment to examine him. It isn't only his demeanor, name, and voice that have changed. His hair is darker, shorter. Gone are the wavy highlights falling into his eyes. They've been cropped into a cleaner, more mature cut. His complexion is still pocked and scarred in places, but clearer than the last time I saw him. He bears a new scar as well, running from behind his left ear to the base of his neck.

The truth hits me like a runaway bus. *Splat.* Ky could be tattooed from head to toe, completely bald, or even missing all his teeth and I'd still be drawn to him.

Why?

Lowering his hand, he locks those two-tone eyes on mine.

I'm naked. Completely exposed. A mess, and he's gazing at me like I'm a drink of water in summer. A cozy sweater in autumn. A first kiss in spring.

Then he's moving, shedding his wintry manner in exchange for something achingly familiar. A relaxed grin reaches his eyes.

This is too much. Ky acted as if he didn't know me with Charley in the room, and now he's reaching for me as if he's found a lost treasure. He's suddenly himself, and I'm not sure if I can handle being so close to him.

Joshua. I love Joshua. Joshua with his piercing blue eyes. Joshua who would do anything and everything to keep me from harm. Joshua who will flip a lid when he discovers I'm not in the castle, and here I am standing in a room with someone he considers his enemy.

I'm confusing obligation with affection. Ky carries the Void because of me and—

He pauses a foot away. No words. Just breaths, and my pulse quick, quick, quickens.

My train of thought switches tracks. "Finale B" from *Rent* takes over my mind's rails.

"Only us."

"Only this."

"Forget . . ."

"Hi," Ky says. It's the most un-epic word in the English language. But then his smile deepens, double dimples forming.

And I'm melting. *Hi,* I mouth. I lift a hand to my throat and shake my head.

His lips press. His eyes see straight through mine. "I know. We'll fix it."

The ache inside lifts. I don't know how or why, but I believe him. I fiddle with the rose-button necklace resting just above my T-shirt's neckline.

His gaze lowers, lopsided grin reaching his eyes. And then . . . oh, then . . .

Ky's arms are around me, enfolding me. His earthlike scent is oxygen. And I'm inhaling, my nose pressed into his shoulder.

At first my arms remain pinned at my sides. But Ky strokes my back, coaxing the tension away, and I relax. My arms slip through his, my hands reaching up and forward and finding comfort in fistfuls of sweater at his shoulders. I open my eyes for the briefest

instant. When did I close them? I take one look at my grimy fingernails and try to pull away. I so need to bathe.

But he doesn't release me. His nose nuzzles my hair, and this
feels so wrong and so right on a hundred different levels. It's just a
hug. A greeting. I'm not betraying Joshua. I'm not.

"It's going to be okay now." He withdraws a few inches. His
hands cup my face. "You're here." His eyes close, he leans in, so
near I can taste his breath—

I lurch back, but the knife ripping my gut remains. Confusion
pins me and I find it hard to breathe. I'm so turned on end, I don't
even know which way is up or where my heart resides.

He doesn't bat an eye at my reaction though. He takes my hand
and leads me to a leather armchair near the window. I sit. Then
he's across the cabin, crouching and opening a trunk. He withdraws jeans, a long-sleeved V-neck tee, a hoodie . . . No, not just
any hoodie. My hoodie. The heather-gray one with "Music Is Life"
screen-printed in cursive on the front. Those are my clothes, from
my dresser, from my bedroom, from my brownstone. No wonder
my drawers seemed barren. Ky had already been there. He knew I
would come. He was prepared.

My hands are cold and fidgety. I tuck them beneath my
thighs.

He returns to my side, places the fresh clothing on the chair's
wide arm. He looks at me and his gaze speaks volumes. How can
so much be said without any words at all?

I run my fingertips over the hoodie's fleece lining. Then I
reach behind me, retrieve the compact with the letter. Draw out
his socked knife.

His hands cover mine, pushing them to my lap. "I have so
much to tell you."

Rap, rap, rap.

He moves to stand beside his desk, rolls his shoulders.

Now that he's not so near, I can think. Inhale. Exhale. I purse
my lips, unsure how to process his words and actions. He was
expecting me. The letter said he'd wait, but how could he be sure

I'd come? Did he and Ebony plan this? When? Why? So many questions I'm unable to voice.

"Come in," Ky calls, all business again.

The door swings inward and a younger, shorter, thinner, non-bald version of Kuna enters. His black hair drapes his face, stopping at his chin. He wears khaki shorts, a white tank, and flip-flops.

Is he not aware it's the dead of winter?

The boy carries a round tray with a silver-domed lid. When his notice falls to me, he offers a curt nod.

"Thank you, Chief Cook Toshiro. That will be all."

Another nod from the boy. "Yes, Captain." He sets the tray on the drafting desk, taps the right side of his chest with one fist, and gives a shallow bow. Then he's gone.

Returning, Ky kneels before me. He removes my sneakers. My socks. "I'm sure you must have a freight's worth of questions." He clears his throat. "I'm sorry about Kuna. And being separated from your mom. I know it's been a difficult week for you."

Tears well, spill, stain. I don't have the energy to fight my emotions tonight. It's too much. My throat burns and I long to sing my heart. To express myself through music. But I can't. I mourn the loss like a death. So much tragedy. But . . . how does Ky know so much?

"To answer your questions, Warren was my mother's father's name. I chose an alias because it's vital I remain discreet. No one can know who I am or where I come from. They'd connect it back to the Second and discover I'm a vessel of the Void. Hard to get people to trust you when you hold the darkest entity known to mankind within your soul. You, Ebony, and Khloe are the only others aboard the ship who know the truth." His gaze locks on mine.

My pulse thrums in my ears. Upon hearing Khloe's name, I feel relief swell. My other half sister is here. I need to see her.

"You will," he says, reading my thoughts again. "But she's fallen ill. Pneumonia. I won't have you catching it and making your throat worse."

My heart longs to meet her. But the feeling is quickly replaced with a surge of adrenaline.

Those eyes.

His touch lingers on my bare feet a few beats longer than necessary.

I bite my lower lip.

Rising, he crosses the cabin and sets a kettle on the kitchenette's stove. Just like in the Second, the ship looks ancient but houses modern conveniences as well. I hope this means a hot shower is in my near future.

Ky turns a knob. *Click, click, click.* A burner lights. "The Callings are losing power. The Thresholds are draining." He retrieves the tray from his desk, then comes over and sets it on my lap, lifts the lid.

Sigh. Steam rises from a bowl of white bean chili, warming my face.

"Why, Em? Why are those things happening?"

I hang my head. Because of me. Something is wrong with me.

"No," he says. "That's where you're mistaken."

I snap my head up. Eyebrows pinch. He . . . heard me?

"Yes. It's real. Our connection. I can hear you. And you can hear me. You just don't know it yet."

But how? Why?

"I've been trying to figure that out myself."

I retrieve the spoon resting on the tray, lower it into the bowl, and lift it to my lips. Mm. Cumin and cilantro. Potatoes and celery. Perfection.

"What have you learned of the origins of the Void and the Verity?"

Can you hear everything I think?

"Not everything. I've learned to tune in to the important things, though. And when you're thinking of me? Well, that makes it a whole lot easier. And now that you're near? It's like the volume has been turned up."

I stare into my bowl. How red is my face right now? *Ever heard of privacy, Ky?*

The kettle whistles. Ky smirks and pours hot water into a basin, carries it over, and sets it on the floor. He lifts my feet and sets them gently into the just-right water.

I wiggle my toes, release a spontaneous sigh. How did he know this is exactly what I need?

Kneeling, he rolls up his sleeves. Right. Left. The sight of the Void—the blackened veins—winding up his arm steals my breath despite the fact it's not a surprise. My own arm throbs. Could it be connected to his pain? He's like this because of me. He could've been free of the Void. Instead he took it on. Again.

This is his secret. Our secret. Does he know he once held the Verity? Is he aware he shared it with Joshua?

"I am. But only because of you."

Seriously, stop. I don't know whether it's good or bad you can hear my thoughts.

"It's good, Em." His crooked smile makes a candid appearance. "It's very, very good."

I drop my spoon into the bowl, and broth splashes onto the tray. Crud. I'll have to watch what I think from now on.

"Don't be embarrassed." His cupped hands dip into the water. "I'm a part of you now. And you're a part of me. It took me a bit to get the hang of reading your mind, and then soon after, speaking to you through thought. It seems you hear me when I think a thought toward you, and I'm betting with focus you can block me, as well as learn to hear me whenever you please. It's just a theory, though. I need to do more research." Excitement fills his tone. He almost sounds like a little kid. He strokes my feet. My ankles. My toes.

I look down and for the first time I realize what he's doing. My throat constricts and my lip quivers. I clamp my teeth to restrain the brewing emotion. Then I watch as he tenderly, selflessly washes and massages my dirty, aching feet.

My heart twists. My throat constricts once more.

This is why the Void entered him. The reason it inhabited Ky instead of Joshua. I still don't understand it.

His hands stop moving. He looks up. Brows draw a V. "David didn't tell you?"

Tell me what?

The expression on his face turns from smooth to sour. "The—" His hands fist beneath the water. "I can't believe he didn't tell you." Then he shakes his head. "Typical."

I touch his arm.

"David and I share the Void, just as we shared the Verity."

Ky rises.

"It split."

Water *drip, drip, drips* from his knuckles to the floor.

He inhales and says, "The Void—it entered us both."

TWENTY-fOUR

she who Holds Her Tongue

His words are a dagger, hitting its mark at the bull's-eye on my chest. I don't know what to feel first. Betrayal? Anger? Relief? If the Void enters the one the Verity's vessel cares for most, that means—

"You love us both." His words are simple. Monotone.

No. How can I know who I truly love when the Verity and Void decide everything for me?

Ky's eyes form two dark slits, making their color indistinguishable.

I lift my feet from the water and stand before him. What do I say? What do I do?

He reaches for my neck, withdraws Joshua's treble clef–heart charm from its resting place beneath my T-shirt.

We stay that way for one long, unblinking moment. I almost, *almost*, think he might kiss me. But then he takes my left hand in his, touches the diamond band Joshua gave me.

My heart is an anchor at the bottom of the sea.

Ky steps away, popping the bubble. "You may use my quarters to change and freshen up this evening. I'll inform the crew you'll be joining us, not as a prisoner, but as an asset. You'll move belowdeck with everyone else tomorrow." He motions to a door on the opposite side of the room. "Washroom's in there. When you're done the chair folds out into a cot. Get some sleep. I'll return in the morning."

Blink. Nod. Swallow.

He walks away. Once he's across the cabin, one foot out the door, he says, "Eventually you'll have to give one up."

Instinctively I close my fingers around my necklaces, as if to shield my two most treasured possessions from his next words.

"You can't have it both ways. At some point you have to choose."

The door slams.

I slump into the chair, open my palm, and gaze toward my chest. At the rose-engraved button, at the diamonds studding the treble clef heart.

They clash.

But they're mine.

Both of them.

As I move to the washroom and draw a bath, Ky's words replay in my mind, raising one final question.

The Void may have split, but it's Ky with whom I shared a Kiss of Infinity, Ky to whom my soul is fully bound.

Why?

I shed my clothes and dip a toe into the tub.

Something tells me it won't be long before I find out.

Sleep eludes me.

So does Ky.

I toss and turn on the pull-out bed. The mattress is too stiff, the sheets itchy. I fold and unfold my arms. Lie on my right side. My left. I wad the pillow beneath my neck, flatten it, and then chuck it to the floor.

"At some point you have to choose."

I flip onto my stomach, press my face into the sheets, and loose a silent scream.

Why is everything such a mess?

"The Callings are losing power. The Thresholds are draining."

Ugh.

When at last I accept my sleepless fate, I cocoon myself in the fleece blanket Ky left for me and waddle to the window. The sea beyond lies eerily still—a reflective plane that seems solid on the surface but if tested would fail to support me. An illusion. A façade.

I hate—*hate*—that it reminds me of my relationship with Joshua.

I question it still. If his love for me is real or merely a product of our childhood bond. Does he love me because he loves *me*, or because he always knew he was supposed to? Would he love me if he could see my mirrormark?

I guess I'll never know. It's not as if I can go back in time and alter the past.

A shiver crab-walks down my spine, and I cinch the blanket tighter around my shoulders. Moonlight reflects off the ocean in wavy white ripples. The ship creaks every other heartbeat and I close my eyes, imagine myself far away from here. No Joshua to deconstruct. No Ky messing with my emotions. There is just me. Alone and confused, teetering on the verge of brokenness.

Who am I? What do I want?

I. Have. No. Clue.

I curl my toes, tense my jaw. Things have gotten so cataclysmically screwed up. Maybe I've never known the answers to these questions.

Who am I?

What. Do. I. Want?

My life was decided for me the moment Joshua kissed my chubby baby cheek. And even now it's the case. I'm the Verity's vessel, so my future is obvious.

But what does it mean that Joshua holds the Void too? How is it affecting him now that I'm gone? Will it spread? Is Ky better with me near? Does he feel the Void less with the Verity close? And how could the Verity inhabit the same space as the Void in the first place? Ky held part of the Verity before, even when he lived with a portion of the Void—does he know? It seems this last question holds the key. Void and Verity together, warring against one another.

I'm missing something. It's right there on the tip of my brain.

Ugh. Why can't I figure it out? This is worse than trying to master the Chopin-Godowsky études on piano.

I touch my bang-matted forehead to the window, shift the blanket up so it covers my ears. I watch the waves as if they hold the answer, the secret treasure I seek just beneath the surface. An exasperated sigh escapes. How much longer until morning? Why does the night always feel so forever?

"Dry your tears," Mom would say. *"No reason to fear the dark. Morning always comes."*

She has always been so sure of everything. When I'd hide beneath the covers, terrified of my own shadow, she'd reassure me. Morning always comes.

Always.

I stiffen. Could it be so simple?

I slide my feet into my sneakers and head for the door. Yes, morning will come, but this can't wait until then.

I've got to talk to Ky.

I'm standing on a ship's deck on the East Coast in the middle of winter. Freezing doesn't even begin to describe the sensation coursing through me. I use the blanket like a cloak, pulling it tighter around me. Never been on a ghost ship before, but my guess is it's not much different from this. Shadows in nooks and crannies, hiding beneath stairs and behind barrels, play tricks on my mind, seem to watch me. Whispering their inaudible secrets.

I take the steps down, down, down until I reach the main deck. No one stops me or orders me back to bed. I'm a member of the crew now. I'm one of them.

What would Mom say if she knew I was a pirate?

I move across the deck, the rubber soles of my Converse

squeak-squeaking over the swabbed wood. It's damp, smells of suds and pine. Ky keeps a tight ship, I'll give him that. He's obviously a no-nonsense captain, and yet there's a sense of freedom here I haven't felt in a long time—maybe ever. A feeling like I could be anyone, do anything, and no one would hinder me.

That's when I hear it. Piano music. Playing softly. The sound is authentic, too rich to be traveling through tinny speakers. The notes transition slowly, an adagio melody flowing from a skilled musician's fingertips. A melody so familiar and near, I know I've heard it before.

It's the song from my coronation. The song from my dreams.

And then I'm forgetting myself, losing my mind in the upsweep as the notes crescendo.

I take a set of curving steps down into the side of the ship opposite the wheel and the captain's cabin. A door waits at the bottom, but it's locked. The music sounds closer belowdeck, but when I press an ear to the locked door, it doesn't seem to be coming from the other side.

I ascend the stairs, still my breathing, and listen. Then I move left. Below me, waves lap and fold and splash. The music is so close. My pulse slows to keep tempo with each struck chord.

Back and forth, back and forth. My shoulders sag. The door I already tried appears to be the only way down on this side. I'm about to give up when I spot an alcove beneath the ascending stairway, so shrouded in darkness it could almost be a wall. I'm there in a breath, thanking the Verity for the door I find within the alcove's secret space.

This one isn't locked.

The second I open it my ears fill with the haunting melody wafting up a spiraling stairwell.

I take the steps one at a time, afraid if I startle whoever's playing they'll stop, or disappear, or cease to exist completely. Toe, heel, toe, heel. The process takes eons, but the music continues, beckoning me deeper.

At the bottom, a timid glow pulses from around a corner. I

skirt it, and a baby grand piano comes into full view, hiding the musician on the other side. It must be bolted to the floor, been here since the ship was built, since before this otherwise unfurnished room had a ceiling. How else would anyone get it into this cramped space?

So beautiful and sad and touching all at once, the song raises an emotion without a title. I stop, avert my gaze to a porthole stage right, unable to look upon the instrument pouring music into my depths. It takes three controlled breaths before I move again. The closer I come to the piano, the nearer I am to losing it. The way the music entwines with my soul isn't something I can explain. It's as if the song was written for me, speaking all my pain and sorrow and loss . . . everything I've felt in the past three months to cover a lifetime.

This is it. This song. It's . . . me.

I tiptoe around the piano, and the composer becomes visible. I can't breathe. Can't move. Can't think. Of course the song seems as if it was written for me. Because when I stand behind Ky, who doesn't even look up from the ivories he's caressing, I catch a glimpse of the handwritten sheet of music before him. The title reads "Ember's Song."

I slip onto the bench beside him, don't make a sound. He doesn't react to my presence and I don't speak. My lashes drift to my cheeks. I cinch the blanket around my shoulders. Listen.

I twist Joshua's ring around my finger, as has become my habit. As if I'm trying to decide whether it fits there or not. This isn't the way things were supposed to happen. Kiss of Infinity aside, I spent three years falling in love with Joshua. But does my past define my future? Do Joshua's choices dictate my own? What about my life? My choices?

What about Ky?

TWENTY-FIVE

Joshua

Desperate times call for desperate measures.

The Third Reflection saying haunts me as I leave Rafaj behind. I am simply doing what I must to ensure the Verity is not destroyed by El's temporary confusion. She has no idea the reason she has feelings for Kyaphus is because of his connection to me. But all will be well soon. Two ingredients? The Unbinding Elixir requires but two ingredients? Obtaining them will be easier than a walk through the Haven. Unfortunately, I must seek the assistance of a traitor in order to secure the first.

As I said, desperate times.

A long-ago memory ascends as I venture deeper into the dungeons, the memory of the day I first saw her. The day my link to her soul became more than a mere complication.

I stood on the back porch of the brownstone beside hers, frowning at the walls and concrete that seemed to spring from every direction. Who would live in such a trap by choice? The Third, from what I had seen so far, was a jungle, but not the kind I had become accustomed to. Trees were present, but appeared artificial, as if included in the landscape for decoration. I enjoy structure, revel in it, but this was too much. Where was the freedom? The pure abandon I felt back home in the Second?

I stooped, collecting a new lightbulb from a low round table. After unscrewing the burst bulb above the rear door, I reached to insert the fresh one in its place, and that's when I heard her.

Her voice came to me as if out of a dream.

The lyrics were dejected and despondent, crushing my heart, not because of what they meant, but because of who I knew they poured from. It was her, the girl I had felt the entirety of my existence but had never laid eyes upon, not since I was a toddler. Makai urged me to wait until he was present to stage a meeting. It would seem like chance, when in truth everything was set in place. But how could I ignore the heartbreak that was my own? I had to see her. I could not delay any longer.

The bulb slipped from my fingers and crashed to the porch. Her song ceased and my heart raced. No turning back. She knew I had been listening. What could it hurt to greet her?

I moved to the wall between our yards and peered over. And there she was, making a run for her back door. She was short, soft, and pale. Her hair was not dark enough to be considered black, but not quite light enough to be a simple brown. Everything about her was in between. Her voice was too beautiful to be singing such a wretched song, her insecurity out of place among such loveliness.

When I hopped the fence and saw her face at last, I was a goner. As much as I made every effort to hide it, there would never be anyone else.

Which is exactly why I must not turn back.

I turn my attention to the task at hand, shoving away the memory and storing it for safekeeping. When I reach the lowest part of the dungeon, determination drives each step. Past the façade to the white-doored cell beside Ebony's empty glass one. I don't even give it another thought before I unlock the door and enter.

My boots scrape smooth cement as I slide into the windowless, white-walled room. It smells of sanitizer and bleach. I blink away the burn and stare at the prisoner lying strapped to a makeshift medical table.

Jonathan Gage's eyes remain closed. Hard to believe I once considered him a friend and ally. His strapped arms and legs twitch, but otherwise he gives no indication he's aware an intruder lurks nearby. His bare chest climbs and descends, and a scar slashes his torso from shoulder to hip. His Guardian tattoo remains stamped on his right breast, a crown encircling a crossed sword and arrow. "To the Crown until Death," it reads. My fists clench. If I could rip the farce off his naked chest, I would.

Kuna was my friend, unlike this wretched swine. And yet Kuna has passed and Gage lives on. In what Reflection is this right or just? I was powerless to stop what happened. If in some way my actions now make up for my past failures, I will forever thank the Verity for the chance to set things right.

I glare at Gage. What does one say to a murderer?

The fluorescent light overhead buzzes as I approach the man who killed Kuna. For a moment I see the man I served beside. The one who helped Makai train me. The one I would have given my life for had it become necessary, as is the Guardian way.

But that man is dead, and I doubt he will ever return.

I lean forward and brace against the table's edge. "I know you are awake, Jonathan."

A menacing grin slithers over his mouth. "To what do I owe this pleasure, David?"

"It is 'sir' to you, traitor."

"Ah, how the tables have turned." His eyes remain closed. "Was it only last autumn I said the same about Kyaphus?" He *tsk, tsk, tsks*. "Tell me, if I am a traitor, why have you come? Surely you have not ventured all the way down here to catch up on old times."

My fingers press harder into the table. "I am here to strike a bargain. Your life in exchange for what I seek."

"And what is it you seek?"

"You know the whereabouts of Isabeau Archer."

"I do."

"Take me to her."

"And why would I do such a thing?"

"Because, should you refuse, I will kill you." My words are blunt and simple. True.

He laughs. "You don't have it in you, David."

The sound of metal sliding against leather echoes around the small space as I draw my sword. In one swift move I wield the weapon, which is more like a third arm, and press it to his neck.

His eyelids flash open, but his gaze remains fearless. Calling or none, he was always good at masking his emotions. A well-oiled machine made to protect and defend.

And kill.

"I see you have come a long way since your wooden sword training days," he rasps, stretching his neck. "What do you want with Isabeau anyway?"

"She possesses an item I require."

"Ha. And what makes you so sure she will give it to you?"

My grip on the hilt tightens. I press just enough to draw a trickle of blood. "She is in the business of trading, is she not? I have a hunch she will be more than willing to exchange what I seek for her servant boy."

Gage winces.

I've cut his ego. Good.

"You will need to trade more than me to procure what you desire." His head turns half an inch and my blade slices, blood oozing onto its edge. Hands clenched and biceps bulging against their restraints, he says, "Might I ask what is important enough for you to enlist the help of a lowly traitor?"

If I was not being extremely gracious tonight, I might give him another gash for sarcasm alone. I lift the sword away and wipe the blood onto his pant leg. "I am in search of a bottle."

Gage breathes easier now. "A bottle, huh? Just a bottle? I don't buy it. If you want me to take you to Isabeau, I'm afraid specificity is required."

"I need a bottle fashioned from mirrorglass." I shove my sword in its sheath and lean over him, my face directly above his. Even if Isabeau doesn't possess the item, if she is on good terms with the so-called Fairy Queen, the Troll will have a way to obtain it. "Do we have a deal?"

"Why, yes," Gage hisses. "I suppose we do."

TWENTY-SIX

NO ONE ELSE

Long after Ky finishes playing, after his fingers slip from the ivories and fold between his knees, we remain silent. Eye contact? Nonexistent. Tension? Thicker than Reggie's triple-layer fudge cake. The echo of Ky's song in my head is the only sound. Haunting me. Raising more questions in my ready-to-explode brain. One stands out among the rest.

How is it possible we are this close? This fast?

My relationship with Joshua developed over a period of three years. But a couple weeks with Ky and we shared the rarest of kisses. I know a Kiss of Infinity stems from somewhere deep inside, from feelings you may not be aware you possess. Still, it seemed crazy.

Until now.

It's as if our paths were meant to cross, our lips destined to meet. I questioned it before, but we must have something deeper. How else could he write a song melodizing my soul?

Is it possible we've met before?

Ky rubs his hands together, rests them on his thighs. If he listened to my thoughts just now, he gives nothing away. He remains cool. Collected. Quiet.

Not like himself at all.

I wish I could know what's on his mind.

"You can."

Blush. *Could you try not to read every thought I think, please?*

He shrugs. "Sorry. It was my connection to you while we were apart. I'll try to refrain now that we're together."

Together. The word stirs something inside me. We're close enough so when either of us makes the slightest shift, our arms brush. The electricity—*our* electricity—is undeniable. I should move away. Stand on the other side of the room. Recoil from the treacherous touch.

Treacherous because it awakens something that has been asleep since he left. Something missing between Joshua and me.

Ky . . . my fingers twiddle . . . *that song . . .* I tuck my hair behind my ears . . . *You've been playing it for me. Haven't you?*

"I'd hoped you heard it." He closes his right hand into a fist, taps it against his knee. "I wanted you to, though I couldn't be sure."

I angle to face him. My knee knocks his. He continues to study his lap as I think, *I did. I heard every note.*

He glances up. Stares at the sheet music before him. "I'd always wondered what kept the Void inside me from spreading after what Tiernan did to me." He speaks without preface, as if he knows what I came to ask.

Duh. Of course he knows. He can read my mind.

"When I discovered David and I shared the Verity, I knew that had to be it. The Verity had to be what kept me from turning Soulless before. But it was more than that too. My desire not to turn Soulless was strong enough to fight the darkness within. You see, each of us who are Called, I wager we all hold a piece of the Verity—a piece of the goodness that stems from the light empowering our Callings.

"When David sent me away, I began to construct my theory. I knew my connection to you would serve the same purpose—the Void is subject to the Verity, for it possesses the soul the Verity loves most. But what would it mean if our souls were bound? Before, I only held half the Verity and a very small portion of the Void. Now the Verity as a whole is bound to half the Void. It's tethered, you see. And not by just anything, no. The Void and the

Verity are now joined by a Kiss of Infinity." He faces me. "What does this mean?"

The question is rhetorical. He carries an answer but that's beside the point. Because the answer he seeks is mine. My mind wanders to day and night, night and day. How the Void covered half the Second in shadows under Crowe's rule. The way the Verity is the essence of everything light and good.

The Void and the Verity were balanced, I think. *The Verity is like the day, the Void like the night. Always existent, but never coexistent.* I watch his face for confirmation I'm on track. But he gives nothing away so I go on. *But now that's changed.*

Jaw pulsing, he nods. "The Void cares a great deal for the Verity." There's a sadness in his gaze. Because he isn't the only vessel of the Void. Joshua cares for me too—loves me—and he won't give me up without a fight.

This should make me happy, to know the boy I loved for so long returns my affection. But the knowledge only adds to my anguish. I don't come away from this without hurting someone. It doesn't matter who I choose. Because either way someone gets left behind.

"Em," Ky whispers, drawing me back to the now. "Does the Verity love the Void? Not the part held by David, but the part it is tethered to? Not a love born out of pity or one stemming from obligation. I'm talking real and true love. A love that would exist even if the Void and the Verity weren't involved."

My lips part out of habit, though it's my thoughts that say, *I . . . I'm not sure.* My eyelashes descend. Chest heaves.

Ky shifts beside me. When I open my eyes he's gathering the sheet music off the piano. It swishes between his fingers as he rises. "The only way to stop what's happening is to find a way to keep the Void from taking over the Verity—from dousing its light." Stepping from the space between the bench and piano, he turns to me. "And to do this we must go back to the origins of light and darkness." He lowers the fallboard over the keys.

The origins. Yes. Exactly. I guess great minds think alike. Then again, Ky and I have always been in sync for some reason.

Even when we fought we had a rhythm, an easiness Joshua and I
never shared. I stand and gaze at him from across the length of the
bench. Watching. Waiting.

"I have a theory." Though his voice hurries in excitement, his
eyes communicate exhaustion. Has he slept at all tonight? The
purple crescents beneath his eyes, along with the slight sag of his
shoulders, suggest he hasn't slept in days. "From what I've found,
the Verity has always existed, but the Void . . ." He pauses, as if
considering his words. "The Void is another story."

If the Void hasn't always existed, then someone—or
something—created it. But who? What?

"That's what we have to figure out," Ky says. "And I need your
help."

What can I do? I'm useless without—

"Stop it, Em. I won't hear you think such things anymore. You
are far from useless. In fact, you are the only one who can help.
Because if the Thresholds drain, only you can get us through to
the next Reflection."

I shake my head. Not true. I can only mirror walk to places
I've been.

"Our souls are one now, remember?" He winks. "If I've been
there, you've been there."

Could he be right? With the song inside, could I be of some use
after all?

"Not of some use. Vital." He skirts the bench, closing the space
between us with each new syllable. "I need you, Em. Can't you see?"

This is more like the Ky I know. Forward. Tenacious. I back
against the wall. The blanket around my shoulders falls, pools
around my ankles and feet. I press my palms to the sleek wood.
The *swoosh* of the ocean beyond the circular window next to my
head echoes my shifting emotions.

Like a wolf on the prowl Ky advances, raw hunger in his eyes.
But I'm not afraid of *him*.

I'm afraid of myself, of these strange sensations awakening the
closer, closer, closer he comes.

"And you need me too." He stops toe to toe with me, leans in, braces against the wall with his arms on either side of my head. "I know you. You've missed me."

It's impossible to think. Again.

"Come with me to the Fourth Reflection." His breath is hot on my face. "I've already spoken with Countess Ambrose. She's expecting us. Expecting you. Together we can fix this."

End the Void? It's all I've wanted—hoped for—since this whole mess started.

"Yes," Ky says. "No more darkness. Only light."

The idea makes my head swim. I've searched for this answer, but to discover I'm not crazy? That Ky believes it's possible too? My heart grows a gazillion times lighter. He doesn't blame me for the burden he carries. Instead he believes in me, in my strengths and abilities.

Lyrics from a *Wicked* song plead to burst from my lips.

"What is this feeling, so sudden and new?"

Except the feeling is far from loathing. Gulp.

Ky's forehead meets mine.

Double gulp.

He grazes his hand down my left arm, mingles our fingers.

I close my eyes, but I don't release his hand.

He kisses my right temple. Places three kisses along the length of my jaw.

My breaths release in gasps. My pulse is a drum line.

He pulls back just far enough so our gazes find each other again. "We belong together, Em. Maybe you aren't sure now, but I know."

How can you know?

Ky smiles then. So genuine. Pure. "I know because I know." He exhales.

My lips part. His breath tastes of peppermint. Why couldn't he have morning breath? It would make the task of keeping my mouth to myself much less daunting.

"I'll make a deal with you."

I arch my eyebrows.

He squeezes my hand, releases it, then paces to the other side of the space and back. "Stay with me. Help me save the Reflections. When we're done, if you wish to return to him, I'll let you go."

I wait. One breath. Two. When he doesn't continue I think, *That's not a deal. That's a request.*

"Sorry." He nears again, fingertips tracing the lengths of my bare arms. "It's difficult to think about anything but kissing you at the moment."

And now I'm blushing. *Please don't let him notice. I'm so confused.*

"For now," he says, ignoring the former half of my thought. His hands cup my face. "Soon all will be clear." And then he withdraws.

And something inside me breaks.

Crud. This is so not good.

"Will you come?"

My stomach churns, whether from the slightly rocking ship or the feelings of betraying Joshua, I can't tell. *Yes, I'll come.*

He crosses to the window beside me, grins into his reflection. "Good. We sail for the Fourth at dawn."

If I stay, one thing has to be clear.

He turns his regard on me. Folds his arms.

If I come, you will keep your distance. No trying to sway my decision or cloud my judgment. This is about the Reflections. The Callings. No more hand holding. No more brooding looks. I lower my gaze to his lips and snap my eyes shut. *And definitely no kissing.*

Ky laughs. He actually *laughs.* "Oh, there will be kissing. But it's not I who will be kissing you."

Eyes open. Brows pucker.

"You're going to kiss me, Ember. And when you do, it's going to be because you've finally admitted to yourself you're in love with me. Not because a Kiss of Infinity tells you to. Not because the Void split and half of it entered me. Because even without those things, in the end, it will still be me."

A little sure of yourself, aren't you? I can't help but crack a smile, enjoy this easy banter between us. I've missed this. Missed him.

"Haven't you learned by now?" He elbows me. "I am always right."

Hardly. I roll my eyes. I'm getting used to him hearing my silent dialogue. I almost like it.

He winks. "We'll see, Em. We'll see."

TWENTY-SEVEN

joshua

"M ove." I sit atop my steed Champion, reins clenched in one hand and my sword's hilt fisted in the other. I press my blade's tip into Gage's back, nudging him forward. It's been this way an entire day, and I've had about enough of his dithering.

But Gage continues through the brush with the same apathetic pace as usual. It's a wonder he can even walk. The Physic on staff at the castle did what he could, but Gage's wound was infected, and without the healing touch of a Physic, or my Ever blood, Gage should not have survived.

Suspicion escalates. Perhaps this Fairy Queen Isabeau spoke of does exist. And if so, has she granted Gage a wish? Enhanced healing of some sort?

He jerks against the rope binding his wrists. "Perhaps if you didn't insist on treating me like a slave, I'd be able to take you to our destination in a timelier manner."

I poke his back again. Champion whinnies. "I seem to remember you doing the same thing to Eliyana during our journey to Wichgreen Village."

He glances back at me and leers. "And I seem to remember *you* supporting that decision. In fact, wasn't it Kyaphus who stood against it?" One eyebrow arcs.

I grunt under my breath. My hands clench the reins and hilt tighter.

Gage's upper lip curls. "Thought so," he says before facing forward again.

Shame falls over me like an axed tree as I shift in the saddle. I've made mistakes, yes. Too many to count. Too many to make up for, if I'm being honest. But I'm right for her. She needs me. Kyaphus may have won the battle for her heart.

But the war's victory belongs to me.

"Here we are." Gage stops.

I sheathe my sword and dismount. Then I slap Champion's rear, and he trots off in search of water and sustenance. No need to tether him to a tree. He always returns when I need him.

Taking my spot beside Gage, I place a firm hand on his shoulder to assure him a sleeping weapon does not mean I'm going soft. Pireem Mountain stands before us, five times the height of New York's Empire State Building. Maples a brownstone deep create a ring around the mountain's base. High above, jagged rocks and narrow paths reside, but legend says a treasure awaits at the top for any man brave enough to venture there.

I've not met any such man. I do know this is the only place in all the Second where the Oden Lily grows—a rare red flower and the key ingredient in the painkiller Illusoden. What other secrets might Pireem hold?

I widen my stance, digging my boots into the sandy earth. "This is where Isabeau's been hiding? The Guardians searched here. They uncovered nothing."

"Because they didn't investigate enough." With a slanting glance he adds, "Perhaps you need a new Commander. Your men are slacking." Bitterness coats his words, and I have to wonder if he misses being a Guardian. He was one of the best. A shame his talent went to waste.

"Where to then?"

"The Mines."

Maple Mine entrances are stationed every fifty feet or so around the mountain's perimeter. Thorny brambles block the way to the nearest one, forcing me to hack at them with my sword.

Every *swoosh* and slice dulls the blade, and I make note to sharpen it at the earliest opportunity. When the path to the entrance is wide enough, I gesture for Gage to go ahead.

Silence settles the deeper we journey. The tunnel slopes downward, but even so the air is breathable due to the shafts above. Once we're well within the mine, the outside light a pin in the distance behind us, my eyes begin to adjust. On either side of us the ends of tree trunks and roots border the walls. The Mine Fairies are busy at work, extracting maple syrup from each tree. The illumination provided by their fluttering wings leaves no need to draw a flashlight.

As Gage continues on, I remain aware of our surroundings and the directions we take. Right, left, left, left, right. The Mines are set up as a grid, not too far removed from the subway system of New York. It makes things easier, at least. A grid, I can navigate. Lines and squares, corners and angles. It's El I'm having trouble with these days. She's unpredictable, a scribbled mess with no starting point and no end.

Hour by hour the gap between us widens, and not just physically. It's as if the longer we're apart, the greater the distance grows. Is she with my brother now? What will he say? The more time they spend together, the more I become the bad guy in all of this. But in the end it changes nothing. According to Rafaj, one sip of the Unbinding Elixir will reverse everything.

Let's hope he's not wrong.

It wasn't too long ago we traveled through the southernmost mines on our return to Haven Island. I suppose I should've noticed the warning signs then. If anyone is to blame for the closeness El and Kyaphus share, it's me. I pushed him on her, insisted he take on the role as her Guardian. I never dreamed they'd fall for one another. Then again, she hasn't truly fallen for him. Her heart is confused. Misled.

I must make this right.

We take another right.

Gage freezes. I halt beside him, fingers twiddling over my

weapon's hilt. "A dead end?" Frustration brews. "I thought you knew your way."

"Tell me, are your men so dimwitted they wouldn't think to check for façades?" He snorts and then walks forward, through the mine wall, disappearing from view.

I scratch the back of my head. Exhale. Of course they checked, but they have a full Reflection to cover. The Guardians are running on little sleep, working in harsh weather with only the rations on their backs to sustain them when they're in the wilderness. Perhaps I need to have a word with Makai about thoroughness. The Amulet Calling remains in full force, it seems. We need to make every effort to do our best as we move forward, and that includes better reconnaissance.

On the wall's opposite side, light blinds me and I am forced to shade my eyes until they, once again, adjust. After a few blinks I scan the scene. Hundreds of Mine Fairies bob in the air, their natural light flickering on and off and off and on, making them appear and disappear again. The sight stirs something in the back of my brain, but I ignore it. Just ahead lies a crystal-clear pool and at the pool's center a maple tree, the leaves in vibrant hues of pink, orange, and green.

I tread with care, craning my neck. A vertical tunnel above the tree goes on for miles. We must be in the mountain's core. I've heard stories of Fairy Fountains. They're said to be Thresholds, though I've no idea where this one might lead.

And if the Fairy Fountains are real, what else, or *who* else, might be?

I skirt the pool to find Gage standing on the other side. A beautiful woman with white-blonde hair and porcelain skin unties his restraints. She wears an airy gown the shade of onyx. When she turns toward me her pleasant smile does nothing to mask the menacing intent behind her eyes. "Why, Joshua David. I was beginning to wonder if you would ever grace me with your presence."

I stop a few paces away, keeping my weapon hand ready. "I have come to make a trade, Isabeau. The life of your servant"—I jerk my chin toward Gage—"for one of your objects."

"I'm not her servant. We're equals." Gage growls the rebuttal, but the way he stands behind Isabeau, rather than beside her, lets on he's either inferior or afraid.

"Hush now, Jonathan." When she moves it's like a dance, graceful, yes, but more akin to a tiger on the prowl. "And I'd much rather you refer to them as artifacts, David. Each one took great effort to acquire, you see." She lifts two fingers, positioning them like a perch.

"Fine then." My neck pulses. Enough with the niceties.

"What is it you seek?" A Fairy flits over and lands on her fingers.

"A bottle made of mirrorglass."

"You get right to the point, don't you? That is a rare item indeed." She strokes the Fairy's wings. The Fairy titters. "As providence would have it, I do possess such an item. However, it comes at a price. Are you willing to pay?" She lifts the Fairy to her lips as if she might kiss it, but instead she snaps her mouth over the Fairy and swallows it whole.

I try to hide my revulsion. If I wasn't aware Isabeau is a monster, I most certainly would be now. "What more do you want? I've delivered your henchman."

"Three gifts." She dabs the corners of her mouth with the hem of her sleeve. "I have Jonathan returned, yes. This fulfills gift number one. For your second offering, I desire something only *you* are able to provide."

Should've known. My hands fist. "How much?"

"Only a small vial's worth."

"Done." My Ever blood is useless at the moment anyway, but she doesn't need to know this. Still, when did my life turn into one of trades and barters? My days are comprised of running from one place to another, extracting information. At least with Nathaniel I wasn't required to pay a price, and all Rafaj wanted was my truth. But not everyone is so generous.

Isabeau snaps her fingers, and in an instant Gage exits through a wall of vines behind her. When he returns he brandishes a small syringe.

Not her servant, my sword. Servant is exactly what he is.

Teeth and muscles clenched, I offer my arm and he draws my blood. He then injects it into a small bottle, corks it, and shuffles away once more.

"Excellent." Isabeau's eyes sparkle. "Now, for your third and final contribution."

I bristle. "I've given you your man and my blood." Not that it will do her much good. "What else could you possibly want?"

"Only one thing more." She lifts her dress and dips a toe in the pool.

This ought to be good. I nod. "Go on."

"You will be headed to the Fourth, where my dear old friend Countess Ambrose resides. She has something of mine. Something I would like returned. She will not part with it easily, I am sure, so you will have to steal it."

My mouth turns down. Steal? I suppose I've proven there is nothing I won't do for El, and that includes employing unconventional methods. "What is it?"

"A rose."

"You want me to steal . . . ? I am afraid I don't follow."

"A rose," she repeats. "It is mine and I want it back."

I shrug. Can't be too difficult to acquire, though my gut tells me there's more to this "rose" than will meet the eye. Still, what's the harm? "Agreed."

"Superb." She wades into the water, dress pooling around her like black tar. Then she vanishes, just as she did at the coronation, leaving the dress floating in her wake.

Where did she—?

"Follow me," a tinkling voice says.

I look down. There, tiptoeing on the water before me, is the most beautiful Fairy I've ever beheld. She wears a crown laced with jewels, and her wings glow a brilliant shade of red. She dives and I go in after her.

So this is her third Mask form. This is how she seemed to disappear at the coronation. How the supposedly invisible attackers—her servants, the Mine Fairies—shot at the guests out of sight. No wonder Isabeau expends all her efforts to keep it a secret.

Isabeau isn't a Mask, the Calling is simply her cover. A way to deter everyone from knowing her true identity.

The Fairy Queen.

TWENTY-EIGHT

A Talent That I Always Have Possessed

Day three aboard the *Seven Seas* and I've been ill the entire time. Ugh. I'm so sick of puking. Literally. *Suck it up, El. Don't let them see your weakness.*

To get my mind off my stomach, I peruse Dimitri's account. A bucket waits on standby, hidden behind the crate where I sit. I'm supposed to be on deck swab duty, but I had to sneak away. Ky will cover for me. He knows our mission to end the Void is more important than a clean deck.

Now where did I leave off? Oh yes. Here.

First Day, First Month, Tenth Year of Count VonKemp

I have been at sea for months but have yet to discover what I seek. I once held out hope my faith in true love might be restored, but alas, the voyage may be futile . . .

I roll my neck. What time is it? I glance out the porthole. Clouds for miles and miles. We're sailing to the nearest Threshold leading to the Fourth. Ky thinks this Countess Ambrose person retains information vital to our mission. The captain has remained true to his word and hasn't tried to sway me since he played my song the other night. This doesn't make much difference though. Turns out Ky just being Ky is enough trouble of its own.

I chew my thumbnail. Moving on . . .

I have visited the Second and Third Reflections but have uncovered nothing of consequence. Now I venture through the Fourth on my way to the Fifth. Perhaps it is in the more distant Reflections I will find my gem. I must dive deep if I ever hope to rise . . .

There it is. That saying. The one etched into the bell. I knew it seemed familiar. Did my Scrib memory pick up on the phrase when I skimmed these pages at first glance?

I turn the book upside down to save my place and mull over Dimitri's words. So far I haven't learned anything new about the Kiss of Infinity. I could skip through his entries, but what good would it do to begin a story in the middle? No, to get the whole picture I have to go in order.

The steps leading belowdeck creak. I jump up and cross to my hammock, shoving the book beneath my blanket.

Tide appears at the bottom of the steps.

I work to slow my breaths.

He lifts a brow. "Lunch is served. Or are you too good to eat with the rest of us scalawags?"

His words could be taken as harsh, but they come off more playful. Sarcastic. I've only been here a few days, but so far it hasn't been so bad. Tide's been friendly enough, as well as a few others. Pirates get a bad rap, but haters gonna hate and all. They're not so bad once you get to know them.

"Now you sound like me," Ky says in my head.

Yeah, yeah. No need to rub it in. I nod at Tide.

He salutes me, a smile longer than Long Island on his toasted face, and heads back up the stairs.

Tide is one of fifteen members of the crew. Actually seventeen if I include myself and Ebony, who's been working with me to draw out the Mask within. So far, nothing. I'm coming to the conclusion Mask just isn't part of my repertoire. Our sessions always end with me puking—because of seasickness—and Ebony throwing her hands up with an exaggerated, "Ugh! Why do I even bother?"

Is it any surprise we've never gotten along? We're as opposite as punk rock and opera.

But Ebony and my lack of Mask are the least of my worries. Ky filled me in. The crew believes we're on the hunt for treasure buried deep in the Seventh Reflection, in some legendary garden known as the Garden of Epoch. Because what else do pirates have to do but search for buried treasure?

Ky's told everyone I'm a Mirror and a valuable asset to the team. But my Verity-ness? That's the part we have to keep under wraps, just as Ky's Void-ness remains hidden.

He wouldn't say more, but I didn't argue. The seriousness hardening his expression was convincing enough.

Not everyone on the crew can be trusted. Got it. The warning from Mom's letter meanders back to me.

"Be chary of whom you place your confidence in."

You don't have to tell me twice. I've been betrayed enough I almost expect it. I reach beneath my blanket, close my fingers around Dimitri's journal—

"Just as I suspected."

I whirl. Look toward the stairwell.

There stands Ebony in all her scrutinizing glory. She's wearing clothes identical to Tide's. How did I miss it? He's always dressed for the beach. But today he wore jeans and a button-down sweater. Should've known it was my deceitful half sister and her impersonating ways.

"You are so not ready to end the Void. You can't even recognize when you're being fooled. Or maybe you just don't care."

Ky shared our plans with her. I was wary to do so, but he felt confident Ebony was better off knowing than not.

Guess we'll see.

She struts over. Grabs my elbow. "The Amulet Calling has faded. Streak is unable to fashion a façade."

So Streak is—or was—the Amulet on board. At least we didn't lose something more vital. As cool as façades are, I'd much rather have a Shield or Mask or Magnet by my side in an emergency.

Three Callings down, four to go.

A bout of nausea lurches. I swallow it back. I will not lose my cookies in front of Ebony.

"Time to work. I've come up with a new angle on your training." The mischief lifting her cheeks does not bode well. "It's more important now than ever we get your Mask up and running. We're down an Amulet and the Physic on the ship is useless if someone needs immediate healing."

She's right. Why does she have to be right? Why, of all people, did Ebony have to be the person I need? I can't deny her strengths. Without her, Preacher would've caught us. And the few times we've trained since, as depleted as I was afterward, I could almost feel something about to occur. Could today be the day my Mask is set free?

She drags me toward the stairs leading to the deck. "You wanted my help? You got it. Four of the seven Callings are still functional for now, but they take much more effort than before. You want to be soft, fine. Stay here and rot in your own vomit. But if you actually want to be worth something around here, you'll stop burying your nose in a book and start acting like the Mirror you are. Matter or don't. But worthlessness is a choice. You decide."

I wrench away and finish the ascent on my own. As I trail her I mouth my inaudible response. *Nobody calls me worthless.*

Nobody.

Who does this guy think he is? Hercules?

Streak charges me from across the main deck, frizzed dreadlocks flapping against his quarterback shoulders like dozens of dried-out snakeskins. His teeth are bared in a wide grin, yellowed and crooked. The closer he moves, the stronger the stench of alcohol becomes, reminding me this guy has probably had his fair share of bar fights.

Oh. Snap.

"A month's worth of chores on Streak!" Charley hollers through cupped hands.

Other crew members howl in response, placing bets for or against me. They've all paused in their daily duties to see "Captain Warren's secret weapon" in action. My blood boils, curdles beneath my skin. It takes every ounce of self-control to ignore the guffaws of the crew. To drown out the stares and knee slaps—all at my expense.

So humiliating.

What I wouldn't give to have Mom here, or Stormy. *Someone* on Team El. A little moral support could do me some good about now. I look to Ebony, who has remained silent. She eyes me. Nods. I can't tell if she's encouraging me or if this is some sort of sick game to her as well. This is her new angle? To have Streak use me as tackle practice—?

"Ooof!" I'm on my backside, pain slicing my tailbone and zipping up my spine. I rub the back of my whiplashed neck, grind my teeth.

Ebony frowns.

Streak lifts his arms like a champion. Yeah. As if taking down a girl half his size and weight makes him so awesome. Spare me.

Charley high-fives the few guys nearest her, smirking as those who lost the bet sulk. I've learned none of their names, aside from Tide.

"Some secret weapon." Charley sniggers. "But you're little, so that's something. We could probably use you as ammo if we run out." The crew roars their laughter. Satisfaction spreads across Charley's face as she hops from her perch on a nearby barrel, struts to my side, and holds out her hand.

I ignore the offer, get up on my own. My palms brace against my knees. I'm so weak. So out of shape. My stomach churns and I clamp my teeth tight. I will not lose my lunch right here for all to see. No way. Not happening.

Ebony waggles a canteen beneath my nose. "Drink this. It will help."

I yank it from her grasp and take a long swig. The water is slightly sweet, tasting of honey. I'm reminded of a moment last autumn. Ky handing me his canteen, the same sweet flavoring inside.

"I'd be careful who you trust," he'd said.

So I keep hearing.

Wiping my mouth with my arm, I straighten and pass the canteen back to Ebony. Before she steps away she whispers in my ear, "You're not focusing. Put your heart into it. All or nothing."

Would she make up her mind? Is she here to encourage or condescend?

Charley whisks her auburn hair into a high pony, cinches it. Red wisps border her face like thin flames. "Ready to get whipped?"

I flex my fingers and then fist them at my sides, my right arm tingling as it has been. The pain seems to be getting worse. Could I have a pinched nerve? Maybe I'd better see the Physic after this session, get some muscle balm or something.

"Did you hear me?" Charley repeats.

I offer no response. Keep the opponent in the dark. Don't let her know my next move. Ebony's instructions from the past few days replay over and over. It can't be as difficult as it seems. My song lives inside me. Problem is my heart is torn, my love divided. How can I ignite my Calling when I'm this confused?

Charley paces away. Stretches both arms over her head, intertwining her fingers and facing her palms skyward.

Streak exits the training square drawn on the deck with chalk. I'm left to face Charley alone. Great. Why do I get the feeling she'll be the fiercer opponent?

A cold sweat dampens my hairline. I roll my neck and shoulders, hop from foot to foot like I've seen boxers do in movies. Except I'm no *Ali* or *Million Dollar Baby*. Why didn't I bother to attend a single sports event at school? Maybe I could've learned a thing or two.

Charley begins to morph. Unlike Wren, she doesn't bother stripping before taking on her Mask form. Her crimson hair lengthens, sprouts from her exposed hands and feet. Her face. The wetsuit she wears stretches with her new shape. She pounces onto all fours, her nose lengthening into a snout, her eyes widening and darkening, almost black. The red wolf in Charley's place snarls, canines bared. She licks her chops, focusing on me—dinner. We're in the middle of the ocean, and I'm facing a hungry wolf with nowhere to go. Peachy.

The crew inhales a collective breath.

My knees shake and I work to steady my breathing.

She prowls, spittle dripping from what looks almost like a grin.

I back away. Glance toward Streak. Then over to Ebony.

Her dark eyes narrow and she gives the slightest nod, as if she's trying to communicate something.

My eyes widen in response. *Hello, a little help here.* Mirror walking with the song inside was one thing, because mirror walking I've done. My Amulet wasn't difficult to master because anyone can imagine a wall. But how do I morph into a Mask when I don't even know what my Mask is? If I had my voice, I'd command the wolf to her knees. Difficult to do when she. Can't. Hear. Me.

Ebony inclines her head toward Charley.

Charley creeps closer.

I close my eyes and run Queen Ember's "Mirror Theory" through my mind. It's memorized. Permanent. I scan every word and line. Picture them. *"Conveys traits relating to . . . the other seven Callings . . . Strengths may manifest all at once, or over time."*

Can I use the Shield in me to attack? But what match is a kick or a punch for those glistening white teeth? What else? *Think!*

And then *he's* there. In the corner of my vision. I turn my head just as Ky steps to the railing on the upper deck. His gaze penetrates my nerves, causing them to burst and dissipate.

"You're a Mirror. You're stronger than she is." I hear him, clear as day, just like all the other times.

Charley's so close I can smell her stale dog-breath. She crouches. Growls.

I have only seconds. No space to think or breathe. I look to Ky and something expands deep within.

I'm a Mirror. Every Calling will manifest itself. I just have to draw it out.

My center warms as if ignited. The Verity? I haven't felt it since the coronation. The sensation of calm overcoming me now is like hearing a classical masterpiece for the first time. I latch onto it for fear its music will end. What brought it back to life?

Ky's face takes over my mind.

No, not what. Who?

At first I try to push Ky away, replace him with Joshua's image. But when I do, the warmth grows cold. So I let Ky in. He shoves and presses, and I let him stay. Something in me releases and my feet lift off the ground. There's the sensation of shrinking, like I'm folding in on myself. Throat constricts. Stomach tightens. My eyes snap open. The world has gone dark. I'm suffocating. A heaviness surrounds me and I heave, move, wiggle to break free of this black cage.

And then I do. I feel so light, like for the first time I'm free of a weight that has been holding me back my entire life. I glance down. My clothes lie in a heap several feet below, and I have the sudden urge to cover myself. But then I see their faces. Streak's broad grin, his shoulders shaking with a chuckle. Charley, returned to her human form, beaming. The rest of the crew's expressions are sprinkled with mixtures of awe and shock, and some even look impressed. And Ky, trying to hide it but unable to withhold the slightest smirk for my sake. What are they all staring at?

I'm moving farther and farther away, carried by my arms or the slight breeze in the ocean air, I can't tell. It's crisper here. Clearer. I'm over the water and my stomach drops, but my body remains airborne. And then I see it. My reflection. But I'm not me, not the me I've always known anyway. Instead I'm the Mask within, the one I didn't truly believe existed until this moment.

For eighteen years I've only ever felt like a caterpillar, trapped in this awkward, clumsy body with a hideous mark on my face. But now . . . now I see what I was meant to be all along.

A butterfly.

joshua

The wish part of the tale was accurate, but the legend never mentioned anything about paying for it. Then again, nothing is ever free. Least of all a wish from the Fairy Queen, especially when her name is Isabeau Archer.

"A deal with the Troll was necessary to secure what is required to detach Eliyana from your less-than-adequate brother."

My right eye twitches and I rub it, ignoring the voice that seems to speak from the shadows. A combination of problems could cause these hallucinations. I'm not getting enough sleep, or any for that matter, and I'm stressed. My Ever blood has gone mortal, weakening the natural strength I've always been accustomed to. I only recently learned I have a brother. Finally, the weight of the Reflections and Callings falls to me. A strange voice is simply a figment of my wearied mind.

Or is it?

I sit up, reach over, and tug on my boots. No use lying here if I'll not be gaining rest. Standing, I survey my surroundings. Dai Island isn't much to look at with its slick, rocky terrain and want for trees. No one would ever guess a Fairy Fountain is hidden in its core.

I'd heard of Fairy Fountains but had never experienced one. According to Isabeau, they're easy to find if one knows where to look. Each Fountain is connected to all the others throughout the Reflections. They're like Thresholds. The difference is you must obtain permission from the Fairy Queen to pass through their territories.

Isabeau controls the pathways between Fountains and sent us on a direct route to the Fairy Fountain of the Fourth—a hidden lagoon in a pocket cave beneath Dai Island, which is where we are now. It's one of five islands surrounding the Fourth's main Island of Tecre.

How much longer until daybreak? If it were up to me, I'd have already crossed to the main island for reconnaissance. If this rose is so valued, it won't be sitting out in the open, and the Fourth's center is full of nooks and crannies. I've been here but once before, during my first year of Guardian training. It was Jonathan who brought me, in fact.

As if on cue, he snores and moans in his sleep.

I cast a glance behind me. Isabeau insisted the traitor accompany me, and he agreed. When did he turn from respectable Guardian leader to the Troll's errand boy? Because that is all she will ever be in my eyes. Queen of the Fairy folk or not, you can't make something what it isn't. Her beauty in her Fairy and human forms may be sights to behold, but they are mere sights, illusions covering what truly lies beneath.

A monster.

Jonathan stirs again, so I move farther down the shore, peering out across the water. The lights of the Fourth's city are fireflies in the distance. I gaze skyward and take in my favorite sight. No matter the Reflection, the stars never change. They're the one thing I can count on to remain constant. They stay where they are, they do not fail. I can look up and see precisely what I expect. Why can't El be that way? Why must she insist on being unpredictable?

I scratch the back of my head. She's a mystery, which is indeed part of what charmed me from the beginning. Now I can't keep up. *Come back to me, El. Come back.*

"You really should get some sleep."

My jaw tightens at the uninvited sound of Jonathan's voice. He's not in error, but I've no intention of letting him in on this information. Instead I continue to move farther away, walking the line between sea and rocky beach. Stones crunch beneath my tread and I kick them up and into the waves. Jogging steps thud behind me and I grunt beneath my breath.

"If you're heading on a walk, I have to come." He's been running but lacks no breath. "Isabeau's orders."

"About that." I shove my hands into my pants pockets, and my sword shifts at my side. "What is going on between you two? Is lackey really your greatest aspiration?"

Out of the corner of my eye I catch him shake his head. "It is a fair price to pay for the wish she granted me. That is all."

"And what wish is that?"

He huffs. "What do you care?"

I shrug. "I don't." It's the most honest reply I can give. What concern do I have for a traitor?

We march in silence, and after a substantial amount of time has passed, I can almost believe we've traveled back in time to when we'd train together in the early hours of the day. What began as a leader-recruit relationship quickly transformed into a friendship. Long after I exceeded the need for instruction, we continued to work out side by side. While other Guardians chose to wait and warm up with the majority, Jonathan and I preferred the quiet minutes before the sun awoke. We'd run along the worn Haven path, our breaths as fog in the air. Sometimes we'd race, while other days we'd jog as if one unit. He was like a brother, another reason his betrayal burned like chaff.

"I had no choice."

I lift an eyebrow at his freely offered words.

He picks up his pace and walks a little ahead of me. I remain silent. This, too, is a tactic we were taught in training. Sometimes the best and most valuable information is given without any interrogation whatsoever.

"My father was Called, and his father before him," Jonathan says. "When the Threshold water manifested nothing in my soul, I was a disgrace to the family. My father booted me out quicker than Preacher can draw and nock an arrow."

We're halfway around the miniature island now. The surface is level enough I can see from one end to the other without effort.

"Moving up in rank as a Guardian became my life. If I could be the best at something, even without a Calling, perhaps my father would be proud. Of course, that wasn't the case."

It never is.

"When the girl came to us, I knew she was the key to getting what I'd always lacked. My first inclination was to offer her up to Crowe, of course. He carried the Void, and though dark, it is powerful. If the Verity could give a Calling, what could the Void do? My first Void injection was painful, but the surge of strength was undeniable. I relished it. For the first time in my life, I felt like I could become the man my father hoped I'd be."

Out of habit, my right fist clenches the hilt of my sword. I've felt it, too, the power coursing through my veins since the Void entered. So different from the Verity. The Verity's presence was—what's the word?—calming? No, it was more than that. With the Verity inside I felt as if life was in constant bloom. I never knew anything different, not until the light left and was replaced by darkness. Only then did I sense the great and tragic loss.

Jonathan clears his throat. "But then a Fairy found me, told me Isabeau was looking for the girl and would offer an even sweeter deal for the return. Something even better than what Crowe could provide with the Void."

We're nearly back to camp now, and the sky is beginning to lighten. "Which was?"

He stops and faces me. "A Calling."

I shake my head. "Only the Verity can give a Calling. One from any other source would be a farce."

His face is as hard as his voice when he says, "A farce, perhaps, but enough. Enough to show my father I was a man. Enough to prove I was worthy of the name Gage." He trudges away, back to our resting place. He's already packed his things and is headed toward our small rowboat when I reach him.

I possess nothing but the clothes on my back and the sword

at my side, so I follow after him. He didn't let on what his Fairy-manufactured Calling is, but there's no question it aided in healing his eyes, which El said were clawed shut by Lark's talons. I almost feel sorry for him. He sought power from the wrong source entirely. Power from darkness only wields more darkness.

The sun blinks over the horizon as I enter the boat. As Jonathan rows to the Fourth's main shore, I ignore the throbbing in my Void arm, attempt to shut out the voice becoming louder each hour. But the fatigue is making the effort too great. When the voice speaks I close my eyes and exhale against it, as if somehow this will carry it away. It doesn't work, however, because the voice's whispers turn to shouts.

"Darkness wields darkness, yes, but much is gained in the night. Rest and solace. Peace. Let me give you rest. Let me . . ."

I don't hear what else the voice says because with each row of the oars, I drift off into the first sleep I've had in days.

THIRTY

sisters again

S he's screaming.

The memory of Mom's shriek haunts me. She's in pain. Being dragged through the Threshold at Central Park's Pond.

Because of me.

Bang! Haman cackles. Wren mourns. Robyn bleeds.

Because of me.

Haman snaps his fingers. Joshua cries out in pain.

Because of me.

Ky dies. Loses the Verity. Takes on the Void.

Because of me.

Coronation guests bawl. Stormy sobs. Kuna dies.

Because of me.

"No," I croak, a weak and wretched sound. "Stop. Take me."

Me, me, me.

I can't continue to allow the people I love to suffer. I won't.

Must.

Destroy.

The.

Void.

Someone laughs.

I flinch.

"You're getting better."

Ebony? Her voice is far away. Muted.

Grunt. I try to roll over in my hammock, but it just swings. I'm mummied in place.

"I knew you had it in you, runt." Ebony again. But the characteristic insult that normally coats her tone is absent, replaced by . . . pride?

I sit up and my hammock makes the ceiling creak. Tide snores from the hammock to my right. Charley rests soundlessly in the one to my left, red hair spilling over the side of the canvas, making it appear as if it's caught fire.

I rub my eyes, letting my vision adjust. What time is it?

"That's it," Ebony says. "You may still have your Confine, Khloe, but that doesn't mean you can't have a little fun with your Calling."

My ears perk. Khloe?

"You're a natural. We must be related."

That does it. I'm out of my hammock and on my feet. After sliding into my shoes and tiptoeing through the crew's sleeping quarters, I take the stairs to the deck two at a time, the rope-coiled railing scratching my palm. A hazy sky greets me, barely lit, suggesting dawn has only just broken.

A girl who couldn't be a day over twelve stands at the deck's center, back turned toward me. Her hair is black frizz, her skin the shade of Mom's favorite cup of Earl Grey. Ebony is across from her, face alight in a way I've never witnessed. Joy adorns her eyes, her customary outfit of arrogance shed for another ensemble altogether.

She's beautiful.

"We have a visitor." Ebony leans to one side, peering at me past Khloe. "May I introduce our other sister." She examines her less-than-pristine nails. "El, Khloe. Khloe, El."

Khloe twirls. Not turns, twirls. "We're approaching the Threshold. You might want to change."

No "Hey, how's it goin'?" No "Good morning, it's nice to finally meet you, sis." She skips right past the formal greetings and jumps into bossiness.

She's definitely related to Ebony.

When she lists her head it's with the grace of a prima ballerina.

Her face is even younger than I expected, baby fat filling out her chin and cheeks. "Countess Ambrose would take it as a sign of disrespect if you were to enter her court looking like you just climbed out of bed." Her words are blunt but not rude. Her smile holds a secret, maybe even a joke. She's only eleven but she sounds years her senior.

I examine my clothes. Yesterday's sweaty jeans and jacket combo sticks to me in odd places, cinched and twisted and stretched. Ebony pushed me to my limit, making me transform to and from a butterfly at least a dozen times. Each instance stirred a passion inside me, awakening the Verity for the first time since I was crowned.

Crowned. Verity. Could taking on the power that comes with being queen have had something to do with the Verity's sudden silence? Was the crown what stopped the Verity from creating a calm within?

I smooth my hair. I removed the mirrorglass crown, but the Callings continue to dwindle. Still, something happened at the coronation when I became the ruler of the Second. I need to run this by Ky.

"Does she always stare off into space like that?" Khloe asks. "Are you sure she's our sister?"

Blink. Huh? My sisters stand with arms crossed and smiles quirked. Both ogle me as one would a crazy person.

"Yeah, pretty much." Ebony shrugs one shoulder. "You get used to it."

Even if I could speak, what would I say? I've never had siblings before. It was always me and Mom. It took a good few weeks to fall into the tempo of having a best friend in Stormy, and only then because she was persistent. But sisters? That's a whole other symphony.

"Have you come to practice with us? I've been ill for a few days, but I'm totally better now. Big brother always makes me stay in bed when I'm sick, even when I insist I'm fine. Ebony's been teaching me how to project. With my Confine in place 'til I turn eighteen, my Calling has limits. Still, there are other ways I can flex my Shield muscles. Isn't that right, Eb?"

Practice? Project? Shield muscles? Eb? This girl talks a mile a minute, launching from one topic to the next without prelude or an opportunity to get a single syllable in.

My older sister stands beside the younger. They may be opposites in appearance, but their personalities sure are in sync. "El's not strong enough." Ebony flips her hair. "Projecting is a whole different level of mastery."

I want to ask what projecting is, to inquire why these two seem so close. Ebony—a.k.a. Bones—mentioned she was the one who transported Khloe to the Fourth upon Jasyn's orders. Could they have bonded then?

"Oh." Khloe bounces on her toes. "I'm supposed to tell you my brother wants to see you. He sent me to fetch you, but then I found Ebony and got excited to practice and totally forgot." She talks with her hands, all flails and flaps.

I nod a silent thanks as I head for the captain's cabin. I need to speak to Ky as well and am grateful for the chance to do so alone. When I reach the upper deck, however, I pause. Observe my sisters for another moment. They laugh and chat, Ebony leaning in to tell Khloe something or other and Khloe nodding. Unprecedented jealousy lances my chest.

When Ky first told me of Khloe, a surge of hope swelled. Could Khloe and I become friends—sisters? Watching her with Ebony now, I have to wonder if the sister ship has sailed. They're so easy with each other. Might I have a chance with baby Evan, if I ever get to meet him? Will anything in my life ever be normal?

Once I reach the captain's cabin, I touch the doorknob and give it a quarter turn. Wait. What am I doing? My hand lifts and knock, knock, knocks.

"Come in," Ky calls.

Okay. Breathe. We haven't been alone since my first night here. *But I can do this, I can*—

I freeze in my tracks. Ky stands across the room, shirtless. His

jeans hang low over his hips, belt undone. Morning's cool light filters through the curved window, softens his winter-worn features.
I almost don't notice he has more than just the one new scar on
his face.

Except my eyes adjust and I *do* notice. I see the burned flesh,
pink and potholed and shiny, on his right pec—the place where
his Guardian tattoo used to be. Inward gasp. The tip of the sword
is still visible, the slightest curve of the crown. But the arrow is
gone, as is the Guardian oath. It appears as if someone scorched the
image clean off his skin. And then there are the yellowed bruises.
The raised lines of healing scars.

The first day of the year screeches back to me like tires on
black ice. Joshua about to propose—again. Me, falling to my knees
in dire agony. Joshua following suit. It was Ky's pain we felt.

Who did this to you? I squeeze my eyes shut. The hurt—
nauseating and suffocating—is too much. My throat constricts.

"C'mon, Em," he says, brushing away my serious thoughts. His
belt jangles. "You've seen me shirtless before." His voice is muffled,
probably from the shirt he's lifting over his head, thank the Verity.
"I don't mind if you look."

Why does he avoid my question? I know he heard me. I can't
help but believe this is somehow my fault as well. That Ky was
tortured . . .

Because. Of. Me.

No one is safe. Everyone I get close to ends up hurt—or dead.
Will nothing ever change?

Footsteps across the cabin. *Shuffle, creak.*

I will myself to hear his thoughts. To search his mind for the
secrets he keeps.

Nada.

I peek beneath my eyelids.

Ky is clothed now, wearing a V-neck sweater, crisp white T-shirt
beneath. Dark jeans. Black dress shoes. Cocky, twisted smile. His
gaze is intense, leaving nothing to question. Must he make his feelings for me so obvious?

I step back. *Ky*... Look down. *Who*...? Swallow. *The scars. The bruises? Who did this?* Look up.

The space between his brows creases. "Some came from Jasyn's Soulless."

And the burn?

His eyes shift. Narrow. He works his jaw before he says, "Next question."

Again I attempt to listen for his thoughts but hear nothing.

Move on. Get that lopsided grin back. *Khloe said you wanted to see me. Is everything okay?*

"Quite." His focus finds mine again, the tension in his expression melting. He wiggles his eyebrows. Lists his head. "Can't I simply want to look at you without everyone watching?"

My heart hits the door behind me. Joshua can't see my mirrormark, so he's always seen me as beautiful. But Ky? What does he see?

"Em . . ." He slides forward an inch, smelling of soap and brine. "You. Are. Beautiful. Every part. Every line and scar and flaw. Every blemish. I love it all. Maybe David is blind to your mark, but that's where I count myself fortunate. He sees the you he wants to see. The you he thinks he can make you. I see you as you are."

My walls vanish. All the tautness between us dissipates.

"And you're the most beautiful thing I've ever seen." Ky is so close now I'm positive he'll touch me. But he doesn't. He doesn't have to.

Because I feel it, the invisible thread connecting us. It's more tangible than ever. Like a force I can't war against. Silence settles, the magnetism present but not as strong.

"Better hurry up." He reaches past me to open the door, ending the moment. "We'll be crossing the Threshold soon."

Wait, I think. *I remembered something.*

"Oh?" He quirks a brow. "Do tell."

I share about the Verity and the mirrorglass crown. Watch his mind work behind his shifting eyes.

"Mirrorglass, you said?"

I nod.

His lips flatten. "I think this bit of information will prove useful when we speak with Countess Ambrose. Especially the part regarding mirrorglass."

Why's that?

"Because." His Adam's apple bobs at the precise moment his lashes lower. "The Fourth Reflection is where mirrorglass was first discovered."

I'd always assumed the ship's captain steered or drove or whatever. Wrong. A guy named Flint is the pilot, in charge of navigation and steering. He wears a shark-tooth necklace and a stoic expression, unblinking eyes focused beyond the ship's bow.

Ky braces against the upper-deck railing five feet away, elbows locked, regard fixed on the sea. His gaze darts back and forth, back and forth, back and forth. He doesn't even glance in my direction when I emerge from the captain's cabin. What's he looking for?

Flint tilts the wheel left an inch. Right two. I shuffle past him, careful not to disturb his concentration. His expression hovers between serious and afraid.

My stomach flips. Great. Now I'm worried. Is there something about the Fourth's Threshold they're not telling me?

When I reach the steps leading to the main deck, I pause and cast a sidelong glance at Ky. Creased lines edge his eyes, span his forehead. I want to reach out and smooth those lines with my fingertips. The urge is so strong I have to keep moving.

On the main deck, the crew works in uniform silence, their miens reflecting the captain's. Streak readies the lifeboats, the cords of his neck rigid. A guy named Sam, but referred to as Gunner, stocks his person with knives, a sword, a pistol. Charley marches past me, a quiver of arrows attached to her hip, a bow made of redwood to match her hair clutched in her left hand.

I clutch Dimitri's journal in my right hand and move to the

railing. Fog engulfs us, floating across and around and through. It's like dry-ice smoke but thinner. A ghost's shadow. Does Flint bear a unique Calling that allows him to find his way blindly? What category would such a gift fall under?

Everyone seems to be dressed in their best. Not gala fancy, more business casual. Collared shirts, slacks, a few ties. Apparently Countess Ambrose is someone to impress. Even Tide, who stocks packs with sandwiches and canteens, has swapped his trademark board shorts for khakis and a polo shirt.

I glance down. Frown. I dug through the trunk containing my things and found the sundress I wore to my eighth-grade graduation. It's a little too tight, pinching my underarms, the middle buckling in places. But at least it falls past my knees. I dressed it up with a cardigan, leggings, and flats. It'll have to do.

Not sure what else to do, I open the journal and turn to the place I left off. But then I change my mind and flip forward several chapters. I know it's here somewhere. I made a mental note of it back in Joshua's study. I lick my thumb, flip one, two, three—aha! I knew it. Perfect.

Twenty-Eighth Day, Tenth Month, Tenth Year of Count VonKemp.

Perhaps the most interesting discovery I have made upon my return to the Fourth Reflection is a substance I am respectively terming "mirrorglass."

Yes!

I have not been here since I was a boy, and the Fourth's beaches are teeming with it. Where did it come from? Was it here when I was a child? The residents have not paid it much mind. I took it upon myself to ask Count VonKemp if I might be at liberty to study the stuff. He allowed it and I have been cooped up in this cramped room for a number

*of months, examining the substance's properties. While my
original intention was to merely pass through the Fourth,
as this is my place of birth, and head straight to the Fifth,
I am fascinated by my newfound discovery and cannot yet
bring myself to move on.*

Sounds like Mom when she was working on a difficult paint-ing. Once she put her mind to it, there was no getting her away from her studio. I had to practically pry her brush out of her hand to get her into the sun once.

Findings:

*Lightweight but strong. Looks like glass, but upon testing
proves to be extremely durable and difficult to break.
   Will not melt when put through mortal fire. (Note for
future study: Might Dragon fire have a different effect?)
   Appears to have a reverse effect of some sort. When
sharp pieces were used to cut the surface of skin, the wound
immediately healed upon drawback.*

I sigh my frustration and turn a page. I know all of this already. Surely there must be something new—

The ship shudders, drawing my gaze level. Streak, Tide, and Gunner lower the anchor as one. Flint skirts the wheel and stands beside Ky. They exchange a cryptic look I can't decipher.

"There it is." Khloe stands to my left. She looks like a doll in her cornflower-blue pinafore dress and Mary Janes.

I knit my brows and snap the journal closed.

"Look closer." She gestures out to sea. Toward nothing.

I squint in the direction of her extended finger. Nothing. Nothing. Noth— Wait. There. Beyond the gray. Something . . . Is that . . . ?

What appears to be a stone arch juts from the middle of the ocean. Jagged rocks loom just beyond, blocking our path. But then the fog parts. Yes. I see it now. The arch leads to something else. It's a gateway. Those aren't just rocks.

They're stairs.

Tide flanks my right. He and Khloe exchange grins. Together they say, "Welcome to the Bermuda Triangle."

cross the bridge

I've seen an underground lagoon hidden beneath the subway. Witnessed humans morph into beasts and vice versa. Walked through mirrors. Fashioned a façade. Transformed into a butterfly. Taken on the Verity. But this? A stairwell in the middle of the Atlantic? At the brink of the Bermuda Triangle?

This is the stuff of legend. Unreal.

What else is there to discover beyond what I've seen? There's so much I don't know about all of this—the Reflections, the Callings, the Void, and the Verity.

But I want to know. I inhale a sharp breath and glance at Ky, braced against the upper-deck railing, elbows locked, knuckles white as latte foam. He could be a statue for how granite-still he stands, expression unyielding. In this moment, he looks more like the stately, cautious Joshua rather than the passionate, take-action guy he is. I don't know why, but the idea turns my saliva to acid.

Weird. I used to loathe Ky. But then . . . I didn't. He's not who I thought he was. He's not who *others* think he is. But I doubt he cares what they think. Ky isn't the type who allows opinions to define him.

His gaze flashes to mine and a muscle in his jaw twitches.

My breath hitches against my will.

A demi-plié smile bows his lips. Flint skirts the wheel, drawing Ky's attention away, and both men bend their heads together. Their hair color is so similar—like caramel-streaked honey. They could almost be brothers. Same peachy skin tone scarred by acne. Same height and build. It's possible. Ky was adopted. Who knows if he has biological siblings he's never met.

I squint, trying to find other similarities between the two. Their lips barely move as they converse. Ky shakes his head. Flint pinches the bridge of his nose. I strain to hear, but the task proves futile. They're too quiet. In fact, it's *all* too quiet.

Something is offbeat.

I scan my surroundings, take in the subtle changes. Normally, the sea's playlist loops at random—*lap, whoosh, spray . . . whoosh, spray, lap.* Seagulls squawk during the commercial break. Wood *tick-click-creaks* in the background. But now? It's as if the layered tracks have been muted. The absence of sound unnerves me.

A hand claps my shoulder. I look right and Streak stares down at me. "Are ya ready, Butterfly?"

I wink at him as if to say, "Aye." Since the crew has seen my Mask, they've gained a new respect for me. I feel less like an outsider and more like . . . well . . . one of the crew.

Streak tromps past me, followed by Charley and Gunner. All three traipse up the steps to join the captain and his pilot. Before I can follow, invited or not, Tide's hand squeezes my bicep. I'd almost forgotten he and Khloe were here. Ebony joins us, turning our trio into a quartet. Her gaze finds Tide and rests there. Is that admiration I see?

Tide leans into me, slides a hand to the far corner of his mouth. "This is bad." His peppermint breath gives me the sudden craving for a candy cane.

"You think?" Khloe twists a frizzy curl around one finger. Despite my younger sister's snarky words, not a trace of sarcasm laces her tone.

Maybe she's like Ebony. But perhaps Khloe and I have some things in common as well.

Tide shifts and laughs, a rich, rumbling sound that reminds me of Kuna. And just like my old friend, Tide finds a reason to smile at a time no one else can.

I miss you, Kuna.

"I mean, worse than bad," Tide says. "This is a problematic situation of epic proportions."

"Don't be so dramatic." Ebony flips her hair.

"My brother will know what to do." Khloe floats away, head held high, not a worry weighing her petite shoulders. Her faith in Ky fills me with unexpected warmth, spreading across my chest, traveling the length of my arms.

Ebony and I exchange a glance. We've fulfilled our Kiss of Accord. She's helped me strengthen my abilities, and I helped her escape. We've no obligation to one another now. No reason to stand so near.

But neither of us moves away. Ebony reaches over, sticks her fingers into the collar of my sweater.

I eye her.

"Your tag was sticking out. You're welcome."

Then I smile. And she smiles. Different from when we were fake friends. This is authentic. Real.

A beginning.

Ebony looks away as if it's too much too fast, so I peek sideways at Tide. Chew on the inside of my cheek.

He shoves his hands into his pockets. It must be obvious what I wish I could ask because he says, "The stairs." He jerks his head, directing my attention toward the rocks. "They're not supposed to be above the surface. The arch isn't either, just its crown. Most of what you see now is usually hidden by ocean, only visible through a window belowdeck."

I yank my cardigan tighter around me. Hug my chest.

"The entire ocean won't drain," he continues. "Because of its unique source in the Verity, Threshold water is comprised of energies rather than elements. You follow?"

I shake my head.

"Hard to explain. Basically, if a Threshold is part of a larger body of water, and the source of that Threshold's energy is cut off . . . only the Threshold water would drain—vanish. It would create a wormhole"—Tide withdraws a hand from his pocket and slices a circle in the air with his open palm—"in the end, leaving a circular waterfall in the middle of the larger body of water. An opening leading to who knows where. You could end up at the far corners of the Seventh or loop back here. Got it?" Fascination shadows his trailing voice.

Whoa. Not only did Tide flip the switch from laid-back surfer dude to all-knowing professor, but my mind has literally bent. Backward. Twice. Nope. I'm thinking about what he said again . . . and . . . make that three times.

That's when Ky joins us. I feel him before I see him. The heat at my back. Breath at my neck. His sudden nearness arrests my pulse. I avert my eyes.

Ky clears his throat. "Change of plans. We eat now. Take no extra weight or supplies. What do we have prepared?"

Lyrics to a popular eighties song scream across my brain. *"Don't stand, don't stand so, don't stand so close to me."*

"I can reheat the pot of chowder from last night." Tide is already stepping away, moving toward the galley. "Give me fifteen minutes." He's gone then, disappearing beyond the galley door.

"I'll help, I guess." Ebony takes reluctant steps after Tide.

Helping someone without getting something in return? She's changed. Softened. There may be hope for my sister after all.

I half expect Ky to leave as well. Instead he shifts closer. Our shoulders touch. Neither of us acts to break the connection.

"Change into something you can easily move in." The hands clasped behind his back release and his arm swings, his knuckles brushing mine. "We no longer have a need to maintain formalities for Countess Ambrose's sake."

Why? Thump, thump, thump. Drum line in my ears.

He wiggles his fingers and they collide with the backs of mine. An accident? I twitch but make no effort to back away. "Because," Ky says, "we're not entering the Fourth as her guests at this point."

I wait.

"I'm not sure what we'll find in the Fourth, but we enter expecting the worst." His voice changes key on "worst," bordering on baritone. He looks at me then, and I turn my head, searching his eyes. His face. He seems to do the same with me as his Adam's apple dips. "I don't suppose I can ask you to remain here?" An arched eyebrow.

The tiny hairs on my hand—the one touching his—raise. I shake my head. *I'm in this.*

He nods. "Good. We need you. But be prepared. With the Threshold this low I can't even guarantee the Fourth is where we'll end up."

I return his nod, and then, before I know what I'm doing, I entangle my fingers with his, squeeze his hand in silent thanks.

And there it is. There *he* is. That smile. The mischief behind those two-tone eyes. Ky is Ky. Not a trace of Joshua in sight.

Before the whole Kiss of Infinity-slash-mirrormark-slash-Verity's vessel thing, I'd never been chosen for anything. Granted, I never cared when it came to sitting on the sidelines. Why whine about not getting picked to play PE soccer? More time to do homework at school, which meant more time with Mom—and later on, Joshua—at home. Back then, I'd rather write a report than partici-pate any day.

But that was then. When I never knew what it was to be part of a team. To belong. To have people need me.

Is this what I've been missing?

My stomach is full and warm from Tide's leftover chowder. But the comforting sensation doesn't last as Streak and Flint work on opposite sides of the lifeboat to lower us into the sea. Some of the crew remain on board the ship. Normally we'd take the *Seven Seas* straight through the Threshold. I guess it sort of sucks the ship through and pops it out the other end.

I've only been through a Threshold once before, and the memory is hazy. I thought I was being dragged through from one side to the other, but was the Threshold actually propelling me? I wouldn't be surprised, given the glowing green light that made the water seem alive. The light—I can only speculate—was a result of the Threshold's source in the Verity.

I gaze through the stone arch and toward the stairs, searching for the same green light in this Threshold. Nothing. With each jerk of the boat my stomach drop, drop, drops and then settles as we hit the water with a *splash*. I'd much rather stay aboard our much safer and sturdier ship, but Ky explained it's safer to leave it here until we know what we're walking—i.e., swimming—into. I'm surprised Khloe isn't remaining back as well. She's just a kid. Surely she'd be safer if we left her here.

Sea sprays my back, squirts into my ears. I lift my arm and swipe at my damp cheeks with my sweatshirt sleeve, burrow down into my hooded collar. Dimitri's journal, wrapped in cords and thick plastic, presses against my rib cage. I couldn't leave it behind. I need to know more about mirrorglass and, well, anything else that might aid us on our journey.

The boat rocks one way, then the other. It's impossible not to lean against the person beside me for support, who just so happens to be Ebony. She doesn't seem to mind, though, because she leans into me too.

Flint and Streak grab oars and row toward the stone stairs. Heave, lift, *slap*. Heave, lift, *slap*.

I should be terrified of what lies beneath those steps. But, strangely, a little thrill jolts through me the closer we get. Ky said they need *me*. Whatever we find in the Fourth, or wherever, we'll find it together.

Seawater sloshes into the boat as the weather awakens. Clouds swirl and lightning blinks beyond the gray, though I can't hear thunder above my pounding heart. My seat is now soaked, but it doesn't matter. I'll be sopping in a minute anyway. The stairs aren't for walking down. They're simply a swimmer's guide. In a larger body of water like this, I imagine it'd be easy to go off course once beneath the surface.

It takes longer than I expect to reach the stone arch. The air isn't cold, but the water saturating my clothes makes it seem colder than it is. At least I changed into a hoodie and jeans. Not as if it makes much difference. Wet is wet, dress or not.

We pass beneath the arch, and the boat dips down a mini waterfall, the air shifting around us. I breathe in, relaxed by the scent of wood smoke drifting on the night air. I'm suddenly warm again. And dry. Blink, blink. Gasp. A hurricane-ready sky no longer looms above. Instead, thousands of twinkling stars dome the atmosphere, dot a Yankee-blue sky.

Joshua would love this, and not just because the sky's color is reminiscent of his favorite baseball team. He loves stars. As long as I've known him, his gaze has never failed to drift skyward at night.

What would it have been like to be raised in the Second with him? Would we have played music on top of his trome back at the Haven, rather than on the roof of my Manhattan brownstone? What if our lives hadn't been so complicated? What if he hadn't kissed me as a baby? Would we still—somehow, someday—have fallen in love?

And it's that single question that makes me realize, no matter what, I will always care deeply for Joshua. Choice or not, a part of me will forever belong to him. Nothing can change this simple truth. It's as set in stone as Excalibur was.

"Until the right person came along and removed it."

I sweep my gaze diagonally across the boat, toward Ky. His right arm circles his sister's shoulders, but he's not looking at her. He's looking at me. A frown draws his entire face, from eyebrows to lips.

My heart wrenches. Why does this have to be so hard?

His gaze lowers, eyelashes that shouldn't belong to a boy brushing the tops of his cheeks.

I long to know what he's thinking. And I can, if I really desire it. For the first time I will his thoughts to be heard without him sending them toward me. I focus. Listen.

Ky grins at his knees. His thoughts become clear.

And. Now. I'm. Blushing.

You thought that on purpose. I'm scolding him, but also not.

He shrugs. *"Can't help it, Em. It's only natural to want to—"*

I cover my mind's ears. *Stop. Don't go there.*

"As you wish."

Sigh. My favorite line from *The Princess Bride.*

Wait, no. Stop. Not now. I will not think of Ky as Westley. I will not think of Ky as—

The boat bumps the stairs, and the invisible link between us vanishes. Streak heaves a coil of thick rope over the boat's edge and loops it around the top step. He leans back, pulls the rope tight, and nods toward Tide.

The boat rocks as Tide rises and leaps into the water. He dives out of view for a full minute before reemerging. When he does, I'm smiling, reminded of Kuna once more. Tide's a Mask, and a water creature at that. I shake my head at the dolphin and think of Stormy. She should be here. My heart aches for my best friend. I wish I could've brought her with me. Is she back to her old, spunky self? I hope so.

Ky moves to follow Tide, but Flint stops him. "I'll go first. Better a pilot captured than a captain. Just in case."

It looks as if Ky might protest, but Flint stares him down. After a second Ky leans back and Flint jumps in the water, grabs hold of Tide's dorsal fin. They dive together while we wait. Ky doesn't look my way again, and no one else makes eye contact either. Everyone is on edge. I feel it in the tension of Ebony's shoulder against mine, in the awkward, deafening silence.

Several minutes later, Tide returns with a thumbs-up. He takes Sam—er, Gunner—down next. Then Charley, followed by Ebony. Member by member, the boat empties. A few are people I've seen around the ship but don't know by name. In the end only Streak, Ky, Khloe, and I are left. Ky is next, but before he enters the water he locks eyes with mine and thinks, *"See you on the other side."*

See you, is all I can think. Why is my stomach in knots?

When he's gone, I begin counting in my head. So far the

longest it's taken Tide to make a round trip has been four minutes and thirty-nine seconds.

At two minutes I take a deep breath. Still plenty of time.

At three minutes I lean forward, peer over the boat's edge. Khloe mirrors my move.

At four minutes I swallow. Where are they?

When we hit the five-minute mark, I glance between Khloe and Streak. The way he flexes his jaw tells me he's nervous too. Khloe, whose faith in her brother could move mountains, even shows worry in the tightness framing her brown eyes.

Then a sensation like a punch to the gut brings me to my knees. My face feels as if it's been pummeled and the skin at my neck stings. My sudden agony is the first sign something is wrong. Because the pain is not my own. It belongs to him, but we're separated by Reflections. Again.

Six minutes. Seven. Eight.

Tide does not return.

ACT III

I see the Light

THIRTY-TWO

The fog Has Lifted

Khloe peers farther over the boat's edge. Streak moves. I rise.

The shift in gravity registers first, not externally but internally. It's similar to the feeling I had the first time I stepped through my own reflection. A distinct change only I would notice. Quickened pulse. Heightened awareness expanding to all five senses. Lyrics to a song I haven't heard in forever play in my mind's forefront. I never thought Zedd's "Clarity" made much sense, but now I wonder if the DJ-turned-record producer was on to something.

Because for every tragedy or crisis, every obstacle or barrier, there's been one remedy, one thing—one *person*—who's given me utter and complete clarity. Joshua's calming was instant, but never lasted. And Ky? He's *"the piece of me I wish I didn't need."* But I do, and I won't lose him. Again.

And just like that, the fog clouding my brain lifts.

The boat *knock, knock, knocks* against the top of the stairs. Streak straddles a bench, loosening us, readying to row back to the *Seven Seas*. Frizzing dreads slap his face, and his biceps flex as he heaves the rope into the boat. *Grunt. Thunk.* He's a silver screen pirate incarnate, from his tattoo sleeves to his yellowed teeth. But I'm not afraid of *him*. No, there are far worse things to fear. Like insignificance. Or having the opportunity to act and not seizing it.

"Brave girl. My brave, brave girl." The pride in Mom's voice carries on her words remembered.

A grin surfaces in response to the Scrib within—to the memory

I recognize as part of my Calling. I always saw Mom as perfect and porcelain, but perhaps I'm more like her than I believed. Her words are etched onto my soul. And no matter where she is, I'm certain she'd still want me to be brave. To do whatever I can to help the others.

Khloe picks her way toward me, distracting me from the silent conversation. My gaze attends her, but my heart listens for Ky.

When she reaches me, she folds her arms and without pretense asks, "What's the plan, El?"

Good question. I press my forefingers to my temples and close my eyes. Ky believes in me. He's saved me time and time again. Now it's my turn. But how can we make it through the Threshold without drowning? Tide was our one-way bullet train into the Fourth. The shallow waters of The Pond, or even the lagoon beneath the subway, were one thing. But the ocean's bed is miles down. We'd die before reaching the bottom, let alone the other side. I've never been there and without Ky's hand in mine, I can't mirror walk my way in.

"Khloe can help."

My lashes snap skyward. I don't even flinch at Ky's direction. His voice in my head is as second nature as singing used to be. I look to Khloe.

Her brown eyes twinkle. "So it's real." Not a question. A confirmation.

My head tilts.

"And here I thought it was only a theory." She laughs.

Did I miss the joke? I glance over her shoulder. Streak rows, puffing through pursed lips. We're nearing the stone arch. Beyond the opening, a storm batters the main ship. Loose sails flap and snap. Someone I can't identify waves his arms wildly from the deck.

"Don't look so surprised," she says. "I saw your expression just now. I've been watching you on the ship too. You shared a Kiss of Infinity with my brother. The connection between you is real." Khloe's words release in a rush. She loses balance and I grab her elbow to steady her.

I move my lips, though no sound emerges, hoping she can read them. *What's. Your. Calling?*

She leans in, peering at Streak, then back at me. "Watch." She takes my hand, yanks hard.

Streak shouting, "Stop, lasses!" is the last sound I hear before my ears flood. The frigid water smashes into me like hundreds of bee stings pelting my body. I claw for the surface, but an unseen weight drags me deeper.

Wham! My head meets something solid. The boat's side? A rock? I'm abruptly reminded of where I am. I gasp for air, but invite a mouthful of ocean instead. The salty water stings my nose and throat, burns as it fills my lungs. I feel my head, but it's impossible to decipher if my hair is damp with blood or water. What was Khloe thinking?

And where is she?

"Stop. Wait."

Ky's voice is my only reassurance. I'm blind. And dizzy. Spots dance before my waterlogged eyes. The pressure on my lungs is too much. I. Need. Oxygen.

But then, just as quickly as it began, the pain eases. I'm no longer choking, and somehow I can breathe, though it feels un-natural. Heavy. As if I'm constantly drinking but never feeling the need to stop and inhale.

This makes no sense. I'm still underwater. I shouldn't be able to— A hand tugs on mine. My head whips left. My heart swells at the sight of Khloe. She's okay and she's . . . smiling? She's—

Khloe. Has. Gills.

I touch my neck. Gasp. Bubbles rise.

I have gills too. How is this possible?

My question will have to wait. Our hands release and we swim freely, but together. Keep close to the descending stone steps, using them as a guide. And then, there it is, the pinprick of green light alerting us to the Threshold's opening. It's faint as if fading with the Threshold's drainage, but it's there.

We swim faster, harder, my heart *beat, beat, beating* as we dive straight through the light. I know we've reached the Fourth when we're suddenly headed up instead of down, following another set of stone steps. Except these are different. Where the steps in the Third were infested with barnacles and seaweed, these are inlaid with precious stones in greens and golds.

When we reach the surface, we crawl up the remainder of the steps onto the landing and collapse. My sodden clothes anchor me to stone.

Khloe props herself up on her elbows. "Bet you've never seen a Shield do that before."

I shake my head, wet hair clinging to my skin.

"It's pretty neat, huh? And it's not just gills. I can adapt to any climate. Change my blood from warm to cold in the desert. Grow fur in a blizzard. Bones taught me how to project my Calling onto others too. It's how I could give you gills like me."

Bones? Ebony taught her this? So this is what they were doing on deck this morning. Practicing.

Too cool. I'm so asking Ebony to teach me ASAP. How awesome would it be if I could project mirror walking?

I wring my hair out and take in our surroundings. We're on a miniature island in an ocean, and a rope bridge extends from the landing to a rocky shore. My gaze follows the bridge. To shore. To—

Myriad emotions wash over me at once. Shock. Pain. Relief. Confusion. I bolt up and crouch in front of Khloe, shielding her like the flesh and blood she is.

Fourth Reflection Guardians line the stone shore beyond the bridge. They're darker skinned like Kuna and Tide. A mixture of men and women. Barefoot. Dressed for a party in their multi-colored sarongs and togas. All bear tattoos on their right biceps, though from this distance I can't tell what the tattoos depict.

Past the Guardian line, a massive Roman-style palace towers, complete with marble columns and a statue of a regal-looking woman in a toga. Archaic symbols I can't read are carved in swirling patterns on the columns and steps. Just like the gems glistening underwater, the symbols are also gold and green. In the distance to the east and west I spy mountain peaks white as cappuccino foam, their snowcaps out of place in this tropical climate. This is the Fourth? It's grander than anything I've imagined but also familiar in a way that feels like home.

Khloe pokes my back, popping my awestruck bubble. I blink rapidly, concentrate on the Guardian line. Each one has a weapon drawn and ready. Spears, knives, bows, swords. Some restrain our crew members. Charley. Flint. Ebony. Gunner. Tide. And is that . . . ? It is. Gage? He's the one restraining Tide. How did he get here and why?

My mind wants to examine the possibilities, to connect the dots. But then I zero in on the line's center and forget them all.

Two men stand there, one behind the other. Ky is in front, beaten and bruised. His right shirtsleeve is torn, revealing his Void-encompassed arm. Even from here the blood on his swollen lips is visible.

Anger surges through my veins, electrocutes my nerves. I'm on my feet, sprinting across the rope bridge. When I'm halfway between landing and shore, the man detaining Ky steps from behind him.

My heart stops, but my feet keep moving.

"El," Joshua calls. Relief softens his cerulean gaze. For a moment I almost don't notice he's holding a sword to Ky's neck.

He's holding a *sword* to Ky's *neck*.

I step ashore, mere feet away from them. My arm reaches, shaking in a desperate plea. *Stop. Please. Release him.*

"El?" Confusion creases Joshua's forehead. His sword hand lowers a fraction of an inch.

But it isn't low enough.

I swallow. Strain to find my voice. The first word I've uttered in days rasps from my lips, loud enough for my ears alone.

"Ky."

THIRTY-THREE

Living in a Blur

All eyes attend us. No one moves. The only sound is water lapping shore, combined with the pulse *tap, tap, tapping* my eardrums in perfect eight counts. We're center stage and our audience waits with breath bated.

"Go back, Khloe," I croak.

"No." I'm not facing her, but there's no denying the tears wavering her voice.

My throat burns worse than ever, so I wave my arm frantically, gesturing for her to get the crowe out of here.

Three, two, one . . .

Splash!

Sigh. At least she isn't as stubborn as her brother.

"El-i-yan-a Em-ber." Joshua enunciates each syllable. Slowly. Carefully. It's as if he's unsure my name and I are one and the same. "It's me."

My right foot slides back, followed by my left. I'm distinctly aware of Ky's mirrorblade tucked into the back of my jeans. I grabbed it before we left, uncertain what the Fourth would bring. Now I have the urge to reach for it but can't quite bring myself to follow through. This isn't Joshua. At least not the one I know. My Joshua is a good guy. A hero. But the man before me is a stranger, cut from the same cloth as Haman or Jasyn or Gage—men molded by weapons and cruelty and revenge.

Gage stands only a few feet to Joshua's right, the only other man here from the Second. Are they together? No. No way.

"What are you doing?" The words are hardly audible. I clear my throat. Who knows how long my voice will last, but I'll take what I can get.

Joshua's brow furrows. The arm holding the sword to Ky's neck trembles. "El, you're confused. But everything will be fine now. I am here. Everything will be fine."

Is his repeated phrase to assure me or himself?

The blade connects with Ky's skin. Blood seeps and drips.

I wield the knife. My arm remains as steady as Ky's unblinking gaze.

"Stay there," he says in my head.

My entire being aches to give Joshua a taste of his own sword, but I stay put.

"Trust me." Joshua's uneven tone mirrors his shaking hand. "Everything will be fine."

Fury flares. Everything is so not fine right now it disgusts me.

"Easy now," Ky warns. "Don't make him angrier than he already is."

Right. "Joshua," I breathe. "Listen. I was wrong to leave without telling you."

And you were wrong to keep Ky's letter from me, I want to add. But I sense now is not the time to demand his apology.

So I give mine instead. "I'm sorry. But it isn't Ky's fault." I gesture toward him, my palm out in surrender. "Let's talk about this." I force a melody beneath my words for good measure. It feels stronger now somehow. Odd. If the Callings are dwindling and the Thresholds drain more each day, wouldn't I be weaker?

"Not necessarily. If the Verity is growing weak, I presume it would be drawing power back to itself."

My eyes widen. What?

"My guess is that each time a Calling disappears, the Verity recharges a little, making it seem strong again. It's having to do less, expel less energy to source another Calling. But it's only temporary unless we can destroy the Void."

Intuition tells me to glance behind me.

No!

Khloe floats facedown in the water. I lug her out, back onto the landing. Turn her on her back.

Ky cries out.

My little sister gasps and gurgles, water flowing from the corners of her mouth. I help her sit. Pat her back.

She blinks and touches her neck. "My gills," she sobs. "I was nearly to the bottom when they just vanished."

Shield is down. Crud. Three Callings remain. Magnet, Mask, Scrib. Now I really wish Stormy were here. It might even things out.

"Eliyana."

I face Joshua again. Does he think repeating my name will remind me of who he thinks I am?

"This man . . ."

Is he refusing to say Ky's name to make a point? He's already ruined Ky's alias. Now the entire crew will know who he is. What will this mean? Will they still follow their captain, or will they turn on him the way Joshua seems to have turned on me?

". . . is our enemy, as is anyone who works for him." Joshua widens his stance, steadies his arm. "I am here to rescue you."

"She doesn't need rescuing." Ky spits on Joshua's boot.

He could do more. Ky is taller and just as strong. Even without his Shield to paralyze, he could take Joshua if he wanted to. So why is he just standing there?

"Because I won't harm someone you care about."

Oh. Wow. I don't know what to say—er, think.

"A simple thank you will suffice."

Thank you. I think my gratitude with all my heart, hoping he feels the sincerity.

Ky nods.

Oblivious to our silent connection, Joshua knees Ky's middle. He doubles over but doesn't cry out.

I voice Ky's pain with a sound resonant of a dying cat and lurch forward. Stop. Wrap my arms around myself as if the pain is my own. *"Don't,"* I sing (sort of). *"Please don't hurt him."*

The tune playing on Joshua's face can only be described as a mash-up of disbelief and heartbreak. His sword clangs to the ground. He releases Ky, who falls to his knees.

It worked. My Mirror song worked. Is Ky right? Is the Verity strengthening with each Calling that fades?

Before I can attempt to comprehend the possibility, a woman's voice says, "Well done. Well done indeed." The voice is accented, but not one I can place.

The Guardian wall parts and the tallest woman I've ever seen floats forward as if standing on a moving sidewalk. She must be six five, six four at least. The Knicks would kill to have her in their lineup, female or not. Her floor-length Grecian gown hangs off one shoulder, a train of sateen fabric trailing behind her. The canary yellow of her gown's fabric plays in stark contrast to her coffee-colored skin. The gown is sleeveless, but her toned arms aren't bare. Coral and pearl bracelets wrap her forearms from wrist to elbow, and a triple-tiered pearl choker encircles her ballerina neck. Everything about her begs attention, right up to her lilac eyes and looping Princess Leia braids.

"*She's a Siren,*" Ky informs. "*This is her Mask form.*"

This is Countess Ambrose, ruler of the Fourth.

Her Guardians take a knee.

The countess halts inches away. Examines me as if appraising something for purchase.

I have to crane my neck to meet her gaze. It's difficult to give her my full attention, though, with Joshua ready to tear out Ky's throat. Ky says he won't hurt Joshua, but what if it came down to life or death? They need to be placed in separate corners before one of them needs more than a Physic can do at this point.

"You must be Eliyana." Countess Ambrose's voice is deep and rich and full of warmth. Like hot chocolate, if it had sound. "Joshua speaks so very highly of you. It is my pleasure to make your acquaintance." She offers her hand, holding it palm down just above my head.

I clench my teeth. My throat aches. I take her hand and curtsy.

Countess Ambrose withdraws her grip, which is not as dainty as it appears, and one corner of her mouth lifts. With eyes fastened to mine, she says, "He tells me you and the rest of this crew were headed here on false pretenses. Is this true?"

False—what? I shake my head. "We're here to seek your help." Ugh, my vocal cords are sandpaper.

The other side of her mouth twists into a wicked grin, as if she and I share a secret. A quarter turn and then, "Let me be clear. I do not tolerate liars in my court." Her expression may stream sweetness, but an undercurrent of steel resonates in her tone. "It appears your captain is the vessel of the Void, and a danger to everyone. He kept this little detail from me upon his prior visit. He must be locked away. I'll not have him spreading the Void the way that wretched man from the Second did."

My face must look a thousand shades of oh-snap. Do I tell her Joshua carries the Void as well? That beneath his shirtsleeves, darkness resides? The confession is on the tip of my tongue, but I can't bring myself to turn him in. I just can't.

Ugh, ugh, ugh.

It's Tide who speaks up. "There must be some mistake, Mother."

Mother? *Tide* is Countess Ambrose's son? I suppose I see the resemblance in their skin and eyes, though his demeanor is much more relaxed than her stick-up-her-rear state.

"A mistake indeed." Countess Ambrose peers down her nose at me. "Shall we?"

Swallow. "Sorry?" What is happening?

"Come. You must be starving. And cold. After all, you've been a prisoner of this Void-infested shark for, how many days is it, Joshua?"

"Five days." Joshua's stare bores into mine. "It's been five days since she was abducted from the castle."

If I didn't know any better, I'd say he's challenging me. Has it really been less than a week since I left the Second? Feels like so much longer.

"That's right." Surprise coats her voice, but it's a sham. This isn't new information to her. What game is she playing? "Please"—a side-long glance at me over her bare shoulder—"you are a welcome guest at my palace." She glides in the direction she came, obviously expecting me to follow.

This can't go on. I won't allow Ky, or the others, to take the fall for something they didn't do. "I wasn't a prisoner."

"Weren't you?" Countess Ambrose asks, her voice rising an octave.

"No," I whisper.

Her steps cease, but she doesn't look my way. "Do you mean to tell me, then, you were with this band of Void-serving pirates by choice?" Do I hear glee in her lilting tone?

"They didn't know Ky held the Void. They're innocent. Let them go." I jog to catch up. Joshua and Ky are now only feet away, Joshua to the countess's left and Ky to her right.

How can I choose between them? Joshua is only trying to protect me. Even so, what are good intentions when they harm others? I stand beside Ky, who's still on his knees. My hand finds his shoulder. "But I knew. And I was with him of my own free will."

Joshua's face is a mask of anger. But I won't let him get away with his lie just so he can imprison Ky and return me to the Second.

Ky straightens but remains on his knees.

Countess Ambrose continues her exit. "Well then, this changes things, doesn't it? Zane, take Miss Ember to the Thatsou Catacombs with the rest of the prisoners. They will have a fair trial in my court on the morrow. We shall see who willingly served the Void or not."

"She doesn't know what she's saying." Joshua matches her pace stride for stride, worry etching the creases around his eyes. "She's confused."

"Now, now." The countess waves her hand dismissively. "We mustn't show favoritism." Before she ascends the palace steps, she adds, "Welcome to Tecre Island, Your Majesty." The "Your Majesty" part is almost a whisper, clearly meant for my ears alone. "Or as you may have heard it called in your Reflection—Atlantis." Wait, what? "I do hope you enjoy your stay."

⸻❦⸻

Atlantis. As in lost city of? I.e., myth? A.k.a. legend? Empire that doesn't exist?

Now I've seen everything.

Atlantis. Just wow.

One of the Fourth's Guardians—Zane, no doubt—flanks my right side, takes my arm, and confiscates my weapon. His grip is firm but gentle, an unexpected reprieve. His right arm bears a band tattoo shaped like rolling waves, and above the band the words "Greatest However Is Water" are inked in deep blue.

"The Fourth's Guardian tattoo and mantra," Ky relays in my mind. *"They hold a deep reverence for water here as Thresholds are sourced by the Verity."*

I nod my internal understanding and return my attention to the Guardian in charge. Zane's shiny bald head and apologetic smile remind me of Kuna, as many things do these days. It was this way when I thought I lost Mom too. I saw her everywhere, in everything.

"I'm afraid you'll have to come with me." The regret in his rumbling accent is unmistakable. He shrugs.

At least I got one of the nice guys. I'm too tired to be pushed and shoved.

With clear effort Ky rises and stands on Zane's other side. The Guardian takes his arm, urges us both forward. One, two . . . ten paces and I'm inches from Joshua. It takes every ounce of courage I have not to shy away from his brooding gaze.

"Can I have a minute?" I ask Zane.

He nods but makes no move to give us privacy.

I don't really need it. The only thing I have to say to him right now isn't for my sake. "The girl." I jerk my head in Khloe's direction. She stands on the island across the bridge. Watching. Waiting. "She's just a kid." Joshua doesn't need to know Khloe is Ky's sister. "I may not have been a prisoner, but she was." The lie comes easily, rolling off my tongue. I only hope Khloe is smart enough to catch on to my plan. "Watch out for her?"

Joshua doesn't make eye contact. His jaw works. "Of course."

Exhale. I glance between Joshua and Gage. Gage and Joshua. "Working with the enemy now?"

Joshua avoids my gaze. His silence is answer enough.

Now for the hard part. I slip Joshua's ring off my finger and push it into his palm. "I can't wear this. Not now."

He flinches. Tucks both hands into his pockets.

My own coldness stings, but what does he expect? How can I marry a man who would go to such lengths? Who would hurt innocents just to get to me? Who would lie about his own darkness but allow Ky to be imprisoned for the exact same thing? I almost remove my treble clef–heart necklace, too, but can't quite bring myself to do it. This necklace is a sober reminder of what I'm leaving behind.

The stony look in Joshua's eyes takes me back to a day last November. "I. Do. Not. Love. You," he'd said.

It was a lie then, one spoken to protect me. If I asked how he feels today, would I receive the same answer? More importantly, would it affect me the same way it did then? Would my heart break in two, or would I feel a weight lift?

As Zane leads us away, the most terrifying realization of all hits me full force.

I have no idea.

I peek over my shoulder one last time. Joshua doesn't watch me leave. Doesn't say good-bye. And I have no clue if the ache inside is for him or for me. Because even though no words are uttered, it *feels* like a good-bye. An ending. A permanent, irrevocable change.

A single tear escapes, blurs my vision for a moment. But no more follow. I have no more to give.

THIRTY-FOUR

HOW BLIND I'VE BEEN

The uneven, stony shore blends into smooth, sandstone-paved ground. We approach the palace but don't enter. My breath hitches as we pass it by. At the crest of the marble steps, situated between the engraved columns, are two towering doors that appear to be made of broken seashells. The mosaic glitters and winks as the sun peers between clouds overhead. Above the doors the words "Palace of Sonsosk" are etched into a marble plaque. Like the Second Reflection, the Fourth is a blend of worlds new and old. Ancient Greece meets beach resort.

Too bad this is anything but a vacation.

Zane leads us around the palace's side. Ky and I bump elbows as we fall in line behind him. We're both still completely soaked, clothes sticking to skin in odd places. Not so different from the first time we passed through a Threshold together, but somehow a thousand Reflections away.

Odd how much he's changed. Or maybe *he* hasn't. Maybe what's altered is *my* perspective. Perhaps now I'm seeing him as he is. Not just the reflection of him, as seen through jaded eyes, but the real Ky. The Ky he's always been.

I'm sorry.

"*Don't be.*" He elbows my side. Half smiles.

No, I think, hoping he hears my remorse. *I've spent my life hating that all people saw was my birthmark. They took one look at me and put me in a category and never took the time to really see me for me.*

"*You still don't get it.*" He shakes his head. "*You think people need*

to look past your mirrormark to see you. But your mark is a part of you.
Love isn't about ignoring the pieces we don't like. It's about accepting the
complete and beautiful whole. See yourself as I see you. Inside and out."
I'm speechless—thoughtless. *Ky* . . .

Before I can think my response, my attention is lured else-
where. The clouds thin and the sun blares high overhead. I shade
my eyes and blink. Smaller buildings dot the area on all sides, as
attractive as the palace with their marble steps and engraved columns, but not nearly as grand. I do a 360 and glimpse the palace
in the distance. How long have we been walking?

We navigate the buildings—homes?—turning right here, left
there. Then we're standing in a marketplace square and, beyond
the homes, a main road stretches along a canal. An arrow sign that
reads "Rahkerlion Canal" points toward it. Merchants sell wares
and shopkeepers dust stoops. Children run and chase and laugh.
Women with swaddled babies chat and sway.

It reminds me of—

The Haven. And I see this place is, in a way, just another
Reflection. Another version of my world. Somewhere beyond the
rainbow. Except I'm no Dorothy and this isn't Oz. We're prisoners,
wide awake with no hope of discovering this has all been a dream.
Things worked out in the end with Jasyn. This time, I'm not so sure.

I want to get a closer look, to experience this new world and
compare and contrast the similarities and differences, but this
isn't a welcome tour. Zane bears a sharp right, leading us down
an abandoned alley. The scent in the air shifts from freshly salted
to dank and mildew tainted. Our path is so narrow we walk in a
straight line now, me sandwiched between Zane and Ky.

A glance up reveals our presence here hasn't gone unnoticed.
More than one curtain flutters in the windows above, fingers
curled around cloth as onlookers peer down at us from their shadowed dwellings.

My pulse accelerates. The tension in the air is tangible, heavier than the moisture weighing our clothes and hair. Something
tells me it isn't mere curiosity that has the natives spying on us.

"It's fear." Ky's true and audible voice makes me jump, his breath raising the hairs on my neck. "They're afraid of me. Of the Void in their midst."

Little do they know another vessel of the Void walks free and clear among them. My anger at Joshua rises from hot to scalding.

At the end of the alleyway lies a trapdoor. Zane lifts it and gestures as if to say, "After you." Ky moves ahead of me and takes the stairs first. I follow close behind. Zane takes his place at the rear and the door slams, echoing through the narrow passage. Our footsteps clap and echo. I shudder.

When we reach the bottom of the long, straight stairway, the scent in the air shifts. It's musty and smelling of sewer. It is, in fact, a sewer. Soft light shines through grates high above, casting shadows. An underground river swishes and tumbles, moving so quickly it would drown anyone who fell in. We walk along the wall beside the river, watching our steps. When I trip, Zane catches my arm and smiles. He's not a bad guy then, just another Guardian doing his job.

Finally, we reach an alcove in the wall that isn't an alcove at all, but a hallway. At the end is a door with three bars lining a small, high window. Zane reaches the door and knocks three times. A man appears, narrows his eyes, and then grunts. The door groans open, mimicking the man's irritated sound. We pass through and the door slams.

I expect to see dungeon cells similar to the ones in the castle but find something opposite. Other. So very Atlantis. On either side of us, small caves, their mouths covered with walls of coral, wait. No door cut into the coral, just a small space between the wall and cave ceiling. How do prisoners get in and out?

We halt at the last cell. "This is the part I hate," Zane says.

"The coral," Ky says before I can ask. "It's poisonous?" He eyes Zane, then looks at me. "We have to climb over."

Zane grunts, jaw tensing.

I gawk. Joshua can't possibly know about this. It sickens me he'd do this to Ky, but he'd never allow anything to hurt me.

Would he?

Ky shrugs. Then he grasps the coral with both hands.

And everything stops. Because Ky is in agony, which means so am I. Even if I couldn't feel his physical turmoil, his pain would still belong to me. He cries out, but still he doesn't let go. The anguish splices through me. In the past I'd be worried for Joshua, but now I almost hope he feels this. That he experiences every jab and convulsion.

The thoughts raise a new sensation. My right arm hasn't been hurting as much since boarding the *Seven Seas*, but this? Now? It's unlike anything I've suffered. I've never been bitten by a snake, but I imagine this to be ten times worse. It's as if poison has been injected into me, creeping, flowing, taking over my bloodstream. Is this what Ky's feeling now, or something else?

He climbs up and over, attempting to touch the coral with as little of his body as possible. But it doesn't do much good. The poison sears his hands. Burns through his clothing. When at last he collapses inside the cell, his body convulses. His palms are red and swollen. His clothing burned and bloody. The layer beneath his sweater is singed, too, revealing the Void snaking up his arm.

Zane's face is contorted, his mouth upside down.

I don't know whether to puke or scream. What kind of sick game is this? We have to get out of here before things get worse. We have to destroy the Void before the other Callings fail.

"I'm afraid you're next." Zane gestures to the empty cell beside Ky's.

I glare at him. I'm about to transform into a butterfly right here and now, but it'll have to wait until Zane is gone. If he knew I could flit over the coral with the hum of a tune, he'd probably put me in a much smaller cage. One I couldn't fly out of.

This is going to smart.

Deep breath. Hold it. Go.

My hands meet the poisonous cage. I'm up and over the wall, each move depleting my energy, my skin begging me to *stop, stop, stop* because oh my chronicles. *Please, stop. No more. Let go.*

I collapse inside the cell. I'm on my knees. *Stay awake. Don't pass out.*

Ky hisses from his cell. Whether it's inside my head or audible, I can't tell. Our internal conversations are so natural now, the difference is indistinguishable. "The Verity, Em." I can hardly hear him. "It protects you from certain elements. It should've shielded you against the poison."

Why didn't it?

Ky rolls his head to look at me through the small coral window connecting our caves. "I think . . ." He wheezes. "With each Calling that dies, you draw in strength, but you lose things too. As long as the Void lives, connected to the Verity by a Kiss of Infinity, it will drain the Verity. You have to fight it, Em. Don't give in to the darkness. I had to learn after what Tiernan did. It was difficult, but it can be done. Do not allow evil to take over. Overcome it."

I draw in a sharp breath. I hurt. Everywhere. But my right arm burns more than any other body part. I look down, push up my sleeve.

And there, spreading up my arm like a rotting disease, are the blackened veins of the Void.

It's a full hour before I'm strong enough to transform into my Mask. I stand in the corner of my cell and strip off my sweatshirt and jeans. I set Dimitri's plastic-and-cord-wrapped journal aside, wad the jeans, and, using my sweatshirt like a knapsack, tie the sleeves together until it creates a nice fabric ball. Then I throw it and the journal over the wall of my cage, let my Mirror song flow, and turn. This Calling still works, but my butterfly is weak and it takes extreme endurance just to make it over the coral. Then I transform to a human and chuck the clothing wad over Ky's cage wall and repeat my alteration into a butterfly. Once I'm beside Ky, who is thankfully sleeping, I change back and redress, double-checking to assure my Void arm is covered. I'd ask how it's possible, but what does it matter? This is happening and I have no idea what to do to stop it.

The Void has to end. It needs to end now.

I kneel beside Ky, examine him from head to boot. The effects of the poison are receding, wearing off like a drug. Ky's shallow breaths shudder his chest. His eyes twitch behind his lids. His mouth is parted. I'd hoped the Void coming upon me would lessen his burden, but his veins remain charred as ever, though thank the Verity the darkness hasn't spread past his shoulder.

I touch a finger to the indent above his lips, trace their outline. It's rare to see him in such a relaxed state. He looks more like a boy than the man I know him to be. Innocent. Fragile.

I want to stay here beside him, watch him sleep and breathe and live. I want to march up to the surface, find Joshua, and give him a piece of my mind. A few pieces, actually.

But I'm starting to see what I want plays the understudy to the lead role I must act. So I repeat the undressing-transforming-redressing process, flitting to the next cage where Ebony and . . . *Khloe* share a cell.

I'm so boiling now I might bubble over. Joshua said he'd take care of Khloe. What in the Reflections is wrong with him?

The ground shakes as if in response to my quavering heart. An earthquake like the one in the Second? More Threshold water draining? We won't know for sure until we reach the surface again, and we can't do that unless we're able to figure out some blasted way out of this twisted dungeon.

I move toward my sisters. They're huddled together, eyes closed, heads bent. Ebony has one arm wrapped around Khloe. She strokes her hair. The older's lips move and I strain to hear. Is she singing? I've never heard her sing.

It may not have the power to heal or command, but it's beautiful. She lifts her head. Her eyes narrow but then she cracks a smile like the one we shared on deck earlier today. She shakes Khloe gently.

Khloe's eyelashes flutter. When her focus rises to me, she smiles too.

I look over them both, taking Ebony's and then Khloe's hand in mine. Ebony resumes her song and I catch on, learning the simple lyrics in no time. Khloe's head rests on Ebony's shoulder. I scoot in beside my older sister. Our heads tilt and lean against one another as we sing the chorus once more. I've never heard this tune, but I like it. Reminds me of a lullaby. Sweet and soft and soothing.

> *"Down by the river, along the dark path,*
> *The Void cannot find me; I hide from its wrath.*
> *Verity beside me, walk with me, don't stray.*
> *And stay with me always 'til night becomes day."*

As our voices rise, I ponder all that's transpired. My coronation. Kuna's death. Mom and baby Evan going into hiding. The Callings failing. The Thresholds draining. Loving Joshua. Hating Joshua. Feeling obligated to rid Ky of the Void. Finding Ky. Falling in . . .

Holy Verity. "I love Ky."

"Duh," Ebony says, her usual candor awakening. "Are you just now figuring this out?"

I blink. Did I say the words aloud?

Khloe beams at me but remains silent. I look from her to Ebony and back to her. "Don't tell him, okay?"

Ebony and Khloe exchange glances. It's Khloe who says, "He already knows."

I inhale a deep breath. Nod. Leave them be as I move to the next cell, where Charley resides. I check on Gunner and then Flint after him. The final cell beside his is empty, as I expected. Tide is Countess Ambrose's son. Of course she wouldn't imprison him.

When I am alone in the last cell, my thoughts take over. Ky already knows. Of course he does. I was confused for so long, but he never was.

Never.

What does this mean? Where do we go from here?

The ground shakes again, rumbles, cracks. I'm thrown off

balance. Fall. Smack my head on the hard, cold floor. I taste blood in my mouth. My ear throbs.

The earthquake grows in intensity. I try to get up but fail. World tilts. Vision blurs. Loose rock and rubble fall from the walls and ceiling. The coral cages begin to break and crumble. I don't have time to shift and escape the danger. But I don't have to. A hand grabs mine and I'm drawn away from danger into the nearest cave.

The world around us continues to fall and break and end. Ky's embrace is steadfast and tight. I curl into him, my head tucked into his chest. After what seems like ages, the shaking dies. We're breathing hard and fast. I look up into Ky's eyes.

He smiles. "I love you too."

THIRTY-FIVE

Joshua

I stare at my reflection. At what I am becoming. The Void continues to spread. Apart from El, it grows stronger. It won't be long before it's reached my heart. Soon it will be too much to hide with mere clothing. My love for her is deeper than ever, but each day she spends with Kyaphus is another her heart is led astray. Which is another day the Verity's power over me weakens.

I must not become like Jasyn Crowe. I refuse.

El's love for me is a dying flame. I did not aid matters by holding sword to my brother's throat, nor by allowing Gage to join me. But I needed his help to create the diversion. With Gage as my witness it was that much easier to get the countess on board with our story. If I could create fear, panic, and chaos among the Fourth's residents, the rose would be a cinch to swipe. I did not imagine my plan would work out so deliciously. Everything fell into place like the final touches on a carved frame.

I kneeled before the countess. "We've come to warn you of the fugitive known as one Kyaphus 'Ky' Rhyen. He is the Void's—"

She held up a hand to silence me. "The man you speak of left two months ago. He retrieved his sister, left the payment promised by Jasyn Crowe for boarding the girl, and went on his way. He posed no threat to me or my people."

"You have been deceived, madam." Gage stepped forward and knelt beside me.

I was not taken aback by how seamlessly he donned his role as my companion. I was, however, unnerved by the fact that we were working as a unit. Am I on the opposing team? The lines have blurred. It's difficult to decipher which way is left or right anymore. All I know is forward. Forward to separate the Void and the Verity. Forward to separate Kyaphus and El.

"You accuse me of poor judgment?" Offense seeped from Ambrose's tone.

"No, ma'am," I interceded, adrenaline coursing. "We only come as your humble servants to warn you. Perhaps we should alert the people—"

She held up her hand once more. "It is interesting you arrive now, at such a time as this. I do not believe in coincidences." She paced the platform in the center of her amphitheater-style courtroom. "Do you?"

I pressed my lips. What was she getting at?

"Kyaphus has sent word he will return shortly. Can you prove he is the Void's vessel, as you claim?"

"On my honor as a Guardian," I said without pause, "I can."

Turning her back, she peered over one shoulder and added, "Let us hope, for your sake, you are not lying. I do not tolerate perjurers in my Reflection."

She dismissed us and we rose and bowed out, following one of her Guardians down the white marble halls to our temporary quarters. I contained my excitement until I was isolated. Kyaphus, returning here? It was perfect. His letter stated he'd wait for El in the Third, which meant she'd be with him. I couldn't have planned it better if I'd tried. My brother would be trapped in one place, with nowhere to run. El would be delivered right to me. All I needed to do was retrieve the rose, supply it to Isabeau, and exchange it for the mirrorglass bottle. Then I'd return to the Fourth, acquire the final ingredient, and serve the Unbinding Elixir to El. She'd be unbound from my brother by week's end.

I turn to one side and gaze at my profile in the mirror, grinning as I mull over how well everything has gone so far. I have to admit, the Void's not so bad. My muscles are more pronounced, my body built. The black veins could almost be a tattoo—

No. I knock the mirror over and it crashes to the floor. I'm on the room's opposite end in an instant, holding my pounding head in my hands.

What is wrong with me? The Void is an unwelcome menace. Its effects are not something to be admired.

Still . . .

I force my thoughts to take a detour, don my long-sleeved shirt to cover my secret, and focus on the task at hand.

Obtain Isabeau's third and final gift. Find the rose.

Whatever it takes.

I am still unsure whether I have the countess convinced. She's seen Ky's arm, yet her expression exudes skepticism. At least the people are terrified and Ambrose is out smoothing the ruckus I created. The little girl El asked me to keep charge of—Khloe, apparently—turned out to be my brother's adoptive sister, which means she couldn't be trusted. I hated sending her with the other prisoners, but what choice did I have? I can't take any chances, not even with a minor.

Clothed and armed, I exit my chambers. Gage is keeping watch outside, ready to alert me at the first sign of the countess's return. Inside, the palace is like a museum with its Greek architecture and grand paintings. When I turn a corner, the next hall hosts square pools and miniature bridges. Whoever designed this place housed a brilliant mind. What I'd give to create again. To be done with this saving-the-Reflections nonsense and do what I want for a change.

I scratch the back of my head. Where did that come from? Of course I want to save the Reflections. For everyone. For El.

But what about me?

I shake my head as if to physically eject the selfishness from my brain. When this is over I may need a few days' sleep to recover.

I scan the hall. Turn down another. Guardians pass me at random, but no one questions me as I make my way around. Why would they? I'm their guest. The man who alerted them to the intruders and the Void. I can obviously be trusted.

Morons, the lot of them.

What's happening to my mind?

At the next corner I pause. A broad grin spreads. It's too easy. Her most prized possession, displayed for all to see?

The indoor garden is a sight to behold, more striking than any I've witnessed. Wisteria hangs from every balcony and column. Roses blossom in all shades of corals and auburns and golds. Parrots squawk and flap from perch to perch. Flamingos wade in the various lily ponds stationed throughout the naturally lit space.

And at the center of it all sits a platform, and on the platform a pedestal, and on the pedestal a single blue rose the color of the night sky.

One hand on the hilt of my sword, I creep forward. Caution has me aware of what lies in my peripheral vision, but hunger to obtain my prize and move on rushes my steps. This could be a trap. Yet not a single Guardian detains me.

I must be a better thief than I believed. Self-satisfaction fills me. Won't Mistress Isabeau be pleased—?

My steps cease. What am I thinking? What am I *doing*? Did I call Isabeau mistress? Perhaps not aloud, but—

I catch my reflection in the nearest pool and all blood drains from my skull. In the time it took for me to venture from my chambers to the garden, the Void spread. Its vines peek above my shirt collar now, threatening to choke my neck. I recoil from the wavy image, and it's in this moment I see it. The more I justify my wrongful methods, the more I convince myself what I am doing is for the greater good, the more the Void and I become one.

But my intentions are pure. How can the Void take over?

I don't have time to ponder the indications. The ground shakes and the garden begins to come apart around me. The flamingos go haywire, the parrots scream, and the pedestal at the center tips.

That's when I sprint for it. Trap or not, the rose must be taken. It's the only way to obtain the mirrorglass bottle, which is the key to undoing El and Ky's bond. Without the bottle, the second ingredient is useless.

I leap onto the crumbling platform and snatch the rose just before it's crushed by a chunk of ceiling. With the thorny stem between my teeth, I make haste for the nearest exit.

Isabeau had better be grateful. My third and final gift is acquired. This rose had better be worth it.

Of course it's worth it.

El is worth everything.

all at once

You know those moments in life that are pivotal and concrete, while at the same time surreal? Like, I'm here, this is happening, but I also question it.

Is this happening?

Is this real?

"My sincerest apologies, Your Highness." Countess Ambrose furnishes a slight bow of her head as she reaches to help me to my feet. She looks out of place among the settling dust and debris. An angel among wreckage. "You must understand my first priority is my people. I couldn't have them threatened by anyone or anything."

I furrow my brows and nod but don't speak. I'm unsure what to believe at this point. Is this woman to be trusted or another Mom would warn to be chary of?

"Zane," the countess says. "Please assist the other members of the crew."

The Guardian with kindness hidden behind his eyes scoots past us, picking through chunks of ceiling and cage. The task is nothing to his broad arms and legs.

Ky rises beside me. Dusts himself off. His fingers twine easily with mine, as if this is the most natural thing in the Reflections.

I squeeze his hand. *Hi*, I think toward him.

"*Hi*," he thinks back, squeezing my hand in return.

"If you will follow me." The countess turns, her toga swishing. "I believe we have much to discuss."

We follow her out of the dungeons, the remainder of our crew falling into line behind us.

Ky puts an arm around my shoulder, leans in to kiss my temple.

Guess everything is out in the open now. No reason to hide anything anymore.

I peek backward, release a sneeze I can't continue to hold in. Then I breathe a sigh of relief when I see each one of us is accounted for.

Gunner and Flint are a little worse for the wear, their faces and arms matted with blood. Clothing disheveled and dirtied. They actually look more like pirates now. The kind that never bathe.

"You think you look much better?" Ky thinks.

Oh, shut up.

He gives an audible laugh.

Cheeks lifted, I shake my head before looking over my shoulder once more.

Charley walks alone, then behind her my sisters walk hand in hand, Ebony leading our youngest sibling like one might lead a lost child. Both have enough dust in their hair and on their faces, they could be ghosts. I reach up and wipe at my cheeks with my sweatshirt sleeve. When I pull it away, a layer of grime cakes the fabric. *Please let the Fourth Reflection have decent hygiene facilities.*

Up and out of the Thatsou Catacombs we venture, but rather than returning us to the surface, the countess leads us through a door that opens to a long—and when I say long, I mean loooonnnnggggg—set of stairs. They're wide and deep, ornamented with the same green and gold stones on the steps curving through the Threshold. Natural light filters between cracks in the underground ceiling, causing the stones to wink and glisten. Sand coats the steps and the air is misted with salt. This entire Reflection smells like a day at the beach. The stairwell seems miles long, climbing up, up, up, plateauing, and then diving down, down, down. Down? How much deeper can we go?

"Right?" Ky says in my head. *"You'd think we'd be in the heart of the ocean by now."*

I roll my eyes. *Wow.* Titanic *reference. Is that really the best you can do?*

"Aww, c'mon. *That was pretty good.*" He puffs out his chest.

Oh brother.

Winking, he lifts our joined hands to his lips and kisses my fingers.

You win, I think.

Ky's crooked grin goes into full-throttle mode, dimples blazing.

When at last—at last—we reach a circular door that could have totally been stolen from the Shire, Countess Ambrose gives three long knocks followed by two short ones.

I half expect a munchkin to pop through a hole in the door and demand we state our business.

But of course one doesn't. After a few beats the door swings inward, opened by a pudgy little man even shorter than I am. The countess lists her head toward him, then enters a chamber as round as the door. Its walls are made of glass, an entrance identical to the one we arrived through straight across from us. We are indeed beneath the city. If we're not in the heart of the ocean, we're somewhere near it. Sea surrounds us on all sides, the water murky for lack of sunlight. A round table fit for Camelot adorns the chamber's heart. Whoa. Cool.

With a sweeping arm the countess says, "Won't you all please take a seat?"

Ky pulls out a chair for me and I sit. Then Zane catches him by the shoulder. "This is yours." He presses the mirrorblade, hilt first, into Ky's hand.

"Thank you." Ky sheathes his most prized possession and takes the seat beside mine. Our hands find the other beneath the table.

Zane stands at attention off to one side, the pudgy man who let us in flanking his left.

The countess takes her place behind one of the chairs.

I watch her. Something's different. But what?

"She's in her natural human form," Ky thinks. "See how her height has changed? And her eyes?"

My own regard narrows as I consider the woman before us. Ky's right. She's a shorter, less glamorous version of her Siren self. Much more approachable, almost motherly. Her nails tap on the chair's wood. When our gazes lock she gives me a smile far different from the one she offered on the shore.

Three knocks, then two short ones on the opposite door. The doorkeeper shuffles over, the short distance apparently winding him as he huffs and puffs around the table. When he opens the door, several people file in.

A burly man with a beard to his naval and a kilt hanging low under his protruding gut.

A dwarf-sized woman with a squarish head and thick glasses.

A couple in their late fifties, the man thin and balding and the woman exhibiting the rosiest cheeks I've ever seen.

"Thank you all for coming on such short notice." Spreading her arms like wings, the countess says, "Welcome to the Council of Reflections."

Something is wrong with Joshua.

The consensus is unanimous.

"He's clearly out of control." The countess's voice carries throughout the chamber. "I recognized it the moment he entered my court. There's a madness in his eyes. A determination I've seen before."

I wrinkle my brow. Raise my hand.

The countess offers a genuine smile. "You need not raise your hand here, *Queen* Eliyana."

My leg shakes beneath the table and Ky steadies it.

I'm pretty sure this is the first time anyone has called me Queen. Highness and Majesty, yes, but Queen? With my name attached? Never.

"As ruler of the Second you are an equal member of this council. Not only that, but you are the Verity's vessel. A woman has not

held that role in a great many years. My grandmother two generations previous was the last female vessel."

I tug my right sleeve down past my hand. I feel the Void pulsing
where it does not belong. The countess knows Ky holds the Void,
too, but she no longer seems concerned about him. Just Joshua.
Why? My nerves manifest in fidgets and stomach cramps.

"Also," the countess adds, "may I say I was quite impressed
with your candor upon the shore earlier? Standing up for what is
right and true is very rarely easy. You are indeed worthy of the title
you bear."

I tuck my hair behind my ears. Both legs jiggle now, and I
smooth my sweaty palms over my thighs. "Um . . ." I glance at Ky,
who nods his support. "Where have you seen it?" I'm afraid of her
answer. "The madness, I mean."

"In Jasyn Crowe, of course."

The notion sends a shudder through me. Joshua? Like my
grandfather? Impossible.

"Is it?" Ky counters in my head. *"David suffers half the Void. It
may have become too much for him."*

You suffer half and you're fine.

*"I've been cautious not to feed it. I practiced controlling my evil urges
for years after Tiernan forced me to drink dark Threshold water."* He
knocks my knee with his. *"Besides, I had the Verity then, just as I have
it now. In you."*

Joshua has me.

"Does he?"

His question stops me. I stare at my ringless left hand. The
Verity keeps the Void at bay. Counterbalances it. Did I cause Joshua
to go dark? Did my actions send him over the edge?

Some vessel of the Verity I've turned out to be.

"David has made his own choices. That's not on you."

The fury behind Ky's thought is almost enough to knock me
off my chair.

Instead I straighten, lean in. Don't want to miss what the countess has to say. That's why we're here, after all.

"The question," she continues, "is why would David go to such great lengths to steal from me?" She lifts one eyebrow and the corner of her mouth at once. "Before the quake, he was in his chambers. My Guardians have confirmed he took off shortly after with what he believes to be my most prized possession." Elbows propped and fingers steepled, she taps her chin. "When I discovered he used you all to create a diversion, I immediately took it upon myself to rectify my error and remove you from the catacombs."

"What did he take?" Ebony chimes in, though the signature irritation in her voice is absent.

The countess eyes her. "A Midnight Rose from the Garden of Epoch."

A low murmur ensues, whispers rising from both council and crew.

"The place is legend," Ky informs me alone, distracting me from the conversation. *"Said to be guarded by a Fervor Dragon."*

Where is it?

"Where else?" When I don't respond he adds, *"Look around you. We have representatives from every Reflection save two."*

I consider the council members. The countess from the Fourth and me from the Second. Kilt-man introduced himself as one of five chiefs from, you guessed it, the Fifth, while the woman half my size hails as a governor all the way from the Sixth.

The elderly couple are not a couple at all, but a brother and sister from the Third. Caretakers who teach of the Reflections and Callings to those in the Third who have ears to hear. Ky is the one who shared with me how most people in the Third lack belief in the Void and the Verity. How the Called there must keep their abilities hidden.

My mind drifts to that November night two months ago when we walked through Wichgreen Village, sat on a bench, and talked after he saved me from Gage. I welcome the memory instead of hindering it as I've become accustomed to doing. Close my eyes and relive his embrace at the village gate. The sound of his voice when he told Gage never to come near me again.

"*Earth to Em,*" Ky says in my head. "*I'm sitting right here. You can have the real thing anytime you wish.*"

I blush and revisit his previous question. *The First and the Seventh,* I think. *There aren't any representatives from those Reflections.*

"*Precisely.*" From the corner of my vision I catch the crook of Ky's mouth twitch. His eyes are for the countess alone, but that smile is all mine. "*The Garden of Epoch spans between the Seventh and First. The Seventh is said to be the only way into the First aside from death.*"

"*The beginning is the end, and the end is the beginning . . .*" Dimitri's words play across my Scrib memory.

Was he on to something? The whole "time is a loop" thing? Are the Reflections a loop as well?

"*That's what they say.*"

Excuse me. I wasn't thinking to you.

"*We'll have to work on that one then.*" Another knock to my knee. "*You need to learn to control what I can and can't hear. Not that I want you to.*" I can't view his full face, but I swear if we were alone he'd be wiggling his eyebrows right about now.

How do you know so much about this? I watch the council exchange words back and forth, but it's like they're on mute. Their mouths move, but the only voice I hear is Ky's.

"*Didn't your mom ever read you Fairy tales as a kid?*"

What, like Snow White *and* Cinderella?

The most indistinguishable shake of his head. He rests the arm opposite me on the table. "*More like* Lament of the Fairy Queen *and* The Scrib's Fate."

Is he joking? *My mom didn't want me to know anything about the Reflections. She pretty much stuck to normal, Third-type stuff.*

Beardy pounds his gargantuan fist on the table.

I jump out of my head—Ky's head—and back into the present.

"I'm no fool," the man says. "Give it to me straight. What are we up against?"

"Now, now, Isaach." The countess lifts her hands, palms out, surrender style. "Let's remain civil."

"We ain't got time for civil, woman." Another fist pound. If the countess is bothered by his disrespect, her face gives nothing away. "Time's a wastin'. I forfeited a Unicorn Joust to be here."

Unicorn Joust? Really?

"Isaach, please," the dwarf woman—Odessa—says. "Let us hear what Ambrose has to say."

"My sister and I agree." The older gentleman raises a hand as if to second a motion. "Go on, Ambrose."

Isaach grunts, crosses his arms, and burrows down into his chair.

Odessa folds her hands on the table and nods for the countess to continue.

"As I was saying, David and his partner, Gage, are nowhere to be found."

My insides flip. So it *is* true. Joshua and Gage were together. Double ugh.

"Fortunately, I would never keep the real Midnight Rose on display for all to see. The one David took was a decoy, which only proves the Void is messing with his mind. He's smart, so he should've figured out it would not be so easy to steal from me. It won't be long, however, before he discovers it is, in fact, a counterfeit." Her grin holds a childlike mischief. It's hard to see her as the cold woman I met upon our arrival. "Anyone after that particular rose would be seeking to use its properties straightaway, especially with a mere three Callings remaining functional."

"What does it do?" Khloe sits on her knees, bouncing like a kid eager for recess.

The countess either ignores my sister's question or doesn't hear it. I'm inclined to give the woman the benefit of the doubt. I have a feeling it's the former though. My curiosity gets the better of me. I will my thoughts toward Ky.

"I've no idea what it does," he thinks.

And here I thought you knew everything.

"Very funny, sassy pants."

"We must move forward." Ambrose rests her attention on Ky and he shifts. Sits a little taller. "Kyaphus, upon your last visit you informed me you seek information regarding the origins of the Void." She makes eye contact with each crew member in turn. "Am I correct in assuming your entourage is up-to-date on things to this point?"

"Go on." Gunner waves a hand dismissively. "We've seen Captain Warren—er, Kyaphus? . . . Sorry, weird name, bro—has been touched by the Void. And we don't care. He's never hurt us. We just want the treasure. Isn't that right, Flint?" He nudges Flint, who sits one chair over, with his elbow.

"You idiot, there is no treasure. It was a cover. He was using us." He keeps his head down, studying the table.

My pulse speeds. Can Flint be trusted? He and Ky seemed close on the ship. But now that he's seen Ky's secret, will he remain loyal?

"No treasure?" Gunner's puppy dog eyes are so pathetic, I almost feel sorry for him.

"No treasure, Gun." As she pats the kidult pirate on the back, Charley's tone hovers between disappointment and pity.

"That's where you're wrong," a new voice says from the second door. Everyone at the table transfers their gaze to where Tide stands. I'd nearly forgotten about the countess's son. Does that make him a count then? Weird.

Tide lifts a book into the air like a trophy. "There is treasure. Just not the kind we expected."

The countess beams. "Ah yes. I believe I've uncovered something but have not had the opportunity to share with my council. Please, Kyaphus, fill everyone in before we proceed."

Ky rises, the legs of his chair scraping as he does. He shoves his hands into his pockets and makes eye contact with each person at the table just as the countess did. When he reaches me he pauses longer than necessary. "First to my crew, I sincerely apologize for keeping the true purpose of our voyage undercover. I worried you would either think I was crazy for wanting to destroy the Void—"

"Destroy the Void?" Gunner again. I suppress the far-from-professional laughter I so want to let go. "Awesome. I'm in. Where do I sign?"

"Would you be quiet?" Flint growls.

"—or not trust me because of this." Ky holds up his right arm, still visible through his torn sleeves. The interruption doesn't seem to have fazed him. "I was wrong to hide the truth, and for that I ask your forgiveness."

Gunner and Tide nod. It's Tide who says, "Yeah, man. No big deal."

Flint continues to stare at the table. I recognize the glaze in his eyes, the hunch in his back. Because I've been there. He feels betrayed. It will take him time to recover.

"As Countess Ambrose here knows," Ky goes on, "I've been searching for information on the origins of the Void and the Verity. There is next to nothing to be found on the subject. Those I've spoken with have said the Verity and the Void have always required vessels. This is how it's always been and always will be."

But they're wrong. A piping hot cup of anticipation brews. Dimitri was on to something indeed. ". . . *all things begin somewhere*," he wrote.

Yes. Yes, they do.

"However"—Ky clears his throat—"I believe I uncovered a clue that has led me to believe the Void was created—by the Verity."

I watch the faces of the council and crew. All hang on Ky's words. He has earned the respect of the countess. Commands the room like the captain he is. He was born to lead. Born for the role he plays.

Though he doesn't take his eyes off the countess, I know he hears my thoughts. He smirks. Rolls his shoulders back. "And if something was created, it can certainly be destroyed. It was you, Countess Ambrose, who told me I was looking in the wrong places. You said if I wanted to discover the origins of the Void and the Verity, I would have to search where one would least expect to find an event in history."

I hear Ky's next line in my head before it's uttered. The answer is so simple. Of course that's where the information would be. Why didn't I think of it? All those hours I spent in the library. All that time consumed examining *The Reflection Chronicles*. I was researching facts, real-life accounts. But I missed what has been right there all along.

All fiction is drawn from fact. Look at my life. I never believed in Fairy tales. In true love or legends or myths. But it's real. All of it. And it always has been. It was simply my perspective that had to change. My mind needed to open, welcome a new reality. And all at once, it does.

With a crooked grin Ky says, "I would have to search in children's stories."

all so clear

This is getting good. We're close. I feel it in the way the Verity warms my center. In how it pushes against the Void threatening to move past my arm. The war inside is tangible. Light versus darkness. Joy fighting sorrow. Life battling death.

I bite my lower lip. It takes everything in me not to burst from my chair and grab the book from Tide, which I'm certain holds a clue vital to our mission.

And he said there's treasure. What waits for us at the end of all this? As far as I'm concerned, the destruction of the Void is treasure enough. What more is there?

"Retrieved what you requested, Captain," Tide says. "Found a copy in the palace archives, just like you said I would." He struts to Ky and plops the book on the table.

I glance at the title—*Once upon a Reflection*. Of course.

Tide backs away, leans against the glass wall with arms folded.

"Thank you." Ky opens the book's cover and flip, flip, flips the pages until he lands on a passage near the center. He holds a finger there as he says, "Before we left the Third I took a risk and filled Tide in on a few key points. If we made it to the Fourth, I knew we could face problems. With the Threshold water low, I wasn't sure what to expect. Chaos? Suspicion? Recent events have put everyone on edge. As half the Void's vessel I must be prepared for every outcome. But if anyone had diplomatic immunity, I knew it would be Tide."

"Pays to be the son of a countess." Tide smirks. Brushes off a shoulder with his knuckles.

His cockiness suits him in an I-know-I'm-awesome-so-why-deny-it? sort of way. I glance over at Ebony. She watches him, an effervescence in her eyes I've never before witnessed. Different from the way she'd flicker her eyelashes at boys in school. This isn't the confident Quinn who believes she can get any guy she wants. This is my sister. Of all the people she could've imitated using her Shield, she chose Tide. And the way she stared at him on the ship? She is so in-like with Tide it's not even funny.

Ky clears his throat and my attention transfers to him. He looks down. The book's pages are yellowed, some of the corners dog-eared. Oh man, would that drive Mom up a wall and back if she saw. Dog-earing a book is equivalent to mortal sin in her mind. Will she return to the Second once we destroy the Void? Isabeau is still out there, revenge hot on her Trollish breath. One more thing to worry about. Even if we reach our goal, there will always be someone else to save. Always.

Will it ever end?

As if in response, Ky begins to read: "*The Scrib's Fate* by Dimitri Gérard."

Wait, what? The same guy who wrote the journal I've been studying?

"'Whence I fell, he left me there.
Lost, nay abandoned; what did he care?
I needed him; away he flew.
I loved him so; he ne'er knew.
When I revealed my soul, my heart,
He turned away; I watched him part.
Without him now, darkness descends.
Where it begins, my light does end.'"

Ky turns the page and continues, "'Once upon a Reflection, deep in the Garden of Epoch, there shone a light lovelier than any human eye had ever beheld.'"

The Verity! Has to be!

"'No human had ever ventured into the garden, for all mortals carry darkness within their souls. And light cannot reside with darkness.'"

This is it. Ky's theory on the Void's origin is based on this very story. I'm so catching on to this allegory thing. Something Ky said when I arrived on the ship empties from a pocket in my mind. *". . . light cannot remain light if in love with darkness. It is impossible."* I scoot to the edge of my chair. Tilt my head. Listen.

"'One day a man happened upon the Garden. With a sharp wit and brilliant mind, he was called to be a Scrib, and he knew in order to enter the Garden he would be required to answer the riddle of the Fervor Dragon who guarded its gate.'" He licks his thumb, flips the page. "'No one had ever solved the riddle. Three attempts were allowed, and three wrong answers forever ensued. Each who came before him was eaten alive by the Dragon, the consequence of an unsuitable response, never to be heard from again.'"

Shudder. Sheesh. Why even try?

"'But as a treasure awaited anyone who could get past the gate, many came and tried their hand, risking their fate at the gate of Epoch.'"

Ah, treasure. What else? I shake my head.

Ky licks his lips.

A thrill darts through me.

"'The Dragon's nostrils flared and her chops watered as she crooned, "What is invisible, but may be held in your arms? Heavier than all the water contained in the sea, but light enough to carry? Surpasses time, but dies with a word?"'"

That's the riddle? Really? It's so simple.

"'Three attempts were not necessary for this particular man. Oh no. He knew the answer, for it is what he had searched for all his days.'"

The words trigger something inside. But I can't put my finger on it. Not yet anyway.

"'"True love," the man replied.'" Ky pauses. Thinks something for my mind alone.

My heart is putty in my chest.

"'The Dragon huffed her disappointment, for her supper would have to wait. She moved aside. Her scaly tail was, indeed, the gate guarding Epoch. She swung it open and the man entered.'"

This is way cooler than the stories Mom used to tell. What else have I missed growing up in the dull old Third? I'm so getting my hands on that book when we're done. I've a feeling there are more stories just as epic. And if they're all true? Even better.

Shifting and combing fingers through his hair, Ky reads, "'The Garden was more beautiful than the man had surmised. Colors he did not know existed decked the flora and fauna. Roses the deepest shade of night bloomed. Trees with bark the color of honey grew tall and towering. The air was crisp, sweeter than the most pleasant of perfumes. Everything was so clear, as if the man had been blind his entire life and was just now gaining his sight.'"

I prop my elbow on the table and rest my face against my palm. My eyelids flutter south.

Ky's voice lowers, awe weighing his next words. "'The Garden itself was a treasure, and the man had no inclination to leave. He was entranced by the beauty of it all. Little did he realize he was not alone. No, the man was being watched.'" Ky turns another page. "'Watched by a rainbow of light. A light with a voice like a song.'"

My breath hitches. I so nailed it. Rainbow light? I was the only one who saw the Verity's true form when it deserted Joshua and Ky, became one within me. The swirling prism left me breathless. And the voice like a song? I never heard the Verity speak, but a Mirror's song is created by a Kiss of Infinity bestowed by the Verity's vessel. I wouldn't be surprised if the Verity itself had a beautiful voice as well. Even the poem at the beginning of this tale has lyrics written all over it.

"'The light was so entranced by the Scrib—the purest soul she had ever beheld—that a longing began in her own soul. She ached to hold the man, to love him, and kiss him, and die beside him. Her soul was the treasure, you see. A treasure any man would have been honored to receive. But it could only be given to one pure of heart and worthy. This Scrib was such a man. And so the light made a choice and took on humanity, sacrificing her perfect state for the flawed body of a mortal.'"

Intuition kicks me in the gut. Ky's mouth turns down and he draws in a deep breath. I ready for what comes next, for the tragic end I'm sure will close this tale.

Another page turn. The last page. "'She bestowed on him the most perfect of kisses, a Kiss of Infinity. But like all men, the Scrib carried his flaws too. Though he'd searched far and wide for true love, and though the light that had become woman was the most stunning creature he had ever seen, alas, he did not love her, and alas, her Kiss of Infinity was not returned.'"

Anger burns. Jerk.

"You can't be forced to love someone, Em. A Kiss of Infinity comes from the deepest part of you."

I can't counter Ky's thought. Because there's nothing to say. He's right. Again.

"'So heartbroken was the woman that darkness descended upon her soul. The great power of the light within was twisted, and soon an evil that had never been known in the Garden formed. Such evil could not exist there. The woman had to rid herself of it or be forced to leave and ne'er return. So though she loved the man despite his unrequited sentiment, the woman had no option but to send the darkness into the one to whom her soul was linked. The Void must have a vessel and the Scrib was the nearest option.'"

The first vessel of the Void. Whoa.

"'And this was the Scrib's fate, cursed to walk the earth consumed with darkness crafted by the woman he did not love. Eventually he grew old and the darkness left him for another, latching onto one who loved the soul infused with light. The switch had to occur, for the light's purpose was to be loved.'"

The Void enters the one who loves the Verity? This makes so much more sense. Ky and Joshua *both* love me, but my love for Ky isn't something caused by the Verity. It's not a result of some forced phenomenon.

I love him because I love him. I loved him before I linked my soul to his. I just didn't know it.

"'And the woman?'" Ky goes on, reeling me in to the final bit of the tale. "'She suffered a fate far worse than death. For she remained immortal, doomed to wander the Reflections forever, lacking the one thing she'd eternally yearned for, the one treasure she had to offer but would not receive—true love. Bitter she became, and so the light could no longer dwell within her. Just like the man, the light abandoned her, searching for a pure soul in which it would thrive. It is said now only death can release the light, for it is through the death of an unloved soul the light abandoned its first vessel.'"

Ky shuts the book.

I sink back in my chair. A tear slides down my cheek and I swipe it with my sweatshirt. This is truly the tale of the Void and the Verity. And two things stand out among every other.

The man—he'd been searching for true love but could not find it. It's Dimitri. He didn't just write this story, this *is* his story. I'm positive. But what happened to the woman? If she remained immortal, is she out there somewhere? Destined to mourn the loss of love and light for all eternity?

What a horrible, despicable fate. My heart breaks for her, whoever she is. I kind of hate Dimitri. His journal remains tucked into my jeans. The feeling of it against my skin causes my stomach to churn.

The second thing, and perhaps the most pertinent, is how the Void chooses a soul. The story says the darkness latches onto the soul who loves light, not the other way around. Which means it is not the one *I* care for most who took on the Void, but the one—*ones*—who care most for me.

Ky.

Joshua.

And here it is. The ugly truth. The only thing that can kill an Ever is a broken heart. Joshua is vulnerable now without his Calling, but even if he regains the power in his blood, it won't matter. Because Joshua still holds half the Void, which means he loves me just as much as Ky does. No matter what he's done, or the bad decisions he's made, deep down Joshua still loves me. And breaking his heart? It will destroy him. If the Void doesn't take over, the heartbreak will.

And then I'm sobbing, right here in front of everyone. Head in my hands, snot on my face, sobbing.

I will always care for Joshua, but it's Ky I've grown to love.

And when Joshua realizes this, if he hasn't already . . .

He. Will. Die.

joshua

I tear off a piece of my shirt and wrap it around my cut palm. Stupid Fairies and their stupid lagoon infested with stalagmites.

I squeeze my eyes and blink away the blur. Instruct myself not to waver, to remain focused. I love El and she loves me. Taking off the ring means nothing. She was upset and confused. Any other would have acted the same. It's the Void in my brother clouding her judgment. I cannot allow it to win. I must be vigilant, attend to the task at hand.

Deliver rose. Take mirrorglass bottle. Acquire final ingredient. Serve Elixir to El.

I stifle a cough with my hand. When I pull it away, blackened blood drips from my fingers.

"You get used to it." Gage cleans his knife on his pant leg. "Same thing happened to me when Crowe injected the Void. You either learn to control it, keep the symptoms at bay, or live with it." He props a foot against a stalagmite and double knots his bootlaces. "I selected the latter, of course. Thanks to your girlfriend it didn't make much difference. Whatever she did to Crowe unfastened the Void from my soul. Give her my regards next time you see her, will you? I doubt she'll hear it from me."

What I wouldn't pay to punch him in his rotten face right now. "You know, I'm getting sick and tired of your moronic comments, Jonathan. Why don't you go throw yourself off a cliff?"

Gage laughs. "We are more similar than you care to admit, my friend. Seems you've chosen the latter as well."

I pick up a stone the size of my tape measure back home and chuck it at him. He dodges it, diving into the fountain at the island's core where we entered.

It is several moments before I'm able to follow. My throwing hand shakes and I grasp my hair to steady the trembling. Whatever Jonathan has done, it is unlike me to lose control. Bile burns my throat and I swallow, bounding into the water after him.

When I reach the Fairy Fountain this side of the Second, Isabeau waits in human form, Jonathan assuming an at-ease stance to her left. This time she reclines on a throne fashioned from twisted vines, Mine Fairies attending her every need. I produce the rose, but the expression she bears is less than satisfactory.

Fury widens her gaze and levels her mouth. She stalks over, snatches her prize, tosses it to the ground, and stomps on it. Then she shifts and transforms, becoming the Troll she truly is.

I back away and draw my sword. The familiar sound of brandished iron never grows old.

Isabeau fills the space, taller and wider than the maple tree at the Fountain's center. "Is it so difficult to decipher a true rose from an imposter?"

I glance at the treaded flower beneath her giant feet. Real? Of course it's real. The petals are crushed and the stem is cracked in two. I blink away the haze that fogs my vision. This is more than mere exhaustion. Am I falling prey to illness? My chest is tight, as if an anvil rests there, pressing in and making it difficult to draw an adequate breath.

"I asked you to do one simple task. One." Her too-long fingernail is shoved in my face. "Yet you are no more competent than this lowlife Jonathan Gage."

My gaze shifts right. A pulsing in Jonathan's jaw lets on he is less than thrilled about his title. Perhaps I can use this to my advantage. It is no longer a question what he traded for his sight—for the Calling that healed him. He meant to offer up El, but that plan fell through. He is the Fairy Queen's slave. I want to ask him if it was worth it, but I refrain.

The Troll growls an exhale. Her nostrils flare with each breath. Then she's shrinking and slimming, softening into her woman state once more. "But I am nothing if not gracious." She turns away and adopts her place on the twisted throne. Her dress cascades around her like a black waterfall, reminding me of the Void oozing through my veins. "You will simply try again. And this time you will not disappoint me. Do I make myself clear?"

I narrow my eyes. "Crystal."

"Be gone then." She waves her hand.

I do not waver.

Her eyebrows arch. "Is there a problem?"

"Why does it matter so much?"

"Excuse me?"

"If this rose is so important, the least you can do is inform me as to its value."

Isabeau leans forward. "You think it wise to push me, David?"

"Have it your way." I feign a quarter turn. She may be devious, but I've always been quick on my feet. "I only ask because knowing its worth may aid in my attempt to recover it." I count down in my head. She can't fool me. If this rose is of any significance to her, she'll relay why. And perhaps then not only can I find it, but I can also use the blossom to my benefit before returning it to Isabeau, the supposed rightful owner.

"Wait," she says, just as I knew she would.

I face her once more, ears alert to whatever comes next.

"I will tell you, David, but on one condition."

Striking another deal with the Fairy Queen is probably not the wisest of choices. "You name it."

"In our youth, Countess Ambrose and I shared a Kiss of Accord."

"Go on."

"I promised her the rose in exchange for her silence on a certain matter. Which is why I cannot simply retrieve the rose myself, otherwise our deal would be broken and I would die."

What's she getting at?

"Requesting you steal the rose is a brilliant plan indeed, but I keep wondering . . . what's to deter my dear old friend from taking it back? You transferring it to my possession does not make it truly mine again."

Her words are irksome, turning my stomach sour. Possessing something *does* make it yours.

"Yes, yes. El belongs to you. She was your love first. You own her . . ."

Incorrect. She's free to make her own choices. She only belongs to me if she wishes it.

"Give her the Elixir. Get your wretched brother out of the way. Only then do you have a chance at winning her heart once more."

I am working on it. Now, silence. I must hear what Her Majesty has to say.

"Her Majesty, is it?"

What? No. I only meant—

"Pay attention, Joshua. Her Majesty is speaking."

My regard finds Isabeau.

"Did you hear me?" Her tone has misplaced its calm. "Why will you not respond?"

"Apologies." I shove the shadow voice away. "If you will repeat what you last said."

Her hands clench the arms of her throne. The vines cut her milky skin, causing her to bleed. But just as abruptly as the wounds appeared, they vanish.

She is the Fairy Queen, an immortal. But then what purpose would my Ever blood serve? It's obviously not intended for her. Could it be for another? Her own immortality doesn't mean her blood heals. Then again, she restored Jonathan's sight by bestowing a Calling. I am not quite sure how her powers function, or to what length they reach. Perhaps she only required my blood for her bartering collection. A valuable commodity if all the Callings revive. What would one pay or trade for my blood?

Need I even ask? A high price has always been placed on an Ever's blood. It is the very reason I keep the seal behind my shoulder cloaked. Very few know the mark, and Evers would prefer to keep it that way. Not that I've met another like me. I'm a rare breed. Of course my blood would be valuable to Isabeau.

"I said . . . ," the woman resumes, "the only way to ensure Ambrose does not come after the rose is to end her existence altogether."

Kill her? Commit murder? "No." I may have crossed a few lines, but that is one I am unwilling to trespass.

"Suit yourself." Her shoulders lift. The Fairies fawn over her. Brushing her hair. Washing her feet. "You were the one who asked. It is not in my best interest to divulge the rose's power."

I weigh the options. Knowing the rose's power could offer a clue as to where Ambrose might stow it. But am I willing to end another's life for such information?

"Yes. Do it."

No. Never.

I offer a mock salute, serves her right, then trudge back through the Fountain, thrusting my blade so hard into its sheath it rips a hole in the bottom. I heave and hold my breath as I hear Isabeau tell Jonathan, "Are you just going to stand there? Follow him."

The water takes me under.

Commence round two.

everything looks different

How did we get here? When did I switch from wishing for Joshua to having Ky on the brain? How did that even happen?

"Stop trying to deconstruct everything," Ky says aloud now that we're alone. His hand finds mine as we make the trek up to the city's heart. "Go with the flow for once."

Go with the flow? Me? Great Scott, you must be joking.

"Funny, Em. Better."

I hum a little tune, getting ridiculously smiley for maybe the first time in forever. With Joshua things were more serious. We had our moments, but for the most part things were tense—intense? Nerve-racking. With him I felt forever on display, auditioning for a role I desperately wanted but that was way out of my league. And, now I see, maybe never right for me at all.

"And with me?" Ky kisses my hand.

Okay, I really need to work on that whole thought-blocking thing. But for now I respond audibly. "With you . . ." I look up and push out my lips. "With you it's more, I don't know . . ." I'm talking with my hands now, trying to get my thoughts out with gestures apparently. Because *that* helps. "It's more . . ."

"Awesome?"

Major eye roll. "That's not what I was going to say."

"Sure it was. I can read your mind, remember?" He taps his temple.

We go back and forth this way the remainder of the walk, living out exactly what I couldn't put into words.

With Ky it's more *this*.

With Ky it's more *now*.

With Ky it's easier and somehow I forget everyone and everything. No worrying about the Void or the Verity. No planning or anxiety or what's-going-to-happen-next mentality.

The closer we move to the surface, the less daunting breathing becomes. I inhale through my nose, ready for sunlight at last. Have we only been underground a day? The sweat stains on my clothes and the grime in my hair make it feel longer. I don't need to lift an arm and sniff to know I'm in desperate want of a shower. My muscles ache and my calves burn. How much farther?

Two seconds later we round a corner and halt before a door. Not circular like in the council chamber. Not a trap like the one Zane led us through. This is plain white. And there, jagging from top to bottom, is a lightning bolt–style crack.

Ky and I exchange glances. Then he reaches forward, turns the knob, and opens the door.

On the opposite side, a decent-sized atrium awaits. Or what used to be an atrium, anyway. The aftereffects of the earthquake send chills up my spine. My jaw goes slack as we wander the wreckage. Crumbled columns. Plants smashed beneath collapsed pieces of roof. The ground is cracked and split, a fountain at the atrium's center lopsided with its statue of a whatever-it-was facedown in the empty pool. Guardians and citizens work to clean up, a long chain of them passing debris down the line to a growing pile.

"I need to go check something. I'll be back." Ky kisses my hand again, then releases it. Crosses to the atrium's other end where he passes through an archway and out of view.

Pushing my hair away from my face, I join the assembly line. Members of our crew pitch in as well. Ebony and Tide lift a lamppost. Khloe sweeps steps and beats a hanging rug. Gunner and Flint provide their best asset—brawn. They all left the chamber hours ago along with the Reflection reps. But Ky and I? We remained behind to speak with the countess privately. Our conversation plays over in my mind as I'm handed a chunk of rock. Pass it along. Take, pass, take, pass. I stare into space.

"You know what you must do?" The countess gazed through the glass, back toward us, while the man who let us in straightened chairs.

Ky assisted him, the task nothing for him compared to the wheezing little man. "We need to learn more about this woman," he said. "The first vessel of the Verity. Is there anyone alive who may know her whereabouts?"

"There is one woman." Face turned toward her shoulder and eyes closed, she spoke in a low voice. "A woman by the name of Dahlia Moon. Isaach told me of her. She resides in the Fifth and may be of some use to you." She crossed to Ky and pressed a small square of paper into his hand.

He stopped where he stood, pocketing the paper without a peek at its contents. "An Ever?"

"Oof!" The little man, who continued to shuffle about the table, rammed into Ky.

Ky stepped back while the man turned up his nose, adjusted his toga, and scooted out the door.

Weird little fella. Never said a word. Very odd.

Once the door clicked closed, the countess nodded. "An Ever indeed. Hard to find one who's lived so long. Keeps to herself. Or so I hear."

I wrinkled my nose. *She hears a lot. How do we know she can be trusted?*

"Because we're not dead," Ky thought.

Touché.

"Hey, earth to butterfly."

I blink. Look left. Right. The line has dispersed, everyone having gone off to attend to another project.

Charley waves her hand in front of my face. Shakes her head. Hitches a thumb over her shoulder. "We could use you down at Kaide Agi Marketplace. You in?"

Chin lifted I say, "Definitely."

The next several hours are comprised of picking up the pieces of this Reflection. Sonsosk Palace atrium is just the beginning. The city is in shambles. All caved-in roofs and eroded walkways. Funny, but this is the first time since my coronation I actually *feel* like a queen. As if I'm doing something worthwhile. The cloudless sky offers no respite, the sun beating down, drawing moisture from my skin. I'm parched. Ready to fall over. But I can't stop smiling.

This is what being queen is all about. Not endless hours in a stuffy castle with servants waiting on me hand and foot. Ruling is about serving. About community and friendship.

I could get used to this.

When the sunset flourishes the ocean horizon, orange melting into indigo, everyone calls it quits for the day. Most head back toward the city center, where word has spread a huge feast awaits anyone who pitched in. But I'm too peopled out, and I long for a moment of solace. I slip away, down the abandoned streets, picking my way to the beach.

In the distance I can make out the faint echo of dance music, and I almost turn around. But then I cross the island's main road—marked by a crooked beechwood sign as Tecre Thruway. When my shoes meet sand and the spray of the sea coos its welcome, I transform from anxious to calm. Once I'm positive I'm 100 percent alone, I shift. Shed my clothes. Spread my wings. The freedom feels natural. As if I've spent my entire life switching between butterfly and girl.

Flit, flutter, flee. First I glide high above the Fourth—above Atlantis. I haven't had a chance to study the map in Dimitri's journal properly yet. Still, I glimpse landmarks my Scrib memory recalls from a glance at that page. The strange, almost unpronounceable names ascribed to everything. The five islands surrounding the main one. The bays spilling into the larger seas to the north and south. The canals running through the cities. I adore New York and the Second is something else, but if I had to choose another

Reflection as my favorite? The Fourth would suit me quite nicely. Something is so freeing about a place surrounded by ocean.

Maybe it's even more like Manhattan than I first realized.

Next I swoop low over the water, my reflection bouncing in the waves. It's the first chance I've had to really observe my Mask form. To take in every curve and color. Strange. Somehow I look like me. My mirrormark is intact, twisting and climbing over my right wing. The edges of my wings are a deep bluish-purple, like the ends of my hair now that my dye has faded.

Part of me wants to remain this way forever. Make the escape permanent. Could I? Would anyone notice my absence?

In the past I wondered as much. Wondered if anyone aside from Mom would miss me if I simply disappeared. But now I know better. I've touched others as they have touched me. Not just the expected like Mom or Ky or Joshua, but the unexpected as well. Reggie. Stormy. Makai. Ebony. Khloe. They all care. And I couldn't leave them behind. I'd never be the same.

My soul swells as I glide back to earth. Donning all my clothing aside from my shoes, I meander along the shore. My toes squish in the damp sand, leaving sunken footprints in my wake. More of those glistening green and gold stones shimmer, washed over with water and foam. I scoop one up and it looks like colored glass. It could almost be . . .

Hold the phone, is this mirrorglass? I examine the stone, holding it up to my eye and inspecting it in the light. Oh my chronicles, it is. But isn't mirrorglass rare? I whirl. There must be hundreds of stones on this beach, if not more. They cover this Reflection. They're in the steps. The walls and floors.

I toss the stone into the air, then chuck it across the water. It skip, skip, skips over the surface.

"I didn't know you could do that."

"Hey, Ebony." I don't jump at her presence or cringe when she stands beside me, feet bare like mine. "Mom taught me. We used to go down to the Hudson when I was little. We'd skip stones and feed the ducks."

"My mother never did anything like that with me." The sadness whispered in her words tugs at my core. "We never just had fun, you know?"

I snatch a couple more stones. Hand one over. "Wanna learn?" Maybe there is something I can teach her after all.

Ebony shrugs. "Whatever. The party felt crowded. I've got nothing better to do."

I should be offended. But I'm not. Because this is her best attempt at a compliment. I take it as such and we stay that way awhile. Skipping stones long after stars dot the night sky. Soon it becomes a game, and we keep score of whose stone bounces farthest. We laugh and talk. At first she's standoffish, but then the wall tumbles. Guess we're more alike than I thought. She puts up a front. Guards herself until she feels safe enough to let someone in.

I ask about Tide.

"He's different." Her lips perk. Eyes crinkle. She's so much prettier without all that makeup. "He doesn't take any of my crud. I like that."

Inquire about Khloe.

"She's the first person to just accept me, you know?" Another toss. It's the farthest stone she's thrown. Go, Eb! "No questions asked. She knows who I am and that's okay."

I question her vast knowledge of things well beyond her years. The Callings. Reflections. Projecting and the Void and the Verity.

She shrugs. "My mother passed on everything she knew to me. It was always 'You can do more. You can be better.' And 'For the Void, Ebony, why can't you be more like me?'" She mimics Isabeau's cool tone. Even her stance alters to mirror that of the woman I've only met once. "Even when my Shield abilities surpassed those of my peers, when I began to learn to project and find strength in the Verity long before my Confine lifted, it was still never enough." Her shoulders relax. She flings another stone at the waves.

I nod. Listen. Was it less than two weeks ago I loathed her? Weird how quickly things change.

"It's what I keep telling you, Em. When something's right it simply happens."

Ky's voice in my head warms me like the Verity. But then, no, not in my head. Breath at my ear. Hands at my waist.

Ebony smirks. "I'll leave you two alone." She faces me. "Thanks." Then she does the weirdest thing ever.

My sister hugs me.

And I hug her back.

It's awkward and distant, but a hug all the same. She pulls away and trudges up the beach, back toward the music and festivities.

"This is perfect," Ky breathes in my ear. "You. Me. No one around."

My entire body flutters as if I'm still in butterfly form. I turn into him. Wrap my arms around his torso. Press my cheek into his chest. "Where'd you run off to earlier?"

His arms tighten around me. "The Threshold."

I draw back a few inches. Gaze up at him.

"The most recent quake left it completely drained. Looks like Niagara Falls on the other side of the island. Ambrose has had to send Guardians to hinder anyone from venturing too close. If they fell in, who knows where they'd end up."

The weight on his shoulders is tangible. I want to grasp it, lift it away.

"We've no time to waste. The quakes become more frequent and severe each time. We have to move if we want to guarantee passage into the Fifth."

I lay my head on his chest again. He sways me, tightening his embrace once more. Does he feel it too? That these moments of peace and calm could be the last we ever share? What awaits us in the Fifth? How long will it take to find Dahlia Moon? What if we can't find her? Where do we go from there?

With each Calling that dwindles, the Verity within strengthens. *I* strengthen. But what happens when the final Calling dies?

What happens if the Void continues to spread inside me? Which will win? Light or darkness? It's a battle against time. Destroy the Void before it snuffs out the Verity.

My mind drifts back to a time when things were less complicated. When my biggest worries were hiding my complexion and avoiding bullies like Blake Trevor. It seems so far away now. Trivial. Were those really my main concerns? I allowed such things to consume me. An unkind word or mean look ruined my day. Why couldn't I enjoy the good parts and let the little things go? Like having Mom to come home to each day. Like having Joshua right next door. Carefree. Happy. Void-less. There are moments I wish I could return to. To truly enjoy what I had. But it's too little too late now. All I have is today.

I crane my neck. Watch Ky. He doesn't notice the change at first, continues to sway with eyes closed to the beat of the tune he composed inside his head.

"I also tracked down the countess and inquired about the mirrorglass crown."

I reach behind me. The journal is still shoved into the back of my jeans. I almost forgot I had it. It's become like a second skin lately. "Did Ambrose know anything?"

"No more than we do. She agreed the crown might have something to do with the domino effect on the Callings and Thresholds."

"Anything else?"

His lips press together. "Like my blade, all mirrorglass has a reverse effect. I'd wager, and the countess concurred, when David wore the crown it kept the Void inside him dormant. When the crown was removed and transferred to you, he may as well have undammed a flood. In the end it's all about choice. Whatever he's doing, his love for you, the Verity's vessel, is not stronger than the Void he's allowing to flourish inside him."

My heart is a thousand mirrorglass pebbles scattered across the shore. How could Joshua allow this to happen? He's always been the one to put everyone else above himself. What could possibly be going through his mind?

"I don't know, Em." Ky breathes against my hair. "And I hate to say this because I know what he means to you, but David is the least of our concerns. Right now all we can do is press forward."

He's right. I know he's right. It's what the Joshua I used to know would do. And he'd expect me to behave the same. Put aside everything else and focus on what must be done.

"If we leave early," Ky says, "we can be at the Fifth's Threshold before nightfall tomorrow. The *Seven Seas* is still in the Third with the rest of our crew. But Isaach has offered to allow us to return on his ship with him."

Except I can't put this aside. This moment. Here. With Ky.

Slipping one arm from around his waist, I reach up, index finger extended. Then I trace the scar running from his ear to his neck. Listen for his thoughts to share what I've wondered since our reunion.

They open like a gate, welcoming me in. I see him tortured by Jasyn's Soulless. Watch him beaten by Haman. And the burn, oh my, the burn.

He tenses beneath my touch. Straightens.

I place my palm against his heart. Feel its pace quicken. Why would he be ashamed of this? Saving a little girl from a fire? It's heroic. Noble. Why hide it?

His thoughts close off, leaving my inquiry unanswered. He looks down. There's a question in his eyes. But also something else.

Longing.

I don't breathe. Don't think. Don't act like myself at all. Because taking action is not my strong suit. Because grabbing a guy by the shoulders and kissing him full on the mouth is not a normal occurrence for me. But I have to do this. I may never have a quiet moment with him again. Our first kiss was under pressure. Desperate. Too fast and too short and I want to remember it more, but I didn't take the time to remember it. I want something I can remember.

I want this. Right now. Because when I kiss him, everything looks different. Because when I kiss him, nothing is the same.

ASIDE

KY

I stumble back and my eyes go wide. For the love of— Well, well, well. Look who was right, as usual.

I knew she'd kiss me first.

Her hands squeeze my shoulders. Her eyes are closed. She kisses me with ferocity. I almost think she's angry, but no. It's not anger. Not anger at all. This is just Em. This is the Em deep inside who at long last is rising to the surface.

I want to fist pump the air. To hoot and holler and yell. But there will be time for celebration later. Because this kiss is her decision. She's confessed her love, but this action confirms her choice.

And she's finally choosing me.

Before I know it her face is between my hands and her arms are around my waist and we're moving. I can't tell if it's her leading or me leading or a bit of both. Regardless, we're traveling across the sand. Kissing and walking and kissing again until I'm on my back, pulling her onto me, careful to keep my distance but also craving her the way I've always craved her.

And I don't want to keep my distance anymore.

joshua

I will not hurt her. This is only meant to scare her into giving me what I came for the first time. The rose does belong to Isabeau, after all. Troll or not, wicked or not, I am out of options. I am out of time.

Under cover of night we creep into the Fourth's palace. We waited until we could be sure everyone had gone to bed. Gage doubles as lookout and backup ten paces behind. Guardians stand at every doorpost and column. The ones remaining, anyway. The earthquake left things a disaster. Columns split in half and steps caved in, the palace looks more like ancient ruins now than architectural genius. It's obvious some cleanup has been done, but there is still much work to do. I hate to revel in the tragedy, but it does leave us an advantage due to the fortunate fact that ruins contain a lot of holes.

When we reach the hall housing the countess's bedchamber, I pause at the corner and peer through the dark. Gage stops, too, so quiet I wouldn't know he was there unless I, well, knew. The roof bears wide gaps that could almost be mistaken for skylights if they were not so oddly shaped. My gaze lifts to the brilliant night sky and my pulse silences. One of the better Third Reflection anthems comes to mind. A song by—what was the band's name?—Switchfoot? I never got around to learning the chords to "Stars" on guitar. Perhaps when this is all over, it's one El and I can sing. Maybe on a night like this. A night when we're together again and the only thing we need to worry about is the chill in the air.

"When I look at the stars . . . I feel like myself."

Never were words more true.

El would be proud if she knew I was thinking in lyrics the way she does. I don't believe she's aware I know that detail about her. She's never shared it with me, but I observe so much more than she lets on. Music is El's oxygen. I've always held a love for it as well, but for her it's different. I wish she were here now, but she's nowhere near. Because I still haven't completed my task.

I still have a job to do.

The countess's chamber doors hang off their hinges. Two Guardians stand like fence posts on either side of the frame, as alert as if it were high noon. I have to laugh at the fact swords are their weapons of choice. They'll be no match for me and Jonathan.

Blade at the ready, I sidestep down the hall. Jonathan follows, staying back and close to the hall's opposite wall. At about the halfway point the Guardians notice us, unsheathe their weapons, and wait. We keep our pace steady, waiting for the last possible moment to attack. We've had enough practice together, and our movements remain in sync.

At ten feet out I glance back and to the right. Jonathan and I exchange nods. Three, two, one, *charge.* The Guardian on the right thrusts and I deflect, turn 360 degrees, and do the same with the left Guardian.

My partner steps in at the precise moment both Guardians thrust their weapons. He hits the left Guardian upside the head with the flat of his blade while I duck, countering my sword against the right Guardian's kneecaps. Wailing, he collapses to the floor. I grip my hilt tighter and rise from my crouch.

Amateurs.

The remaining Guardian backs against the wall, rubbing his injured head, sword arm shaking. He can no doubt see this match is already won. Still, he stands his ground, parrying right, ready for one of us to make our next move. I've got to hand it to him. I admire a man who will stay and fight in the name of the one he's sworn to protect. Such a man is one I'd trust with my own life.

But not today.

I jerk my chin toward Jonathan. He closes in on the Guardian, who lowers his weapon half an inch. No question who will win this standoff. I don't see what my partner does next because I slip from the hall into the countess's bedchamber.

Perhaps this will be easier than I anticipated.

Her bed lies at the room's center. Chunks of ceiling act as obstacles, but I dodge them without issue. When I'm at her bedside I pause, watch her chest rise and fall, rise and fall. My vision blurs and unwarranted rage fills me. I narrow my gaze. She's fooled me once. I'll not tolerate her doing so again.

Remain calm. Keep your head. I am only here to scare her. I will not harm her.

"Unless she gives you no choice."

No. It's not a choice. I refuse.

"We shall see."

I climb onto the bed. When I'm straight above her, she wakes. Her eyes and mouth widen at the same time. I cover her mouth to stifle a scream, though even if more Guardians showed up, I doubt we would have much trouble taking them.

"Listen carefully," I whisper in her ear. "I am going to remove my hand in a moment. The only thing, the *only* thing that is to come out of your mouth is the location of the true Midnight Rose."

She nods, eyes frantic. Her gaze shifts right.

I follow it and squint into the night. There, at the chamber's other end, on a table domed in glass, is the rose. Of course she would keep it near. If she values it as much as Isabeau seems to, she'd want it close. I move to get up, lifting my hand—

The countess jerks her head up and bites down.

My teeth clench.

"Do it! You have a right to defend yourself. You are justified in this."

No.

The countess's eyes change. She's shifting into her Siren state.

"*Do it now. Before it's too late. If she speaks with her Siren voice, you'll be done for. You'll never find the rose. Never achieve what you've worked so hard for.*"

What choice do I have? The voice is right.

Free hand trembling, I raise it in the air. I pause. But then the countess opens her mouth and my hand comes down.

The blow is hard.

The blow is deadly.

The countess does not wake.

ACT IV

Her voice

upon the water

"Welcome aboard the *Iron Lass*. I do hope ye enjoy the voyage." Isaach winks, then brandishes a pint, uncorks it, and chugs. Ale leaks and courses down and around the corners of his mouth, flecking his beard with alcohol droplets. Gone is the sour demeanor he wore during the council meeting. This man is a swab-bucketful of just enough drinks and not enough kilt. My gaze avoids him when he lounges on a nearby barrel, legs wide and drink punching the air. Unicorn Joust indeed. This man should not be allowed near weaponry of any sort. Ever.

Our crew goes to work, joining with the *Iron Lass* bunch to ready the vessel. It's not as large as the *Seven Seas* and designed more like a Viking ship, with one sail at the center, lengthy oars protruding from either side, and the head of a Dragon carved into the wood at the bow. Yes, I finally learned the difference between stern and bow. I'm a true pirate now. Savvy?

My sisters and I share one oar, which is heavier than it first appears. We're setting sail from the south side of Tecre Island, opposite of where we entered through the Tecre Sea. Just getting out of what I've been informed is Sarames Bay is difficult enough. Countess Ambrose didn't come to see us off and Tide didn't show either. We waited, but Ky figured our resident surfer dude decided to remain behind with his people. Makes sense but a glance at Ebony's heartbroken expression has me irked. Tide, at the very least, could've said good-bye to her.

Dawn breaks but the air remains chilled. My face is numb

and I rub my hands together, blowing hot breaths between them. According to Ky it'll take all day to reach the Fifth's Threshold. My arms scream from the burn brought on by rowing. But the work feels good, just as it did when we helped clear the Fourth's wreckage.

Each day I grow stronger, more confident. When I happen upon my reflection it's leaner, more toned. My round face has lengthened. My cheeks are more defined. It's been awhile since I even bothered to feel self-conscious of my mirrormark. I was worried about change, terrified of what it would bring, but perhaps it's for the better.

The old me would never be able to handle what's happened. The old me would have fallen apart over Joshua's betrayal. Yes, it hurts, but it won't break me. I won't let it. As Ky said, Joshua makes his own choices. I can't be blamed for them, and I won't be made to feel guilty for his despicable actions.

Joshua and I have been through so much and not enough. Through everything and nothing. Through beginnings and endings.

Joshua and I have been through . . .

We're *through*.

The wind picks up a few miles out and a horde of dark clouds brews in the distance. Even from here I can see the lightning flashes within them. A natural squall or something caused by the draining Thresholds? Captain Isaach is passed out, and Ky orders us to draw in our oars. We do so, locking them in place. He struts to our trio, brows knit and eyes searching the waves.

He's thinking what I am. Drat. We're headed straight into a storm and it may be another side effect of the Void's hold on the Verity—the Verity's connection to the Void. I rub my right arm, which still hurts, but I've gotten used to the ache. Is that good or bad?

"It's neither," Ky assures my mind. *"Believe me, there's no other way to cope with the pain but to live with it."*

Wind whistles past my ears. I lift the hood of my sweatshirt. *What should we do?*

"*What do you suggest, my queen?*"

I'd roll my eyes, but the seriousness in his thought makes me think better of it. My gaze descends. This is really the first time anyone has looked to me for guidance. The task is harder than it seems, and I make a note to put together my own council when and if I ever return to the Second. I'd include Mom and Makai and Stormy. Maybe I'll earn some points back with Preacher if—

"*Em?*"

I chew the inside of my cheek. *See who has one of the three remaining Callings. If we're lucky maybe there's a water Magnet on board who can help calm the storm.* Unlikely, but all avenues should be exhausted before we buckle down and wait. Man, now I really wish I'd brought Stormy.

"*Good idea,*" Ky thinks. "*Why don't you go ahead and shift, scout things a few miles out. Don't fly too close to the gale, but get close enough to report what we're up against.*"

Aye, aye, Captain.

He turns, moving from crew member to crew member, asking if they're Called and if any are Masks or Scribs or Magnets. Not that a Scrib could do much, but who knows? Maybe someone carries knowledge of hurricane survival. What could it hurt?

I move to the stern, crouch behind a crate, strip off my top layer of clothing. Then I release the song within. My voice has grown stronger, clearer. I let the lyrics surround me. Wait for the familiar feeling of weightlessness.

But nothing happens.

Try again.

Fail.

Again.

Nothing.

Ten times. Ten times I sing my Mirror melody—the notes their own symphony—and neglect to transform. No. Not again. The Verity has absorbed another Calling. My voice is stronger because of it, but what does this matter? I'd hoped Mask would be the last to go. Nothing is ever so fortunate.

My heart an anchor at my feet, I don my clothes. Head across the ship to give Ky the worse-than-sucky news. But before I reach him, Ebony stops me.

She's gotten super easy to read. The mischief perking her cheeks lets on she has a plan B. Hands on her hips, she quirks a brow. "Trouble in the butterfly department?"

"What are you thinking?"

Lips curving at the corners, she says, "I think you're ready."

"Ready for what?"

"What else?" She flips her hair. Her Calling may be gone. Her makeup and nice clothes absent. But she's Fifth Avenue as ever, all attitude and class. Poise. "I think it's time we teach you how to project."

If you'd told me two months ago that Quinn Kelly—in any shape or form—would one day teach me how to not only harness the Magnet within but project it, I'd have laughed. "Magnet what?" I would have said. "How much crazy-sauce did you eat last night?"

Good thing no one ever asked. They'd totally be saying, "I told you so," right now.

"Again!" Ebony's shout barely carries over the storm's roar. "Don't go soft on me. Draw out the Magnet. Be the Magnet."

Oh sheesh, she sounds like my old PE teacher. "See *the ball*. Be *the ball*."

I swipe the rain from my eyes. Slick my hair off my face for the hundredth time. What I'd give to have Stormy here. What's she been doing in my absence? If only there were such a thing as phone calls between Reflections. I wish with all my heart to see her. To tell her about everything that's happened. To confide in her about Joshua. And Ky. Ebony has opened up to me, but I haven't crossed that street yet. I'm still feeling her out I guess. Waiting to see if she's for real this time.

"What are you waiting for?" she calls through cupped hands.

Ugh. Fine. I put thoughts of Stormy on hold, free my song again. My sneakers slip and slide on the rain-ridden deck. I'm on my knees. Back up. Ack, I'm down. Splinter through the heel of my palm. Lovely.

We didn't hit poor weather until a couple hours in. Ebony and Khloe put their heads together, working to figure out what my Magnet ability might be.

"Water?" Khloe suggested.

Ebony shrugged. "We could try it."

And we did. It was the most obvious since Stormy is the only Magnet Ebony and I have met.

Nada. Zilch. Water access denied.

"Wind?" Khloe offered. "Fire?"

Nope and nope. The storm drew closer, and still I'd summoned nothing. Except this isn't just a storm, it's a typhoon. Five bucks says we're overboard before we reach the Threshold.

"I'll take your wager and raise you ten," Ky thinks. *"We'll make it."*

When did you become Mr. Optimistic?

"When I realized you loved me."

Yesterday?

"Try two months ago."

Why am I not surprised?

"Remember what I told you about Magnets?" The weather is too much and I've no clue where on the ship Ky is.

Sort of? Question? Statement? I'm too soaked to tell.

"C'mon, Em. Scrib is working fine. If anyone can remember, it's you."

I'm on my feet again. Trip. Bite my tongue. Taste blood. Magnets, hmm . . .

They have to maintain extreme focus. And the focus exhausts them, drains their energy.

Ugh, my energy is already drained. I'm starting a step behind.

"What else?"

I will my brain to recall our conversation that night at Wichgreen Village. So much information. Such a small span of time. But . . .

They summon things. Elements. Matter. Energy.

"Try earth!" Ebony calls, breaking my concentration. "The sand at the ocean bed. See if you can summon that. You could make an island for the ship to wait on until the storm ends."

I shake my sore arm. Grab the hem of my sweatshirt and ring it out. My feet squish in my sneakers. Wind sends the rain down at a diagonal. Still, I home in on my song. Earth, huh? I'll give it a whirl.

Annnnnnddddd no.

"Try energy!" Khloe again.

I shake my head. What energy? Where? How do I even wrap my brain around the concept?

Ebony makes a time-out T with her arms. My sisters and I huddle together, bodies racked with shivers. "This isn't working." Sniffle. Cough. "We should just hunker down and wait for the storm to pass. I'm useless."

"You are *not* useless," Ebony says. "We just haven't found your niche."

My niche. Right. "How do you summon energy? How is that a thing?"

"Too bad Tide's not here." Khloe bounces on her toes. Her soggy curls hang like wet rotini.

"That's it!" With a side hug to our youngest sister, Ebony squeals, "Runt, you're a genius!"

"I know." Khloe's smile is like a painted doll's.

"What'd I miss?" I glance between them.

"Remember what Tide said?" When she says his name, Ebony lights up like the Lincoln Center fountain.

My conversations with Tide were few and brief at that. "He said . . ." It's coming back to me. "The Thresholds are comprised of energies rather than elements and—"

"If a Threshold drains"—Ebony's interruption is rushed and bubbling—"it would create a wormhole. Which is why you have to summon the Threshold now. This storm is a warning. By the time we reach the passageway into the Fifth, it could be too late."

Holy Verity, could I summon a Threshold? And not only that,

project the ability onto another? Could my sisters and I work together to draw the Fifth Reflection Threshold here to get us out of harm's way? It's worth a try.

I scoot back. Widen my stance. Close my eyes. The Verity springs up. I feel the power of my Calling surge, the spark before a blackout. Something tells me this is it. This is the last time the Verity will generate a Calling before going silent once more. And then it won't be long before its light is doused entirely.

All or nothing. Make it count.

The ship rocks and tilts and I'm forced to brace myself against the railing. Thunder gives a standing ovation with its rounds of applause, while lightning flashes a curtain-call warning. Like the earthquakes, there's no doubt this storm is anything but supernatural.

Which is why we cannot fail. *I* cannot fail. We *will* make it to the Fifth in one piece. We *will* find Dahlia Moon. We know a broken heart created the Void. Could the opposite rescind it?

The theory formed last night. Wide awake, I paced my room, mulling over the notion. If we could track down this immortal woman who was the first Verity's vessel, help her find true love as she desired, could the Void be conquered?

Perhaps Dahlia Moon will have more answers.

Ebony waves her arms in frantic arches. I scan my peripherals, then try to block the chaos and find my calm. Around me, everything falls apart. Flint clutches the mast as if his life depends on it. Gunner mans the thrashing sail along with a few crew members I don't recognize. Ky runs to and fro, barking orders, assisting where he's needed. Charley is perched on the lookout while the remainder of the *Iron Lass* crew pours buckets upon buckets of water back into the ocean. Isaach, of course, is still passed out, water sloshing over his gut and up his kilt.

It's madness. Here. There.

Everywhere.

Countess Ambrose's final warning buoys in my memory. "The deeper into the Reflections you venture, the more opposition you will face. I have heard rumors of those who worship the Void."

"Like the Soulless?" I asked.

She gave a solemn shake of her head. "Soulless have no free will. No minds of their own. The ones I refer to are known as Shadowalkers. They revere the darkness. Bow to it."

Ky bristled at her words.

I shuddered. Who would have thought such people existed?

A wave crashes over the railing, drenching me with the very real and life-threatening present. Ignore anxiety. Ignore danger. I have one task now. No use worrying about anything else but how to get us out of here.

"Projecting is a cinch," Khloe said before we hit the squall. "Think of your Calling like a wire running between you and the Verity, connecting you to your ability. You take it in"—she drew her hands to her chest—"then push it out." Her palms shoved away. "Most people stop there, but Ebony showed me how to keep pushing until my power is more than my own."

As if in slow motion my mind travels to the Fifth's Threshold. I read about it in Mom's journal, and there was even a small sketch for reference. I recall the passage, letting the words wash over me.

Twelfth Day, Sixth Month, Thirtieth Year of Aidan's Reign

Mom was only eight when she penned the entry, though, as was her custom, the words read as if written by someone years her senior.

The king has returned from his outer Reflection travels, and as always he has come bearing gifts. As he has no daughters of his own, he is always kind enough to shower me with items he might bestow upon his own children, if he had any.

He did have one. Just not yet.

This time he arrived with pastels from the Fourth's Kaide Agi Marketplace and a miniature canvas depicting a painting of the Threshold leading from the Fourth to the Fifth—Yanlib Sea Threshold. The king relayed it is one of his favorites, and by far one of the loveliest Thresholds to behold.

And there, illuminating the page opposite the entry, was a sketch of a waterfall that seemed to cascade from the clouds. The sketch caught my eye immediately, and I stored it away in my Scrib memory bank. A curtain of green liquid at the center of the sea. Mom used pastels rather than her go-to charcoal. The water reminded me of Oz's Emerald City, all green and glowing. A sight one would never expect to find, but there it is. Existing. Doing its thing.

Image clear in my mind's eye, I focus with all my soul. Willing the Threshold near, inviting it with my voice, my song a serenading lullaby. Normally I'd stop there. Concentrating on me, myself, and I. On what *I* can do. Instead, when I feel the energy well inside me, I thrust it away. My face contorts and my knees buckle. It's all I can do not to fall over. My sisters didn't mention anything about pain. Feels as if I'm slicing in two. Me igniting the Magnet within, and the Magnet within igniting me.

Oh, if Alicia Keys could see me now. It'd bring a whole new meaning to "Girl on Fire."

I can't do this. It's too much. I'm exhausted to my core, haven't had enough time to hone this avenue of my Calling. I can't—

I can't.

But *we* can.

A deep inhale prepares me for the scorch. And boy, does it *scorch. Ouch.* How does Khloe do this and keep a straight face? Is it one of those things you get used to like the ache of the Void? I certainly hope so, otherwise I won't be inclined to project ever again.

Pull, *ouch*, push, *crowe*, pull, *snap*, push, *gah!*

The squall rages on. The waves threaten to turn us bottom

side up. I want to pause, see if my projection is working, but I can't
risk losing focus. I may not be able to get it back if I do. I draw the
image of the Fifth's Threshold here, expand it out and away, left
and right, to Ebony and Khloe. Together we can do this, together
we will make it.

A flash of green light. There. Through the torrent. Another
deep breath. *Come on, come on . . .*

The Threshold flies toward us as a tornado, fast and furious.
We're headed straight for it. Or it for us. Can't tell. The light flick-
ers, like a lightbulb about to burn out. Then the curtain proceeds
to come down on itself, the water folding over, the fall shrinking. Soon it will create the wormhole Tide mentioned, just as the
Threshold in the Fourth did.

Hurry up, you blasted Threshold. We don't have all day.

It hits us full force. One more breath before the air is vacu-
umed away. There is only water. We should be drawn through.
Instead we remain stagnant, frozen between there and here. Oh
my Void, we're going to drown unless we do something. The
crew needs to row. But if I lose focus and speak to Ky, ask him to
give the order—

"I've got you, Em," he says in my head. *"Don't let go."*

Pull and push, pull and push. Draw in the Calling, project it
out and away. My lungs are flaming. Can't hold my breath much
longer. I'm going, going, on the verge of gone . . .

We burst free, buoying to the surface of what I can only hope
is the Fifth. Sun beats white hot. The ship and crew are logged
with water. We're floating along a murky brown river. Red and
purple canyon walls surround us on all sides. The scent of wet
dirt coats the atmosphere. A desert is the last thing I expected to
find in the Fifth. With its enchanting Threshold and chief who
looks as if he migrated from the rolling green hills of Scotland,
sand dunes and cacti were not included in the picture.

Then again, the Reflections never cease to amaze me. I should
learn to anticipate the unexpected by now.

I collapse to my knees, but I'm not alone. Everyone on board gasps and chokes. Some are passed out, the length of time underwater too much for them. Those who lasted perform CPR on the weaker ones. I smile to myself, not because I'm glad they need revival, but because I don't.

I really am stronger than I believed.

When I gain my bearings, rise to a stand, it's Ebony who says, "Well done. I knew you had it in you." She claps me on the back. "That was kind of awesome, sis."

It's the first time she's referred to me as such. And it's in this moment, something between us shifts. No façades. No walls. She *is* for real. I can trust her.

And now I'm beaming.

Ky appears beside me, one arm wrapped around Khloe. "We made it," they say in unison, then chuckle. Though they're not related by blood, the sound of their laughs rings similar.

Hands on my hips and chest expanding, I take it all in. So this is it. The Fifth. It's not much to look at. *Oh well.* I shrug. As much as I long to sleep for days, we don't have that sort of time.

Dahlia Moon, here we come.

joshua

"*You had no choice. You did what was required to obtain your goal.*"

"Get out of my head!"

The voice that emerges from my mouth is not one I recognize. It's angry and bitter, splintering through the canyon like a nail through rotting wood.

The voice inside, however, is one I've become all too familiar with. This voice has been eating me alive for days, but more so since I slunk away from the Fourth, the countess's blood hot on my hands. I can no longer slough it off as exhaustion. The voice taunts me, driving me mad, relentless in its sinister assurances.

"*Come now. Surely you don't mind my presence. The company must be welcome. The life of a murderer is a lonely one—*"

"I am not a murderer!" The last word echoes, returning to haunt me again and again with each step. My entire body itches and burns. I am surrounded by desert, but my state has nothing to do with the Fifth Reflection climate.

The Void is taking over. I am running out of time.

"*Tell me, Joshua, how does it feel to be a murderer?*"

My internal vexation mimics Haman's hiss, mocking the memory of our confrontation at the subway Threshold. Back then the words were a jab, cutting at my guilt over my mother's death. A death that was an accident. A death that was not my fault, just like the death of Countess Ambrose.

It was an accident.

I did not intend to kill her.

It is not my fault.

"Keep telling yourself that," the voice jeers.

I shove the countess's son forward, prodding the boy's back with the tip of my sword. Since when did I become a murderer, and now a kidnapper? My criminal record grows thick, but I'm so close. I can't give up, not when I've come this far. I pick up my pace, clutching the mirrorglass bottle in my right hand.

Once Gage and I delivered the true Midnight Rose to Isabeau, we parted at last, then I returned to the Fourth alone, eager to find my brother and El in the catacombs where I left them. But they were nowhere to be seen, and anxiety mounted among the Reflection's residents.

"Something is amiss," a shopkeeper murmured to his customers as I crept between buildings in the marketplace. "The countess is usually up with the sun. Passes through every morning, tasting the baker's bread, chattin' with the coffee roaster. Unlike her not to show."

The countess's body hadn't been discovered yet, but it was only a matter of hours before the tides would change. I couldn't risk remaining in the area. If I got caught, the countess's death traced back to me, all my hard work would be for nothing. Still, I required information as to where Kyaphus had taken El. The countess most likely would have known, but the woman was useless to me now. My best option was her heir. But of course I couldn't take his meager word for it. I brought him along to ensure he relayed the truth. He protested at first, insisting the crew had nothing I desired.

"Listen closely. I will find the whereabouts of your captain. With or without your help." I lifted him by his shirt collar, and his feet dangled aboveground. The extra strength I'd received from the Void was paying off.

"Hey, man." The boy's hands shot into the air faster than Ever blood heals. "I'm sure we can work out a deal."

I lowered him but kept my grip tight. "What is it you want?"

"There's a girl on board the ship. Ebony. Leave her alone and I'll do whatever you ask."

"Done."

I didn't give him time to request a Kiss of Accord, and he didn't attempt it. Perhaps the kid is smarter than he looks.

Fortitude carries us farther from the Fifth's Fairy Fountain, closer to the canyon's end. Isabeau was more than accommodating once she had her precious rose. Now we trudge through this forsaken desert land. I bear no interest in Kyaphus's reasons for dragging—stealing—El away. It only matters that I catch up to them before things turn irreversible. If the Callings expire entirely, if the Thresholds finish draining, that's it. The Verity's light will extinguish, and the Reflections as we know them will never be the same.

"How much farther to the nearest compound?" The sound that trips off my tongue is again foreign to me. More animal than man.

Tried or Ride or whatever his name is walks with hands behind his head. "I told you, I've only been here once. I think it's at the end of the canyon."

"You'd better be right, kid. For your own sake."

I want to vomit from my own cruelty but refrain. I must keep my wits if I'm to question the people of the Fifth. This Reflection is known for its smaller clusters of people, and most who live here are native born. Rare to have strangers or visitors, which makes my job a crowe of a lot easier. If El and Kyaphus have been sighted, the people here will know.

A small hut at the crest of a winding trail ahead catches my eye and I aim for it, nudging the boy's arm with the flat of my blade so he adjusts his course. The sun beats down and I blink against its rays, longing for the winter of the Second. I'd welcome snow over sand any day.

The trail takes longer to climb than anticipated, or perhaps I have nothing to gauge time against anymore. Up close the hut looks more like a small cottage, out of place in this terrain with its cobbled walls and potted flowers in the windowsills. It almost seems familiar, as if I've seen it somewhere before.

I shake away the notion. Throat parched and legs weak, I shove the boy left, keeping my sword level with his chest. Then I lift a fist and pound the door. Someone shuffles around on the other side. The curtain in the window to my left flutters. I lean to the right and shade my eyes, peering through the glass but unable to catch much of anything through the caked dust.

When I draw back I catch a glimpse of my reflection. Then I recoil, dropping my sword and clawing at my face. This is me? This is the man I've become? No, not a man at all, but a monster. No different from the Troll. No better than Jonathan. How could I have allowed this to happen?

"For power."

No, for El.

"Not for your precious Eliyana. You did this for yourself."

The door cracks and I shield my face with my arm, all too sure whoever it is will not help me if they see not who but what I am.

The door flies wide and a woman steps over the Threshold. Her belly has reduced since I saw her last. She cradles a baby, bouncing him the way I've seen countless mothers do. I lower my arm and her confused expression pales to dread.

My knees knock and I collapse at her feet.

"Joshua!" Her shout echoes the fear widening her eyes.

I can't move. I gaze at her, tears streaming as I croak, "Elizabeth."

meant for me

How much farther? Every joint and muscle aches. I'm dirty and tired and basically done. I blow a breath onto my palm and sniff. Grimace. I'd ask someone for a stick of gum, but yeah. Doubt Ebony has a random piece of Juicy Fruit lying around in her pocket. And if she did I bet I wouldn't want it anyway. Because *eww*.

The hike through the canyon along what I've learned is the Docolora River is uncomfortable at best. My jeans are stretched out from constant wear and have begun to sag low on my hips. My hair is so tangled a bird could make a nest out of it. I'd be lucky to get a brush through it even after a wash and condition, neither of which is probably anywhere in my near future.

Isaach leads the caravan with the *Iron Lass* crew close behind. The draining Threshold we passed through—Nabka Threshold—looked more like a pond by the time we left than the lake Isaach said it's supposed to be. The alcohol seems to have worn off, as the bearded man's steps are sure and straight now. We follow single file, the path growing narrower with each step. At one point I'm forced to turn sideways in order to scooch between two boulders. A bout of claustrophobia kicks in and I'm half inclined to turn back. But I'm sandwiched between Ebony in front and Ky behind. Nowhere to go but where everyone else is headed.

When we reach the slenderest patch of the pass, I'm sure we've hit a dead end. But wait. No. Hard to see when everyone is taller than me, but is that . . . Are they . . . Yes. They're getting down on all fours, crawling through a low tunnel. Funny how almost drowning didn't freak me out, but the idea of going through this hole in the earth causes my pulse to amp. Is it long? Sturdy? What if it caves in? What if we get stuck? Death by suffocation or a rock to the head is so not the way I want to go.

Khloe enters, then Ebony. Ugh, fine. I'm on my knees, breathing deep, then scuttling forward. I can't see a thing and the only sound is the shuffle of my sisters in front of me, the pant of their shallow breaths. Low oxygen makes my chest constrict the farther we crawl. I wish Ebony would move faster.

"Really, Em? You faced the most sinister man in the Reflections and this is what scares you?"

If you're going to make fun of me, you can just leave. The sand and pebbles grate my palms. My knees are sore and there's a crick in my neck. For crying out loud, will this tunnel ever end?

"I keep telling you," Ky thinks. *"If you don't want a response, you have to block me."*

And how am I supposed to do that?

"Think of it like self-defense. Take your thoughts captive. Keep your mind guarded. Make a conscious decision to—"

Ky's thought dies. Cuts off. We're talking radio silence. *Ky? Hello? You okay?* I hear him move behind me, but his mind has muted.

"See?" His voice returns. *"Exactly like that. Go somewhere else. Anywhere but here."*

Anywhere but here, huh? It's worth a try.

Still moving, I work to focus. That's really all any Calling is—focus. What I've been doing since honing my abilities. Using my mind, my heart, to find the strength within. Love ignites my Calling, as I discovered at Nathaniel's that cold November night on Lisel Island. When I tried to ignore it, do away with it, everything was more difficult. But when I let it in? Invite it? My Calling comes alive—the *Verity* comes alive. Of course it does. Because the Verity was meant to love, to be loved. It all makes so much sense now.

Nowhere to go but forward, I close my eyes. I continue crawling, but I'm not here. I think of the Verity, of the woman it became. Of the heartbreak she endured. My thoughts take me to what I imagine to be the Garden of Epoch. Trees at every angle. Roses the brightest hue of red. A river with a waterfall the clearest crystal blue. Pouring, splashing, foaming at its end. I picture myself walking along a cobbled path, and as I walk, hedges sprout on either side of me. I envision an orchard filled with any fruit one might wish to eat. As I pick an apple, more trees spring up around me, shielding me.

"*You're doing it,*" Ky thinks. "*I can't hear you.*"

I move through the trees, breaking free of them. *But I can still hear you.*

"*Only if you want to.*"

I do, but for now I allow myself to shrink back into the solace of the trees. It's quiet here. I love Ky, but this is nice too. Needed. A first-in-forever minute alone where I can think anything and no one knows but me, myself, and the Verity.

I remain that way, lounging against the apple tree of my mind, crunching on the sweet fruit. When we exit the tunnel, I rise and dust off my jeans. Ky gets up beside me. He's beaming.

"You're my favorite," he says aloud.

I smile up at him, but my thoughts linger in my private corner. A little mystery will do him some good. Because some things need to be left unsaid—unheard.

Some thoughts are meant for me alone.

"Gather 'round, friends, and hear this tale."

Isaach's wife, Breckan, gestures for us to join her by the campfire. Her sapphire eyes dance in the flames' light. Her hair is as fiery as Charley's, who is apparently a native of the Fifth. The woman's voice is young and vibrant, but the laugh lines framing her smile let on she's older than she sounds. She wears a dress fashioned from stripped cloth similar to the one modeled on our redheaded crew member.

And there's another thing too. Something I didn't pick up on until now. The men wear stripped cloth at their belts, one on each corner. The colors are vibrant, and the cloth dances and sways with each body move.

The Verity's true form plays at the forefront of my mind. Could the cloths be like the dyed hair tassels of the Second? A sign these people serve the Verity? What tokens of loyalty did I miss in the Third and Fourth? I make a mental note to pay better attention. Knowing who stands with the Verity with just a glance could be useful in the future.

I watch as the other tribe members huddle in, some resting on halved logs or the desert ground, others standing in groups of twos, threes, and fours. Aside from Charley, who seems at home among a group of women who could be her twins, our *Seven Seas* misfits remain banded. We squeeze onto a log, out of place with our non-orange hair and drab clothing.

Our arrival at the Nitegra Compound was welcomed with a horde of questions and wide-eyed stares. The Fifth is apparently the least populated of all Reflections, and even more so now with the draining Thresholds. Isaach explained the Nabka Compound near the same Threshold was abandoned the day the lake began to drain. No one wants to live in the desert without ample water and a passage out. Need I explain?

"Me great-great-great-great-great . . ." I lost track of how many greats he used. ". . . grandpappy discovered the Fifth," the chief explained. "Brought his tribe and settled the first compound. Over time the tribe grew and split in two, then three. We eventually grew to five—Nitegra, Nabka, Mancheco, Uptuck, and Koweapnan." He held up four fingers, confirming he'd been drinking again. Or maybe the tongue-twisting tribe names scrambled his brain. "Our tribe is the best, though. Ain't that right, Breckan?"

She smiled sweetly up at him, patting his pronounced gut with her dainty hand. Adoration shone from her eyes. It was apparent in the way she hugged him. In how she watched him walk away.

Now she's center stage. I glance at Isaach who sits just beyond her. The same admiration I saw in her now radiates from him. His gaze never abandons her. The constant smile she bears conveys that she doesn't question her husband's love.

I reach right and slip my hand into Ky's. He squeezes it, tracing the top of my thumb with his. With Joshua I carried so many doubts. Worries. Was our connection real? Manufactured? But with Ky? I don't wonder for a second what goes on in that mind of his. And not because I can hear him most of the time. It's because when you know, you just know. And knowing is a beautiful thing.

"Quiet now, quiet." Breckan makes a sort of lower-the-volume movement with her hands.

The tribe's chatter dies. The fire *snap, crackle, pops*. Smoke wafts toward us, makes me blink too much. I lower my head, watch Ky's thumb move back and forth over my skin. He has a freckle on his knuckle. I curve my lips.

"*The Legend of the Shadowalkers*," Breckan begins, "is a tale as old as the Reflections."

Chills raise the hairs on my arms. Countess Ambrose mentioned Shadowalkers, beings who worship the Void. Breckan says they're legend, but I have a feeling, like the story Ky read in the council chamber, the Shadowalkers are very real indeed. I'm betting Jasyn Crowe was a Shadowalker. He chose the Void, relished its power. Is that really any different from worship?

"Legend says," Breckan continues, "tha first Shadowalker began as a vessel of tha Void."

I look up just as Breckan casts a backward glance toward Isaach. A teasing, playful look. He lifts the pint that might as well be glued to his palm, then winks. Something tells me they're sharing an inside joke meant for the two of them alone.

"Corrupt was tha vessel. Loathsome." Her face contorts, as if she's donning a scary mask. "Rather than fight against tha Void, tha vessel welcomed it. It began with a single bend of the will, but soon became more. Even tha Verity's vessel could do nothing ta stop it. For when tha Void's vessel began ta love himself more than tha one who held tha Verity, that's when things went south."

A low murmur passes like a wave over the tribe. Some excited. Some in awe. They must've heard this story before, but still they take it in as if they're hearing it for the first time.

"When tha Void moved on ta another, tha previous vessel remained loyal ta tha darkness. Followed tha new vessel everywhere and soon convinced others ta join as well."

Tiernan. Jasyn. Gage. All willingly surrendered to the Void. No one forced them like with Ky or the Soulless.

"Heed me warning, friends. Listen to me words. For here is tha moral of me tale. We all have a little darkness in us, but tha choice is yers. Will ya fight it?" She puts up her fists. "Or will ya bow?" She flourishes her arm in a wide sweep. Stare intense, she lets her gaze pass over us all, as if allowing her words to sink in. Then, after what seems like eons, she backs away and sits on Isaach's lap.

He kisses his wife full on the mouth and she returns the sentiment with fervor, grabbing his face between her hands. The tribe hollers and whistles. Someone begins a song on the bagpipes. Children rise and dance in circles around the fire. Knee slaps, claps, guffaws, and giggles. All are present. All should lift my spirits.

But my mood is not so joyous. My heart droops and I lean my head on Ky's shoulder, blocking my thoughts as I wonder . . .

Has Joshua chosen the life of a Shadowalker?

FORTY-FOUR

joshua

W here am I?"

My eyes awaken to darkness. It consumes me, pulling me under. I see and feel nothing. I cannot recall what hour it is. Is it day or night? How long have I been out? Am I still out? Blackness is my only company, weighing heavy on my soul. I try to claw at it, but I cannot move. My arms feel pinned at my sides, and my legs are filled with lead. When I inhale it's as if I'm breathing smoke. An attempt to choke it away is futile. The fumes will not recede. Have I died?

"In a way, yes," a voice says, though it is not the sinister hiss I've come to know recently. This voice is much more horrifying, because this voice is not foreign, as *this* voice sounds like my own.

"Who are you?" I ask.

"Who else?" he says. "I am you."

I try to sit, though I have no way to decipher if I am lying down or standing up. It's as if I am in a state of limbo. There is no north or south, no right or left. There is only darkness and my own voice taunting me in my head.

"This is what you wanted, isn't it? You've kept me suppressed for so long, but I've longed to be released. When you finally began to unlock my chains, I knew it was only a matter of time before you allowed me to take over completely."

Head pounding, I attempt the smallest movement. A roll of my wrist or a turn of my head. But I remain stationary, imprisoned in the darkness of my own mind.

"Doesn't feel good, does it?" he asks. "To be trapped inside yourself? Welcome to my world."

I want to draw my sword, but my fingers won't so much as twitch at my sides. "Who are you? Where am I?" The desire to pass out again presses on my eyelids, but I force them wide. "Do not play games with me."

"I told you. I am you, or a version of you. You may call me Josh, if you wish."

A guttural sound emits from my throat. If I could, I'd clench my fists and punch this imposter in his invisible face. I always hated when someone slipped and called me Josh. It's not my name. "Where am I? Do not make me ask again."

"The light in your soul has been captured. Taken over by me, the most selfish, most shadowed part of you."

It cannot be. "Release me, you swine." My soul thrashes. "Release me or I'll—"

"You'll what?" Josh jeers. "You are helpless now that I have at last risen to the surface. And we have a job to do. The Elixir—"

No! What have I done? What could I have possibly been thinking? This isn't the way. "Don't you touch her." The words seethe, hot coals on my own head. "You go near her and I swear I'll—"

"Again with the threats." I can almost envision my evil side with arms crossed and eyes narrowed, a wicked smile plastered on his face. "You have no power over me anymore. I am free. And I'll not be returning to my prison."

With all my might I lash against the darkness, against the Void I so foolishly allowed to spread. My muscles burn, but I don't relent. My chest feels as if it may explode as Josh continues to hiss in my ear.

"Allow this. Welcome it."

"No!"

"This is your punishment."

"I can do better. I can do right. I can be good. I can overcome."

"She deserves better than you."

I cease my fight.

Josh isn't wrong. After all I've done, lying, bartering with traitors, murdering the countess . . . do I truly believe El would have me? No doubt she'd take one look at me and see the horror I've become.

I exhale and rest, the darkness like a ton of bricks pressing in. I don't think of it as giving up, but more like letting go. A release of sorts. The Void has latched onto my mind now, a virus taking over the network of my brain. I am no longer Joshua, but Josh. The Void is in control. The release lifts a burden I can no longer bear.

I close my eyes and El's face fills my mind as I drift off to sleep.

calling to me

I can't remember where or from whom, but at one point I heard time is like a river. Maybe it was Disney's *Pocahontas*, or perhaps it was that super-nerdy kid Greg in fourth grade who always went on and on about *The Legend of Zelda*. Either way, I'm stealing the phrase. Because as we follow the shore along the Docolora River, one thing is certain.

You can't stop time.

It's always flowing and changing. You can try to pause its course, even alter it. But it continues moving and eventually builds up and bursts free, pouring over the dam you created. The flow of time is inevitable. Fight it or go with it. But no matter what you do, you can't turn back. I think Dimitri was wrong in that regard. He said time is a loop, but how can it be?

No one can change the past.

I rub my droopy eyes, checking to ensure, once again, that I didn't leave Dimitri's journal behind. I read late into the night until the last flicker of campfire faded. The chapter on mirrorglass only confirmed Ky's assumption that the crown had something to do with recent catastrophic events. I draw it to the surface of my mind, using my Scrib memory to recall every detail.

Second Day, Twelfth Month, Eleventh Year of Count VonKemp

I have confirmed mirrorglass may be molded into weapons

and tools when melted by the flame of Dragon's breath.
Dragons are sly, vicious creatures. To behold their breath
and live to tell the tale would be a rare feat indeed, making
items fashioned from mirrorglass a valuable commodity.
Should one come across such an item, I would advise he
guard it with his life.

My gaze falls to Ky a few feet ahead. His bare back is toward me, his shirt wrapped around his head like a turban. His mirrorglass blade is sheathed at his side. I've never asked him who originally gave it to him. I'd search his thoughts, but I have a feeling that's a story he needs to share when he's ready. Instead I let my mind wander back to Dimitri's words. Let them sink in like the last note of a truly profound piece.

What is perhaps truly the most fascinating feature of
mirrorglass is its effects on light and darkness. The reverse
effect seems to turn darkness into light and vice versa. If I
had not witnessed it with my own eyes, I would not believe
it myself. But when exposed to light, the mirrorglass turns
dark, and when darkness hits it? The stuff reflects back
light. It is quite the sight to behold.

And this one revelation explained so much. Ky and I were awake until dawn discussing it. When Joshua wore the crown, it turned his darkness light, keeping the Void dormant as Ky said. But when I took it on? The crown only served to suppress the light. It's why I felt a sudden loss of warmth and peace at the coronation. The reason my connection to Ky grew stronger. The Verity was silenced for a time, allowing the Void in Ky to work its way in through our intertwined souls. When I finally removed the crown at the brownstone, it was too late. The damage had been done, my connection to Ky and the Void more solid than ever. It found its way into me, latching on through my growing love for the boy before me.

The knowledge brings joy and sorrow in a single wipe of my

brow. Joy because it wasn't some problem with my blemished soul that caused the Verity to grow weak. Sorrow because had I not been connected to Ky by a Kiss of Infinity, the Void never would've found its way in to begin with.

When King Aidan wore the crown, his soul was not linked to Jasyn's, so the crown would not have hurt the Verity within. It may have dimmed it, and I'm guessing because of that Aidan would not have worn the crown often. But even with the light docile, darkness wouldn't have found a door. It was my soul bond to Ky that made the difference. But how can I regret saving him from becoming Soulless? I don't know who I'd be without him.

I look at Ky again. His scars shine in the sunlight, his rose and thorn Shield seal standing out among the wreckage of his skin. The image brings another to mind. *Joshua* bruised and bleeding. *Joshua* doing everything in his power to protect me from taking on the Void. As selfish and coldly methodical as his actions come off, everything he's done has always been about one thing.

Saving the people.

Saving me.

Chewing my bottom lip, I mull this over as we make the trek to Dahlia Moon's. Not because I'm changing my mind. Ky or Joshua? But because Joshua was my best friend—my only friend—for a long time. We have a history. Ky may be my present, my future, but Joshua? He's my past and that doesn't change overnight. It never changes.

Because no one can change the past.

Isaach relayed Dahlia lives at the canyon's east end, only half a day's walk from the Nitegra Compound. Breckan drew us a map on a flat red stone, pointing out the Reyaub Cliffs to the west and the Nabka Forest to the north, admonishing us to stay along the river's shore. "As long as ye can find tha river, ye can find yer way east or west. It's like a path, ye see?" She smiled then bogged us down with packs full of food, supplies, and water.

"The Fifth's desert is wicked." She bustled about her hut, riffling through baskets, arms loaded with whatever she could scrap.

"Hard ta keep yer wits about ya when that noon sun hits. Rest beneath tha shade when ye find it, and sip at yer canteen every ten minutes er so. And don't ferget what I said before. Stay near tha river if ya know what's good fer ya. Good luck."

With a wave the odd couple sent us on our way. Charley elected to stay behind, whittling our group down another notch. Six of us remain, and everyone's been filled in on our mission. Ky didn't see a reason to keep things hidden any longer.

"You all deserve to know what we face in the days ahead." Mopping his face with his shirt, he made eye contact with each of us. "If anyone wants to stay back, he or she is welcome to do so."

We listened and some exchanged glances. In the end, only Charley bowed out. I searched Flint's eyes, looking for something I could trust—or suspect. He hasn't said much since the Fourth, and Gunner does most of his talking for him. Still, the pilot tagged along, hands shoved in his pockets and back hunched. Now we march in silence, our tasks wheeling through my mind.

Find Dahlia Moon.

Inquire about the first vessel of the Verity.

Locate said vessel.

Destroy. The. Void.

I shared my theory with Ky during our all-nighter. We sat under cover of the Fifth's stars, legs dangling over the edge of a cliff, sharing a canteen of sweet cactus juice and a handful of grapes.

"Is it possible?" I popped a green grape into my mouth, the juice oozing tartness onto my tongue.

Ky took a swig. Wiped his mouth with the back of his arm. "Makes sense. We'll have to mention it to Dahlia. If the Void was created by lack of love, why wouldn't true love be its weakness?"

Leaning back on my elbows, I nodded. The night was cool but not uncomfortable. Maybe the desert wasn't so bad. We sat that way for some time. I didn't want to fall asleep and give up the moment.

But daylight always reigns. And what did it bring but white-hot doubts beating down with the sun's rays? What was I thinking?

The desert is awful. Everything appears better at night. Now I'm rethinking the notion I know anything about destroying the Void. Maybe this is all pointless.

"*The Fifth's desert is wicked . . . Keep yer wits about ya.*"

Breckan's words are a bucket of ice down my back. Blink. Step. Straighten. Nearly there. We left before dawn and the sun is almost directly above now. I wipe the sweat seeping into my eyes, shade them. Where—?

"I see it! I see it!" Khloe jumps up and down, spunkier than she should be after half a day in the heat.

We pick up our pace, canteens rattling against our packs. My sweatshirt wrapped around my waist loosens and I cinch it snug. We follow the winding hill path, the way jutting into the rocks, then back out. When we near the top, the house comes into full view. In the shade of the canyon wall our destination grows clear. That's when I stop. Take a step. Crane my neck. And then I'm holding my breath, covering my mouth with both hands. Because I've seen this house before. I know it. All at once I don't care about my aching legs or my heat exhaustion or anything but shoving past the crew and bursting through the door.

This is Mom's dream house, the one she drew in her sketchbook-slash-journal. The one she labeled "Someday." The stone chimney. The hedge of rosebushes. The ivy framing the door. The foliage is dried out and the structure is a little dilapidated, but it's here.

"Mom?" I call once I'm inside. "Mom? Are you here?"

"Eliyana?" Her voice is faint. Muffled. Far.

Biggest sigh of relief ever. "Mom. Where are you? Where's Evan? I can't see anything."

Footsteps thud across the stone floor.

I whirl.

A baby cries. Another sigh. My brother *is* here. He's okay. Have he and Mom been in Dahlia's care this entire time?

I move deeper into the cottage, past the front window shedding a miniscule amount of light. I run into a stool. *Ouch.* Why is it so dark? My pulse reaches my ears. Something's off and it's not the lights alone. "Mom, this isn't funny anymore." Dumb thing to say. Because Mom doesn't play jokes. Not like this.

As my vision adjusts, the faint outline of the furniture and floor plan becomes clear. But still no sign of my family. I search all two rooms. Nothing. When I return to the front, Ky and the others have piled into the entryway.

"Is she here? Is Dahlia Moon here?" Khloe rises on her toes, stretches her neck.

I shrug. Open my mouth to answer that no, no one seems to be home, but the desert sun has certainly induced hallucinations of some sort. Maybe the cottage doesn't even look the way I saw it. Maybe I only imagined it was the one in Mom's drawing. I've missed her. Much has crowded my mind these days, but I've never forgotten Mom and Evan.

Shuffle. Creak. The crew shifts, turns their heads. A figure steps out from behind the open front door. A man, tall and dark, with black veins running the lengths of his arms, across his bare torso, around his neck, over his face.

The crew backs away, giving him room. Everyone except Ky, who pushes Khloe behind him and draws his mirrorblade. "Em, if you were ever going to mirror walk, now's the time to do it."

His comment throws me off. Does he really think I'd abandon the team?

"Had to try," Ky says in my head.

I'm not going anywhere, I reply.

The man moves toward me, stepping into the thin sliver of window light. I wouldn't know him except for those eyes, cerulean blue and him as ever.

"Joshua?" His name sounds as if I've spoken it in another language.

He shakes his head. Bares his teeth. "It's Josh now." A roll of the neck. A crack of the knuckles.

I knit my brows. *"Joshua."* Now my voice is shaking. "What's happened to you?"

He doesn't respond. Doesn't try to hug me or talk to me. And I realize, even with his eyes, he's not the same at all.

One more step toward me, then he does a full 180 and rounds on Ky. "Hello, brother," Joshua—Josh?—snarls.

Brother? I can't see Ebony, but a "What the bleep?" would be fitting right about now.

"Reunited at last," Josh says.

Khloe steps out from behind her brother. Hands planted on her hips and stance wide, she says, "We're not afraid of you."

The Ever draws his sword.

"Joshua, don't!" I sing.

A glare over his shoulder. "I told you." He spits to one side. "It's Josh now."

Then he runs his blade straight through Khloe.

I'm on my knees, scrambling to my younger sister's side. Drawing her into my arms. Patting her hair. Her eyes roll into her head.

Ky is frozen, blade held fast at his side.

Josh wipes his bloody sword on his pants.

I press my soaked face into Khloe's curly mop. Whisper an inaudible, blubbering, *"No."*

Ebony is with me now, wrapping her arms around my quaking frame, resting her forehead on my shoulder.

Like everything else, this is because of me. I look up at Josh now. He's just staring at Ky. Waiting. Waiting for what?

Lyrics to Passenger's "Let Her Go" burn through me . . .

"Everything you touch, surely dies . . ."

No. This is not my fault. If I doubted my choice before, I sure as crowe don't now. I find my voice. "How could you do this?"

Josh doesn't cast a glance in my direction. His regard is trained on Ky. Still he doesn't budge.

With care, I transfer Khloe into Ebony's arms. It takes every ounce of willpower I have to rise, but I manage. The Verity is hard to notice, but I sense it, flickering like a dying flame in the pit of my soul.

"Answer me!" My internal scream turns audible. The sound echoes through the small space.

Josh gives no indication he hears. Not a flinch. Not a twitch.

I pound my fists on his back, which feels rock hard against my touch. How did he get like this? How could he allow the Void to take him? I'm inclined to keep blaming myself. The Verity is meant to keep the Void at bay. But this isn't on me. I won't let it be. Joshua made his own choices.

And, like a true Shadowalker, he chose the Void.

A sob emerges as I take a step back and yank at my hair. At long last I catch a glimpse of the Ever tattoo above his right shoulder blade. It's barely visible, but it's there. Beneath the blackened brambles. It's simple. Beautiful. Perfect.

Joshua's seal . . . is a heart.

It should've turned black like the rest of him.

I clutch my own heart to keep it from falling out of my chest. The Void is everywhere. I shove away the image of Jasyn Crowe. This is Joshua. *Joshua.* He's a good guy. Because beneath it all there must be a chance he can return. Our mission becomes more desperate than ever, Joshua added to the list of those we must save.

The rest of the crew makes no move to attack. They don't breathe. Don't blink. Because after what's just happened, no one dares get near Josh—the Void.

Ky is the first to speak. A statue, his mouth scarcely stirring. "Wrong move, David."

"We'll see." He slips his hand into his pants pocket and withdraws a small bottle. It's lovely, made of what is unmistakably mirrorglass.

As he faces Josh—his brother?—Ky's nostrils flare. A single tear escapes his green eye and slides down his cheek.

Josh lifts the mirrorglass bottle and collects the tear, swishing it around and holding it up to the light. Then he turns and offers the bottle to me. "Drink." His tenor borders on robotic.

I recoil. "Excuse me?"

"Drink, El. Or so help me I will finish off every last one of them."

In the past I wouldn't have believed such a threat, not from Joshua. But now I bite my lip to keep it from quivering. I hold my ground so I don't crumple. Mirrorglass reverses. What will this reverse?

Josh brandishes his sword once more. He won't do to Ky what he did to Khloe. The beating in the Fourth was one thing. Joshua can take the few punches he gave Ky then, because whatever happens to Ky happens to Joshua. That alone was my first tip Joshua's not all right. No matter his hatred for Ky, Joshua wouldn't hurt him and risk hurting me. But killing is different. And without Ever blood to restore him, Ky's death would end all three of us.

So Josh levels his weapon at Ebony.

Second thought not required. When I saved her from becoming Soulless it was selfless. Now the act is for myself as much as for her. Whatever she's done in the past, she's my sister. And not just by blood either.

I snatch the bottle from Josh's hand, glaring as I tip it ceiling-ward. Ky's tear slides from the glass onto my tongue. Flavors bounce and change, reminding me of the blueberry girl from *Willy Wonka and the Chocolate Factory*.

At first the tear is sweet. I taste our reunion on the *Seven Seas*. My confession in the catacombs. Our kiss on the Fourth's shore.

The tear turns sour.

I'm transported to the night Ky kidnapped me. Knocked off my feet by his cruelty. By the way he so easily stabbed Makai.

The taste melts to bitterness.

Anger rises. Ky working for Haman. Ky taking me from the castle and leaving Mom behind.

"Em." He reaches for me.

It makes no sense, no sense at all, but I withdraw from his touch. Emotions war. Love, anger, hatred. Which one is right?

Ky's face pales, the life and light vanishing from his complexion.

Black veins climb up his bare torso, up his neck and slack jaw. I've never seen him look this afraid. This helpless.

Josh alters too. The Void drains from him, gradually receding into nothing. Because the Void inhabits the one who cares most for the Verity's vessel. Whatever drinking the tear has accomplished, Ky's love now far surpasses Joshua's.

I inspect my right arm, plain as the left now. The Void has vanished from me as well. Ky bears the full weight of it. And something inside me snaps. Even so I can't bring myself to touch him, to hold him, to tell him everything will be okay. I'm glued in place.

I fight against my invisible restraints. "What have you done?" The question is for Josh. I expect to find him gone and the real Joshua returned, but even without the blackened veins, his stare remains stone cold. Heartless.

"A few more seconds should do it." He folds his arms. Leans away. His gaze never leaves mine.

A few more . . . what? "What are you—?"

The flavor on my tongue vanishes at last. Bitterness turns to nothing. I'd never know I drank . . . What did I drink? I can't . . . I can't remember. My eyes close. Head hangs.

A tap on my shoulder.

I whip up my head. A man stands before me, darkness covering every inch of his skin. The only light he carries is in his eyes, one green and one brown. Who is he? He almost seems familiar, but why? I step away, take the most comfortable place in the room. The place that feels safe.

The place beside Joshua.

FORTY-SIX

josh

I wouldn't believe it unless I was seeing it with my own eyes. The Elixir worked. That old coot Rafaj wasn't so insane after all.

"Mirrorglass reverses, my boy." Bony finger pointed, he explained further, "The stuff is plentiful, particularly in the Fourth, but to find an object crafted from it? That is a rare find indeed." He hacked several times, and I was certain he might pass out before finishing. Fortunately, he didn't. "There are few who possess a touch gentle enough to shape the small stones into something else, and even fewer who can tame a Dragon long enough to use its breath for melting. For it is not the glass itself that is rare, but the one who knows how to use it."

I listened intently, soaking in his every word. I knew my brother's blade caused a reverse effect when withdrawn from a wound, but what would the bottle do?

"Two ingredients are needed for the Elixir," the old man croaked. "The bottle, as I have mentioned, and a single tear."

Seemed easy enough, but I waited, all too aware more was required than met the ear. No doubt retrieving the specific tear needed would be a feat in itself. I moved deeper into Rafaj's cell. "Whose tear?"

Knees wobbling, he rose, using the stone wall for support. "To unbind two souls, here is what you must do." His finger lifted in the air, and then he stroked his pointed chin. "Using the mirrorglass bottle, collect a tear shed by the one you wish to be forgotten."

All right, that would be Kyaphus. Shouldn't be too challenging.

"It must be a first tear, and it must be one produced from a broken heart. That, I am afraid, is nonnegotiable."

The difficulty rose a level. Still, it was achievable.

"Serve the tear to the one you wish to do the forgetting. Once it touches her lips, the process shall begin. It should be mere moments before they are unbound, failing to remember the other altogether."

Eliyana is stubborn, and I knew persuasion would be key. And I was right, of course, because here we stand. Not only did the Elixir swipe her memory, unbind her from my brother, but it erased the Void from my soul as well.

"You idiot," my good side says in my head. *"The Void entered Kyaphus because he loves her most now. You've ruined everything."*

I laugh at my own joke before I think it. *I believe that was you.* I put his voice on low, keeping it just loud enough, but not so much I can't hear myself think.

"I'll fight you. You won't win this."

On second thought I mute him completely. I'll catch up with him later, fill him in on what we've accomplished with the Void at our fingertips. Kyaphus carries the full agony that comes with housing the darkness, leaving me free to control him and it. I get the power without the pain.

El's expressions shift between confusion, anger, fear, and longing. Lower lip trembling, she sobs his name. "Joshua?" Her hands quake. "Joshua, what's . . . ?" Her head shakes and her eyes squeeze shut. "What's happening to me?"

I draw her in and caress her cheek with my thumb, acting as the man she believes me to be. "Everything's going to be fine now." The lie is too easy.

She sighs and leans into my touch. But just as quickly, she recoils.

I curl my fingers into my palm, and my fingernails pierce my skin. This is nothing less than what I expected. Rafaj warned me of the side effects, of her probable confusion, but I can handle it. With my brother out of the way, there's so much I can accomplish.

"Ember."

The sound of his voice curdles my blood, but I don't act. There is no need.

El faces him, her own expression a mask of confusion.

"Ember."

If he calls her by my mother's name one more time, I may be forced to pummel him. He's no longer connected to her, which means a good beating won't hurt me in the least.

I grin at the notion.

He reaches out.

She does not move. Until she does.

When she breaks eye contact, I know for certain I've succeeded.

When she breaks eye contact, I know the bond is broken.

When she breaks eye contact and places her hand in mine, I know she has forgotten him for good.

ASIDE

KY

This can't be real.

Why is she standing beside him?

Why is she holding his hand?

I know the Void consumes me, but I'm still me. Nothing's changed. I fight against the darkness, shutting out the heinous thoughts threatening to win me over. I've practiced this for years, since Tiernan gave me my first taste of evil.

"Let me out!" Kyaphus, otherwise known as my evil twin, bellows.

Shut up, I tell him, pushing him deeper. *I'll handle this.*

I take a step forward, and Ember moves closer to his side. It's not that she looks happy to be there. Quite the opposite. Her face is like a ghost's. She's terrified. But the difference is she knows him. He's familiar. It's me she doesn't recognize.

"David, what have you done?" The words release on a growl. I'd raise my knife, but if she doesn't know me, she doesn't know my blade won't kill him either. Starting a fight would make things worse.

"Only what was required." He removes his hand from hers and places a protective arm around her shoulders. "I saved the Callings. The Reflections. The Void is no longer intertwined with the Verity. Which means everything should return to normal soon."

My throat constricts. "At least heal her then." I gesture toward Khloe, who lies in Ebony's arms, bleeding, but not quite gone. "Please." I hate to grovel, but if it's what's required to save the only family I have, so be it. "She's innocent."

David raises his right brow.

Em looks up at him.

When he cuts his palm on his sword, letting his blood drip onto Khloe's wound, I know it's only a show. A way to prove he's the good guy. I don't care about his reason though. I only care that my sister survives.

Time ticks like a bomb ready to explode.

Khloe's eyes open and she gasps.

My chest grows tight, but a relieved sigh escapes.

The problem may be rectified for now, but our goal remains the same. The Void must be ended for good. Only then will we truly be free.

I glance at my crew, searching for someone who might stand by me. Of all people, it's Flint who joins my side. Ebony helps a bloodstained Khloe up, supporting her as they hobble over. But Gunner backs away and out the door. I watch him run, disappearing from sight.

My gaze finds Ember's then, except she's not Ember anymore. She's El again. She stares at me with vacant eyes. I think of how much I love her. I think of her song. But it does me no good.

She can't hear me anymore.

FORTY-SEVEN

DUSK IS FALLING

That man with the mismatched eyes won't quit watching me. He's kind of creepy, to be honest. Ebony tried to convince me I know the guy, Ky something or other. I just shook my head and asked her to leave me alone. Maybe I can't trust her after all.

Maybe I can't trust anyone.

I step outside through the cottage's back door. Dusk is falling over the canyon, but it'll be hours before the temperature cools off enough for my taste. The house sits on a cliff. And behind it, a rope bridge spans at least a mile-wide gap between two flat-topped hills. Below, a gorge looms, river rushing around the menacing rocks. Mom says it's Elang Creek Threshold and leads into the Sixth, a quick escape in case she needed one from Isabeau.

Isabeau. Right. I attempt to organize my thoughts, remember the things I seem to have forgotten. But my brain is scrambled eggs, and while some things are easy to recall, others are . . . well . . . not. It's as if they're blurred, present but with a sort of film covering them. And don't get me started on the pieces that have vanished altogether. Tracks scratched off a disregarded CD.

Like, where were we before we found Mom?

She, baby Evan, and a guy by the name of Tide (who I recognize but hardly know . . . I think?) were gagged with hands and feet bound in a hollow space beneath the kitchen floor. Ebony threw her arms around Tide and he hesitated only a moment before embracing her and lifting her off the ground. Joshua claims he arrived only moments before we did, so he didn't have time to release them. His story seemed valid. He may have deceived me in the past, but he wouldn't lie about this. What reason would he have?

Last clear memory I can muster, I was in the Fourth, skipping rocks with Ebony at the seashore. And that in and of itself is weird. When did Ebony and I become friends, and why? I know we're on good terms now, but the context is warbled. Then there's the girl, the one Joshua saved with his Ever blood. Where did she come from, and who does she belong to? She looks at me a lot, too, though it doesn't bother me as much as the creeper's.

Ugh. I kick a stone and it slides across the red dirt, over the cliff's edge, and into the gorge. The water is so far down, the rush of the wide river pronounced enough, I don't hear a splash. The stone goes over and then . . . nothing. Kinda like these memories I can't quite place.

Someone squeezes my shoulders. I jump, but then they squeeze harder. Sigh. I reach back and pat the top of Mom's hand. Her, at least, I remember. With a signature kiss to my temple, she asks, "How are you feeling, brave girl?"

I scratch my head. Because that's what you do when you're . . . "Confused."

She comes around to face me. The calm in her voice doesn't match the panic in her eyes. She glances past me, then back, past me, then back again.

"Mom, what is it?" What's she looking at? I want to look over my shoulder, but the slant of her lips warns against it.

Tight hug. Can't breathe. Her mouth finds my ear. "Listen, we don't have much time before he retrieves me." She pulls away. Smiles too sweetly. Kisses my forehead.

Retrieves her? Why do I get the feeling she's overdoing the affection as some kind of act?

"Joshua cannot be trusted," she says through pursed lips. "Something has disturbed him. I am unsure what, but he trapped me, your brother, and the boy Tide."

Dread churns. Spider-walks my nerves. "Where's Evan?"

She pulls me close again. "Joshua has him. It is why I cannot say more. Regina has gone to fetch Makai. She was outside when Joshua arrived and was able to slip away unseen. I have no idea how long it will take them to return."

The mention of Reggie injects a dose of hope. My favorite cook in all the Reflections was here? Maybe my memory isn't so poor after all. I know Mom and Evan, who the first time I held him smiled straight at me as if we'd been best buds forever. Makai and Reggie are on their way, both of whom I recall to a tee. Maybe they'll bring Stormy. Crowe, I wouldn't even mind if Preacher tagged along. How horrible can things be as long as I recognize those closest to me?

"Just remember," Mom whispers in my ear. "Be chary about those in whom you place your confidence. Joshua threatened to hurt your brother if I tell you too much. I am reluctant to put anything past him at this point in time. He carries a madness I recognize all too well."

Madness. A pinprick in my brain. Someone mentioned something about madness. And Jasyn Crowe. The memory feels recent. I'm in a room. Ebony is there, and the leader of the Fourth . . . ? But the rest is hazy at best. Why can't I remember?

"Mom, what doesn't Joshua want you to tell me?" The words are a runaway subway. Urgent. Ahead of schedule.

She lists her head. Once again her gaze falls to the door behind me. "Kyaphus. Do you remember anything about him at all?"

The guy with the Void? "I've never seen him before in my life."

Her mouth turns down. "Promise me this: if he attempts to speak with you, if he finds the chance, listen."

I nod. Anything for Mom. Always.

After one last kiss to my cheek, she shuffles back toward the house. "Supper will be on soon. We will wait for Dahlia's return together."

My ears perk. Dahlia Moon? Of course, that's why I came, right? To find the Ever woman with answers regarding the Void and the Verity. I don't know how I know that, and the source of the information is once again a fog. Still, it's another memory restored. Yay, me.

"How do you know her?" I ask before Mom enters the house. "Has she been caring for you? Did she help deliver Evan?"

Mom does a half turn, a genuine smile perking the corners of her lips. The panic melts from her complexion, replaced by a secretive look I know all too well. "Dahlia comes and goes. Sometimes she is here, sometimes there. Evers get antsy, you know? They never remain in one place too long because they are around for *so* long. But yes, once you left the Second, she arrived to care for your brother and me."

What does my leaving have to do with anything? "How do you know her?"

"You know her too. She goes by an alias to keep her Calling hidden, as many Evers do. She bears many names, in fact. I believe her favorite is the nickname you bestowed, though. Your 'Fairy godmother' is quite fond of you, my darling." Mom slips inside without another word, leaving me more confused than before.

The one I bestowed? What—?

I shake my head. There's only one person I've nicknamed. One person who has said those exact words verbatim. Which means Dahlia Moon is none other than the sometimes crazy, always bubbly, Fairy godmother incarnate Regina a.k.a. Reggie Reeves.

FORTY-EIGHT

josh

My brother is on his knees. I kick him in the rib cage again. His head slumps to his chest and his shoulders heave.

What a pathetic excuse for a twin.

He lifts his head. "What did you do to her?"

I pace to and fro across the living area, keeping one hand on my weapon's hilt at all times. "That is none of your concern."

"Give it up, David." He spits to one side. "Do you honestly want her this way? Confused? Forced to be with you because she knows of no other option?"

"There *is* no other option."

"You've fooled yourself." He hangs his head once more.

"No, *brother*, it is you who has been fooled into believing her love for you is true."

His head snaps up and tilts to one side. "You keep calling me that. Why?"

"Because, unfortunately for me, we're brothers. Fraternal twins, in fact." I draw my sword for good measure. "And the only—the *only*—reason she feels anything for you"—I touch his shoulder with the tip of my blade—"is because of your connection to me." I return my sword to my side.

He squints and his mouth opens as if he might speak. Then he seems to think better of it and clamps his jaw. Good. He's learning. At least that much can be said for him.

"This is what we're going to do." I drag him to a stand and shake him a bit to force eye contact.

He's reluctant, but his gaze meets mine.

"You are going to tell me everything. Where you have been. Where you are headed. And then you will walk away. You will never contact her again. Do I make myself clear?"

He nods. "Crystal."

I can tell he's lying, but the detail is trivial. If he won't walk, I'll make him.

"Now tell me." I shake him again. "What are you after?"

"A way to destroy the Void for good."

The idea is laughable, but I keep my tone neutral. "And exactly how are you going to do that?"

The front door swings wide and bangs against the wall, causing both our regards to flash in that direction. The Second castle's head cook stands there, a menacing scowl on her plump face. "What in Sam Hill is going on here?" Regina Reeves's hands plant on her generous hips. "If I didn't know any better, I'd say you two boys were having a brawl."

Makai Archer appears behind her. My lesser half inside me punches the air. I suppress his joy. The Shield may bear an effect on Joshua, but he will do nothing to stop me. The Void will not be destroyed. Its power is too great. If anything, we must discover a way to let it flourish. Jasyn Crowe made too many mistakes to count. I will be different. I will control the Void the way he never could.

"*Moron,*" Joshua shouts. "*Don't you see? You can't control the darkness. The darkness controls you.*"

Silence, prisoner, I think.

"Makai, get ahold of your man." Regina moves aside and the man advances on me.

I shove my brother to the floor and level my sword at Archer. "You don't want to do that, Commander."

He should disappear using his Shield ability, but he doesn't. Perhaps the Callings are returning in the order they vanished. Ever failed first, then Physic and so forth. Shield didn't die out until later, so it serves to reason it would not have returned just yet.

Same with the Thresholds. It may take time to reverse what was done when Eliyana and Kyaphus shared a Kiss of Infinity. Joshua and I may disagree on what happens with the Void, but at least we can come to terms on one matter.

Eliyana is mine—ours. The only one she will share a Kiss of Infinity with is me.

"Joshua." Makai's tone relays warning. "Do not force me to disarm you. If you do, you do not want to know what comes next."

I tilt my head back and laugh. "Oh, please. You're twice my age and half as strong. Do you really believe you can best me?"

The man in the prison of my soul smiles.

Makai attacks.

I lunge, but he's quicker than I anticipated. He dodges my move, darts behind me, and wraps my throat in a choke hold. "Drop the sword, Joshua."

Clenching the hilt tighter, I stretch my neck.

"I said drop it." His hold contracts.

My weapon clangs to the ground as I gasp for breath. My arms are twisted behind my back with so much force my shoulder pops from its socket.

I refuse to yield. With a shove to the pain, I jerk and lurch, biting down hard so a scream cannot release.

"Stormy! Preacher! Wren! Robyn! Give me a hand!" Archer's bellow is too loud in my ear.

My fellow Guardians are on me, holding me back as I lash and struggle. Teeth bared, I emit a growl. "This isn't the end. The Void will prevail."

"Do you realize how idiotic you sound?" the man in my head asks. *"They're going to throw you in the dungeons with Rafaj if you keep this up."*

Shut your mouth, captive. I continue my fight all the way to the cellar. Continue until they tie me to a pipe. They release the countess's son and the man who arrived with Kyaphus. Stormy, Preacher, and Robyn leave without a second glance. But Wren lingers, giving me that look she always gives.

"Why are *you* here?" I let my head fall back against the pipe.

"Why do you think, Joshua?"

Her wounded tone does nothing to faze me, though I feel it pinch my other half. "You shouldn't have come, Wren."

She yields one long glare before going the way of the others and bolting the door behind her.

Darkness shrouds me, not a shaft of light in view. But I don't mind, as I welcome the shadows. They comfort me as I drift off to sleep.

joshua

At last he's out. I thought he'd never leave.

Without my dark side to war against, my task grows simpler. I tug against my invisible restraints, making the slightest movements in my effort to be free. I will undo what I've done. As much as I hate to work with my brother, I see now destroying the Void is the only way. My experience has shown me as much. The power of the darkness is too great a temptation. Kyaphus is stronger than most, it seems, but who's to say he won't end up like Jasyn Crowe?

Josh walks that path now. And, like the Void, he must be terminated.

FORTY-NINE

set me free

Night is in full bloom now, and the slightest chill begins to descend, draping the canyon like a light dusting of snow. Only, without the snow.

I cross my arms and rub my biceps, feeling a forever film of grime even after my bath earlier. I can't decide what bothers me more. Joshua's guard-dog act or the vessel of the Void's lingering gaze. Both leave me unsettled. A deep sense of loss coats every thought and emotion. A sense something is missing. Yes, my memories are spotty, but it's more than that.

If only I could figure out what.

So much has been misplaced. Joshua claims I was taken by pirates, but how was I captured? And why? None of it makes sense, and something deep inside rings an all-too-recognizable bell.

Joshua has lied to me before.

Mom says he's lying now.

I'm keeping my mouth shut around him until I find out why.

How long until Reggie and Makai arrive? They have to travel through two Reflections to get here, and the Threshold we used to enter the Fourth has drained. Mom says Reggie left yesterday, but there's no telling how far they'll have to travel to the next nearest passage into the Fourth. I'd mirror walk and pull them through, but I've no clue where they are. Besides, I haven't attempted mirror walking since leaving the Second. The Verity inside still feels like a flicker. When will everything be normal again? Has it *ever* been normal?

Joshua has Mom terrified, refusing to put Evan down if she can help it. Ebony and the girl Khloe whisper behind his back, and the other two guys, Flint and Tide, are under lock and key along with the man Joshua claims is enemy number one in all the Reflections.

Kyaphus Rhyen.

As if on cue, footsteps scuffle behind me. I didn't hear the back door open, but there's no question who has followed me out here. Doesn't Joshua know when to give it a rest? I've heard the same thing over and over since our reunion. I was kidnapped. The trauma messed with my memory. But he's here now and everything's going to be fine. The Callings and Reflections are safe. The drained Thresholds should fill up and return to normal. But nothing is normal, not when I hardly know who I am or how I got here. Not when the Verity lies dormant in my soul.

I loose a frustrated scream. Grab at my hair.

Joshua clears his throat behind me.

I brace myself for another conversation I'm not in the mood to have.

"Ember."

I whirl. Terror grips me. I back toward the cliff's edge, toward the mouth of the rope bridge. The man before me looks different from earlier today. The blackened veins that covered his entire body have begun to shrink, reaching only as far as his jaw, revealing his face. The expression there can only be described as anguish.

"Please," he says. "I'm not going to hurt you."

"How'd you get out?"

"Makai and Reggie are here. They've brought reinforcements, including Stormy and Robyn."

Stormy is here? And Robyn? Their familiar faces fill my memory and I emit a half sob, half hiccup. I've never been so happy to remember anything in my life. But . . . how can this guy know those names would give me such relief? "My name's not Ember," I say.

His entire face points south from his furrowed brows to his drawn lips. When he reaches out, I stumble backward, end up straddling rock and bridge. I'm leaning so far I might end up in the gorge if he comes any closer.

"Would you just listen, Em? Please."

I promised Mom. I bite my lip. Nod. "Okay."

His stare bores into mine. His jaw muscles flex.

What's he doing?

The ground shudders.

I bend my knees to keep from falling. Whoa. Another earthquake? How is that possible?

"Lower your walls, Em," Kyaphus says. "Let me in."

This guy really is off his rocker. Lower my walls? Let him in? What game is he playing?

That's when I hear it. The music. At first the tune is faint and far away, floating along the night air in a whisper. This song, I've heard it before. Once, perhaps. Or twice? It's so achingly familiar. I long to put lyrics to its notes.

The Void's vessel smiles. "That's right, Em. Remember."

I tilt my head. Lower my eyelids. Lyrics I didn't know I had in me roll in a sonata across my mind. They're not out loud. Because this song is my soul. And sound can't do it justice.

> *"I can walk through my reflection,*
> *Use my Shield as a deflection,*
> *Sing the song of my complexion,*
> *But it's nothing without you."*

A breath in my mind. Dim but real. I continue . . .

> *"I can heal and I can fight,*
> *My memory is bright,*
> *Through a façade I bear good sight,*
> *But it's nothing without you."*

Without who? Have I lost someone? Is this why my memory loss has been so painful?

> "If love is what ignites me,
> Then the Verity inside me
> Cannot win unless you're beside me.
> I'm nothing without you."

The song inside dies just as a sound like earth splitting amps my pulse. Dust rises and pebbles dance. It is another earthquake. Joshua said the Thresholds were fine.

He was wrong.

My hands grasp the poles anchoring the bridge in place. I peer beyond my shoulder. The water below churns in hunger for a fresh body.

I'm losing my balance.

The cliff's edge is crumbling.

And I'm falling.

The Void's vessel grabs me.

And everything comes back into focus.

I look into his eyes, but the monster before me has vanished. In his place is the man beneath. Kind, two-tone gaze. Crazy-adorable crooked smile. Hair of gold with a heart to match.

"Ky." His name is a wake-up call to my soul. I used to think "I See the Light" was about Joshua. But now, *now* I see the difference. Because it's like the fog has lifted. Because, with Ky, everything is new.

"Hold on!" he shouts.

The cottage windows rattle. The draining Threshold calls to me, but Ky's grasp keeps me from falling.

For now.

I look down. The water drains faster than anything we've witnessed. Which means whatever Joshua—Josh—did to make me forget Ky, to break the soul bond we shared, it didn't quite work. Ky's tear. And the bottle? Somehow it erased my memories of him. But erasing memories can't change what actually happened.

Joshua can make me forget Ky, but he can't alter the events of the past. Such a feat would be impossible. Ky and I shared a Kiss of Infinity. My mind has forgotten him, but my soul?

Never.

Somehow I know Ky's touch is the only thing binding us. I feel it in the very real and tangible energy passing between our fingertips. If we disconnect, my memory of him will fade once more. If he sets me free, he'll be lost to me. But our hands are slipping, the cliff is breaking. Much more of this and we'll both end up sucked through the Threshold. And if it creates a wormhole? Who knows where we'll end up, or if we'll even arrive at the same place. And even if we did, would I know him? Is this touch thing a fluke or a permanent fix to what Joshua—Josh—did?

Ky's fingers tighten, but he's weak. Weary. The Void may be rescinding, the light in him fighting it off, but the darkness is too much for him right now. He's not strong enough to hold us both up. He can't pull me back and I can't let him fall. One of us needs to remain here. To fill Makai in on what we've discovered. To look after Mom and Evan. To question Dahlia—Reggie.

My fingers loosen.

"Don't!" His arm flexes and shakes.

I want to tell him I love him. I want to kiss him good-bye. Instead I ask the question I already know the answer to. "Find me?"

His face contorts. The sight is a dagger to my heart. "Always," he says.

My fingers splay.

I let go.

CODA

KY

Em is not gone, she's only lost. This isn't forever. It's merely the beginning.

"I've seen a lot of heartbreak over the decades." Dahlia removes the kerchief tying her black braided hair. "But nothing so tragic as the original vessel of the Verity."

We've transformed the living area into a council session room. The couches have been pushed back and chairs added so everyone can take a seat. I choose to stand, finding a spot at the wall near the front window. I much prefer a place where I can observe, and from here I have the best angle.

Em's mom paces the kitchen, bouncing her baby boy as she walks. Commander Archer casts regular glances in her direction. When she meets his gaze she smiles, then returns her focus to their son.

Flint and Tide sit on either side of the fireplace, knees bowed with hands clasped between them. Their tired expressions raise a hair of guilt. They really need some rest. We all do, but this takes precedence. I'll have to promote both men if we ever end up on the *Seven Seas* again. While others in my crew abandoned our cause, these two have proven themselves worthy of far more than their current titles.

"Get to the point, Regina," Preacher says, using Dahlia's Second Reflection name. "We don't got all night." I stifle a smirk. I've known the old grump long enough to decipher the difference between a teasing word and a nasty one. He may seem as if he's annoyed, but the slight perk of his whiskers says he's the opposite.

"Cool your jets, Saul." She waves her kerchief at him. "I'm gettin' there."

Wren slumps in her chair, her sister, Robyn, perched on the chair's arm beside her. I don't know why they chose to bring Wren of all Guardians. A bad attitude is the last thing we need. She is familiar with David, though, and that may be of use in the future.

Stormy sits cross-legged at one end of the sofa. Her shoes are off, eyes as bursting as her stick-up hair. I know she, at least, will do everything she can to help us find Em.

I move my gaze right, to Ebony and Khloe. My sister lies with her head in Ebony's lap. The older girl strokes my sister's black curls with a touch so gentle, my heart warms. I dwell on the feeling, use it to drive the Void another inch down my neck. The pain it causes makes my nostrils flare, but I've learned to keep the ache quiet. Hope fuels me. In whatever small way, I am still connected to Ember. I may have been deleted from her mind, but I doubt anything could be strong enough to remove me from her heart.

That is my belief anyway.

"I've encountered her just once," Dahlia continues. "Years ago. During a visit to the Sixth. She keeps to herself like an Ever. Immortality does that to a soul, ya know? Everyone you knew is gone, only to be replaced with more who will pass on before your time. It can be a lonely existence at that. Gotta have a strong heart to endure so much loss." She pounds a fist to her bosom.

I shift my stance, crossing one leg over the other.

"What's her name?" Stormy fiddles with the fringe on the throw pillow in her lap. "The original vessel?"

"Like me," Dahlia says, "she bears many names. I knew her as Sonja. Some claim she was the mythological Medusa. Others swear she was the despicable Queen Vashti from the book of Esther. But the most popular and perhaps most often told tale is the one of the Fairy Queen."

A story my mother told us as kids rises to my mind. *The Lament of the Fairy Queen* always made Khloe cry. I, on the other hand, found it a little dull. The story is meant to leave you feeling sorry for the Queen in the end, but I never failed to come away peeved. In my opinion the Queen deserved what she got. I guess it depends on how you look at it really.

The last person I expect shoots from her chair. "David should be included in this. It isn't right." Wren storms from the room, leaving everyone frozen with jaws slack. When I hear the cellar door creak open, I follow after her, Makai in tow. But by the time we reach the door, Wren is dragging David along by his elbow. She shoves past us and they sit side by side on the love seat. Makai and I exchange a hefty glance. Okay then.

"Tell them," Wren orders. Maybe she will be of some use after all. While the others seem timid around my apparent twin brother, which I still hesitate to believe is true, Wren doesn't bat an eye near him. "Tell them what the old man said about the Fairy Queen."

I arch both my eyebrows.

David glares.

"You want to find your girlfriend or not?"

He looks away.

"I don't like it any more than you do, but if we want to end this and find her, we'll all have to work together."

Wow. Song continues to surprise me. Being wrong about people is one of my favorite things. And it appears I was mistaken.

David's hands remain bound behind his back. He adjusts on the cushion and leans forward, staring at the rug when he clears his throat and begins, "The Fairy Queen is real . . ."

The tale he relays leaves us all speechless. Even Khloe sits up to listen, knees pulled to her chest like when our mother would storytell.

But it's Ebony who's brought to tears. She swipes at them and stares at her lap. "All this time, and I never knew. My own mother and she never told me who she really was." Her hands form fists at the center of her crossed legs. "I should've known. Everything she taught me. Her vast knowledge of the Reflections and Callings. She was shaping me to be just like her." Head whipped up, she says, "Does this mean I'm not a Shield? Is my power some sick inheritance from my wretched immortal mother?"

No one answers. We have none to give. All we can do is take the missing pieces as they connect. The Fairy Queen. Isabeau. The Midnight Rose, which remains a mystery until Dahlia stands and says, "So that's what the woman is up to." She rounds on Makai. "You'd best be moving Miss Elizabeth along, you hear? I won't have no Fairy Queen up in here puttin' her to sleep forever." Shooing him into the next room, Dahlia goes on and on. When the door shuts down the hall we can still hear her muffled rants.

So the Midnight Rose is a weapon, one plucked from the Garden of Epoch. And anyone who drinks its dew will sleep forever. I've never heard anything so insane. Good thing Em isn't here. She'd flip out if she knew Isabeau continued to seek revenge on her mom.

Then again, that was the old Em. The one I've come to know in recent days would probably lead the Troll's death march.

When Dahlia returns to the room, she claps her hands. "We know what we must do then." Her lips curl. "Pack your bags, people. It's gonna be a wild ride."

We stare at her, waiting for whatever we seem to have missed.

With a slap to her knee, Dahlia says, "The only way to defeat the Void is to reverse what happened between Isabeau and Dimitri those many years ago. And to do so we must move back in time."

I smile because I know exactly what she's getting at. *The Fairy Queen's Lament* mentions a fountain in the Seventh, and more specifically in the Garden of Epoch—the Fountain of Time.

Whatever David did to mess with Ember, it won't matter if we can find the Fountain. If we can find it, the clock can be reversed. If we can find it and travel back in time, perhaps more than Ember can be saved. I know because I've tasted its water but once, and recently too. A single sip from a vial given to me by a stranger. A sip I used to venture into the past to save a little girl from a fire.

My burns feel fresh as I close my eyes and picture Em's face.

The course to the past is calling.

acknowledgments—
a.k.a. blessings of 2016

This year. Oh, this year. *Unraveling* couldn't be a more perfect title because it not only fits El's journey, it fits mine too. This book was a labor of love. You hear authors talk about "blood, sweat, and tears" a lot. No words could be more fitting. This story had me in tears more often than not. I was sure it would never get finished, and even if it did, would it live up to the beautiful cover Kristen Ingebretson (thank you!) designed?

Only you, dear reader, can answer that question. So thank you, once again, for joining El, Ky, and Joshua on their journey. I hope some of your questions have been answered and that you'll stick around for the conclusion. Never forget that you're stronger than you know. I believe in you. You're awesome.

To my editor Becky Monds—the dedication of this book rings true. Your patience and grace this year went above and beyond. You are a true gem and I am so blessed to work with you. Thank you doesn't seem good enough for all you've done. This book is here because of you. I can only hope it's worthy of the person to whom it is dedicated.

To my TNZFiction team. Holy Verity, you guys blow me away! Jodi Hughes, Paul Fisher, Allison Carter, Amanda Bostic, Daisy Hutton, Kristen Golden, Kayleigh Hines, Karli Jackson—you work so hard for me behind the scenes. Because of you I get to see my books on Barnes & Noble shelves. Your efforts bless me. Love being a part of this publishing family!

Matt Covington, you've done it again! Thanks for creating two more gorgeous maps.

Julee Schwarzburg, you clean me up nicely. Thank you for saving me from loads of embarrassment with too many "likes" and adverbs.

Dad and Jodi (Mom)—you love on me when I need it most. Thanks for being a haven when I need a break from life.

For my girls who never cease to be my biggest (and most patient) fans. I love you both more than I can possibly say. Thank you for being the best daughters this mama could ask for.

John and Brooke (and kids)—you guys gave me a home when I needed one. Words can't express my appreciation. Your family brought light and joy to a super-hard time. Also, Pie Face was awesome. Just sayin'.

Aunt Terri—this book never would have been finished if you hadn't swooped in and saved the day when my laptop crashed. You bless me over and over. I love you so much!

Nadine Brandes—this year has been tough, but you've remained a light throughout. From our trip to see Marissa Meyer to ACFW to your release-day surprise, you've remained a friend through and through! Hugs!

Thanks, as always, to my author friends who time and time again offer their love and support (and sometimes chocolate and coffee)—Mary Weber, Shannon Dittemore, Christen Krumm, Neysa Walker, Becky Dean, Krista McGee, Lorie Langdon, Laura Pol, Cara Putman, Kristy Cambron, Melissa Landers, Emileigh Latham, Elizabeth VanTassel, Lauren Brandenburg, Alexis Goring, Rachelle Rea Cobb, Rachel Hauck, Katherine Reay, Dana R. Lynn, Rhonda Starnes, and any and all other author friends I have failed to mention. You all encourage and inspire me every day.

To my IRL friends and family who never fail to love on me or answer the phone, whether I'm jumping for joy or in crazy hysterics—Karine Krastel, Carolyn Schanta, Janalyn Owens, Staci Talbert, Kim Baschke, Kay Larson, Rachael Larson, DD Cason,

Kristy Neufeld, Lilly Wheeler, Sheryl Cooper, Zara Pearson, Cassia Pearson, Jarom Pearson, Deanna Zedicher, and Kjelse Rittmeyer.

To my online friends who are always there with a GIF or a sticker or a word of encouragement to brighten my days—Mandi Alva, Hope Ortego, Abby Woodhouse, Brian Asriel Newman, Trina Ruck, Angela Godon, Melanie Kilsby, Steven Mannasse, Brittany Nelson, Ari'El Gracia, Sunday Gracia, Sarah Perry, Mindy Seta, Karen Bissell, Immanuel Gomez, Gabrial Jones, and Elizabeth Meyer.

To my amazing street team and online support (fan club)— you guys are the icing on the cake. All your reviews and excitement and fangirling/boying over *Unblemished* floored me. I'm so blessed by your time and encouragement. Thank you for help- ing spread the word about this series and for all the amazing notes and e-mails I've received. Whether you are #TeamKy or #TeamJoshua, I am 100 percent #TeamYou.

To Caiden Carrington. You know why.

And last but never least, to my Creator YHWH. Chris Tomlin got it right. *"You're a good, good Father. It's who You are . . . and I am loved by You."* I only made it through this year and this novel by Your grace and strength. You carried me. I owe all to You. You are the light within me, the calm to my storm. Blessed be Your name. Amen and amen.

Don't miss the thrilling conclusion to the unblemished trilogy!

unbreakable

Available May 2018!

To learn more about
Sara Ella and her
upcoming books, check out:

Website: saraella.com
Facebook: writinghistruth
Twitter: @SaraEllaWrites
Instagram: saraellawrites
YouTube: Sara Ella

about the author

Once upon a time, Sara Ella dreamed she would marry a prince and live in a castle, and she did work for Disney! Now she spends her days throwing living room dance parties for her two princesses and conquering realms of her own imaginings. She believes "Happily Ever After Is Never Far Away."

ᴖᴋᴗ

Visit Sara online at saraella.com
Facebook: writinghistruth
Twitter: @SaraEllaWrites
Instagram: saraellawrites
YouTube: Sara Ella